BETWEEN
DARKNESS
AND DAWN

MARGARET DUARTE

Omie
PRESS

Book Cover design Yocla Designs by Clarissa

Publisher's Cataloging-in-Publication Data

Names: Duarte, Margaret.
Title: Between darkness and dawn / Margaret Duarte.
Description: Elk Grove, CA : Omie Press, 2017. | Series: Enter the between, bk. 2.
Identifiers: LCCN 2016917579 | ISBN 978-0-9860688-4-3 (pbk.) | ISBN 978-0-9860688-5-0 (Kindle ebook)
Subjects: LCSH: Women--Fiction. | Self-actualization (Psychology)--Fiction. | Spiritual life--Fiction. | Quantum theory--Fiction. | Alzheimer's disease--Fiction. | Paranormal fiction. | BISAC: FICTION / Visionary & Metaphysical. | FICTION / Fantasy / Paranormal. | FICTION / Occult & Supernatural. | GSAFD: Occult fiction.
Classification: LCC PS3604.U241 B47 2017 (print) | LCC PS3604.U241 (ebook) | DDC 813/.6--dc23.

This book is dedicated to my sons, Todd and Jon, my daughter-in-law, Martina, and my granddaughters, Angelina, and Tessa. You are my life and my inspiration.

Summer

2001

The second path of initiation begins in the South,
the place of innocence and trust.

I had always thought that my mind belonged to me alone, that I could isolate, even insulate, it from the world around me. I was prepared to share my possessions, my talents, my body, but my mind—never.

I was wrong.

BETWEEN
DARKNESS
AND DAWN

Chapter One

A S THE BAY BREEZE WHISPERED across the barren hills of Bayfront Park, the first day of summer dawned on the horizon. The city of Menlo Park lay only two miles west, yet this land, surrounded by salt ponds, marshes, and sloughs, had the feel of another planet, on which we were all alone.

"Out-of-the-way places like this attract weirdoes," my mother said. "Anyone could be hiding out here, and we'd be defenseless. Good Lord, whatever were you thinking?"

Although she lagged behind me a foot or two, I didn't need to turn around to know that a frown marred her perfectly groomed face. I caught a whiff of her Shalimar perfume, so alien to our surroundings, yet so like my mother, the scent of orange, lemon, and vanilla, of tradition and order. It played games with my head, made me wonder if I was doing the right thing.

We had walked half a mile into the 2.3-mile trail that ran the perimeter of the park, past a red pump house and salt and tidal ponds full of water birds with stilt legs. Ahead, a sign alerted us to the upcoming nesting areas for burrowing owls and advised us to remain on the designated path.

I waited for my mother to catch up to me.

"I was hoping we could celebrate the summer solstice together and attune ourselves to the rhythms of the natural world," I said, forestalling any comments she might have about the smell of natural gases and decaying algae that infiltrated the morning breeze.

"It's half past seven, and we're surrounded by" —she turned in a slow circle, eyeing the star thistles, wild mustard, and assorted grasses visible in the dawning light— "bugs, mice, and squirrels. Oh, Marjorie, what's gotten into you?"

Now, there was a question far easier asked than answered. Part of the strength that had anchored my mother before and after my father's death of cancer and had helped her follow her life's path with such fierce determination, made her resistant to listening to my altered worldview. If she opened that door, even a crack, it would lead to far too many uncertainties. If she allowed herself to wonder, if she exposed herself to arcane possibilities, it would cause doubt and rattle her faith. Yet, if the universe existed as she had led me to believe, we wouldn't be here today. There would be no way for the spirit world to contact ours.

I wouldn't be hearing voices.

Mother peered at me through narrowed eyes, waiting it seemed, for a creditable answer.

I resumed walking, all too aware of the renewed pain my answer would evoke—for both of us. "When you told me last March that I was adopted, I was too upset to take into account how difficult telling me this must have been for you. I'm sorry."

My mother increased her pace to keep up with me. "I should never have shared that information. You caught me by surprise."

We had both been caught by surprise. And we'd both experienced the pain and scarring resulting from a secret withheld for twenty-eight years and suddenly exposed like a gaping wound. My hope was to treat this wound before the infection of misunderstanding and mistrust settled in. If it wasn't already too late.

"You had no choice, Mom. Not after I ran into Veronica."

"Hey twin stranger," Veronica had said on our first meeting. "Who do you think was adopted? You or me? We're identical. What are the chances we're not related? I know you're curious, because I sure am. If you don't get an answer, I'll clue you in on mine."

The trail turned left to follow a series of unirrigated hills with brown grasses and drought-tolerant plants. "You also told me that you didn't know the identity of my birth parents," I said, "only that my mother was a descendent of the Ohlone/Costanoan Esselen Nation, and that she died soon after giving birth to me."

"Why are you bringing up old news when you know it causes me pain?" my mother asked, matching me stride-for-stride.

"Because I found out who she is, Mom. Her name is—"

My mother swung around to face me. "*Was*, Marjorie. You found out who she *was*."

"Not exactly..."

Her face took on the unyielding appearance of stone; an expression I knew was due to her deep sense of loss at the change that the exposed secret of my adoption had brought into our lives.

We started walking again. At this rate, it would take hours to complete the park's perimeter trail. A jogger sped by. Good. Maybe this would ease my mother's concern about getting mugged by a weirdo. "Remember how I told you I was hearing a voice and thought I was losing my mind?"

Silence.

"The voice belongs to—"

"She is dead," my mother said.

If only I could believe, as I once had, that dead meant dead and that the deceased went to heaven, hell, or some place in between and couldn't—wouldn't—come back to haunt us. "I know, but—"

"She...is...dead," my mother repeated, each word a hammer to the nail of my spirit. "She gave birth to you and died. Case closed. I'm the one who loved you and sacrificed for you, day in and day out, for twenty-eight years, and, by God, I'm the reason you are who you are."

I wanted to hug her and communicate, as words could not, that I would always love her for raising me the best way she knew how and for being here today, trying to support me, when it was obvious she'd rather be at morning Mass, even the confessional. But I could sense by the way she was clenching and unclenching her fists and stumbling along the perfectly level path that this was not a good time.

"You were two weeks old when I adopted you," she said, her words nearly drowned out by the swooping, base-heavy sound of an overhead jet. "Doesn't that count for anything?"

I halted. Met my mother's flashing blue eyes. "Of course, it does, but—"

"Then why are you choosing her over me?"

Was it true? Was I choosing one mother over the other? I hadn't asked for the untold story of Antonia's life to infiltrate mine. I'd been content living a neat, orderly existence, scripted and directed by those I considered stronger and wiser than me. I'd believed myself to be the only child of Gerardo and Truus Veil, of Italian and Dutch ancestry, when in fact, I was a twin daughter of Irish descendant, Bob Mask, and Antonia Flores, a Native American. It's a bit hard to carry on as before when you discover that the foundation on which you've built your life is fiction. My current worldview needed major stretching to assimilate Antonia's messages from the beyond: *Marjorie Marie Veil, there is something you must know. You must listen. Time is running out.*

"My birth mother...Antonia...is speaking to me," I said, "and I have to find out what she wants, so I can make her stop."

Mother's eyes bored into mine as if she could bend me to her will. I couldn't blame her for trying. It had worked often enough in the past. Only recently had I begun stepping away from my cultural and familial environment and attempting to follow my own path. "Hogwash. Dead people don't talk."

How I wished that were true.

A hawk screeched from above, and I remembered what my friend Ben *Gentle Bear* Mendoza had said about the call of a hawk; how it often signals changes to come.

"Why are you carrying on in this way?" my mother asked.

For the same reason you would if our positions were reversed. "I don't mean to dishonor or blame you, Mom, but if I don't go to Big Sur, the land of Antonia's people, and use the Earth's medicine to find out what she wants, I'll risk spending the rest of my life in regret."

"Don't talk to me of primitive medicine like some pagan squaw," my mother said, her eyes glistening with an odd light, some kind of misguided triumph. "You were raised Catholic and, by God, you'll remain a Catholic if I have anything to say about it."

My vision blurred, and for a moment, my mind went blank, unable to comprehend my mother's sudden cruelty. She had always tried to control me with the force of her will, but this was different. She had never resorted to name-calling before.

Over the last few months, I had tried to accept her reasoning—and excuses—for withholding knowledge of my adoption and of my twin. And I had hidden my hurt as best I could. But I wasn't about to stand back while she discredited my birth mother's heritage and spirituality. "By *squaw*, I assume you're referring to my Native American ancestry. But the pagan part, no."

"The occult, false idols, animal worship."

My body throbbed with the thrust of a thousand needles as I stared at the woman who had turned into a stranger. I should've been prepared for her reaction. The angry look in her eyes should've warned me to back off. But I had carried on, ignoring the signs, so desperate to explain, so desperate for her approval.

"It's witchcraft," she said, her right hand opening and closing as though she were about to slap me.

A soft breeze cooled my hot, prickly skin and lifted my hair. "What do you know about witchcraft, other than what you've seen on TV?"

"It deals with magic, sorcery—the devil," she spat out. "It means you're not a Christian."

If honoring the traditions of my Native American ancestors meant I wasn't a Christian, she had a point, but, really, was Jesus all that into the Euro-American idea of *Christian*, or was He about tolerance and kindness, fellowship and love? "I don't think Christianity and Native spirituality should be at odds, that's all."

"You're talking about the occult, Marjorie! About praying to eagles and worshiping rocks."

She wasn't about to give an inch. Understandable. I had been there myself not all that long ago. I had feared wide, open spaces and vast expansions, limiting my existence to what I could see, feel, and hear. "I'm not talking about the occult, Mom, at least not in the way you think. I'm talking about shamanism, the belief of my ancestors, not witchcraft or magic, though they may have some things in common."

Her face turned a mottled red, not a good sign.

"I'm not joining a cult or losing my faith," I continued, "only supplementing it with something that'll bring me closer to God. There's power in the universe that I hope to tap into, using the spirituality of my ancestors."

"By worshiping a bunch of pagan gods and talking to spirits?"

I took a deep breath. My mother wanted to keep things as they were. Again, I couldn't blame her. My determination to discover a new part of me was forcing both of us to question our values and our concepts of reality. It was like I had shed my skin and appeared as someone else, someone she didn't recognize as her daughter. She didn't deserve my desertion after all the years she had cared for and loved me. But Antonia had planted a seed of determination inside of me, to discover who I was, who I was meant to be. And to prove I wasn't crazy.

How could my mother continue to be so unreasonable in the face of what I was going through? Unless, that is, she equated the voice I was hearing to mental illness, rather than as part of a wake-up call as Dr. Mendez had suggested.

"You revere Mary and believe in angels and saints," I said. "And you talk to Saint Christopher when you travel."

"That's different."

"The church has statues and a serpent that depicts the devil."

Mother's teased and sprayed hair lifted in the breeze. She opened her shoulder bag and pulled out a scarf. "They're just symbols."

"What do you think totems are?"

"We don't worship the statues. They're just reminders."

"Same with totems."

"You make it all sound so...so...reasonable," my mother admitted grudgingly, as though trying to discern the flaws in my defense of a nature-worshipping spirituality, which she considered evil.

"That's because it is…"

Why was I putting her through this? What was the use? We were speaking different languages.

"Guess I'm just trying to fill that big empty space inside of me," I said.

"Cliff could have done that for you."

Oh, dear God, not again. "With sex?"

Mother raised a hand to her chest. "Marjorie Marie Veil."

She loved my ex-fiancé as if he were her own son, and she still hadn't forgiven me for our break up. "Marry him, honey, before it's too late. He's handsome. He has money. He'll take care of you."

"No, Mom." I would no longer play the role of pleaser and conformer, waiting for deliverance.

"Oh, I forgot," she said, "you're too busy pining over that Morgan fellow you met in Carmel Valley."

I thought about the man I loved and would soon marry, his green eyes, his kind, understanding ways. Little did my mother know that Morgan was the reason I was here today, attempting to make her understand. He had asked me why I was punishing her. "Is it because she loves you too much and wants to protect you, or because she can't let you go?"

"Even Morgan will have to wait."

"Men don't wait, Marjorie. They find someone else. Grab the brass ring while you can. You may not get a second chance."

"It's only a brass ring."

She shook her head and frowned at me. "You've changed since seeing that…that…Indian guru."

"Transpersonal psychologist," I corrected.

"And since taking off to Carmel Valley on that so-called retreat. All that talk about Earth Medicine and the Medicine Wheel and totems and gemstones. I'm surprised you're not burning incense and staring at psychedelic designs on the wall."

She came to another halt. "You aren't involved with drugs, are you?"

"Of course not."

For a blessed moment, my mother remained silent, then, "I feared the primitive would come out in you sooner or later, the Indian part of you."

Apparently, her fight for my soul wasn't over.

"Are you saying this primitive knowledge is passed on through the blood?" I asked. "If so, you must also believe in the sacredness of it, and that I need to discover that part of me."

Mother made the sign of the cross before heading off again. "I don't want to hear this."

This conversation was far from a matter of want. For either of us. "My desire to change isn't something bad," I said. "Actually, leaving an unrewarding job and ending a painful relationship is healthy. I'm just moving on."

"I wouldn't call throwing away all you've built up over the years, moving on."

"I'm getting unstuck, that's all, knocking down my tower of blocks and starting over before it's too late."

"Life isn't a game, Marjorie."

"And neither is my desire to let go of things that no longer serve me. For once, I'm choosing how I want to live."

"And what will you live on, manna from heaven?"

My mother knew I had made enough money in the stock market to guarantee my financial security for years though she had considered it stealing at the time. "Where'd the money come from if not from someone else's pocket?" she'd asked, making me feel guilty for accomplishing something for which she admired and praised my ex-fiancé.

"You always listened and obeyed. At least while your father was alive."

"And now I've stopped?" How I wished I could make it all better. For her—and for me.

"Yes."

"And is that so bad?"

Mother hesitated, then released a sigh. "I *am* proud of your strength and the way you've conducted your life so far, but—"

"You don't agree with the path I'm taking."

She glanced at the surrounding terrain. "It's so primitive."

In the world my mother knew and subscribed to, one didn't question authority or break old, worn-out structures. Part of me understood her concern, considering the pain she and I were currently going through, but that didn't lessen the disappointment I felt at the way she was repudiating all my wants and needs. "How about you wait in the Jeep while I finish my walk?"

Mother's face cleared for an instant before wrinkling up again. "You mean to that sacred path you've been talking about?"

"It's called *The Great Spirit Path*, otherwise known as the *Stone Poem*."

"How can they call this a park?" she said. "It's nothing but dirt, rocks, and weeds. And what's that irritating sound?"

"Turbine engines. They pump methane and other gases out of the decomposing materials buried below the surface and use them to make electricity. This is an old landfill, Mom. I thought you knew..."

"You think God's going to talk to you out here on a garbage heap?"

"Consider the sound as the rhythmic beating of the heart or the beat of a drum. Any steady rhythm, even one of pumping machines, can serve as a shortcut to meditation."

Mother shivered. "I don't think I'll ever understand you."

That's okay, Mom. Just love me enough to let me go.

We had reached the northeast corner of the park, another mile to go before completing the circle back to the parking lot. In preparation for today, I had gone over and over the exact words I would use to convince my mother of the existence of another reality—one I hadn't even known existed three months ago. Only now did I realize that one's concept of reality isn't changed by words, but through experience. In order to redirect my life on a course of my own choosing, I would have to let go of my mother's beliefs and learn to rely on my own.

The Dumbarton Bridge rose over the San Francisco Bay like a steel ocean wave. Sunlight shimmered on West Point Slough. And the tidal salt marsh shivered and sparkled as though dusted with glitter. Such beauty, yet… It didn't soften the realization that misunderstandings, compounded by guilt and the need for self-preservation, produced enough emotional shrapnel to pierce and wound the heart in unspeakable ways. Wounds that, even when healed, would forever leave scars.

When we reached *The Great Spirit Path*, I handed my mother the keys to my Jeep, took a brochure from the box installed at the beginning of the trail, and started my walk.

Alone.

☽☽☽

"Welcome to The Great Spirit Path Sculpture," I read out loud. "The rock clusters ahead of you—of raw, unhewn stone—have been assembled into a stone poem, inspired by American Indian Pictographs." I skimmed over the poem's history—how it had been conceived by Menlo Park artist S.C. Dunlap, how its four stanzas were spread over a 3/4 -mile trail, and how it was the largest sculpture of its kind in the world—all the while wishing that my mother would've joined me on this walk as a sign of her support. She had withheld the true story of my birth and nationality for twenty-eight years. What other truths had she kept hidden?

What untruths had she allowed me to believe?

Cluster four was a pictograph of the words, *I walk*. I ran my fingers over the stones and called out, "I WALK." At cluster number five, I called out even louder, "WITH THE WIND BEHIND ME."

As I continued to follow *The Great Spirit Path* over the small hills and undulations, I read the meanings of the poem clusters that followed to myself.

When I reached cluster nineteen, I took a deep breath.

"I RELEASE ALL MY FEAR."

The park was beginning to fill with families, dog walkers, bicyclers, and joggers, but no one appeared to notice the crazy blonde calling out the words to the poem.

At cluster twenty-five, the stones formed a cross, reminding me of the Medicine Wheel that Ben *Gentle Bear* Mendoza had introduced me to in the Los Padres National Forest. He had helped me find the stones to create my own sacred wheel and then showed me how to set it up and take the first step in the direction of the East. I treasured those stones and those memories. In fact, I carried them with me wherever I went.

At the point of the cross facing south, I asked Mother Earth for guidance, in the way of my ancestors, and vowed to remain open to her message, regardless of what may emerge.

A loud screech broke the silence.

The hawk again.

I shaded my eyes to follow the flight of the magnificent bird as it swept past me and up toward the sun.

Something drifted to my feet.

I stooped to pick it up. A tail feather, by the looks of it. Flat with horizontal bands running across its length and a black stripe towards the tip. I stroked the feather's soft, downy surface, then unzipped my belted pouch and placed the hawk's gift inside with my treasured stones and mouse totem. I'd received the mouse-shaped stone from Joshua, a child I'd befriended and learned to love in Carmel Valley and who would soon become my son. The totem—a reminder to examine what is right in front you—felt cool to the touch and filled me with comfort.

After hurrying past the last twenty-eight clusters, I called out, "AMEN," and started to dance.

I danced to the rhythm of the breeze pulsating through the vegetation below me, the birds soaring above, and the park's persistent engines. I danced in thanksgiving and because it felt right. I danced to the choreography of my earth life.

"I'm glad your father isn't here to see this," my mother said from behind me. So, she hadn't waited in the Jeep after all. Instead, she'd been watching me make a fool of myself.

"Somehow, I think Dad would've understood," I said. He would've understood my attempt to break through the rigid wall of ideas and belief systems that separated me from the rest of the world. He would've understood my need to release and let go of my old shell and find a new home. He would've understood my sudden need to shout and dance, rather than keep a stiff upper lip.

My mother, however, thought me crazy, because she couldn't hear the music.

"Maybe you should see a psychiatrist instead of a psychologist," she said, "someone who could prescribe something to stop the voice you've been hearing. Then you wouldn't have to turn your back on everything you've worked for, everything you've been taught."

"Dr. Mendez told me that what I was going through wasn't a medical emergency, but a spiritual one," I said, "something I should confront rather than suppress with medication."

"Don't you think, if the dead could talk, your father would've reached out to me by now? What makes Antonia so special? Why would God allow her to talk to you, but not allow Gerardo to talk to me?"

I'd been asking similar questions myself over the past few months, but the answers hadn't come. What I did know was that I needed to find out more about my birth mother—who she was, what she wanted—and, in the process, discover the same about myself.

"I'll pray for you," my mother said, her eyes moist as though mourning the loss of my soul.

What was the use? I'd been trying to lead her through the door of change, but she wouldn't step through it. What I saw before me was a park. She saw wasteland.

In order to connect with the mother who had given me life, I would have to break free of the mother who had spent a lifetime trying to protect it. But knowing I was doing the right thing didn't make it any easier. *I'll pray for you, too, Mom.*

"Come on, I'll take you home."

Chapter Two

MAYBE IF WE HADN'T ARGUED. Maybe if my mother hadn't lashed out at me and called me a pagan squaw.

Maybe then, I would've waited until morning and said a proper goodbye, instead of driving off during the night, putting an even greater distance between us.

Big Sur. Images of mountains, forests, and ocean drew me, balms for my wounded soul. I was running away from one mother and reaching out to the other. How long would my journey last this time? What lessons, what teachers, would it hold?

I could've called Dr. Mendez. He would've put my mind at ease, assured me that everything was okay, that I was doing the right thing. "You need to push past your perimeter of comfort and safety," he told me during our first therapy session. "Slow down, follow some blind alleys, let the truth catch up to you." When I responded that I was scared, his comforting words gave me the courage to move on. "Freedom comes at a price. Is your mother your protector or your keeper? Is your home your castle or your prison? How will you know unless you break the bonds for a while? Your heart has been silenced for too long. Let it be the expert."

A parade of vehicles surrounded me, their headlights piercing the dark, all illuminating the same path. But I wouldn't stay on this highway for long. I would be turning off soon, to a place close to the trees.

☽☽☽

Big Sur. Big South. How I loved those words. To me, they symbolized freedom and hope, this ribbon of dark highway, my yellow brick road; Big Sur, my Oz. Once there, I would find the way to my center, and then, hopefully, my way back home.

The sun was rising, but fog veiled the road with an eerie mist, giving me the sense of entering a new world. I checked my rear-view mirror. Gray fingers misted the road behind me, making it difficult to focus on what I had left behind.

I lowered my window and breathed in the thick, icy air, marveling at the scent. Pine forest? Kelp? Iodine? Whatever, it smelled wet and wonderful.

Robinson Jeffers' poem, "Return," came to mind, how it spoke of allowing life to run to the roots again, down at the Sur Rivers. It was time to allow Big Sur's miraculous healing waters to pour out of the mountainsides and into my soul. Like a slab of clay that had been wedged, kneaded, and punched into malleable softness, I was pliable, responsive, and ready to surrender.

Ten miles south of Carmel, I spotted the Rocky Point Restaurant perched high on a cliff above the dissipating June fog, a perfect place for breakfast and a fantastic view.

The host led me onto a heated terrace overlooking the Pacific Ocean. Solid, dignified boulders protruded from the churning water, reminding me of mothers watching over their children. Vigorous waves splashed against the stable rocks. No orders, no signals, no directions from the elders; no whistles, no rules. The waves appeared fearless, energetic, and mischievous, slapping against the rock-mothers' laps and encircling their rock ankles with foam-inducing play.

After placing my order, I focused on the hypnotic churn of the ocean. Glittery sprinkles blanketed the water's surface all the way to the horizon, and blobs of seaweed floated like powdered cinnamon on top of foaming coffee. There, right in front of me, lay the antidote for the emotional difficulties I'd been experiencing—nature therapy, instead of books and gadgets and antidepressant pharmaceuticals. Been there, done that, skimming across the surface of life, rather than pausing and holding my breath long enough to notice, let alone partake of, the generous gifts of nature. How tragic, that I could name the make and model of my car, the brand of my clothes and shoes and the vast number of manmade items in my possession, but could only name a fraction of the plants, trees, animals, birds, clouds, and rocks that made up my world.

Breakfast arrived. Canadian bacon, poached eggs, and country potatoes. I gasped at the size of it. Enough to feed two people. Twice. "I'll get a container for the part you can't eat," the server said, confirming that my jaw-dropped expression was nothing new. I dug into my meal, knowing I wouldn't be eating like this for a while, not in a camp kitchen with limited cooking supplies and my equally limited camp-cooking skills.

I left the restaurant sated and reflective, only to notice a butterfly land on the Harley parked next to my Jeep. What a contrast. Gossamer and steel, wings of iridescent yellow and orange quivering against slick, shining metal.

"Like it?" a male asked from behind me.

Transfixed by the glistening, almost translucent wings of the butterfly, I sighed. "Absolutely beautiful."

"It's a *Fat Boy*," he announced. "Just added those chrome pipes. Gave it an extra ten horsepower. Too powerful for a lightweight like you."

I turned and met the man's flat brown eyes. "Sorry, I was talking about the butterfly."

A lift of his brow. The shake of his head. A grin. "Well, I'll be..."

Mr. Harley's longish, windblown hair and tanned face appealed to my senses. But something about him triggered an emotional truth that made it through my memory-filter as significant. *You've met men like him before, only to rock you off center.*

His glance wavered between me and his bike. "At least the butterfly knew something good when he saw it."

I grinned in spite of myself. "What makes you think *it* was a *he*?"

"Because *he* appreciated my bike, of course. And because *he* just landed on your shoulder."

"Really?"

He hooked his thumbs through his belt loops and smiled.

"Oh, I get it." I chuckled at how easily I'd been duped. "No butterfly on my shoulder."

Another shake of his head. "Babe, you're either a good loser or a good actress."

"I'm a terrible loser," I admitted, grimacing at the term, babe. "I thought it was a lot funnier when the joke was on you."

He lifted his hands and shrugged in a you-hurt-me-first fashion. "How would you feel if all I noticed was the butterfly if he landed on *you?*"

"Relieved," I said.

He folded his arms and narrowed his gaze. "Not the answer I expected."

"Oh, there you are, honey."

We both turned at the sound of a sultry voice belonging to a woman blessed with looks rarely seen outside of Hollywood. Her full auburn hair lifted in the coastal breeze as if encouraged to do so by a photo-shoot fan. Her eyes were light brown, her skin iridescent.

She reminded me of the butterfly.

Harley Guy signaled for her to come closer. "Hey, Claudia, I just met a woman who prefers insects to *Fat Boys.*"

Her full lips stretched into a polite smile, then curled into a grin, as if she'd caught the punch line to a joke. *Nice, too. Darn.*

She angled her head and presented me with a demure Lady-Di smile.

This goddess, shy?

Well, there was nothing shy about her outfit: red spandex top, brown fringed-leather jacket, and black leather pants and boots.

I pulled out the keys to my Jeep and unlocked the door, feeling loneliness weigh down on me. How I wished Morgan were here with me now. "Nice to meet you."

"Maybe Cecil and I will be seeing you around," Claudia said with an eager note in her voice.

I opened the door and tossed my takeout container onto the passenger seat. Strange. For a moment there, I sensed that Claudia was lonely, too. *Nah.* Not with that hunk she was with. "You never know," I said, though I doubted it. By the looks of her, tent-camping wasn't her style.

She pulled on a full-face helmet and buckled it under her chin.

Cecil's half helmet struck me as more of a choice of style than safety. Or maybe it was a sign of defiance. *Full helmets are for pussies.* He straddled his Harley and ignited it into life.

It rumbled. It roared. I took a step back.

Claudia smiled an apology, then slid her visor down and swung onto the elevated seat behind Cecil.

Broad handle bars. Monster chrome headlights. Nothing skinny about that machine.

Another, louder, roar.

I raised my hand in farewell.

Three months earlier, I would have been impressed with this couple's obvious wealth and good looks.

Now, I was just glad to see them go.

☽☽☽

After another sixteen miles down Highway 1, I turned into the entrance to the Pfeiffer-Big Sur State Park and drove past the Big Sur Lodge to a dollhouse-sized building where I verified the number and location of my campsite.

Shafts of sunlight penetrated the branches, needles, and leaves of the redwoods and oaks that formed a canopy over my reserved spot, highlighting my temporary allotment of paradise—as well as that of my neighbors. Cramped into their small space were two family-sized tents, a giant gazebo, tables, chairs, a camp stove, a sink, a stack of deflated air mattresses, and... Jeez, was that a portable loo?

Currently, all was quiet, my neighbors nowhere in sight.

It didn't take long for me to figure out that pitching my tent would take a while. After spending a week camping in the Los Padres

National Forest two months before, the process should've been second hat. But the tents we had used then were small and strictly functional. Unlike this one.

I unfolded the instructions, which started with a tip: *Always practice at home before your first trip.* "Woulda, coulda, shoulda," I grumbled before dumping the tent parts to see what I would be dealing with: ground cloth; tent; rainfly; stakes; main body pole; vestibule pole; rainfly pole; tent stakes.

Back to the instructions. *Enlist help of at least one other person to assist you to assemble the tent.* "Yeah, right."

Trial and error got me as far as spreading the ground cloth, stretching the tent over it, staking the tent corners through the stake rings, and snapping together the flexible, collapsible poles. Now for the tricky part. *Make an X shape over the top of the tent with the body poles and insert into the pole sleeves. May require some pulling, stretching, and adjusting.*

At this rate, I'd be lucky to get the darn thing up by nightfall.

"Looks like you could use a little help."

I glanced over my shoulder.

The speaker had the face and figure awarded to people who eat well, take their vitamins, and exercise. Her hair was gray, though she looked no older than forty, and her clear blue eyes sparkled with good humor.

"You bet I could, if you're offering."

"Happy to help out a fellow camper in need," she said.

I would've reached for her outstretched hand if my own hadn't been balancing the flexible main body pole like a telescopic fishing rod.

"I'm Anne," she said, her bracelets jingling.

I dropped the pole to the ground. "I'm Marjorie. Care for a drink?"

"Water would be lovely," she said, eyeing my *Olympic Dome 4-Person Tent.* "That's a pretty fancy house you're erecting. Four bedrooms?"

"I know it's a bit much," I said, pulling bottled water out of my ice chest, "but I wanted plenty of space. The ad said it would set up in five minutes."

"Ads can be misleading."

I handed Anne her water. "I figured that out about an hour ago."

Anne uncapped the bottle and raised it in a salute before taking a sip. "Seems I came just in time."

"I'll treat you to baked beans and hotdogs after..."

"Twenty-four grams of protein, twenty-seven grams of fat, fifty-five grams of carbs. Not part of my usual diet, but today, I'll make an exception."

With Anne's help, the rest of the tent went up in minutes. She compared erecting a tent to ceremony, the instructions a test. "Sometimes you have to nix the instructions and trust your intuition," she said. "For instance, I always use more ground stakes than called for, just in case my handiwork isn't as sturdy as it looks."

"Wow," I said. Clear-view windows; mud mat; front and rear vestibule; rainfly; blue dome; interior pockets for stashing gear. A little over the top, but it had seemed like a good idea at the time.

Anne took a step back and inspected my new home. "Eddie Bauer, with all the bells and whistles. Did you bring a groundsheet and mattress?"

"Yep. And a sleeping bag and pillow."

"How about an extra blanket? It gets pretty cold at night when the fog rolls in."

The thought of fog creeping in and engulfing the campsite gave me a moment of unease, but I shrugged it off. "In some ways, at least, I came prepared."

"Good." Anne pointed to her right. "The bathrooms and showers are thatta way. Be sure to use them before bedding down, so you won't be searching for them after dark. Did you bring a gas stove?"

"Yep. In the back of my Jeep.

"Good, I'm hungry."

ƊƊƊ

The tent looked inviting, with the inflated air mattress, sleeping bag, flashlight, blanket, bottled water, and just about everything else I could imagine needing inside, including a catalog for the four-day

Esalen Institute workshop that Dr. Mendez had signed me up for while I was here. Something about opening up to further growth and eliminating accumulated patterns that numb the perception. "Don't limit your life experience," he'd said. "Extend your spiritual family with people who will provide you with new learning experiences."

The smell of barbecued beans and hot dogs wafted through the newly operational camp kitchen.

"I could get used to this," I said.

Anne turned the hot dogs and stirred the beans. "Hate to break this to you, but the reason it's currently so peaceful is that your neighbors from the Circus Camp next door are out sight-seeing. Enjoy the quiet while it lasts."

"I wondered why there weren't any vehicles," I said. "Looks like they haven't finished setting up yet."

"Notice the air compressor?" At my nod, Anne said. "What do you think they'll be doing when you're all hunkered down to go nighty-night in that cozy tent of yours?"

"Oh no."

"And they've got three kids."

"Kids are cute."

Anne's brows shot up, and she slapped a hand over her chest. "Not these. No one watches them. They're everywhere at once." She sighed. "You'll find out soon enough."

It felt like I'd just been sucker-punched. "Maybe I shouldn't have pitched the tent."

"I was thinking about moving to a quieter site myself, but" — Anne paused, then shook her head— "there probably aren't any other spaces available. And, to be quite honest, I don't like the idea of camping too far out on my own."

With a brave smile, I assured her, "Well, now you have me. That is, if you don't mind helping out a greenie camper every now and then."

Anne reached over and patted my hand. "We'll help each other."

Chapter Three

IT HAD BEEN A ROUGH NIGHT, just as Anne had predicted. When the Circus Campers returned, which wasn't until well after dark, they fired up the generator, and while the parents pumped up the air mattresses and incited each other with vulgar profanities, their children ran wild, shouting and squealing, blissfully unaware of the camp's quiet-time rules. The little rascals even made a couple of tight spins around my tent before their parents herded them into their canvas den. Once the children were bedded down, the parents started in. And they were worse than the kids. I gritted my teeth and stuffed Kleenex into my ears, figuring it had to be alcohol that was making them so jovial—and loud. They caroused until the wee hours of morning, just minutes, it seemed, before I unzipped my sleeping bag to face the day.

At last, the camp was still. It was also foggy and cold—something brought home to me the minute I stepped out of my tent. Insulated clothing swaddled my body, but all those layers would make using the bathroom a chore. Good thing Anne had urged me to check out the facility before bedding down. I hoped my memory would serve me now, because even my flashlight couldn't penetrate the thick, wet mist.

Needless to say, I wasn't in the best of moods when I got back to camp. If I didn't fire up the camp stove soon and restore my resolve with some hot coffee and the remnants of yesterday's Rocky Point breakfast, I'd probably call the whole trip off.

The rush of the Big Sur River, the descending *caw* of a crow, and the peacefulness of the surrounding redwood grove gradually negated some of the camp's inconveniences. By the time I had finished breakfast and stowed my supplies in the cargo space of the Jeep, my mood had lifted. And a plan started to form.

If I drove slowly and kept my eyes focused on the road, I should be able to locate the Visitor Information Center for maps and brochures offering tips for exploring.

While driving through the fog at a crawl, I had second thoughts about the sanity of yet another one of my hare-brained ideas. I'd heard Big Sur described as "the greatest meeting of land and sea," but this was more like the meeting of land and *sky*. I could understand Jack Kerouac's question on visiting here: "What the hell is this?"

Fortunately, the Visitor Information Center was only a short distance down Highway 1, and, fortunately, I was driving a mere twenty-miles-an-hour, otherwise, I would have missed the turn. The sole woman in charge appeared to be having a less than perfect morning. With a polite smile in place of conversation, she handed me a trail map of the Los Padres National Forest, along with a smaller, less intimidating map of the hiking trails for the Pfeiffer State Park. We might as well have been the only two people on earth, considering how a curtain of fog cut us off from the rest of the world, but that didn't inspire her to friendliness. It took effort on my part to pry out the information it was her job to share.

Back at camp, I picked up my daypack and checked its contents: compass, first aid kit, pepper spray, whistle, mouse totem, journal, pen, maps, and water. No better way of shaking off my recurring sour mood than by a vigorous hike.

My map pointed out a trail that started at the far end of the parking area and headed uphill into the yeasty and fecund redwood forest. The fog had lifted, and as I walked the path, the sounds of light traffic and children frolicking near the Big Sur River faded into silence. I followed Pfeiffer-Redwood Creek until I came across a sign that directed me to the Valley View Trail.

My vigorous hike soon morphed into a senior-citizen stroll. I meandered through warm pockets of air, where the sun had penetrated the dense redwood groves, and through icy pockets of canopied shade. Wind gushed through breaks in the trees and whistled past my face and ears. A plane droned overhead like a giant bee, and, for a while, the only other sound was the hypnotic thud of my boots on the dirt path. An occasional insect buzzed by, followed by the *caw, caw* of crows searching for food. Ahead, lay the carcass of a small bird, the feathered skin shriveled and folded in on itself—a leg, a bone, a bit of flesh. The sign of death and decay amid such beauty brought me to a halt. And that's when I realized I had left the marked trail.

The sound of cascading water struck me as odd. My map had specified that I cross four wooden footbridges and several creeks before reaching the waterfall, and I hadn't crossed even one. Plus, this didn't sound like a sixty-foot waterfall. Not enough force.

Before me, lay a clearing carpeted with the grays, rusts, and browns of fermenting vegetation, bordered by vines, wood ferns, and maples.

And nearly camouflaged by the underbrush was the earthy brown sculpture of a woman.

The sounds of chirping birds, buzzing insects, and cascading water gave way to the sound of blood pumping in my ears.

I sank to my knees on the forest floor.

What tools had the artist used to create such true-to-life features out of what appeared to be plain, unembellished mud? And why here? People didn't leave works of art out in the middle of nowhere, unprotected and exposed to the elements.

No way will anyone believe me, and I left my camera behind.

I grappled with the zipper of my backpack for my journal and pen, hoping to capture some of the sculpture's details with words and amateur sketches.

From my left came the dry muffle of weight on dead leaves.

Goose bumps skittered across my neck and arms.

What was that?

I dug into my backpack for my pepper spray.

Instead, I caught hold of my mouse totem.

A rustle in the greenery. The snapping of brambles.

"Hello?" I said.

The silent presence moved, stopped.

My guidebook had mentioned the presence of gray fox and coyotes out here, even bobcats and mountain lions. At any moment, I would feel the weight of something wild plunging onto my back, its teeth sinking into my neck.

The mouse totem, symbol of trust and divine focus, pulsed in my hand.

Forget about trust.

Forget about divine focus.

I stuffed the totem into my backpack, got up, and ran.

$$☽☽☽$$

On reaching camp, I crept into my tent and gave in to a fit of shaking.

"Yo? Marjorie."

My teeth chattered like a *Yakity-Yak* wind-up toy. "In here," I said, my voice barely strong enough to clear the canvas walls.

Anne peeked through the tent entrance as though playing hide and seek. "Hey, what's up?"

"You'll never believe it."

Vertical lines appeared on her otherwise smooth forehead. "Looks like you could use some coffee."

"Anne—"

"Coffee first. Then we talk."

I followed her out of the tent, filled the coffeepot with bottled water, and set it on the camp stove to perk, the simple routine settling my nerves.

My new friend, I decided, had strange taste in clothes. Who, for instance, wore a long skirt while out camping? The skirt showed much use, but its orange, black, and silver pattern of suns, stars, and moons still managed to look bold. A long-sleeved blouse—some kind of netting attached to a tank top—hung over her skirt and was cinched by an elastic belt with a cat-faced buckle. She must've been in a hurry getting dressed because the cat's face was upside down, rhinestone eyes and all.

Anne glanced up and smiled as though aware that I'd been watching her. "Got anything yummy to go with the coffee?"

"You'll find *stroopwafels* in the round tin next to the mugs."

Her eyebrows lifted.

"Dutch for 'syrup waffles,'" I said. "Two thin layers of baked dough with caramel syrup filling. Mom's parents, my Opa and Oma, were from Holland and introduced me to them when I was a kid. Along with chocolate sprinkles called *hagelslag* and a spiced cookie called *speculaas*. Anyway, if you put a *stroopwafel* over a hot cup of coffee for a few seconds, the filling softens, and it'll taste and smell like it just came out of the oven."

"Sounds heavenly."

"It is, believe me. The Dutch are experts at satisfying the sweet tooth."

While Anne poured the coffee and topped each mug with a *stroopwafel*, her bracelets jingled like car keys.

"I never take them off," she said.

She'd caught me staring again, though she hadn't lifted her eyes from her task. "Never?"

"Haven't for years. You get used to them, honest. They stay clean, too, because they get washed every time I do."

"Are they real?"

"Gold, silver, and bronze. Otherwise they wouldn't hold up to the abuse."

"And all the rings on your fingers?"

"Garnets, amethysts, agates. Never take them off either."

I thought of the stones in my belted pouch, markers for my Medicine Wheel. "You're probably going to tell me they have healing powers."

Anne grinned, and I couldn't hold back a grin of my own.

I liked her.

"I like you, too," she said.

Whoa. Was she reading my mind?

Anne glanced at the abandoned Circus Camp next door. "Until now, I've made it a point not to get too chummy with the other campers, but for you I've made an exception. Hope you plan to stick around for a while. I'd love the company."

"Same here," I said, tempted to give her a hug for showing up when she had. After this morning's scare, I didn't have much confidence in my ability to hold out for an extended stay. "And the earrings?" I asked, unable to curb my curiosity about Anne's colorful, offbeat ways; especially now that I suspected she might have psychic abilities like me. "Do you sleep in them, too?"

She laughed. "Yep."

"Don't they hurt?"

She pushed several gray curls behind her ears. They sprang right back. "They tangle in my hair now and then, but usually they're okay."

"Why stars?"

"You mean instead of diamonds and pearls?"

I nodded.

"My jewelry talks to me. It sings. It protests. It giggles."

"That could drive one crazy," I said.

"Or keep one sane," she countered.

Wild card, Ace, Jack, or Seven?

"Psycho or eccentric?" Anne said as if I had spoken out loud.

Something twisted in my chest. Either she was reading my mind or she could mirror my thoughts in an observe-and-guess fashion. Both ideas unsettled me.

After we'd finished the entire pot of coffee and nearly all the *stroopwafels*, Anne said, "Okay, now tell me what you saw."

"You're not going to believe it," I said.

Her smile encouraged me to blurt out what I'd seen and how I'd sensed being watched.

She looked into her coffee mug as if reading tea leaves. "First of all, it's dangerous leaving the trail."

"I know, but—"

"Never do that again, unless someone's with you."

I had already figured that out for myself, but, darn it, one reason I had come to Big Sur was to contact my dead mother, and that meant spending time alone. I would have to find a way.

Anne shook a finger at me. "Oh, quit looking like the world just came to an end. I'll trail you if it's privacy you're after, as long as I'm close enough to hear if you call for help."

She'd done it again. Read my mind. "I do need to be alone sometimes," I said.

She got to her feet. "Let's go see that sculpture."

"Just a sec."

I rushed back to my tent for my camera.

Chapter Four

"IT'S GONE!" The weight of disappointment bore down on me as I kicked at the bare spot where the mud sculpture had been. "It was right here."

"Are you sure this was the place?" Anne asked.

The clearing, the dried needles and leaves, the vines, the ferns. "Positive. Look, the ground's matted where the statue once was. I wish you could've seen it, Anne."

The clay was still damp as if I had interrupted the artist. Maybe that's why I had felt as if I weren't welcome.

Anne walked in a slow circle, inspecting the area as though it were a crime scene, then bent to pick something off the ground.

I hurried over, hoping for a clue, any clue, as to where the sculpture had gone.

She ran her finger over the object's dull triangular blade. "It's a potter's knife for cutting clay. The pointed tip prevents the tool from dragging on the clay's surface." Our eyes met. Anne grinned. "And you thought I didn't believe you."

"A sculpture in the middle of nowhere? Sounds kind of far-fetched, even to me, who'd seen it."

"In Big Sur, anything's possible," Anne said. "It's a haven for musicians, artists, and writers."

"Like Jack Kerouac and Henry Miller," I said. Part suffering alcoholics, part literary geniuses, Kerouac and Miller shared stream-of-consciousness narratives about life in Big Sur, to which, in my current state of mind, I felt oddly attracted.

"You're leaving out artists of the clay sculpture variety," Anne said, "but I can remedy that."

"How?"

"By taking you on a field trip."

My last field trip had been a high school excursion to Yosemite National Park, rushed, but full of good memories. "Okay," I said, though there had been an exquisite example of local art right here.

Until it disappeared.

While Anne continued her inspection—which seemed rather a waste of time at this point—I toed the duff beneath my feet. What kinds of insects and animals thrived below the decaying needles, twigs, and leaves? I imagined centipedes, ants, beetles, worms, slugs, and spiders, quivering and slithering out of sight.

The sound of rushing water and the raucous outbursts of what my visitor's brochure had identified as a Steller's jay joined with the tinkling of Anne's bracelets in a series of mismatched rhythms and pulses that had my body itching to supply the missing beats.

"By the size of the footprints alone, it's clear that someone, besides us, has been walking around here," Anne said, recapturing my attention.

"You think someone stole it?"

Anne shook her head. "More likely the artist moved it. Tell me again about how you sensed a presence."

Although the sun still cast its warm glow through the trees, my skin felt chilled. "I sensed a looming shadow and heard something moving and breathing."

"What did you do?"

"Said, 'Hello.'"

Anne rolled her eyes. "Tell me you're kidding."

"Then I ran like hell."

"See what I mean about going out alone?" Anne pointed toward a sunny spot of matted pine needles. "How about we sit down for a while and enjoy the silence?"

Birds calling and water splashing hardly amounted to silence. Peace, maybe. Silence, no. Ignoring my previous musings about what lay beneath the forest floor, I sank onto the carpet of leaves and needles, which accommodated me like a favorite chair. I blew out my breath and, with it, my disappointment over the missing sculpture. The solution to the mystery would present itself, if not sooner, then later. Might as well relax and enjoy the moment.

Anne sat in a perfect lotus position, eyes closed, her long skirt hiked up past her knees. She looked like a tripod, balanced as she was on her bottom and folded legs. Which was good, because she appeared to be in some kind of trance, and I didn't want her toppling over.

My thoughts drifted to Antonia, long dead, but not silenced. I needed to know what she wanted. Her inability to move forward was as restraining as a mental ball and chain, her limbo, my limbo. Unless she instigated some kind of communication, I had no way of reaching her—and releasing myself.

Anne opened her eyes. "Tell me about your mother."

A quiver shot through the fault plane of my spine like a low-intensity earth tremor. "Jeez, Anne. How do you do that? I was just thinking about her. At least about one of my mothers. I have two, my birth mother and the mother who adopted and raised me."

"You send out some powerful messages, easy to tune into," Anne said. "I sense you were thinking about your birth mother."

I'd learned in the past three months not to question what I didn't understand. After all, I was hearing voices when no one was there and experiencing unreal realities that would challenge even the most open minded. Yet, according to some reliable sources, I was not headed for the looney bin any time soon.

"Go ahead, hon," Anne said. "I'm a good listener."

Talking about Antonia saddened me, and I didn't know where to begin.

"At the beginning," Anne said.

Invisible needles pricked my skin. Who was this stranger I was about to spill my guts out to? I stared at Anne's clear, open face and saw no malice there. Maybe sharing would help get me out of this midway place, this space of inertia, this in-between. "I don't know much about my birth parents, other than that my mother had an affair with my father. His name is Bob Mask and he was married when they had their fling. My mother, Antonia, gave birth to identical twins...Veronica and me...nine months later. She must've told my father about our births, because he ended up raising Veronica. He took her to Maryland. Can you believe it? For twenty-eight years, my father and sister lived on the opposite coast, and I had no idea.

"Anyway, I stayed behind with my mother. Soon after, she died."

Anne closed her eyes, said nothing.

I picked up a twig and started digging through the duff and litter in front of me. "For some reason, my father wasn't informed of Antonia's death until long after she'd left with Veronica, and I was put up for adoption. Gerardo and Truus Veil took me in as an infant and raised me as their own. It was quite a shock when I ran into my twin a couple of months ago in Carmel Valley."

I took a ragged breath, fighting the anger that overcame me whenever I thought of all the years Veronica and I had missed being together. "I'm having a hard time with that."

"So is Antonia, I presume," Anne said.

"She's dead." I had already told Anne this, but felt compelled to tell her again. Her comment implied that Antonia still felt pain and regret due to her past actions. I suspected this to be true, because of Antonia's persistent haunting, but why would Anne presume such a thing?

My twig had made it through the thick layers of outer duff and litter and was now piercing the earth. "Truus, my adoptive mother, doesn't understand why I want to delve into the past and expose what's over and done with. You'd think Antonia's life meant nothing, instead of holding the key to a part of me I didn't know existed."

"Understandable. Truus probably feels threatened."

"She's not used to me questioning my spirituality, that's for sure, or questioning who I am and what I can give."

"Ah," Annie said, "pulling back the curtain of Oz."

"That about sums it up. Anyway, Antonia was a descendent of

the Esselen tribe, whose territory once extended from Carmel Valley to Big Sur. That makes me part Native American. Learning about the philosophy and spirituality of my ancestors, and how they interacted with nature, is important to me. It brings me comfort."

"Paganism," Anne said.

"I prefer to call it Earth Medicine, but yes, that's what my mother calls it. And when she says the word, she spits it out like it's something dirty."

I sorted through the pile of coarse woody debris that I had unearthed in my excavation—nonliving stuff in various stages of decomposition that bridged the living vegetation above the ground and the soil below. "Actually, she freaked out."

Anne chuckled. "I can imagine."

"I tried to explain that her Christian beliefs and those of the Native American didn't necessarily collide."

"But she would have none of it."

"How'd you know?"

"Elementary, my dear. I'd say many Christians feel the same."

"She thinks I'm communicating with the devil."

A slight scowl twisted Anne's lips. Then it was gone. "Are you willing to explore and be surprised? Are you willing to discover new things about yourself and find your own sense of truth?"

Explore? Discover? Get out of limbo? "Yes, that's why I'm here."

"To experience, or to observe?"

"Experience," I said. "I've observed myself into a self-inflicted prison, always following other people's rules and expectations, their road maps instead of mine."

"Well then, it's time to step into the storm. Because, my dear, your path will not be an easy one."

"Yeah, tell me about it," I said, then caught myself. Had my life path thus far been any more difficult than that of most people I knew? Hell, no. I had so much to be grateful for.

"Do you trust me?" Anne asked.

"If not, I wouldn't be here with you, now." I said. "How about you? Do you trust me?"

She smiled.

"Oh, yeah, I forgot. I send off some powerful vibes."

"Now, don't get defensive."

I jabbed the stick deeper into the ground. "How would you like it if someone could get into *your* head?"

Anne glanced at the mound of rubble I'd uncovered, apparently not impressed. "I send out vibes just like everyone else. Besides, I can't read your mind all of the time, only when your thoughts wave like red flags."

"Why are you helping me?" I asked. I'd been fortunate in making as many friends as I had in Carmel Valley. How could I be that blessed again? Was it true that people came into our lives to support us when most needed?

"Everyone needs help now and then," Anne said, "to steady them as they learn to become themselves."

"But you hardly know me."

Her eyes met mine. "My dear, we've known each other since the beginning of time."

Her words made my skin crawl, but in a pleasant way. "Anne, you're so weird."

"You've got that right."

I chuckled. Shivered.

"There was a time when women always helped women," Anne said. "I mourn the loss of those times."

"I think Antonia, and at least one other ancestor, have been trying to help me."

"Ah, the voices."

"Jeez. You know about them, too?"

She ignored my question. "What language do they speak?"

"I hear them in English, which makes sense when it comes to my birth mother, but the other voice I've been hearing, Margarita Butron, spoke the Costanoan language and maybe a smidgen of

Spanish. How I'm able to understand her, let alone hear her, remains a mystery."

"Do you see them as well?"

I dropped my twig into the earthen hollow and scooped the dirt and duff on top. "I saw Margarita once, in a mirror. It's a long story."

Anne smiled as if she knew how I felt. "Scary?"

"More like spooky. It blurs the separation between what's real and unreal. Everything isn't as black and white anymore."

She nodded. "More like a foggy gray."

"Yeah, until the sun comes out."

"And it always does."

With dirt-encrusted hands, I patted the earth. "Yes, thank God."

Anne leaned forward and placed her hand on mine. "Did you seek help?"

Swallowing became difficult. "Yes, a modern-day shrink, who specializes in transpersonal psychology."

Anne's raised eyebrows prompted me to add, "That was my first reaction, too. Dr. Mendez believes that medical science and spirituality go hand-in-hand, and he talks about the collective unconsciousness and the holographic universe. Stuff I'd never heard of before, but helps make sense of some of the crazy things happening to me lately. He steered me in the right direction, for which I'll always be grateful."

"Thank God for that," Anne said, making me wonder if she knew more about transpersonal psychology than she was letting on.

"So instead of drugging me and giving me months of therapy, he shipped me out of town on a journey."

"Were you afraid?"

"At that point, my life had taken such a sharp turn that fear took a back seat to figuring out what to do."

Tears formed in Anne's eyes, giving me the impression that she either felt my pain, or identified with it in some way. "So, you were all alone?"

"Not exactly. I had a hitchhiker. A stray cat I named Gabriel."

"After the angel?"

"Angel and messenger."

"Where is he now?"

"With my soon-to-be adoptive son, Joshua."

Anne threw up her hands, the stacked bangles on her arm sliding to her elbow with a jingle that could have been mistaken for glee. "And the plot thickens."

"If by plot, you mean change, then yes, my life and relationships have changed due to the weird things that have happened to me. But when it comes to understanding, I have a long way to go. There seems to be nothing linear or forward moving in my life right now, no rational cause and effect, just roadblocks and wrong turns. Anyway, Joshua was mute and orphaned when I met him. But he's not mute or orphaned anymore."

No request for clarification from Anne. "Do you miss him?"

I bit my lip before answering. "Whenever I think of him, my heart hurts to the point of breaking, but he's with Morgan now."

She placed a light hand on my shoulder. "The man you love?"

As I lifted my grimy hands and sniffed the moist, musty odor of humus and dirt, I realized there had been something therapeutic about my dig. "Yes, and maybe someday, I'll tell you about him, too."

"So why are you here instead of with Morgan and Joshua?"

Something in Anne's voice caused me to glance up. "Because I'm not ready for a relationship until I figure out what Antonia wants and regain some degree of normalcy in my life. Before that, it would be crazy to draw the two people I love most into my world."

Anne looked away, and I wondered about her life. She must've suffered greatly to be so understanding of my pain.

"When I think of them," I said. "I want to end this search. I want to turn my back on the world and seek a safe haven where my sole concern would be to love Morgan and Joshua. To be safe, insulated, and isolated. I want to hoard my possessions, and my love."

Anne observed me without a flicker of judgment in her eyes. Bless her heart. "But?"

"Then I'd become even more selfish than I already am, and I'd never know if I was destined to be and do more."

Anne placed her hand over the small mound of earth that I'd patted into place like a fresh grave. "How do you plan to contact your birth mother?"

This question was never far from my mind, a question for which I had no answer, other than to wait, hope, and seek solutions from outside of myself, as well as from within. "I don't know. She's dead, yet she isn't. Sometimes she talks to me" —*You are not who you pretend to be*— "And sometimes I hear her crying, usually when I'm meditating in my Medicine Wheel."

"So, you practice the medicine of your ancestors?"

"The Esselen didn't make use of the Medicine Wheel, but it's the best way I know how to experience, if not understand, the essence of Native American spirituality." I pulled a fist full of stones and semi-precious gems from the pouch around my waist. "These are my marker stones."

"Good for you," Anne said. "So, you found a teacher?"

"My friend, *Gentle Bear*, led me through the first step of the Medicine Wheel. The direction of the East."

"The path of initiation," Anne said. "And in Big Sur, you want to experience the second step of the Medicine Wheel, the direction of the South, where you seek the return of the trust and innocence of a child and the opportunity to re-capture the wonder of being alive." She grinned, making me wonder how she could be so knowledgeable about a spirituality outside of most people's radar.

"As I told Morgan on our last day in Carmel Valley, if I don't learn to trust again, our relationship won't stand a chance. But that's not all. I need to learn how to say no to what hurts me, so I can say yes to love. I crave security but something inside of me still needs to be born."

"Which hopefully will become a reality for you here in Big Sur," Anne said. "Where energy messages are sent to us from all of creation."

And where I may find the teachers I need. "Do you practice Earth Medicine?" I asked.

"No, dear. Currently, we're not on the same page, maybe not even in the same book. But that doesn't mean we can't help each other find what we seek."

"Are you married?"

The twinkle left Anne's eyes. "Not anymore and not in the way you think."

I was about to ask what she meant by that when she stretched out of her lotus position and rose to her feet. "Let's get back to camp. Maybe later, we can figure out how to contact your mother."

We. I liked the sound of that.

☽☽☽

I returned to my campsite hungry and ready for a nap, but a nap I wouldn't get. Not with three squatters inside my tent. At first, I thought that maybe I had taken a wrong turn, but no, this was my Eddie Bauer-room-for-four palace. "Hey. What are you three varmints doing in my tent?"

The smallest of the three, a freckle-faced girl with curly blonde hair, squealed, and the two boys nearly knocked me down in their attempt to escape.

"Hold it," I said, hands raised. "You've got some explaining to do."

"We were just playing," the tow-headed girl said, as if trespassing were no big deal.

"You were playing in *my* tent," I pointed out, "and in *my* private space."

"Well, *you* weren't here," she said. The girl couldn't have been more than six years old, but she certainly had spunk.

The two boys, around eight and nine, looked on, apparently happy to let the little girl, whom I assumed to be their sister, speak for them. But I wasn't about to let them off the hook. I turned to the tallest, figuring he was the oldest. "And what've you got to say for yourself?"

The brown-haired hoodlum looked me straight in the eye. "Sorry."

He reminded me of Joshua. Except Joshua would never have gotten into this kind of mischief. Neither would he have been squealing with laughter as these kids had been when I entered.

Too bad.

A quick inspection of my tent revealed that my sleeping bag and pillow hadn't been disturbed. No damage done. "Do your parents know where you are?"

"Mom got a job at the Big Sur Lodge and Dad in park maintenance," the blonde pixie said. "Christopher's watching us."

"And who is Christopher?"

"I am," the tallest said, his fawn eyes wavering.

I looked at him in surprise. "*You're* in charge?"

He blushed.

I eyed the other boy, who still seemed to be searching for an escape route. "Hope you guys are hungry, because I'm starved."

All three looked at me as if I had sprouted wings.

"You didn't hurt anything as far as I can see," I said, then quickly added, "though that doesn't make it right."

All three nodded in unison.

"Okay, so your parents aren't far off, but I still can't believe they're leaving you unsupervised. Don't they read the papers?"

The trio continued to stare at me, probably wondering what I was about to do next. I backed out of the tent and retrieved my camping stove and food from the cargo hold of my Jeep, relieved that I'd had the foresight to pack everything away. The kids could've burned themselves, started a fire. "Do you guys like hot dogs and chips?"

A slight hesitation, then, "Yeah!"

The three delinquents were actually kind of cute. Christopher was a dead ringer for Alfalfa of the *Little Rascals*, lean and gangly with dark hair, light skin, and freckles. His brother, oh dear, his brother. I tried not to laugh. He was more reminiscent of Spanky, short and stocky, with a baseball cap way too big for his head. And the girl, well she looked like a disheveled Shirley Temple.

Alfalfa seemed to have a sense of shame at least. He blushed when I held up a plate. "The hot dogs will be done in a jiff," I said. "Go wash your hands so you can put mustard and catsup on your buns and take some chips. I also have water and Diet Coke."

Spanky grimaced. "Diet?"

"I like Diet Coke," the girl said.

Her brothers groaned and, right on cue, gave her a look of disgust.

What would it have been like to have had brothers and sisters while growing up? I grew up alone, craving a sibling, only to find out six weeks ago that I had an identical twin sister. And that we were as different as night and day.

The kids filled their plates and attacked their food, barely breathing between bites. "Anyone for seconds?" I asked when they had finished gobbling down their respective meals. All three nodded. "Jeez, when did you last eat?"

"Last night," Christopher managed to say through a mouth full of food.

Poor kids. "Okay." I pointed at Alfalfa. "I know your name is Christopher." I turned to Spanky. "So, what's your name?"

"He's Nathan," the little girl said.

"And you are?"

"Holly."

"And how old are you, Holly?"

"Six."

"How about you, Nathan?"

Holly started to answer, but I held up my hand. "I want to see if Nathan can talk."

He snickered behind his hand. "I'm eight."

"And you're nine, right?" I asked Christopher.

"Ten," he said, arching his back and thrusting out his chest.

I raised an eyebrow, implying that a ten-year-old should know better than to invade a stranger's tent.

Christopher dropped his gaze and shifted his feet.

I picked up the plates and started to clean up my makeshift kitchen, figuring that, with their stomachs full, the kids would run off.

Instead, Nathan asked, "Can I help?"

"Well...sure," I said. "You can put the used plates and napkins in the trash bag."

Holly squeezed in next to her brother. "I wanna help, too."

A sense of warmth wrapped my heart, and, as I gave Holly a chore, it occurred to me that the three children had invaded my camp for a reason. They were here to help me experience an important component of the second path of the Medicine Wheel, that of innocence and trust.

My friend, Ben *Gentle Bear* Mendoza, had referred to the Southern direction of the Medicine Wheel as the "Way of the Child," and to walk it, he said, "You need to reawaken the child within you and recapture the wonder of being alive."

Done with their chores, the threesome looked at me in silence.

I remembered a game called *Snapshot* I had played with my parents when I was their age. "Okay, I need someone to be a camera."

All three kids volunteered at once. "Me. Me. Me."

"You'll each get a turn," I promised. "Let's start with Nathan."

Nathan blinked, as if surprised by the sudden attention. He glanced at his older brother before stepping forward.

"Christopher, I'll need you, too."

Christopher nodded and waited for instructions.

Holly shifted from one foot to another. "Whatta bout me?"

"For now, watch and learn."

I motioned to Christopher. "You'll guide the camera, which will be Nathan, to a spot that interests you. Nathan has to keep his eyes closed until you tell him to open them and take a picture. You'll snap the picture by tapping Nathan on the shoulder. Got it?"

Again, Christopher nodded.

"Okay, Nathan, when Christopher tells you to, open your eyes without moving any part of your body. For five seconds, stare at what's in front of you. Then Christopher will tap your shoulder and you'll snap your eyes shut and tell us what you photographed."

Nathan demonstrated surprising knowledge of the critters raiding the campground tables during his turn as camera. He photographed a western gray squirrel, a Merriam chipmunk, a crow, and a Steller's jay.

Christopher showed more interested in the surrounding vegetation, photographing brambles of poison oak, blackberry, and stinging nettle. "The stuff you need to stay clear of," he said. "Because you'll get stung or get a rash that hurts like the dickens, especially if you get it you know where."

By the time it was Holly's turn to be the camera, we were laughing and screeching like kids in a grammar school playground. In fact, we were having so much fun that we didn't notice the return of their parents.

"What the hell are you doing to my kids?" yelled an angry female from the direction of the Circus Camp.

"It's Mom," all three kids said at once, their bodies tense. They looked more terrified now than they had when I'd caught them in my tent.

"I should have you arrested," the heavyset woman sputtered as she came our way.

The kids looked at me wide eyed. What did they think I was going to do, tell on them?

"Christopher, get your fat ass back to our camp," the woman screamed with the force of a cyclone. "You, too, Nathan!" She grabbed Holly by the arm and yanked her to her feet. Holly winced and smothered a gasp.

Next, the blasted woman turned on me. I half expected her to pull out a rolling pin. "Don't you have anything better to do than mess with other people's kids?" she screamed as if from a great distance.

Inside I was fuming, but I didn't want to make a scene in front of the kids. Their mother was doing a pretty good job of that on her own. But when she called Holly a snot-nosed brat, and looked like she might strike her, I lost it.

"Do you have any idea what it feels like to be called names by your mother?" I said. "Someone you love and adore. Believe me, your daughter will remember it till the day she dies. Is that what you want? For her to remember you with a hole in her heart?"

Holly pulled free of her mother's grasp and dashed off toward her tent. But I wasn't done. "Why are your kids here with me, anyway? A perfect stranger. When they should be with a sitter? Allowing them to run around unsupervised and get into all kinds of trouble may cause you to regret it someday. You'll wonder why they don't come to see you, why they don't bring over the grandkids, why you're all alone."

She stared at me for several seconds before turning and walking away.

I sank to my knees, shaking. I had just told Holly's mother some of the things I should've told my own.

Instead, I'd cut and run.

Just like Holly.

Chapter Five

"IT SLOWS YOU DOWN, my dear," Anne said when she came by my camp the next morning and caught me straightening up my tent.

"What does?" I gave my pillow a vigorous shake and plopped it on top of my sleeping bag, deciding that this mega tent was one hell of a shelter; the kind of hideout I craved every now and then, where I could feel insulated and in control. No bushwhacking, no carving my own trail, no testing myself or taking a risk. A place where I could stay as I was and where I was, rather than face the struggles that awaited me outside.

"Your tent," Anne said. "It's magnificent, but—"

"I love this portable cottage." I patted my pillow for emphasis. "It's colorful and roomy, and—"

"Hard to put up and take down," Anne said with a laugh.

She had a point there. This weighty monster was a bit glampy, though I wasn't about to admit it. "It makes me want to stay put," I said.

Anne frowned as if I'd given the wrong answer to an important question. "It limits you."

"So, what do you suggest?" I wasn't exactly thrilled with her choice of morning topic. Sure, I was here to connect with nature, but there were limits to how close I wanted to get.

Anne backed away from the tent and beckoned me to follow. "Why not stretch your boundaries a bit and sleep under the stars?"

I bit my tongue to keep from admitting that the thought of sleeping without a roof over my head gave me the willies.

Apparently, Anne already knew me too well. "Does the thought scare you?"

"I'd feel so unprotected," I said.

"What kind of protection is that portable shelter of poles and polyester?" Anne asked, jabbing her finger at my fortress.

I knew she was teasing, considering she must occupy a tent as well, but I couldn't keep still. "It protects me from bugs and snakes."

"They can still get in. And don't say it protects you from people, because just yesterday, I heard the shouting of an irate woman coming from the direction of your camp."

The memory made me smile. Telling off Ms. Circus Camper had felt good. In fact, it released emotions that had been simmering below the surface for too long. Come to think of it, the Circus Camp had been noticeably quiet since then. "Okay. The tent makes me feel more secure, like I'm in a cozy little cocoon."

"All in your head, my dear."

I scanned our surroundings, taking in the lingering fog, the moisture dripping from the trees onto the spongy earth below, and the nearly imperceptible breeze, then eyed my tent with its apartment-size rooms, windows, and vestibule. "Sorry, Anne, but for now, it offers my only security."

She shrugged. "I have a surprise for you."

"I like surprises, I think."

"You'll love this one. Although, fair warning, you may be a bit shocked."

)))

Anne led me to a pool of water surrounded by a lush accumulation of ferns, sorrel moss, lichen, and majestic redwoods. Sheets of sunlight streamed through the flat needles of the trees and dappled the greenery below, while water spilled from a mossy, rock ledge protruding from the midst of brambles and vines.

As we stepped onto the springy floor of the cathedral-like grove, something previously hidden from view caught my eye. Mud sculptures. Twenty or more. All of the same woman and child. I dropped to my knees, trying, but failing, to absorb what my mind refused to accept as real. Like the sophisticated sand art creations in beach competitions, the details on these sculptures—from the fine strands of the figures' hair to the smooth texture of their clothing and skin—appeared to have been carved by a master. Water gushed into water, birds cawed, and sunrays pierced my skin, all adding to the magical quality of the scene. I tore my gaze away from the artwork in front of me and directed it at Anne. "How? I mean—"

"Pull yourself together, hon, and I'll explain."

"How could you keep this from me? I thought we were—" I was about to say friends, but really. I had just met this woman. What did she owe me, besides nothing?

"The artist's name is Adam," Anne said, "and I had to get his permission before sharing his secret with you."

"Is he some kind of recluse?"

"He's staying here until—"

A rush of heat spread over my face. "Is he a criminal?"

"No."

I blew out the breath I'd been holding while waiting for her answer. "So, what's the problem?"

"He has Alzheimer's, Marjorie, and his doctors believe he belongs in a medical facility. However, he'd rather die than be stuck in some hospital bed, surrounded by other confined and dying people."

Even without knowing the man or his circumstances, I blurted, "But what if he gets lost or hurts himself?"

"That's why I'm here."

"You?"

"I'm his care manager."

I took in the pond and the wet, slippery rocks surrounding it. "What if he slips and falls? It could happen in a split second, when you're not around."

"It's an experiment of sorts," Anne said, apparently not swayed by my dire predictions. "We hope to prove that access to nature is far better medicine for people with Alzheimer's than confinement. Plus, since contracting the disease, Adam has formed a dislike of water. It's nearly invisible to him and therefore disconcerts him. He doesn't like to drink it and prefers not to shower or bathe in it either."

"So where is he now?"

"With Brock, his personal care aide, who's probably having a heck of a time getting him squeaky clean."

The whimsical expressions on the sculptures' faces and the fluid positions of their bodies brought a lump to my throat. "They appear so happy, as if they're playing. May I take a closer look?"

"Sure, but be careful. The sculptures are made of mud dried in the sun instead of reinforced and kiln-baked clay, so they're fragile."

I walked the springy carpet of needles surrounding the artwork and marveled anew at Adam's talent.

Anne ran a light finger over a sculpture of the child. "I provided him with the tools, taught him a few basics, and he took it from there."

"You taught him well," I said.

She waved away my complement. "No one can teach what he's able to do."

"You sculpt, too?"

"I have a studio in Monterey, part of the tour I have planned for you. That is, if you'd like to see it."

"Are you kidding? You bet I would."

"Tomorrow, I'm picking up groceries for Adam. Part of another experiment, to make sure he gets plenty of fruits, veggies, vitamins, and herbs."

Only part of my attention remained focused on Anne. The other part was trying to decide which sculpture touched me more, the one of the woman watching her son at play, or the one of the child trying to catch a butterfly.

"So, how about Wednesday?" Anne asked.

I started to nod but hesitated at the sound of rustling branches and leaves.

An old man stepped from the bushes into the clearing. His long, wispy beard lifted in the breeze, reminding me of the angel hair we used to spread over our Christmas tree when I was a child. "Is that Adam? He looks like a...a..."

"Classy tramp," Anne said.

Disheveled, yes. Classy, no. Then again, first impressions are often deceiving.

Another rustle and out of the underbrush darted what looked like a dog, slender, thick-furred, with a long, pointed snout. The creature didn't wag its tail in greeting, but held it out, horizontal and stiff. I re-experienced the pounding heart and urge to run I had experienced the day before. Actually, it wasn't a dog, but a—

"Coyote," Anne said.

I remembered how the coyotes had howled and yapped at night during my stay in Carmel Valley. "Since when do coyotes approach humans? What if it has rabies?"

"There's nothing normal about this situation," Anne said. "But don't worry. Buster won't hurt you."

The coyote's yellow gaze met mine, and the half grin on his face gave the impression that he was amused, if not downright laughing at me. I glanced at Adam. He was staring at something hidden in shadow. I followed his gaze, but saw nothing.

A breeze kicked in, causing the towering redwoods to shift and sway. Shafts of sunlight broke through needles and branches and revealed what had caught his attention—a sculpture.

"Sunwalker," I heard Adam say just before my world went black.

☽☽☽

Something cool pressed against my forehead, and I opened my eyes. Anne hovered over me, her usually sunny face set in a frown. She dabbed at my face with a wet cloth, her bracelets jingling with a high, clear pitch. "What are you trying to do, give me a heart attack?"

I attempted to sit up. "I've never fainted in my life."

She pressed me back down. "Easy does it."

"The sculpture," I said. "Anne, there's one of me."

"Try to sit up now. Thatta girl."

I searched for the old man, but he was nowhere in sight. "Where'd Adam go?"

Anne patted my head and smoothed my hair. "You scared the bejesus out of him, passing out the way you did. Maybe bringing you here wasn't such a good idea."

"Did you see it? There's a sculpture of *me*." I twisted around, afraid it would be gone, but there it was, just as I remembered.

"Odd that it has no eyes." Anne said.

It did look kind of spooky with those hollows where the eyes should've been. Otherwise, it looked just like me. "How'd he do it? I mean, how'd he know? He never saw me until yesterday." Another glance at the sculpture and there stood Adam again, appearing a bit curious, maybe, but not upset.

"Can you sit up?" Anne asked. At my nod, she supported my back as I rose.

I stared at Adam. He shook his head as if to clear it.

"He called me Sunwalker," I said.

Anne glanced at Adam and gave him a thumbs-up. "He probably won't remember."

Though my head ached and I felt nauseous, I had an irrepressible urge to confront this man. He hadn't just happened to sculpt a replica of me, days, maybe even weeks, before my arrival.

And he hadn't just happened to know my Indian name.

"There's a spiritual dimension to AD that we don't yet understand," Anne said, "which seems to grow in magnitude as the physical mind and body wither. Adam sees things, Marjorie. He claims that he encounters the spirits of the deceased."

His clothes weren't torn or dirty, just bulky—army surplus stuff—quite practical for camping, and his long white hair was pulled back from his face and secured into a ponytail with an elastic band.

What stood out, though, was his posture—a bit slumped, but relaxed and graceful.

"At first, he may look pale and insignificant," Anne said. "Like a nonentity. But on closer inspection, you'll notice his quiet dignity, gentleness, and strength. Then, of course, there's his art. It's what keeps him going."

She motioned for Adam to sit with us and, to my surprise, he did.

Not a word passed between us, and in time his calm presence communicated with something inside of me.

Just as I was beginning to feel the boundaries between us dissolve, he stood.

I heard a jingle. He paused at the sound, then put his hand into his coat pocket, pulled out a ring of keys, and fingered them one at a time.

I turned to Anne. "What are the keys for?"

"They're his totems."

A gold-plated BMW emblem dangled from the key ring with small studs of what appeared to be sapphires and diamonds. "Keys as totems?"

"Yep," she said.

Adam shuffled over to a work in progress and knelt in front of it.

"But the keys themselves are of no use to him now, right?"

"Yes and no," Anne said. "There's a mini computer attached to the key ring that has Adam's daily routine programmed and offers advice and directions if he gets lost or confused. It's sort of like a Palm Pilot, GPS receiver, and wireless modem all in one. It also alerts me if he's in trouble."

"Which makes you what? Some kind of cyber nurse?"

She ran her fingers through her hair, causing the curls to stretch and spring back like the swell and contraction of ocean waves. "It's a new project, still primitive in execution. He's lucky to be involved, but a lot can go wrong."

"What if he loses them?"

"He cherishes those keys, so I doubt it. But just in case, we also put wireless sensors in his clothing." Anne chuckled at the look on my face. "Kind of high tech, don't you think? It's like he's a member of some exclusive club."

"The society of the senile and helpless," I said.

Anne considered me in her calm, thoughtful way, taking no offense at my sarcasm. "More like the society of souls with one foot in heaven." She patted my knee. "Watch and learn."

"Does that make him the patient or the doctor?" I asked, still unconvinced that she was doing the right thing.

Anne called me what sounded like "smart ass" under her breath. "Actually, Adam's an extraordinary human being, advanced for his time. When he was diagnosed with Alzheimer's, he immediately began to study the disease and came up with a remarkable theory. He considers AD as a 'remembering,' a going back to a collective mind shared with nature and with God, a mind that connects everything. Not empty space, but spirit."

"He believes AD breaks down the barrier between our mind and the Almighty's?" I asked, liking the sound of it.

"That about sums it up." Anne got up and stretched her legs. "He felt the need to immerse himself in nature and give his body the opportunity to acclimatize itself, so eventually, when further dementia set in, it would know what to do. As do animals, plants, and insects. He believed that the bright, natural light of outdoors and the aroma of God's clean earth would relieve his agitation, depression, and sleep disorders."

"You mean, in place of drugs and sedatives, which have side effects," I said, realizing how close I'd come to relying on prescriptive medications myself instead of seeking out the root cause of my problems. I would've done just about anything to stop the voices.

Thank goodness, Dr. Mendez had set me straight.

"Exactly. The intellectual stimulation of being outdoors helps exercise his mental muscles. I also provide him with folic acid and Vitamins B6 and B12 in hopes that they'll slow the progression of the disease."

"Sounds like a good plan," I said. "Everything being natural and all. Sort of like treating the patient, instead of the disease."

Anne smiled, apparently pleased with my guarded acceptance of her holistic approach to AD. "Adam and I made a pact. We would progress with his experiment as long as he could prove that his mind knew what to do, unless, of course, he became a danger to himself or to others. He signed an advanced directive putting all in writing, and so far, so good."

With Anne's help, I rose to a stand. No longer nauseous. Headache gone. "Hope it works. That would mean—"

"That until now, we've been going about the treatment of Alzheimer's all wrong," Anne finished for me in a voice that shook.

"What a breakthrough that would be," I said.

"I'm a licensed vocational nurse as well as a geriatric care manager and have been trying for years to prove that nursing programs need to integrate the spiritual into their course work. Adam is experiencing a crisis of spirit, as well as an illness of body. His sense of identity and purpose is shaken, so he needs help spiritually as well as physically."

Anne searched my face and seemed satisfied with what she saw there. "He had to abandon habits and rituals of a lifetime, and for a while this caused him to become listless, bored, and pessimistic. But then he discovered mud."

"He sure did," I said.

Adam was working his clay, and we watched him for a while before I said, "So many sculptures of the same woman and child."

Anne's eyes puddled with tears. "They're all of his wife and son. His wife died thirteen years ago, and his son is now grown. Adam is working feverishly to memorialize them as he knew them, before his memory fails."

"They look so happy."

"That's how he remembers them."

"So, why isn't he with his son?"

I thought of how I'd left my mother for reasons hard to explain to those accustomed to judging by outside appearances.

"There's little honor in growing old these days." Anne said. "Adam is selfish, yet selfless, weak, yet strong. He's trying to do what's best for his son, and for himself as well. Sometimes one can't do both and must choose."

51

I knew the feeling, trying to do what was best for Truus, but also what was best for me. Sometimes one can't do both and must choose.

Maybe Adam and I had something in common.

"He's trying to figure out what it means to be alive," Anne said. "And what it means to die."

I swallowed with difficulty. "Thanks for bringing me here."

Anne shrugged. "Actually, Adam wanted to meet you. He was the one you sensed yesterday when you came across the sculpture he was working on. He says your mother's here and has a message for you."

Something cracked inside of me. I felt like crying, but held on. "Anne, he called me Sunwalker, which is the name my birth mother gave me before she died. He must know her."

Anne crossed herself. "Then he may be the key."

》》》

When we got back to camp, three children occupied my tent. Again. The bravest, young Holly, jumped up, not appearing the least bit upset at being caught trespassing a second time. "Are you a pervert?" she asked, addressing me.

Anne laughed.

I ignored her and asked Holly, "What's a pervert, dear?"

"I think it's a—" Holly searched my face for clues.

"It means you're bad," Nathan said. "Dad says people like you should be locked up."

Holly's eyes widened and she backed up a step, before edging forward again. Brave girl.

Anne chuckled. "This is getting interesting."

Christopher, who had been silent until now, spoke up. "I don't think you're bad just because Dad says so."

"Now that's my kind of guy," Anne said.

"Are *you* gay?" Nathan asked, addressing Anne.

This time I chuckled, suddenly able to see the humor in the situation.

"Do you know what gay means?" Anne asked.

Nathan shook his head.

"It's okay," Holly said. "I like gay."

"Me, too," Nathan said.

Christopher looked uneasy. "Dad'll kill us if he finds us here."

"Yeah," Nathan and Holly chimed in.

"Well, goodbye then," I said.

They took off like rabbits.

"Parents like that really screw up their kids," I said as I watched them race back to their camp. "They learn by what they see and hear."

"And by instinct," Anne added.

"They're getting no guidance. Unless you consider punishment after the fact as guidance."

"They're getting lots of freedom, that's for sure." Anne said. "Jealous?"

I surprised myself by saying, "Yes. Children need restrictions for their security and well-being, but they should also have the right to an opinion and to make some of their own decisions. My mother's lack of trust in me caused her to try to control my life and activities, not only as a child, but even now."

Anne was wise enough not to comment.

"Look at Holly," I said. "She stands up for what she believes in. She hasn't been broken. At least, not yet."

"Broken by whom?" Anne asked.

"Her parents, teachers, church, society, life."

"You think she'll lose the power of her convictions?"

"It depends," I said. "She's got spunk, that's for sure."

Anne continued to stare at the Circus Camp, though the children had long disappeared into their tent. "They do think for themselves, judging us on what they observe, rather than what they're being told."

"I wouldn't have done so at their age," I said. I had always been the perfect child, always following the rules, never questioning authority.

"So, you're just getting to that now?" Anne asked.

"Yeah," I said, "after twenty-eight years."

"So, who's got the better parents?"

"One of life's contradictions, I guess."

We stood silent until Anne said, "I have some meditating to do. See you Wednesday."

"Wednesday?"

Anne shook her head. "I knew you weren't listening. That's when I'll be taking you to my workshop."

I looked at her blankly.

"Oh dear, Adam really shook you up, didn't he?"

"You have no idea," I said.

Chapter Six

EVEN COCOONED IN MY sleeping bag and zipped inside my waterproof tent, I sensed fog blanketing my world, and it gave me the feeling of being completely alone. Yet strangely, I didn't mind. The fog served as a reminder that I had things to clear up, things to do.

Anne would be busy today, which was good. Although I enjoyed her company, I needed time alone to set up my Medicine Wheel and sit in the place of the South, where the process of contacting Antonia and discovering my true self would begin.

As I struggled out of my sleeping bag and into my clothes, I recalled what Ben *Gentle Bear* Mendoza had told me about the Southern direction of the Medicine Wheel. "It's a place to identify and erase old beliefs, attitudes, and attachments that no longer serve you, the unhealthy habits, ideas, and emotions that you carry around for no purpose other than to perpetuate old hurts and behaviors and keep you from moving on."

After a lukewarm cup of coffee from my thermos and a granola bar, I belted the pouch containing my spiritual tools around my waist and stepped out of my tent.

Sporadic shafts of sunlight penetrated the wet, drooping branches and needles of the surrounding redwoods. Not ideal hiking conditions, but the fog had lifted enough for my purpose.

I followed a gated road into an old oak forest. The path was well marked and firmly packed due to many hikers on their connect-with-nature adventures. I passed a primitive cabin, and then, with Anne's warning about not leaving the trail still ringing in my ears, I stepped off the marked path.

Following what appeared to be a trail made by a series of four, rather than two, legged species, I felt like a researcher on an expedition to a remote corner of the world. Before regrets for an ill-advised detour could set in, I found the perfect spot for what I intended to do, a flattened circle of soft, spongy earth surrounded by a protective wall of trees and underbrush that I wouldn't be able to identify without a field guide. At least I knew not to sit on the reddish-green leaves of poison oak vines or the shamrock-like leaves of stinging hedge nettle, thanks to Christopher's warning during our *Snapshot* game, and it didn't look like I was invading the den of a raccoon, skunk, or fox. All I needed now was an hour of uninterrupted time.

I set my stone markers on the smooth earth, thinking of how the Medicine Wheel represented the four directions, North, South, East, and West, and also symbolized an encircled cross. I lit my smudge stick, let it burn for thirty seconds, and extinguished the flame. When the stick began to smolder, I fanned the smoke toward me with the hawk tail feather I had found in Bayfront Park and inhaled its grounding, aroma. The burning sage, heather, and cedar had an herbal, woody scent, different from the lemony, black licorice scent of the frankincense and myrrh I'd become accustomed to in church. Regardless, it reminded me of how, as a child, I'd watched the priest put incense into the thurible and swing it forward and back, forward and back—with the censer clicking against its chain on each back swing and smoke wafting out to cleanse and purify the altar.

Using the smudge stick and feather, I cleansed the area above my head, toward my feet, and in the four directions. Then I sat, facing north, in my sealed and strengthened space. I placed a candle next to the smoldering smudge stick on the seashell in the center of my circle and lit it, symbolically opening myself to my own source and to the One Source. Finally, I rested my hands on my knees, palms up, and closed my eyes.

Bird chatter—*seet-seet-seet-seet-turrr; chick-dee-dee; weze-weze-weze-weze-weet; zir-zir-zir-zir-see-see*—filled the space around me, signaling all was well. I breathed in and out, allowing my body to relax, then picked up the black notebook Dr. Mendez had given me at the end of our first therapy session. "I would like you to keep a journal, starting today," he'd said after handing it to me. "Personal revelations can come as a whisper in the night, a fleeting thought, or, as in your case, a voice in your head. Record what you hear and see. Share what you have been taught to keep to yourself. Later, we will try to decipher and understand."

What negative behavioral patterns did I need to erase from my life before I could open to the questions that haunted me?

The first thing that came to mind was the certainty that I could no longer be what others expected me to be, starting with the expectations of my adoptive mother. I loved her. I respected her. And I was grateful for all she'd done for me. But feeling obligated to justify my actions and behavior to her was no longer an option. It was time to let go of her life story and adopt my own.

I drew a stick figure of Truus in my journal, and as I snuffed out the candle and smudge stick and dismantled my Medicine Wheel, I recalled childhood memories of her gentle touch, how she tested my forehead for fever, rubbed my back in concern, kissed my cheek. My throat clogged. I cleared it.

No backing down now.

I dug a hole through the mounds of fermenting duff, tore the page that contained the stick figure of my mother from my journal, and buried it. *I love you, Mom, and I thank you.*

Eyes centered on the grave-like mound, I began to sing a song to celebrate the occasion of making peace with at least part of my personal history; a song Ben *Gentle Bear* Mendoza had taught me during our time together in the Tassajara wilderness. *Nya Ho To Tya Ha. Oh Ho Mo Ne Me.* I didn't know the meaning of the words, but their effect on my spirit had all the meaning in the world. Dots of sunshine formed patterns on my eyelids as I continued to bellow out Ben's spirit-song. Every inch of my body seemed to open up and absorb the pulsating energy that surrounded me, until finally, I'd had enough.

I sagged backwards onto the soft, spongy earth. *What now, God?*

A rustling from between bushes and underbrush.

Jeez. Not again.

The parting of strangling brambles and vines.

I sat up, heart racing, my skin a mass of goosebumps.

I should've listened to Anne.

Too late now.

Adam and his sidekick, Buster, stepped into the open.

"Oh, my gosh," I said between ragged breaths. "You scared me."

Adam edged forward, his eyes focused on my journal.

"Are you okay?" I asked.

He continued to stare at my journal.

I wanted to pick it up and shove it into my backpack, but something—call it intuition, a sixth sense, empathy—cautioned me to hold back.

Adam scratched his head, then headed back through the curtain of underbrush, followed by the coyote.

I sagged back onto the ground. *I think I hear you laughing, God.*

The earth's warmth worked its way through my jacket to my muscles and bones. Looking up, I followed the length of the elegantly fluted redwood trunks shooting straight into the great blue sky.

Just as I was getting around to thanking God for the gift of my surroundings, Adam returned—holding a book.

He settled next to me as though we were new best friends.

I sat up with effort, my body heavy, uncooperative.

Adam traced the scrolled design on his book's cover.

"Your journal?" I asked.

He nodded.

"Do you want to show it to me?"

He nodded again and put it on my lap.

I traced the scrolling on the cover as he had done. His journal likely held some of his most private thoughts and faded memories, unrecoverable if lost. "Do you want me to read it?"

"Yes," he said, and for some reason, I shivered.

I turned to the first page, dated **March 21, 1996**.

"You started this journal five years ago?"

"Five years ago."

Jeez. While I was trying to erase portions of my past, Adam was being robbed of his. I shook my head at the irony.

I have Alzheimer's, Adam wrote. *Oh, dear God, I have AD.*

Dr. Peters says my disease is in the preclinical stage, caught early using new imaging technology. The symptoms at this point are hardly noticeable and can last for years. The next stage is called mild cognitive impairment, MCI for short, where I'll start having memory lapses and trouble making sound decisions. Then comes mild dementia, followed by the moderate dementia, where I'll grow more confused and forgetful and will need extra help with daily activities and self-care. Apparently, my personality will change, too. And not for the better.

I don't even want to think about the severe stage of AD, when I completely go to hell. Thank God, Kathleen died peacefully with me at her side and will never know. How long before I become a burden to my friends and my son? How long before I'll no longer be capable of managing my day-to-day life or planning my future?

I've always heard that life isn't a dress rehearsal, that it is short and meant to be enjoyed. Only now do I fully comprehend what that means. All my life I've lived for the future, always trying to get somewhere other than where I was. I have an eight thousand square foot home, a BMW, a king-cab diesel truck (Ford, American made), and a shiny red Corvette. My key chain is heavy, an apt symbol of my accomplishments. Yet, lately, I feel as if it's weighing me down.

What I wouldn't give to go back to the time when Kathleen was alive and we were so much in love. We were rich in ways I hadn't realized.

Until now.

On the page dated **March 21, 1998**, Adam wrote:

Two years ago, today, I was diagnosed with AD. Currently, I'm headed for the mild cognitive impairment stage, still able to drive, thank God, but getting lost more and more. I always make sure there's plenty of gas in the tank, so I can make it home after many wrong turns. Rich people are supposed to live longer than poor people, damn it. Trouble is, I have a disease that high-tech medicine can't fix or cure. Lucky me.

On **June 21, 1999,** Adam wrote:

The cost of nursing home care is shocking. And it's not covered by insurance or Medicare! Yeah, yeah, I can afford it, but for how long? Anyway, I can't remember how to use the VCR, and I can't ask my son for help because he doesn't yet know I have AD. How much longer before he figures it out?

I can't bear for that to happen.

Patrick, my attorney, introduced me to a nurse and geriatric care manager named Anne. I guess he's her attorney, too. Patrick has arranged for her to take care of me. We talked about an Advanced Directive otherwise known as a Living Will and that I have to write down my wishes for future care and treatment. There's a special form designed for people with dementia. Patrick said I can give Anne the authority to make decisions for me for when I'm no longer able, and to let her know my preferences. The directive is not only for my protection but also for hers, in case someone tries to sue her on my behalf.

I continued to skip ahead, since Adam's journal was a long one.

June 4, 2000: *I'm getting lost a lot, but I refuse to give up my car. Anne says I'm beginning to ask the same questions over and over.*

November 12, 2000: *I got in a car accident today. Just a fender bender. But they took away my license, even though it wasn't my fault.*

March 21, 2001: *I left home today. No one knows where I'm going, except for my attorney, and Anne, of course, who's going with me. I left a note for my son, telling him I was taking a trip and not to worry, though I know he will. I'm changing my name to Adam and will find my Eden in Big Sur, the Big South, God's country. That is, until I reach the final stages of this damn disease and need round-the-clock care.*

I looked up and met Adam's eyes. He was crying. So was I.

"Would you like to have it back now?" I asked.

He shook his head no.

"I'll return it when I'm done reading it, okay?"

"Okay."

"Adam," I said. "Why did you call me Sunwalker?"

"I don't know," he said.

☽☽☽

I was surprised, and a bit disappointed, that three particular youngsters hadn't invaded my tent while I was gone. I checked out the Circus Camp and noticed the car was missing. Clouds were forming. It looked like it might rain. I fixed a peanut butter and jelly sandwich, crawled into my tent, and opened Adam's journal to where I'd left off.

The handwriting had changed. Soon I discovered why.

April 30, 2001: *Anne is writing this journal for me. I can no longer do it for myself. Sometimes, even with Anne's help, it takes hours to put into words what I want to say. Like how I feel about my son. I want to hold him, transfuse all I have and all I know into him, make him strong, but mostly happy. However, I can't give him what I have and what I know. Maybe our blood types don't match. Or maybe my love, my concern, all that I have, would smother him.*

During most of his life, I've tried to stand back and watch him fall, hoping the excruciating pain I felt as a result wouldn't kill me. His looks of disappointment, hurt, and anger nearly broke my heart. I watched his chin come up—a good sign as far as it went—and wondered why love had to hurt so much. I would give my life for my son, yet I've never let him know. There are no words to convey to him what I feel. Guess, he'll have to discover it for himself.

I used to be such a big shot. Look at me now.

☽☽☽

When a drop of moisture fell onto the page of the journal, I realized I was crying. I heard the patter of rain on the roof of my tent and, for a moment, wondered if God was crying, too.

Anne crawled into my tent, her hair and clothes misted with rain. "Guess a mega tent comes in handy after all."

I managed a weak smile.

"Hey." Anne's earrings and bracelets jingled. "What happened to you?"

I held up Adam's journal.

"Ah, and I thought you were missing me."

"It's so sad that nothing can be done for him."

"Says who?"

I patted the book on my lap. "Adam."

"His last entry was almost a month ago. His attitude has changed since then."

My look must have appeared skeptical because Anne added, "Girl, he's got one foot in heaven, and if we watch and listen, we may get a glimpse of it, too. What you see as lack and limitation is part of what helps him feel so grateful."

"He doesn't seem grateful to me."

The expression on her face softened. "There are good things happening to him now. He's plugging in."

"Sure," I said, not believing it for a minute.

Chapter Seven

ANNE'S STUDIO WAS NO MORE than a cubbyhole in a former cannery warehouse along Ocean View Avenue. "It's nothing fancy, I'm afraid," she said as she unlocked the door and gave it a shove. "Studio space in Monterey is expensive, thus limited, but thanks to a friend, I was able to get a whopping 500 square feet, including a sink, without breaking the bank. Many artists are going the communal studio route these days, but, as long as I can afford it, I prefer to pay extra for a place of my own."

I stepped into the neat and orderly studio and right off noticed an electric wheel fitted up against the wall in front of me. "You do wheel-thrown work?"

Anne's lips twitched. "I do sculpture now and then, but throwing gives me the greatest thrill." She pointed out a series of adjustable shelves holding jugs, jars, and vases in a wild array of styles and colors. "I start with freshly thrown pieces, then stretch, pinch squash, even drop them."

"Sounds violent,"

"Sometimes it is. At other times, it takes a gentle touch to bring a creation to birth."

To the left of the wheel stood a long workbench with a storage area underneath for what appeared to be large containers of plaster and glazes. I saw a scale for weighing, a radio splotched with clay and paint, and a deep porcelain sink. The concrete floor sloped towards a drain as though the room were a giant shower stall. Anne drew my attention to the bank of fluorescent lighting mounted on the ceiling.

"Full spectrum fluorescents mimic diffused daylight without the distraction of windows."

"Makes me want to slap down a glob of clay and start doing some punching of my own," I said. I'd only taken one art course in college as part of my GE requirements. We were assigned to mimic Pablo Picasso's method of collage. Ha. I barely passed with a C.

Anne crossed her arms, her expression thoughtful. "Feel inspired, do you?"

The variety of objects and forms on the shelves made me wonder how it would feel to create something so original. "Hard not to be in this place."

"Another place to bring out the artist in you," Anne said, "is an art gallery, which I'm proud to say, we have plenty of in Monterey County. Budding craftsmen often start with something functional like a bowl, while others go hog wild."

"Like you?"

Anne shrugged, though I knew my comment had pleased her. "More like Adam. He came as quite a surprise. I introduced him to a primitive form of clay sculpture, using the mud along the bank of the pond. A little art therapy, I decided, would do him good. He could use it as a symbolic language to express himself, like telling stories with his hands. He enjoyed touching the clay and manipulated it for hours. However, I had no idea he would have such great, untapped talent. It's remarkable, really, to have such a command of the form without years of schooling and practice. On top of that, Alzheimer's, even at the mild stage, robs one of the ability to perform complex tasks and to organize and express one's thoughts. Something remarkable, something unexplainable is going on. It's almost scary to watch."

"I know what you mean," I said. "It's beyond remarkable the way he reproduces with his hands the images he sees in his mind. It's like he's channeling into a collective unconsciousness that most of us aren't aware we're privy to." Out of the corner of my eye, I caught what appeared to be a stainless-steel refrigerator butted against the opposite studio wall. "What's that?"

"A kiln," Anne said. "Want to see what's inside?"

"You bet."

Anne's bracelets jingled as she disengaged two latches on the outside of the kiln. "There are a variety of kiln styles. Mine happens to be the front-loading kind." She blew out a breath and opened the door. "It's like Christmas every time I open it. I never get over the thrill of seeing my pieces fired."

The kiln was filled, side-to-side, bottom-to-top, with forms of all shapes and sizes. "You made all this?"

"When the mood strikes, I'm a regular assembly line. This happened to be a bisque firing, where the clay pieces can touch without fusing, so I was able to put smaller pieces inside of larger ones, even stack them, to get as much as possible into the kiln. But when the pieces are glazed" —Anne rolled her eyes— "it's a different story. If glazed pieces make contact during firing, they're stuck together for life, like a bad marriage."

Anne pulled out what appeared to be a squirrel teapot, its tail the handle, its nose the spout. I laughed, a merry sound like the jingle of Anne's bracelets. "Cute, cute, cute."

She handed it to me. "Feel the texture."

I cupped it in my hands as if it were a newborn, which in a way it was.

"It's a bit fragile," Anne said, "since it still needs to be glazed and fired."

I ran my fingers over the teapot's surface, appreciating every detail. "It's rough, yet smooth."

Anne lifted it from my hands and set it on the work surface. "At this point, it's porous and strictly ornamental, until glazed and fired again."

A thought struck me. "Why don't you fire Adam's pieces so they don't dry out and crumble over time?"

"Because they'd self-destruct in the kiln. His pieces are made of pure mud, with nothing added to strengthen them and lessen the degree of stress during drying and firing. I wouldn't know what temperature to fire them at or what color they'd turn on doing so. They could turn red, tan, brown, even gray or white."

"All clay comes from the ground, right? So, what's the big deal?"

Anne took an odd-shaped vessel out of the kiln and placed it on a shelf. "Clay, or in Adam's case mud, can be dug from the ground and prepared by slaking, sieving, and returning it to its plastic state, but that's very labor-intensive and needs special equipment, which I don't have. I buy the ready-made clay in a moldable state and packaged in sealed bags. For hand building and modeling, I use 'open clay' favorable for limited shrinkage as well as safe drying and firing, which is different from the clay I use for throwing."

"How about giving him some of your ready-made clay to work with?"

She waved her hand, dismissing my suggestion. "Believe me, I've thought of that, but it would be too much work to haul the clay and finished pieces back and forth. Adam rarely creates anything small..." She paused and appeared to think for a moment. "I guess I could try using clay with fiberglass in it. The glass fibers fuse with the clay during firing and give it greater tensile strength and resilience. But it would take a kiln larger than mine to fire some of his pieces."

She turned back toward the work area and clapped her hands. "So, what would you like to do today?"

I picked up a chunk of clay wrapped in plastic. It reminded me of the Play Dough I played with as a kid, except this was a grayish brown instead of bright pink, yellow, green, and blue. "Working with this looks like fun." Did I just say "fun?" When was the last time I'd really enjoyed doing something creative?

Anne appeared pleased with my answer. She tore a chunk of clay from a large block sealed in a bag and cut it into pieces with a wire, then lifted one piece of clay at a time to shoulder height and slammed it onto the pieces below.

"Wow," I said, impressed with the violence of it.

"You can get rid of a lot of frustration this way," she said.

"I guess so."

She handed me a chunk of clay and kept a sizable portion for herself. "Frank Wilson, Professor of Neurology at Stanford School of Medicine, says that we are creatures identified by what we do with our hands. So, we need to free our hands from our keyboards once in a while and introduce them to play."

She folded her piece of clay in on itself, using the heel of both of her hands and exerting a downward pressure. Then she rocked the clay up toward her body with her fingers, and down again with the heels of her hands. "This is called Ox-head kneading, where you coax the clay into a workable state."

I thought back to another childhood memory, that of watching my mother make bread. The sensory pleasure she had derived from handling the fresh dough had manifested itself in the relaxed, almost meditative, expression on her face. This feeling of well-being—that everything was right with the world—had filled me with joy, equal to that of watching the bread rise and bloom in the oven. Later, my mother "upgraded" to a bread-making machine, which took care of the mixing, kneading, rising, and baking and, as a result, robbed the activity of much of its joy.

"Try it. You'll like it," Anne said.

And I did.

She left me to it, saying something about unloading the kiln. But she could've left the building for all I knew, so entranced was I with the effort and joy of this child-like play. I hadn't played in years. Too many years.

Apparently, I had some catching up to do.

"Good job," Anne said, in what seemed like minutes. She handed me the wire she had used earlier. "Now cut the clay and check for lumps, air pockets, and foreign objects. If it's still uneven, continue to knead."

It was, and I did.

Anne hummed to herself, doing who knows what, until I finished preparing my clay. Cut, push, pull, squeeze.

Like chewing gum with the hands.

"Enough!" Anne said finally. "Your clay's ready for the next step. But before you go any further, I'm taking you to an art gallery for inspiration."

This woman was leading me places I needed to go. I'd be a fool to object.

☽☽☽

"Few materials are as responsive to a sculptor's hands and tools as clay," Anne said as we walked into the Flowering Bloom Gallery on Highway 1 the following afternoon. "It's plastic when moist and yields to the slightest pressure."

Although we had come here to inspect the *ceramic* artwork, I was immediately attracted to a magnificent glass vase displayed on its own pedestal near the gallery entrance.

"Glazed ceramics are related to glass," Anne said as we paused in front of the glass display. "Glazes are part glass, you know."

I didn't, but then again, there was a lot about art I didn't know, illustrated by my barely passing grade in the subject while at school.

"I can't begin to tell you how glass is sculptured," Anne said, noticing my absorption with this particular piece. "Although I do know it can be blown, cast, molded, pressed, rolled into sheets, and spun into threads."

"This vase looks hand blown," I said. It had an iridescent surface, shaded from gold to emerald to purple. I thought of Picasso's three-dimensional collage technique, with its assembly of different forms. "Do you think it's made of glass layers?"

"Your guess is as good as mine," Anne said. "The light coming through the gallery's floor-to-ceiling windows adds to its beauty, don't you think?"

Forms appeared to float in the walls of the vase, implying motion. When I moved, the colors changed. "Look," I said. "It even radiates color onto the surrounding surfaces."

"It's lovely," Anne admitted. "But we came here to check out the ceramic pieces, so let's get with it."

I turned away from the vibrant piece of glass and noticed a man standing behind a counter. I smiled a greeting, and he smiled back, but graciously allowed us the freedom to roam without interruption.

Anne maneuvered me away from the glass display to a ceramic piece that was equally beautiful and absorbing. "Ceramics are made of clays that become plastic or fluid when mixed with water," she said. "But once they're fired, they can never become fluid again."

There were several expressive ceramic sculptures that took on human form, some headless, some armless, some looking like *Star Wars* aliens, but none with the gut-level attraction of Adam's. I regretted that his work would disintegrate over time.

"Is there a piece you particularly like?"

"Actually, yes." I indicated the statue of a naked woman with no face, who appeared to be hugging herself protectively. "It reminds me of Antonia, though I don't know why."

"Maybe because she looks like she's in pain."

"Could be," I said, then sighed—not a sigh of dejection, longing, or pain, but rather of deep contentment. "I love it here, Anne. It's peaceful, yet full of energy."

"There's energy here all right, a life force that's translated through each artist into action. It's all about keeping the channel open and not worrying if it's good or valuable or permanent."

"Are you implying that anyone can do something like this?" I asked, incredulous.

"I'm saying it doesn't matter. No one will ever think and respond the way you do. So tomorrow, I suggest you just go for it. Whatever you create will be beautiful."

"My mother thinks I'm losing my soul," I said, allowing a nagging worry to surface that I'd attempted to bury during my Medicine Wheel ritual.

"Which mother?"

"Truus. According to her, Antonia is the reason behind my spiritual downfall."

"I don't agree about the soul-losing and spiritual downfall part, but

I can understand her concern. You're taking a risk trying to express your truest self, and you'll be misunderstood and condemned."

"It's reckless," I said.

"Yes, and you may reach the point where you can never go back."

"I feel like such a bitch, pushing my agenda to the point where it hurts my mother and Morgan and Joshua. I wonder if I'm being selfish seeking to discover myself in this way."

"Well, there are bitches and then there are bitches," Anne said. "Don't let guilt hold you back. Prevail against it. Guilt is a sign that you've chosen what you think others expect of you as your standard of behavior and disavowed your own self-directed will. It's the price you must pay for your freedom."

"You remind me of my sister," I said.

"That's good, yes?"

I nodded. "She's the good kind of bitch."

"I like her already."

"She wants to be a Drug Enforcement Agent and loves to wear red."

"Does she have tattoos?"

The thought made me laugh. "I forgot to ask."

"Probably a great big red one in the shape of a heart," Anne said. "I hope to meet her someday."

"I hope you do, too." We were getting sidetracked, but I didn't care. It felt good talking to someone who understood where I was coming from and where I hoped to go. The only other person I'd come across who did so was Morgan. Thank God for Morgan. "Anne, I've made so many mistakes."

"Big, fat, hairy deal! If you want to follow rules to perfection, Big Sur isn't the place for you. You can't be self-conscious or afraid of doing something wrong. You want an authentic personal vision, girl, not hollow imitations. Speaking of which... Do you dance?"

I shook my head. "Too self-conscious."

"Then I know just the place where you can frolic with your inner bitch."

I groaned. "What are you getting me into?"

"Yourself."

Ah, now things were getting really interesting. "If you expect me to get all dolled up, no deal. My tent may be big, but I didn't bring many beauty supplies."

Anne's bracelets jingled as she patted me on the back with the confidence of a seasoned event planner. "Just leave it to me."

"I've been doing a lot of that lately," I said. "Following the leader."

There was a moment of silence, and I thought I'd offended her.

"Just tell me when I step out of line," she said.

I smiled. "Actually, you're good for me."

"You're good for me, too," she said.

Chapter Eight

"E VERYONE NEEDS A CREATIVE OUTLET," Anne said as we entered her studio the next morning. "Otherwise we lose track of ourselves."

I heard her, but wasn't actually listening, distracted by the medley of textures, shapes, and colors of the clay conceptions shelved in a part of the room I hadn't noticed before. What visions, what emotions, what experiences had Anne captured and translated when creating these figurines, bowls, vases, and abstract forms?

Anne picked up a textured and glazed piece that resembled a crouched figure and handed it to me. "Through art we find ways to understand the conflicting emotions inside of us."

I thought of the framed lithograph I had planned to buy several years back while visiting a seaside gallery with my mother. It was a Bev Doolittle, titled *The Spirit Takes Flight*. Etched on a plaque below the painting had been a quote by Chief Seattle. *We are part of the Earth, and the Earth is part of us*. Something about the images camouflaged in the painting had made my spirit soar. Unfortunately, it didn't have the same effect on my mother. "Are you out of your mind?" she'd asked. "Why would you want to hang that disturbing picture anywhere in your house? A patch of ground with a bunch of leaves and rocks and... Dear God, is that a snake?" Torn between the desire to purchase the print and an equal desire to appease my mother, I had opted for appeasement. Better to give in than immerse myself in the thick cloud of censure she wore around her like a cloak and was more than happy to share with the ones she loved.

"Most of us spend our adult lives producing, accomplishing, and setting goals," Anne said, bringing my attention back to the figurine I was holding. It reminded me of the statue I'd seen in the Flowering Bloom Gallery of a naked woman with no face, who appeared to be hugging herself protectively. Both pieces, though expressed by different artists in different ways, gave the impression of people in deep pain.

"Today you're going to discover something free of that," Anne said, "something you can give yourself to for no benefit that you can see. But first you need to relax, and, by that, I mean play, make a mess, let the clay get under your nails."

I handed the figurine back to Anne.

She brought out the clay I'd prepped the day before and slapped it onto the head of the potter's wheel. "I'll teach you a few basics and then let you loose. Pretend you're in Kindergarten and have found a new toy. Don't worry about getting it right. You don't have to get an A."

"Gotcha." I tried out the seat attached to the base of the housing wheel. Though not very comfortable, it provided easy access to the tray in front of me.

"This wheel is electric," Anne said. "There's a foot pedal to speed it up or slow it down. I suggest you let it go at a slow, steady speed. The slip tray catches the water and slurry as you work, but don't let it overflow. I'm not giving you any throwing tools besides a sponge, a towel, and water. Today, you'll just use your hands."

Water, element of the Southern direction of the Medicine Wheel, takes the shape of the container it's poured into, the way the physical manifestations in our life take the form of our thoughts.

"Got it."

"Water is an important lubricant throughout the throwing process," Anne said, "but don't use too much. It's best to use a little, often, and sponge it on. Re-wet your hands and the clay before each move, always keeping a film of water between them."

Water, the great in-between, expresses differently under varying conditions, can be solid like ice or transformed into vapor.

"The clay smells kind of moldy."

"That means it's aged," Anne said, "and bacteria and mold have had time to develop."

Bacteria? Mold? I backed away from the wheel.

"Mold and bacteria contribute to the workability of the clay," Anne said. "So, consider it a good thing."

"Right!"

Anne patted my back. "Okay then, have a blast. I'll be back in an hour or two."

I shooed her away, anxious to begin.

She noticed and laughed. "Wish I had a mirror so you could see yourself right now."

"Bye," I said, my heart pounding.

Once I got the potter's wheel spinning, I touched the cool, wet clay's center. Like my center, it waited to be transformed and discovered. I let myself go limp, allowing all resistance to float away, and, while listening to the steady whir of the turntable, I positioned myself into the slip tray and leaned over the wheel head.

Eyes closed, I cupped my right hand around the clay, resting my thumb on top. Then I overlapped my right hand with my left and squeezed. I continued to work by feel, reminding myself to every so often release my grip and re-lubricate my hands. Pull, stretch, pinch, squash, my hands moved as if possessed.

I felt an opening beyond the mind through which I passed, becoming part of something greater, some kind of eternal flow. Something magical coursed through me and through my fingers, speaking a language beyond rationality and words.

I forgot about time.

I forgot about control.

I forgot about myself.

I opened my eyes, turned off the wheel, and, as with a dream on waking, recall of where I'd gone and what I'd done, faded so quickly that I couldn't hold on to it.

Anne returned while I was washing my hands.

I heard a gasp, but ignored it, having no idea what I had created and feeling a strange reluctance to find out. "Marjorie," Anne said in a strained voice. "What is it?"

"Not a squirrel teacup," I quipped.

Silence, except for the sound of Anne shifting around and turning the wheel. "It's not of this world."

Curiosity got the better of me. I turned from the sink, but Anne blocked my view. I stepped around her.

Whoa. "Did I do that?"

All I remembered was the cool feel of the clay and the exhilaration of molding it with my hands. Hands that had developed a mind of their own, tearing, pressing, pulling, everything just flowing together.

"I thought you were going to make a cylinder or a bowl," Anne said. "What happened?"

"I don't know."

"Think you could do it again?"

"Not in a million years."

Anne ran her fingertips over the flowing moist clay. "Sometimes it's hard to know where inspiration comes from. But in your case, I have to agree. You're an amateur. You shouldn't have been able to accomplish something like this. Even after years of working with the medium, I couldn't have." She pulled up a stool and sat down. "Adam's kind of talent, I can rationalize as a case of acquired savant syndrome, where AD allows for some kind of superhuman mental capacity. But *this* really gives me pause. Do you have any idea what provoked you to create this piece?"

The creation looked unfamiliar, as though some unknown part of me had escaped and manifested itself in the clay. "Not a clue."

"What about Antonia, your birth mother? Was she an artist? Do you think she was streaming through you?"

"As far as I know, the Esselen weren't potters or sculptors," I said, sensing that the inspiration had come via a different route.

"I don't think this is about reproducing a lost art," Anne said. "Rather, the receiving and transmitting of a message from something out of this world. Contrary to what many believe, inspiration isn't earned. It isn't permanent or solid, but ephemeral."

I peered at the sculpture, following its caverns, its protrusions, looking for clues. Something had worked through me, all right, some power greater than myself. "Have you ever heard of the zero-point energy field?"

"It's a universal information field that contains the quantum energy from which we create the physical world," Anne said. "Some theorists believe that the zero-point field holds the history of every soul and connects us all together. Mystics and practitioners of holistic medicine refer to it as the *Akashic Record* or *Book of Life*."

How fortunate I was to be able to share my experience with someone receptive to, and tolerant of, the unexplainable. "Dr. Mendez refers to it as a holographic field or collective consciousness, some kind of super dense sea of frictionless energy and information that we can tap into unconsciously. It's like the whole of the universe was inside of me and I downloaded something from there and it translated through my hands into the clay. Does that make sense to you?"

Anne laughed. "I'm an artist, remember? So, yes, I know what you mean, but I've never created anything as mind boggling as this."

"As you said, I was the receiver and transmitter of a message from outside of this world. What the message means is a mystery. Maybe we'll find out when the time is right. That's how things have been going for me lately. I let go of my questions and wait."

)))

I was still awake fretting over the day's surprises when a small, bundled-up form entered my tent. I reached for my flashlight and snapped it on, revealing little Holly, eyes wide and likely blinded by the sudden, intense light. My heart pounded in delayed reaction. "You scared me."

"Sorry."

I aimed the flashlight away from the child as she edged forward. "Why aren't you in your tent sleeping?"

"I'm not tired."

"Then go to your momma's tent."

"She said not to bother her. Anyway, she snores. So does Dad."

"I'm sure they don't want you wandering off."

"It's okay."

It was *not* okay. But she was here now, so I'd do my best to keep her safe. "Well, come on in then, and I'll fix you some hot cocoa."

She sat at the foot of my sleeping bag. "With marshmallows?"

"Yeah. It comes that way. Instant, you know."

She inspected the space around us, full of dark shadows, yet intimate and cozy with its cocoon-like fabric walls. "I like your tent."

"Thanks. I like it, too."

I slipped out of my sleeping bag and into my down jacket. "Stay here where it's warm."

I had a stash of bottled water, untouched since I'd sampled the water coming from the camp spigot. I retrieved the packaged cocoa from the cargo hold of my Jeep and closed the lift gate softly so as not to wake Holly's parents.

She stuck her head through the flap of the tent as the water started to boil. "Who are you hiding from?"

"No one, honey."

"Mom says you are."

No comment.

"It's okay," Holly said. "I hide all the time."

"From who?"

"My brothers, mostly. Dad says I'm afraid of my own shadow."

"Yeah, me, too."

My shadow side, my disowned darker side, where my weaknesses and foibles resided, the aspects and traits of myself that I found disturbing and was afraid to explore. I needed to descend into and accept that side of myself in order to break free of its hold. Did this child have a shadow side, too, a darkness she needed to explore?

If so, was there anything I could do to help?

I handed Holly a mug of cocoa and fixed one for myself. "When you've finished your drink, I'll loan you my flashlight, so you can find your way back to your tent. Tomorrow you can return it, unless you'd like to keep it. I have another one."

She twisted the mug in her hands. "I better not. Mom'll ask where I got it."

"Then just drop it off whenever you get a chance, okay?"

"This cocoa is good, the best I've ever tasted," Holly said, dodging my question like a seasoned politician.

The cocoa was instant, nothing special, but I knew what she meant. Things always taste better when you share it with someone you care for. Unfortunately, the caffeine and sugar would likely keep me awake the rest of the night. Hopefully, it wouldn't have the same effect on Holly.

"Thanks for being so nice to me," Holly said.

"You're welcome, honey. Everyone needs a friend now and then."

"Like Adam?"

"Adam?"

"The old man who makes the mud carvings. He's my friend. But it's a secret. I promised not to tell."

"You're telling me."

"That's because you're his friend, too. He told me when he was making the mud carving that looks like you."

I shivered. "The one he made before I got here."

"He knew you were coming."

"Did he tell you my name?"

"He called you Sunwalker. Is that your middle name?"

My body felt like it was going into spasms. "Sort of."

Holly's eyes narrowed. "I only shake when I'm scared."

This kid was sharp. "You better get back to your tent before someone misses you."

"They only miss me when they need something."

I sighed, saddened by the many forms of abuse disguised as love.

Chapter Nine

ANNE PROPELLED HER VOLVO sedan down Highway 1, driving the narrow, winding road as though it were a racetrack instead of an obstacle course.

I thought we would miss our destination altogether, but no, Anne had things under complete control. Without warning, she braked, swerved off the road, and screeched into a crude pullout to our right.

"You must have an angel on your shoulder," I huffed.

"Oh, quit being such a fussbudget," Anne said, her moon and star earrings dancing like fishing lines.

I gave an unladylike snort. "I'd rather drive with a ninety-year-old granny."

Anne took no offense and pointed into the distance. "Look!"

Nestled between the trees, on a large volcanic rock, surrounded by crashing surf and shifting sand, stood The Point Sur Lighthouse.

A rush of emotion brought a lump to my throat.

I love lighthouses. They stand tall and firm during times of difficulty, serving as beacons, guiding, protecting, and comforting.

I released my grip on the console and relaxed my feet.

"Feel better?" Anne asked.

"The access gate is locked, and there's no one here."

Anne waved her hand. "The docent will show up soon enough."

"You called ahead?"

She clucked. "Rest up, worry wart. We've got a three hundred and sixty-foot climb ahead of us, one-mile-round-trip."

I straightened my spine. "Good. I need the exercise."

"Now, remember why we're here," Anne said. "To meet with the beacon that will help us navigate the waters of materialism and wealth and the sea we call life."

"To see the light," I summarized. Who or what would serve as my beacon as I attempted to pull back the curtain of Oz? Was there an access point for what I was searching?

"And to access our third eye," Anne said, touching the center of her forehead.

Anne could slide between depth and humor as naturally as an otter at play, and sometimes I couldn't keep up with her. About to comment on what a crazy and wonderful person she was, I heard the distinctive roar of a Harley. "You've got to be kidding."

"You got a problem with Harleys?" Anne asked.

"If it's the one I think it is, yes."

Sure enough, in roared the massive Fat Boy with its monstrous wheels and fenders and a chrome headlight the size of a boulder. And riding it were Cecil and his centerfold sidekick, Claudia.

Anne twisted in the driver's seat to get a better view. "Tassel handlebars. Nice touch."

"It certainly gets your attention, doesn't it?" I said.

For once, Anne wasn't in tune with my mood. "Wow, fork tubes the size of tree trunks."

"Wait until you meet its owner," I said. "You might take a different view."

"Can't wait," she said.

The docent pulled in next to us, unlocked the gate, and led our small caravan into the parking lot at the base of Pt. Sur's giant rock formation. After we'd stretched our legs and paid our fees, an elderly couple drove in and parked their Ford Taurus next to the Harley.

How were two old people going to make it up that hill? The place hardly looked disabled-accessible. Neither Anne nor the docent appeared concerned, so I put my misgivings aside.

As we began our half-mile walk along the curvy, paved road, the docent introduced herself as Linda and, in typical tour-guide fashion, started right in with a litany of lighthouse facts. "It's one of the few remaining examples of a complete, self-sufficient, turn of the century light station," she said, before I switched my attention to the old couple walking several paces behind us. They had to be in their late seventies, and I marveled at their stamina.

"The lighthouse has been in continuous operation since 1889," Linda said. "It's on the National Register of Historic Places and—"

"Who operates the light?" Cecil broke in. He edged past Anne and me to the front of the line, Claudia trailing him, leather-clad-hips swaying.

"Quite a distraction," Anne whispered, eyeing the couple as if they were hot celebrities who had strayed out of Hollywood.

"You bet," I said, once they were out of earshot. "When they're around, nothing else seems to matter."

Anne chuckled. "It looks like they're joined at the hip. Though it's kind of romantic the way she's holding his hand."

"More like clinging," I said. "Like she's afraid to let go." Why would a woman with a body and face of a siren need to cling to anyone?

Anne gave a soft whistle. "I've always wondered what it would be like to look like that. Big Bambi eyes. Thick lashes. Lips plump like ripe fruit."

"Don't forget the hair."

"Yeah, like in those intense hydration shampoo ads. And I always thought those pictures were doctored."

I poked Anne in the side. "She's looking at us."

"Probably wondering why we're staring."

"Nah, she's probably used to that. More like wondering how anyone's hair could look so bad."

Anne ran her fingers through her curly locks. "Speak for yourself. I'm a goddess."

On seeing this handsome couple advance toward her, Linda brightened as if experiencing a mini power surge. For a minute, I thought she hadn't caught Cecil's question. But apparently, she was too practiced for that. "The Coast Guard operates the lighthouse, but the California State Parks and the Central Coast Lighthouse Keepers maintain the buildings and conduct the tours."

Cecil was either fascinated with Linda's answer or a good actor, because he gave the appearance of hanging on to her every word. As he continued to question her, I spaced out, which had been my intent in the first place. To let go and keep the channels open for those energy messages sent from all of creation that Anne had talked about.

The massive, offshore rocks, the crashing surf, and the panoramic views of the ocean and mountains provided all the ingredients for a meditative state. In fact, they took my breath away. What there was left of it, anyway. I was definitely out of shape.

Speaking of which...

I peered at the old couple now walking several yards behind us and slowed my pace, motioning for Anne to go on without me. The pair seemed engrossed in their surroundings—and each other—not in the least bit perturbed at missing the field trip spiel.

Eventually, our group made it to the summit, only to meet a chilly wind blowing in gusts around sandstone buildings, restored barns, and a visitor center. Linda pointed out a blacksmith and a carpenter shop. I tried to envision the people who had once lived and worked here. What had life in such an environment required in personal sacrifice? How had they dealt with the loneliness and isolation?

Linda mentioned a ghost tour.

No thanks. There were enough ghosts in my life already.

I hung back some more, deciding it was time to introduce myself to the old couple and see if they needed a hand. The rest of the group continued on, oblivious to my desertion.

When the couple caught up with me, I asked, "Are you okay?" They smiled and nodded, but I noticed the strain on their faces. "How about we take a breather? We can catch up with the others later."

"That sounds like a mighty fine idea, young lady," the man said, wobbling as if he might topple.

I reached out with the intent of offering my support, but ended up shaking his hand. "My name is Marjorie."

His hand felt skeletal, yet strong. "Nice to meet you, Ms. Marjorie. I'm Bill, and this is my wife, Emily."

For the first time, I noticed Emily's striking blue eyes and prominent cheekbones, currently pink with cold. "This is a tough hike," I said. "I'm amazed at how well you're doing."

Emily reached for Bill's hand and gave it a squeeze. "We came here on our honeymoon, fifty years ago—"

"But it didn't seem this steep at the time," Bill finished for her. He smiled at his wife with the love-struck expression of a newlywed, and my chest grew warm, in spite of the outdoor chill. Suddenly, this couple didn't appear bland anymore.

"Ready to catch up with the group and tackle those stairs?" I asked after a short rest.

"Guess if we can make it to the top," Bill said, "we've still got a few miles left in us."

By the time we'd climbed the spiral staircase to the lamp tower, Linda had reached the end of her spiel. "Point Sur's Fresnel lens was replaced in 1972 with an electric incandescent lamp. In 1975, the incandescent lamp was replaced by a rotating aero-beacon mounted on the fog signal room's roof. The aero-beacon was later moved into the light tower to protect it from the wind. Light from today's aero-beacon is visible for 23 nautical miles."

I sighed, glad we'd made it, then left the elderly couple to themselves. They were doing just fine without me, giving each other the strength they needed.

The docent turned to head back down the stairs. And that's when Cecil recognized me. His wide-eyed look and sudden smile implied that I'd just made his day. "Hey, aren't you the Butterfly Lady?"

Anne looked at me with question marks in her eyes.

"Yep, that's me. And you're the Harley Guy."

Cecil's eyes strayed to Anne. "And who's this New-Age goddess you've teamed up with?"

"The Good Witch of the South," Anne quipped, "fierce protector of simple, kind folk."

He struck his forehead with his palm. "Of course."

She reached out her hand. "Been waiting to meet you with bated breath."

"A witch, with a sense of humor," he said, shaking her hand. "I like that. The name's Cecil." He turned to his partner, and I sensed the special bond missing between them that had been so evident between Bill and Emily. "And this is Claudia."

"No nickname?" Anne asked in mock surprise. "Harley Guy, Butterfly Lady, Good Witch of the South, and..."

"Not that I'm aware of," Cecil said, as though daring Anne to come up with one.

With an I'm-not-going-there smile, Anne winked at Claudia, who made no response. Apparently, she was as zoned out as I'd been much of the morning. Or maybe she just didn't give a darn.

"Hey," I whispered to Anne, when Cecil and Claudia turned to follow Linda down the stairs. "What happened to all that talk about navigating the waters of materialism and wealth?"

Her eyes hardened. "Once I was attracted to men like Cecil, like a moth to a flame. But not anymore. They want to own you and then proceed to feed off you like vampires, leaving you weak and them strong—at least until their next feeding."

"You sound bitter," I said, surprised. During the short time I'd known her, Anne had come across as tolerant to a fault of other people's foibles, including my own. "You must have gotten burned."

"Cremated, darling. This is my second life, and I'm back as a warrior."

"Anyway," I said, "he already has a girlfriend."

As I watched the northwesterly wind push the sand across the narrow neck of Big Sur Point, I realized that, in the matter of a few hours, I'd seen the difference between the relationship I once had with Cliff and the one I now had with Morgan. Like the Big Sur Light House and the northwesterly wind, I wanted to cast my own light and push the sands of my own life story. Cliff hadn't understood this, Morgan had. Like Cecil, Cliff had walked ahead of, rather than next to, the woman he loved. *His* life's agenda, not mine, had taken priority in his mind. Morgan, by contrast, had released his urge to fence me in, thus freeing me to pursue my own path, strengthened by the assurance that he would wait for me and care for Joshua until my return.

I had accessed my third eye, and the flash of my future with Morgan, as seen while observing Bill and Emily, the elderly couple honeymooning after fifty years of marriage, assured me that I was headed in the right direction.

Chapter Ten

"HOW'S ADAM?" I ASKED over coffee at my campsite the following morning. The fog that had plagued the Pfeiffer Big Sur campground practically since the day of my arrival had lifted, which bode well for a warm, sunny day.

Anne inhaled the steam misting from her mug. "Pretty good, considering. He has a routine going that's just about automatic, but it's never a sure thing. If one link in the routine breaks, then the links that follow are lost. The mini-computer attached to his key chain helps. As do Buster and Adam's personal aide, Brock." Anne shifted on the log we were sitting on and blew into her coffee, sending out another stream of vapor. "Somehow, Buster, barely more than a pup, sensed Adam's predicament from the get-go and elected himself guide dog. It's almost as if he has an innate ability to sense nonverbal communication and mirror it back."

"Holly knows about Adam," I said, offering Anne a blueberry scone. I was all out of *stroopwafelen*.

She patted her stomach and shook her head. "Yes, Adam told me. But so far, she and her brothers have kept his existence to themselves, thank God, considering who they have for parents."

"I'd like to believe they're just watching out for their kids."

Anne quirked an eyebrow. "If they were watching out for their kids, they wouldn't leave the little tykes alone as often as they do. This is a family-friendly park, but that doesn't guarantee their safety." She set down her cup and extended her legs in a long stretch, her sandaled feet poking out from beneath her long skirt.

Who wore sandals while out camping and hiking, especially in this variable weather?

"Want to go see Adam?" Anne asked.

"Sure." I grabbed the empty mugs and took them to the community faucet, my primary source of water now, ice cold and straight from Mother Earth. Water, like emotions, shouldn't be bottled, but allowed to run free. Happy water, I decided, tasted better. A small bird crept up the redwood nearest me, poking its thin curved beak into the bark as it climbed.

"Maybe Adam can beat AD," I said on my return. "Miracles like that happen all the time, you said so."

Anne stood and did a yoga-style stretch. She inhaled and raised her arms over her head, then exhaled and bent forward until she was touching her nose to her knees. One second, two seconds. My muscles tightened protectively. "You're not being realistic," she mumbled through the folds of her skirt.

I put down the rinsed mugs and tried to imitate Anne's stretch— *hold, hurt, hold.* But I couldn't get my nose within a foot of my knees. "Isn't there a way to slow Alzheimer's down?"

"That's why I'm here, dear. I spend time with him, make sure he's eating right, and provide him with vitamins, herbs, ritual, and ceremony."

"Ritual and ceremony?" This surprised me coming from Anne, though it shouldn't have, considering she had the worldview and lifestyle of a modern-day hippie.

"I use a little Christianity mixed in with the wisdom of other religious traditions, add a little Native American philosophy, and even a pinch of white *magick* to help him accept the will of the Divine."

Her methods intrigued me. She intrigued me. Maybe we were more alike than I'd realized.

"I'm leading him on a journey, my friend, kind of like the one you're on, to discover his internal beauty and forgive his body and himself."

I nodded, though not sure I agreed with Anne. As far as I could tell, Adam and I were not on the same journey at all. While Adam was *losing* his mind and trying to *hold on to* his past, I was *releasing* the hold of my past in order to *discover* my mind.

"Ritual and ceremony help him access whatever it is that can heal him," she said, "so he can die in peace rather than resentful and angry."

The stretch Anne had performed earlier was beyond my ability, so I resorted to a more attainable variety. I bent down and touched my toes, reached to the right, reached to the left. "What about medical science?"

With a smile that appeared suspiciously like a challenge, Anne put her hands behind her back in a prayer position and brought her head down to the front of her knees. "At the moment, medical science offers him little hope, other than drugs to slow down the process."

Was this woman made out of rubber? "So, you're his nurse, medicine woman, and priestess."

"Witchdoctor," she said, coming out of a forward bend that required the flexibility of a contortionist.

I smiled—couldn't help it. Witchdoctor sounded appealing, considering medical science more or less gave up on people like Adam. Still, I felt the need to make another argument in favor of traditional medicine. "Shouldn't he be in some kind of care facility where he'd be more comfortable?"

"In prison, you mean?" Anne asked, eyes smoldering.

When I didn't answer, she shrugged. "Anyway, we can't make the choice for him."

"Says who?"

"Officials with Adult Protective Services, the Geriatric Network, and the Public Conservator's office for starters. Would you like me to go on? Adam made his preferences clear—in writing. He wasn't merely involved in the planning, he instigated it. Anyway, he has a right to be on his own. He's in no eminent danger, he's not suicidal, he's not homicidal, he provides himself with food and shelter—"

"Oh, come on," I said. "He can't cook, let alone use the camp stove. He can't even remember where he puts things much of the time. How can he provide for himself?"

Anne's expression softened. "Simple. He hired me. He also hired Brock to help him bathe, accompany him on trips to the doctor, and act as a sitter when I'm not around." She paused, let out her breath. "I won't force him into a shelter, Marjorie. I won't take away his dignity."

"You call this dignity?" I blurted, feeling an urge to burst into tears. What was wrong with me? I hardly even knew the man.

"Open your eyes, girl." Anne spread her arms wide and turned in a circle. "This is holy ground, a place of compassion, honesty, and love. I'm trying to make his journey worthwhile, regardless of the outcome. Adam is learning what it means to let go...and to die."

Let go and die. Was that what my adoptive father had learned to do after he was diagnosed with terminal cancer? I had caught him crying once when he thought he was alone. But I never heard or saw him cry again. He remained kind, loving, and upbeat until the end.

God, how I missed him.

A sudden thought entered my head.

"That's it, Anne. Antonia hasn't learned to let go and die."

"Some people aren't open to the light when it comes for them," Anne said. "They don't say *yes* to it and therefore stay in the dark until they're ready to be brought out of it. Something must have been left undone."

"Yes, but what?"

Anne's gaze bored into mine. "Watch Adam. He may have some answers."

A man with AD. Was that possible?

☽☽☽

Adam was working on a mud sculpture when Anne and I arrived, his hands wobbly as he manipulated the wet clay. The intertwined trees, scrubs, and brambles, the gushing waterfall, and the sunrays oversaw all as if the greatest Creator of all were watching.

"He looks so peaceful," I said.

"He's happier now than when he was in good health and had the world by the tail," Anne said. "He once told me that some of his acquaintances, who were strapped for cash, laughed more often and expressed more joy than he ever did. He had tons of money, but no time to live."

No time to live. That sounded like the path I'd been on. Until Antonia came calling and rocked my world. I was obsessed with the same goals that drove the Silicon Valley company I worked for: speed, productivity, and the constant need to upgrade.

"Adam's peace shows up in his sculptures," I said, "which aren't being preserved."

"That's the beauty of it, don't you see," Anne said. "No ego is involved, no prestige, no pressure. For once in his life, Adam's doing something that's not about money and fame. It's amazing, really, how, in spite of AD, the messages get through from his mind to his fingers when he works with clay."

"Kind of like those sand mandalas Tibetan monks create," I said. "Only to destroy them on completion to demonstrate the impermanence of existence. Or the beach sculptures people construct out of sand and water. Hours of work and then, poof, they wash away with the tides." Although I got it in my head, the concept didn't translate to understanding with my heart. Something told me it was important to preserve some of Adam's work, that it had a purpose and was meant to be used.

He was sculpting with such intensity that, at first, he seemed oblivious to our presence.

"Answers arrive in many forms," he said when we reached his side. He studied his mud creation with a faint smile.

"He's found his sanctuary," Anne said softly. "He's receiving thoughts and impressions from outside of himself."

As I had in Anne's studio. "Maybe Dr. Mendez's suggestion is true, that the world's like an ocean and we're all connected like a spiritual community of some kind."

Anne slapped her thigh and raised her hands, bracelets jingling. "Hallelujah. I believe we may be on the same page after all."

I grinned at her enthusiasm. "That would make our belief in the separation of our consciousness an illusion."

Adam stopped working on his sculpture and looked at me. Something appeared in his eyes, a new intelligence, just before he said, "You can't please your mother."

"What?" Maybe I'd misunderstood him.

"Prepare your mind," he said. "She'll contact you when she's ready."

My vision blurred.

Another nudge to my side from Anne. "Remember what you said about the separateness of consciousness being an illusion? This isn't coming from Adam. He can no longer reason to such an extent. The spirit world is active around him. He offers no resistance."

I stared at the grizzled old man, feeling as though I had entered a dream, where the impossible happens and makes perfect sense. He had not only read my mind but also that of my dead mother.

Adam turned away, as if nothing of importance had transpired between us, and resumed work on his sculpture.

"Adam?" I said.

He turned and tilted his head.

"Do you know my mother?"

He blinked several times and scratched his head.

"Does she want to tell me something?"

He looked at me, yet through me.

Anne placed her hand on my shoulder to steady me. "Adam, tell us about the sculpture you created of Marjorie."

Adam followed the direction of her gaze to the clay piece I had found so disturbing. Why hadn't he given it eyes? He looked startled for a moment. "Antonia?" He cocked his head and turned to look into my eyes. "She said you were coming." A hesitation, and then his face cleared. "Sunwalker."

A fog-like dizziness overtook me, creating the sensation of my brain floating free of its physical boundaries. I caught Anne's arm for support. There was no way Adam could've known Antonia's name, let alone the name she'd given me before she died.

91

Unless she'd told him.

Was Antonia attempting to contact me through Adam?

If so, I was one step closer to discovering the meaning of her message from beyond the grave.

Chapter Eleven

WHEN ANNE OPENED THE DOOR of the kiln, I got a sense of the separation and wonder a mother must feel on seeing her newborn for the first time. *By what miracle has this child been created—in me, through me?* Anne, too, had a look of heightened anticipation about her, given the flush of her cheeks and the slight tremor of her hands. "Even after years of working with ceramics," she said as she birthed my sculpture from the belly of the kiln, "I still get excited when I see a fired piece for the first time. Firing is the most critical part of the ceramics process. It converts weak clay into a strong, durable, form."

Weak into strong.

"It shrank," I said.

Anne chuckled and held it to the light. "Clay shrinks over ten percent from its raw to its fired state." She rotated it in her hands. "Good. No cracks or warping."

No mold. Blemish free.

"The color is different, too. It looks whiter. Smoother."

"That's part of the thrill, Marjorie. You never know what your piece will look like after a fiery 1,940 degrees in the kiln. When you submit something to heat, it becomes something else."

At my silence, Anne broke off her inspection of my handiwork and scrutinized me instead. "Well?"

"I feel alienated from it, as though my work and someone else's got switched in the kiln."

"I call that the 'Are you sure that's my baby?' syndrome," Anne said, "which often happens at the bisque stage. You've been separated from the piece for a while and the energy of inspiration has worn off. It has also changed in color, size, and texture."

"Maybe if I feel the peaks and hollows, I could recognize it tactilely, you know, experience a rebirth rather than a birth."

Anne nodded and handed over the bisque piece.

I closed my eyes and explored the fired clay with my fingers, trying to remember. Pull, stretch, pinch, squash. What had inspired me? What invisible guide had directed my hands? Familiar warmth flowed through me, along with the desire to connect with the lost part of me that had somehow manifested itself within the clay and survived the fiery kiln, only to come out stronger. *No warps, no cracks.*

But the answers didn't come.

I opened my eyes and handed the piece back to Anne. "It's painful to look at, yet it invigorates me and makes room for hope. Does it do the same for you?"

"For me, it's like hearing a disturbingly beautiful symphony."

Anne set the piece on a turntable and spun it slowly, studying it from all angles. "You could brush on some colored stains or experiment with different glazes. Maybe blue. It looks fluid like water and sky..."

A picture of my sister came to mind, with her passion for red— red leather jacket, red boots—my strong, courageous, passionate sister. Then I thought of my red-skinned ancestors, warm, simple, trusting. "No. It has to be red."

"Are you sure? Red is an odd color, hard to control. It does strange things in the kiln, sometimes even turns black."

"The more shades of red the better," I said. "Do you have an air brush?"

"And what do you know about air brushing?"

"Absolutely nothing. But I'd like to try spraying the color on."

"Wow, aren't you brave all of a sudden."

"You said art was something we can give ourselves for no benefit that we can see."

"Spraying on the color with an airbrush is good for gradual color transition," Anne admitted. "It gives a soft, light-and-shadow effect, where the colors blend and seem to melt away at the edges. It's a technique I use when a work is unusual in shape and size, such as this one." She gave the sculpture a final slow spin. "Tell you what. I'll demonstrate how to use the spray gun and compressor and let you practice on newspapers. Then I'll show you where I store the glazes and you can experiment with different shades on some of my bisque rejects."

No one trained me for this. What if I mess up? "Maybe you better teach me how to paint the glaze on too, just in case the air brush doesn't work out?"

$$\mathcal{D}\,\mathcal{D}\,\mathcal{D}$$

It was well past noon by the time Anne had finished with her instructions. "You'll find some energy bars and bottled water in the fridge," she said, then waved goodbye and left me to it.

The idea of air brushing the piece appealed to me. It seemed so freeing, so easy. In actuality, it was neither. Each time I aimed the gun at the newspaper, envisioning a soft, sheer dusting of color settling on its surface, I ended up with blotches and splats that reminded me of the damage done by those paint guns used as toy weapons. The airbrush would clog, or the compressor would kick in, and the new surge of power would blast the paint—and its musty, sulfuric fumes—out of control.

About to call it quits, I heard a voice. *Put the gun away.*

Whoever it was, I had to agree. It was time to put the gun away. Too violent. Too unruly. I turned on the radio, not bothering to change the current rock-and-roll station to one more suited to my taste. I didn't have a clue as to what I was doing, and I definitely wasn't transmitting any insights from the depths.

Time to regroup.

Nodding to the Rolling Stones, I rotated the turntable. The fluorescent light played off the bisque surface of the sculpture, shadow and light, shadow and light.

Then a small window opened in my mind.

I'll call it Darkness and Dawn.

Drums pounded, guitars strummed, and voices wailed as I continued to rotate the sculpture. How soft and malleable the clay had once been in my hands and how hard it was now due to the inferno in the kiln, temperatures of unimaginable heat, hot enough to melt glass.

The Rolling Stones sang about the color black, and as their loud, piercing music vibrated around and through me, I picked up a paintbrush and dipped it into a jar of crimson glaze.

"Red. It has to be red."

I dabbed the glaze onto one section of my sculpture. Assertive ruby swipes of color brightened the surface before fading into dull patches as they dried. *Red is good*, the voice said. *Now a dab of green. There. Yes. And there. Now brown.*

While switching glazes from Holiday Green to Walnut Brown, I lost control. And as the Rolling Stones continued to sing about painting things black, I wondered if maybe I should've left the piece alone.

☽ ☽ ☽

On her return to the studio, Anne turned off the radio. "*You*, listening to rock and roll. Why does that strike me as odd?" She eyed my handiwork and her mouth tensed. "So, you decided not to use the air brush after all."

"It wouldn't cooperate," I said, unmoved by what sounded like disappointment in her voice. "Let's say, I faced a bit of resistance."

Her eyebrows nearly disappeared into her curly gray hair.

"I knew from the beginning this work wasn't mine," I said. "If it's ruined, it's ruined. No big deal."

"But—" She blinked and cleared her throat— "I had it scheduled for a showing at the gallery on Saturday."

I broke into a sweat, as if the room had turned into a kiln set to bisque firing. "Don't you think you jumped the gun a bit?"

"I didn't think your muse would allow you to screw up this badly."

Maybe I should have listened to the Rolling Stones and painted it black. "Actually, I wouldn't have wanted it displayed in public anyway. So, no big loss."

Anne gave the turntable a spin and watched as the reddish, greenish, brownish conglomeration twirled like a ballerina doing a not-so-perfect pirouette. "You were willing to display Adam's."

"That's different."

"Hypocrite."

Though I hated to admit it, she was right. I'd been anxious to share Adam's work, but was averse to sharing my own. "Too late now."

Anne squinted as if in pain. "I should've warned you that certain glazes don't mix well on the same piece. And red is so... finicky."

At that moment, I came close to understanding how Adam must feel. As soon as you start concentrating on the outcome instead of the process, the joy is gone. "If it's any consolation, I had a ball ruining this piece, Anne. I really did."

One more glance at the work of art turned aberration and we walked away, no longer worried that it might fall and break or be stolen. It was just a glob of altered earth, manipulated by human hands, inspired by mind and spirit.

Chapter Twelve

HOLLY, CHRISTOPHER, AND NATHAN were up early the next morning. No surprise. Not much for three kids to do in a shared tent half the size of the one I had all to myself. But they were quieter than usual. No running wild, no shouting and squealing. What was going on?

Nestled in my synthetic cocoon, I listened for clues. The words "fireworks" and "parade" drifted my way, reminding me of what day it was: The Fourth of July.

Firework shows always start just before dark and last into the forbidden hours of night. Magical patterns launch into the sky. Cylinders of yellow, orange, red, and green travel outward, explode, and then shower down like willow branches, or burst into chrysanthemum-like flowers and spheres of colored stars. Memories of the popping, the whistling, and the rumbling, along with the quiet energy of the kids' excitement in the chilly morning air, caused the child in me to rejoice and the adult in me to mourn a deep loss. When was the last time I'd felt the emotional, almost magical, intensity of joy and excitement in a world otherwise focused on competition, achievement, and the drive to acquire?

I threw back the cover of my sleeping bag. Cold air latched on to me and wouldn't let go. I pulled on my insulated clothing and prepared a pot of coffee on my camp stove, then tossed a handful of trail mix into my mouth, the burst of fruit and nut flavors lifting my mood.

"Marjorie," Holly called out. "We're going to a parade!"

I waved at her, but didn't call back. The last thing I needed was to upset her parents.

"Holly, shut your trap, or the trip is off," yelled a disgruntled male from inside his tent.

Holly giggled and waved at me. What a trooper.

I had made no plans for today, but with Anne around something was sure to come up.

As though conjured up by my thoughts, Anne walked up and said, "Hey sport."

"How do you do that?" I asked. "I didn't even hear you coming."

Her earrings caught a ray of sunlight and sparkled like mini firecrackers. "I walked on tip-toes so I wouldn't attract the kids' attention."

"You don't like those cute little munchkins?"

Anne grimaced. "It's their parents I prefer to avoid."

"Yeah, they're hard to warm up to." I poured two mugs of coffee, never tiring of the joy I felt on smelling a fresh brew.

"Brock's watching Adam," Anne said, "which frees me up to show you something at the studio."

I pictured the sculpture—abandoned on the turntable—and felt a knot in my chest.

"As long as we avoid Alvarado Street because of the upcoming parade, Monterey should still be relatively quiet."

"The kids sure are excited," I said, handing Anne her coffee. "Doesn't that just bring it all back?"

"Don't know about you," Anne said after taking a long sip, "but I plan on being right there in the thick of things when the fireworks get started. Want to come along?"

"I don't do crowds well." I craved space. Heck, I needed solitary confinement.

"That's part of the fun, silly. It wouldn't be the same if we were the only ones there. Just think, it's 2001, two hundred and twenty-five years since the adoption of the Declaration of Independence, a time to renew dedication to our principles, our liberty, and our God-given unalienable rights."

"Okay, so it takes the collective energy and appreciation of a crowd to make the Fourth of July celebration what it is, but—"

"If you're afraid you'll get lost, I can tie a rope around your waist like *Chango* the wharf monkey and keep a tight grip on the other end."

"Ha, ha." I'd already been down that route with my ex-fiancé, which had led to the complete opposite of what our forefathers meant by liberty and independence.

ꙮ ꙮ ꙮ

The streets of Monterey were livelier than usual, but we made it to Anne's studio in less than an hour. Anticipation of the upcoming festivities filled the air, and I couldn't block its positive effect on my mood. I entered the workshop with a smile, no longer dreading what I might see.

Anne headed straight for the kiln, opened the door, and reached inside. "I decided to fire your piece anyway, just to see how bad it could be."

When she withdrew my sculpture, I gasped. "What did you do to it?"

"Just fired it, sweetie." She placed my handiwork on the turntable and gave it a light spin. "It speaks, girl. I don't know quite how, but I feel included in something, just short of bliss."

My body heated up as if Anne had raised the room's thermostat to ninety. The piece looked even more magnificent than had the original. There was no way I could've accomplished this on my own. Mud. Glaze. Heat. What made it so special?

"You've served as an instrument, my girl. Beyond the clay, behind the shape, texture, and color, something shines through... Radiantly."

Thank goodness, I hadn't painted it black.

"We can show it at the gallery after all," Anne said, her face beaming.

"I don't think so."

Anne sighed, and for the life of me, I couldn't understand my reluctance to share something I had considered an abomination only minutes before. "It's not for sale."

"Who said anything about selling it?" Anne asked. "Two days ago,

100

you were vehement about displaying one of Adam's sculptures at the gallery, and now you've become as protective as a new mother."

Mother; birth; possession; ownership. Something from deep inside of me, something unfamiliar and totally unexpected, had materialized in the form of a sculpture. Exposing that part of myself involved crossing a bridge from a life of certainty to one of uncertainty, reaction to action—and then burning the bridge behind me. My mother had tried to create the perfect world for me, but that kind of control wasn't possible. I'd learned that much during my stay in Carmel Valley and continued to do so while here in Big Sur. The illusion of emotional safety blocked progress toward self-discovery. And that was no longer an option.

It was time to open a new door instead of staring longingly at an old one.

"If Adam can share a piece of himself, so can you," Anne said.

Nothing outside of yourself, including a piece of glazed and fired clay, can give you what you think you're missing. "It *is* inspiring."

"It uplifts. It reaffirms. It arouses," Anne said.

I shivered and pulled myself from its hold. "If Adam agrees to show one of his, then—"

"Three days won't give him enough time to complete a sculpture using my reinforced clay," Anne said, "but maybe he can get one done in time for the gallery showing in two weeks."

It was time to give myself permission to change my life story. "Okay, if he's in, I'm in."

Even as I said it, sparks went off in my head like a premature Fourth of July fireworks display. In celebration or warning? Only time would tell.

꠨꠨꠨

The fireworks at the wharf had made me feel like a kid again. I'd cried out in excitement and celebration right along with Anne and the rest of the impassioned crowd, not only in celebration of the Independence of our great country— "Sovereignty of the people!

Independence forever!" —but also in celebration of my expanding sense of freedom and independence.

And now I was tired.

Too bad the Circus Campers weren't.

Holly, Christopher, and Nathan were too wound up to sleep. Understandable. But their father's behavior was less easy to comprehend—and to forgive. Beer made him mean. He screamed at the kids and cussed at his wife, so often I lost count.

Worry would haunt the little sleep I would get that night.

Chapter Thirteen

N O," ADAM SAID when Anne asked if he would like to go to her studio to work on a sculpture. He bent down, scooped a handful of clay from the bank of the pond, and squeezed it until muddy water ran down his arm. Buster yawned and rested his scraggly head on his paws, eyeing us with what looked like amusement.

"The coyote's smiling again," I said.

Anne squatted in front of the dog and scratched behind his ears. "Actually, dogs and coyotes don't smile, but yes, it does look like Buster's laughing at us. The Native Americans call the coyote 'trickster' for the jokes it plays on humans."

"He doesn't play jokes on Adam," I said.

"No, you don't, do you, fella?" Buster squirmed with what appeared to be pleasure as Anne rubbed his hairy back. "Anyway, lightness of being supports healing."

Lessons from a smiling coyote? "Adam agreed to do a piece for the gallery, right?"

Anne stood and the dog whimpered, following her with his yellow-brown eyes. "Yes, but he didn't say when or how. Looks like we'll have to bring the clay here."

Another delay. With only two weeks until the next gallery showing "How long will it take for a sculpture the size of Adam's to dry?"

"Probably a week," Anne said, still eyeing the dog. The relaxed expression on her face and the faraway look in her eyes implied that her thoughts were elsewhere.

"So, if it takes Adam four days to sculpt, and it needs a week to dry, and then it still needs to be bisque fired, glazed, and re-fired... Anne, we'll run out of time."

"There'll be time enough," she said. "Brock's on call. It'll take him less than fifteen minutes to get here. Let's go get that clay."

We paused to wave at Adam before heading out of the grotto, but only Buster appeared to notice. He gave a short yelp and appeared to grin even wider.

)))

Two hours later, we were back, lugging our clay burdens on our shoulders, but Adam was no longer in the grotto. I tried not to let my impatience show or let on that I had a painful stitch in my side. Darn, the clay was heavy.

"He can't create if he's not in the mood," Anne said, shielding her eyes from the sunrays shimmering off the pool of water.

I paused to listen to the raucous chirping and chattering of hidden birds and the whisper of the afternoon breeze as it swooshed through the redwoods, oaks, and pines, marveling at the gentleness of nature's music and feeling a sense of tranquility take hold. When would I learn that some things just couldn't be rushed?

"Come on," Anne said. "He's probably having lunch."

As we neared Adam's campsite, I heard squeals of laughter.

"Oh, oh, guess who?" Anne said.

We stepped into a clearing of soft wild grass just as Holly announced, hands on hips, "Brock said it was okay, so mind your own business."

"Holly, let's go," Christopher pleaded. "Mom and Pop are looking for you."

Holly stomped her foot. "I haven't said goodbye to Adam yet."

"Hurry up before we get in trouble."

Holly shot off, tangled curls flying. "Adam!"

"What a handful," I said, envious at the girl's tenacity.

Anne dropped her bag of clay. "Thank God for her love and innocence. It just streams from her."

"And her trust," I said, my throat tightening. "When do we lose that?"

"Too soon," Anne said. "Too darn soon."

"Hi Marjorie! Hi Anne!" Holly called after giving Adam a peck on the cheek. "We have to go now."

"See ya," Anne said.

I raised my free hand in farewell just before Holly and Christopher disappeared through a break in the underbrush.

Adam stood—smiling.

"We brought you some clay," Anne said, pointing at the plastic sack I still lugged over my shoulder like a burden basket of gripes and grudges. "And there's more where that came from."

Was it my imagination, or did Adam's eyes dull just a bit?

"You can work with it here if you like," Anne said, nudging the bag of clay at her foot. "All you'll need is a piece of plywood as a base and a bucket of water."

"In the grotto." he said, his voice barely audible amid the piercing chatter of birds.

Anne yanked the bag of clay back over her shoulder with a grunt. "Your wish is my command."

Adam nodded, but made no move to follow us. Neither did Buster. Instead, he raised his furry head and sniffed the air.

When we reached Adam's outdoor studio, Anne dropped the clay and huffed.

I let the bag of clay slide off my shoulder and land next to hers. "Okay, so now what?"

"We leave Adam alone and check back with him later."

☽☽☽

When we returned that evening, Adam and Buster were still hunkered down next to the unlit fire pit where we had left them. Adam stared heavenward, shoulders slumped.

"Whatcha doing, Adam?" I asked.

He pointed at an opening between the trees.

I crouched beside him and squinted at the star-studded sky until I grew soft and weepy. What was he thinking? What was he feeling?

"Be back in a bit," Anne said, heading in the direction from which we'd come. "I'm meeting Brock at the Lodge to discuss this weekend's schedule."

Before I could react to her desertion, Adam said, "Look!"

"Wow," I said, not wanting to disturb the tranquil mood by asking him what he was referring to.

"I'll follow that star home," he said.

Guilt gripped me. All I'd been concerned about lately was getting Adam to create a damn sculpture, when instead I should've been concerned about his health and well-being. Actually, he was doing a better job of adjusting to the changes in his life's journey than I was. What could I learn from him?

"Do you know what it's like?" he asked.

I wrapped my arms around me, suddenly chilled. Was he asking if I knew what it was like to lose my mind? "Yes. I think I do."

"You have AD, too?"

"No, but sometimes I think I'm losing my mind."

"Did you go in for...um...help?"

"Sort of."

"Did they figure you out?"

I thought of Dr. Tony Mendez, how he had guessed that I was hiding things. "In order to help you Miss Veil," he said. "I need to know... What have you not told me?"

"Sort of."

"I hated that place," Adam said. "There were pictures...of...of brains on the wall."

Dear God, he'd been through hell.

"They asked me questions, and... I got mad."

"Me, too," I said.

"I didn't know the answers, so I..."

"Ran?"

"Yes."

"Me, too. Doctor's orders."

It was almost dark now, except for the moon and stars. I hoped that Anne would remember to bring a flashlight on her return.

"There is no cure," Adam said.

I made a choking sound.

He turned his attention from the stars to me. "You sound in despair."

The simple statement caused my throat to swell and tears to slide from the corners of my eyes. Adam, a man who was losing his mind, had sensed my mood and given it a name, thus unlocking a door to my heart that had just about rusted into place. I wanted to go back to Morgan and Joshua, but couldn't until I'd contacted Antonia. Or until she'd contacted me. She was caught between dimensions, lost between worlds and, in a way, so were Adam and I.

I sensed Adam watching me. "I hear other people's thoughts," he said.

I froze. *Just like me. What a pair.* "I've been hearing other people's thoughts, too, Adam. It scares me, but I try to listen."

Adam shifted closer to me.

"Normally I don't take on other people's problems," I said. "I have enough of my own. But I care about you, Adam. I'm just not very good at showing it."

"I miss my son," Adam said.

"Where is he?"

Adam took in a shaky breath, but didn't answer.

I put my hand on his shoulder. "Why don't you let us contact him for you?"

"He'll come after me."

"Isn't that his choice to make?"

I felt Adam's body sag next to me. "I won't be a burden."

Chapter Fourteen

I HAD BEEN CAMPING at Pfeiffer Big Sur State Park for four-teen days now, seven over the usual park limit. Doctor Mendez had worked hard to "bend the rules" and procure fifty-six consecutive days for me in the same location. It took some doing, but somehow, he'd convinced seven people to rent this space for seven days each and then pass them on to me. I had thirty-nine days left, and here I sat in my mega-tent no closer to contacting Antonia. Of course, I hadn't been trying that hard. There had been many distractions.

What surprised me, though, was that Antonia hadn't contacted me either. Should I just wait it out, as Adam had suggested— "She'll contact you when she's ready"—and continue hanging around until she made the first move? Maybe she was okay now. Maybe she had resolved what had been bothering her. But if this was the case, why was she communicating with Adam, a complete stranger? Was it be-cause AD somehow dissolved the barrier between her world and his? Or did Adam's lack of the need to control—what she might say, what she might demand—open him up to her message?

I crawled out of my tent only to find myself separated from the rest of the world by a swirling curtain of morning fog. The tempta-tion to crawl back into my sleeping bag and wait for Mother Nature to be more cooperative drew me with a force that proved hard to resist. In two days, it would be my twenty-ninth birthday. Twenty-nine and still searching.

After starting my campfire, I heard a trembling voice penetrate the fog. "Marjorie?"

"Holly? Over here, sweetheart."

She materialized out of the mist as if the fog had taken on human form. Her outstretched arms guided her into the dome-like clearing created by the heat of the fire. "Could you make me some hot cocoa?"

I motioned for her to sit down. "It would be my pleasure."

"I know you think I'm brave, but I'm scared," she said, scooting as close to me as the physical constraint between familiar strangers would allow.

I put a saucepan of bottled water onto the fire to heat. "It's daytime and your parents and your brothers are nearby."

She peered at the grayness all around us and pulled her pink jacket more tightly around her footed pajamas. "Daddy says there are 'Dark Watchers' out here."

Darn that man. "He did?" I'd heard of the Dark Watchers legend: giant human-like phantoms, shadow people, only seen at twilight, silhouetted against the night sky, along the peaks of the Santa Lucia Mountains, staring into space, seemingly at nothing.

"I think they're watching me," Holly whispered.

Yeah, me, too. I shrugged, hoping to downplay her fear. "What's wrong with that? You aren't doing anything wrong. Maybe you make them happy."

She bit her lip as she considered this. "They see me visiting Adam."

"Maybe they visit Adam, too."

"They do. Adam talks to them. I've seen him."

"So, if Adam isn't scared of them, why are you?"

"I don't know. I just am."

I emptied a package of cocoa into a mug and added a spoon. "Someone very wise told me once that fear is just an illusion."

"What's an illusion?"

"Something that's not real."

"It's real to me."

She had a point there. Though most of our fears are about things that *might* happen, but likely never will, they seem real indeed. "Tell you what. You're welcome to stay here whenever I'm gone. As long as you take good care of my things."

She nodded, her curls jiggling in silent imitation of Anne's bangles. "Okay."

"But you'll have to let your parents know where you are."

She avoided my eyes. "Is the water ready yet?"

As I blended hot water with the cocoa in her mug, mini marshmallows floated to the top. I inhaled the sweet, chocolaty aroma. "At least tell one of your brothers, okay?"

She reached for the steaming mug, still avoiding my eyes.

I stirred the cocoa before handing it to her. "Is your family staying here long?"

Holly tested the cocoa with the tip of her tongue before taking a sip. "Dad and Mom's summer jobs here pay for the park fees. Otherwise we'd be homeless."

"Doesn't the park supply some kind of dorm housing for its employees?"

"Not for their families. Anyway, Dad says camping here is like getting a free vacation."

"What about school?"

Holly shrugged, keeping her eyes on the mug. Marshmallow foam lined the top of her lip, reminding me of a milk ad, except with an angel instead of a celebrity. "Adam has a God jar."

It took a moment for me to adjust to the change in subject. "What's that, dear?"

"When he has a problem, he writes it on a piece of paper and puts it in a jar. Then God takes care of it."

Let go, let God. "What an excellent idea, just letting God handle things." A matter of not trying so hard. Allowing the battle between what you know in your heart and what you've been taught to believe time to play out. Watching, listening, and staying on track. Even if that track leads away from all that's familiar. Holly and Adam—direct and uncomplicated—served as golden threads to the spiritual side of the universe.

"I can make you one," Holly said. "There are lots of jars around here that people forget to put in the trash. I'll wash one and decorate it for you."

"Why thank you, sweetie. I could sure use a God jar right now, a reminder to let our father in Heaven handle things when I feel out of control. And since you'll be tent-sitting for me, I'll pay you five dollars a day."

"Then I'll have a job," she said, eyes bright as firecrackers on the Fourth of July.

I added lukewarm cocoa to Holly's mug, more conducive to warding off a child's fears than the steaming hot variety. "But you can only tent-sit if it's okay with your mom and dad."

The brightness left her eyes. "They don't like you."

Even considering the source, the words stung. "Probably because they don't know me."

"Dad says women who travel alone are asking for trouble."

"What do you think?"

"I get into more trouble when I'm with my brothers."

Little girl pout, Buddha brain. How right she was, though sometimes "getting into trouble" is a necessary ingredient in life, an ingredient I had purposely avoided—until my dead mother came calling. "You're pretty wise for your age. Now finish your cocoa and head back to your tent before your family wakes up and notices you're gone."

Holly gulped down the last of her drink and wiped her lips on the sleeve of her jacket before handing back the mug. "Thanks, Marjorie."

"You're welcome, Holly."

She got to her feet and disappeared into the mist, entering a world I wasn't part of and to which I didn't belong.

☽☽☽

After straightening up my campsite, I decided it was time to visit Anne's lodgings for a change, instead of her always visiting mine. I knew more or less which direction to take, considering she always approached my place from the east. And her dugout shouldn't be too hard to find. Just be on the alert for some kind of bohemian grove, with dream catchers and dried flowers dangling from tree branches in celebration of nature and summertime.

As it turned out, there were no dream catchers and dried flowers dangling from the trees. Instead, the lace windsock, paper lanterns, and scarf-like sheets flapping in the breeze were a dead giveaway. As was the yurt, with its lattice perimeter and umbrella-like roof. Colorful Moroccan panels skirted its walls, which included two vertical windows and a door.

Wonder how long it takes to put up and take down this mega shelter.

"Hello," I called.

No answer.

I knocked on the door. A real wooden door. "Anne, it's Marjorie." No answer.

Her Volvo was parked in the space next to the yurt, so she couldn't have gone far. And it was a bit early to relieve Brock at Adam's camp. Maybe she was still sleeping. Ha. It would be nice to discover that Miss Fit-as-a-Fiddle was a late riser.

I tried the door. It was unlocked. I opened it a crack. "Anne?"

I didn't encounter the groggy, disheveled person I had envisioned. Instead, Anne was dressed in a flowing white robe and kneeling in front of a small altar fitted against one of the rounded sides of the yurt. The altar held two lit candles—one gold, one silver—two bowls—one filled with water, another with what appeared to be salt—plus, a chalice, a bell, a wand, and a small cauldron.

I must have gasped, because Anne opened her eyes and held up a hand to silence me before rising to her feet. "I bid you hail and farewell," she said four times, facing a different direction with each incantation. Then she added a farewell to a Lord and Lady, while circling the interior of her yurt, counterclockwise, with what appeared to be a magic wand.

Saying *my skin crawled*, just about summed up my reaction. It felt as though I was encountering a complete stranger, someone performing some kind of Wiccan divination.

"You can come on in now," Anne said as she began to dismantle the altar and put the ritual supplies into a small drawer on its side. "I'm a porta-pagan," she said into the silence. "I carry my altar with me."

"Do you practice witchcraft?" I managed.

She stared at me for a moment before answering. "I'm too lazy to be a full-fledged witch, my dear. I just fill in the empty spaces with some earth-based religious practices. And, in case you're wondering... No, I don't have any supernatural abilities. The forces I use are right here for the taking, available to all."

"Not like the witches on TV?" I said, trying to keep the conversation light while my brain wrapped around this new development. Our friendship had taken a sudden turn. Witchcraft was something I didn't understand and, in truth, didn't want to understand. Could I muster the courage to withhold judgment and continue on as before? A seed of mistrust had been planted in my heart, a new awkwardness. The way she dressed should've tipped me off. Modern-day hippie, my foot! More like a priestess, shaman, witch doctor, and nurse all wrapped into one.

Anne studied me, blue eyes gleaming. "There are many types and traditions of witches. Ask a hundred witches a question and you'll get a hundred different answers. However, all in all, we try to live in harmony with nature and take responsibility for the environment. I happen to be a solitaire. I find all the info I need in books and through practice. I make up my own rituals."

"You make them up?"

"As I go. Sure. Whatever works for me is real for me. Guess you can call me an eclectic Wiccan. I borrow from Hawaiian and Native American traditions as well."

Anne reopened the drawer in her altar and pulled out a small silver octagon. She held it up, and I recognized it as a St. Christopher medal, almost identical to the one hanging from the rear-view mirror of my Jeep. "Have you ever prayed to Saint Christopher to protect you in your travels?" she asked.

I remembered once using this same argument with my mother—and failing. "Of course, I'm Catholic."

"So am I," Anne said.

"You can't be both," I blurted, though I should've known better. Hadn't I been attempting to experience the mysteries of the Native American Medicine Wheel in my search for understanding, while, at the same time, holding on to the rituals offered by the church of my upbringing?

A faint smile crossed Anne's lips as she took note of my uplifted palms. "Did you know that convent and coven come from the same root?"

I didn't, but also didn't see the significance.

"Have you ever made chicken soup for a sick friend?"

I pulled my telltale hands into fists. "Of course. Who hasn't?"

A flash of sympathy burned through Anne's widened smile. "How about wearing a lucky outfit or carrying a lucky charm?"

I thought of my mouse totem. "Sure."

"Have you ever knocked on wood?"

"Okay, okay, I get the picture. These are all forms of *magick*, right?"

Anne clapped her hands. "My God, she's getting it!"

I ignored her sarcasm. "I also believe we should live more simply and focus less on the material—"

"Are you going somewhere with this?" Anne asked.

"Well, I'm interested in the spiritual, New Thought, New Age, and the beliefs of my ancestors."

Anne stared at the medal in her hands. "So?"

"Well, I'd never become a Wiccan, but—"

"No one's asking you to. Wiccans are smart enough to realize that their religion isn't the path for everyone."

"Will you quit interrupting? I'm trying to say that I might be able to incorporate some rituals of the Wiccan faith into my life."

"I'm so relieved to hear that."

"Darn it, Anne. I'm trying to understand."

"I know, sweetie, I'm just playing with you." She put the medal back in the drawer of her altar. "We're both attempting to live spiritually and in tune with nature, just going about it in different ways. Anyway, I have bad news. Adam didn't feel inspired to use our reinforced clay. Although he did use our piece of plywood as a base for a beautiful mud sculpture of his wife holding his son."

"Can't you try firing it anyway?"

"I did, and it exploded in the kiln."

"Darn," I said, disappointed, but not surprised.

"However, your sculpture is already at the gallery," she said.

"What!"

"I was afraid you'd change your mind now that Adam wasn't carrying through."

"You *are* a witch," I said, not half as upset as I thought I'd be.

Chapter Fifteen

"CATCH," ANNE SAID on approaching my campsite the following morning and tossing what appeared to be a credit card in my direction.

I caught the rectangular piece of plastic and turned it in my hand. "What's this?"

Anne held up another card, grinning like an actor in an ad for a vacation rental. "Your room key."

"My...? What are you up to now?"

"I reserved two bungalow rooms at the Big Sur Lodge for tonight and made reservations for dinner, so hurry and gather your stuff."

I crossed my arms in explain-please fashion.

Anne eyed my clothing: a fleece shirt, baggy nylon pants, and sturdy hiking boots. "Since we're going to the gallery tonight, I figured you'd like to take a proper shower and dress up a bit."

I looked down at my outfit, not quite the height of urban chic. "As you well know, I didn't come prepared for gallivanting around town. So, what do you suggest I wear?"

Anne sized me up, her hand cupping her chin, her index finger tapping her cheek. "Looks like we're about the same size, so I'll lend you something of mine."

One look at her flamboyant skirt and gauzy blouse and I rolled my eyes. "Oh goody. Can't wait."

Anne's grin widened. "Trust me, you'll look fabulous."

"It would be nice to take a leisurely shower," I admitted. "And French braid my hair and put on some makeup. That is, if I remember how."

"I'm sure it'll come back to you," Anne said. "Let's go."

I retrieved my as-yet-unused makeup case from the cargo hold of the Jeep, rumbled through my suitcase for some underwear, and was about to leap into Anne's Volvo, when I remembered promising Holly that she could watch my tent.

"What's up?" Anne asked, noticing my hesitation.

"I have to leave a note for my tent sitter that I'll be gone."

Anne rubbed the back of her neck. "Tent sitter?"

The puzzled look on her face lightened my step. For once, I wasn't the one asking questions. "Be right back."

$$\mathcal{D}\,\mathcal{D}\,\mathcal{D}$$

"I passed on the fireplace rooms since we won't be spending much time here," Anne said as we walked toward the Lodge bungalows with our overnight bags. "No phones, televisions, or alarm clocks either."

"Maybe I'll treat myself to a long soak in the tub instead of taking a shower," I said.

Anne checked her watch. "You've got two hours. I'll meet you at four o'clock sharp. That'll give us time for a glass of wine before dinner."

"Which means no nap," I said, longing to crash out on a soft bed with fresh, clean sheets for an hour or two after my bath.

Anne went on as if she hadn't heard me, "I left an evening dress with a matching cardigan and sandals in your closet. Go make yourself beautiful."

Evening dress, right. "You're so bossy."

"A prerequisite for being a good caregiver," Anne said. "Anyway, I'm fitting right into your plans."

"You make it sound like I'm using you."

"Actually, no. You're allowing yourself to receive the gifts being offered. And believe me, that's a big step for most people. Simply put, you're a pretty sharp gal." Anne spun around and headed for the cabin next door. "See you at four."

The spacious room had its own deck and, just as Anne had predicted, no electronic gadgets to distract from the restful atmosphere. The comforter and shams on the bed looked like homemade quilts with diamond patterns in greens, browns, and rusts. White wainscoting stretched halfway up the wall, the rest of which was painted a soft beige. The brown oak shutters covering the windows would block out the sunlight come morning. A nice change.

As I took this all in, part of my mind fretted over what kind of bohemian outfit I would find hanging in the closet? At first glance, I liked what I saw, at least as far as color and texture were concerned. The sleeveless column dress was made of some kind of taupe metallic with a lace overlay on the front bodice. The matching cardigan had lace-detailing on the scalloped sleeves and hem. Shine and lace; what a combination.

I slipped on the taupe sandals. A bit tight, but at this point, I wasn't complaining. On the dresser lay a matching purse and pearl dangle-hoop earrings. Anne had thought of everything.

A long soak in the tub no longer appealed to me. Anxious to get into that dress, I would shower instead.

Promptly at four, I opened the door and nearly collided with Anne—a transformed Anne—in a swingy shift dress of black mesh over a tan lining, with silky bubble appliqués on the hemline. The neckline was high, and a silky bow drooped over her left shoulder.

"Wow!" I said. "Black, with no wild stripes or flowers."

She fluttered her lashes and curtsied like royalty. "I didn't want you to think I was an inflexible, obsessive, compulsive, schizoid loner, who focused only on one narrow point of interest to the point of paranoia. So, I wore my 'bubble-duty' dress."

I gave my best rendition of a wolf whistle. "You look absolutely beautiful."

"You should see me in my nurse uniform."

"I can imagine," I said. And surprisingly I could. I'd always compared nurses to angels anyway.

She lifted her hair from her ears.

"Diamonds," I said, "and they're not even shaped like moons and stars."

Anne looked me over and clucked in approval. "How do you like the dress I picked out for you?"

I twirled, feeling like a princess. "I couldn't have done a better job of it myself."

"You look fantastic," she said. "Especially with your hair French braided like that."

"I feel fantastic."

Anne linked her arm through mine. "Then let's make this a night to remember."

☽☽☽

"You're spoiling me for camping," I said as the Big Sur Lodge host escorted us to our table. "I may not want to go back to sleeping in my tent."

"Well, I'm sure you can get the room for as long as you like," Anne said.

"Don't tempt me," I said, though I knew I wouldn't do it. I had come here to get closer to nature, to my mother, and to myself, and I wouldn't accomplish that under a comfortable roof with every convenience at my fingertips. I wouldn't be able to smell the fragrance of decomposing foliage mixed in with the woody and piney scents from the tall canopies of trees. I wouldn't be able to feel and absorb the warm energy of the sun or the soft breezes on my skin. I wouldn't be able to sense the enormity of the space around me.

"What kind of wine would you like?" Anne asked after we were seated. The question took me back to Carmel Valley, where Morgan had asked me the same question. A picture of his green eyes and dimpled smile filled all the space in my mind, and I fought back tears.

Anne cleared her throat. "How about a local wine?"

I stared at the wine list through blurry eyes. The first selection

119

was Morgan Sauvignon Blanc. I blinked. Held up the list. Jabbed at it with my finger. "Anne, look."

"'Rich melon and pineapple, lovely balance, crisp, and fresh,'" Anne read from beneath the wine selection. "Hey, isn't Morgan your boyfriend's name?" Her eyes danced with apparent pleasure at the serendipitous discovery. "So, for you it's 'Morgan Sauvignon Blanc' and for me 'Storrs from the Santa Cruz Mountains.'"

Over Anne's *Sautéed Filet of Salmon and Linguini* and my *Chicken and Portobello Mushrooms*, we talked and laughed, and, finally, after thoroughly stuffing myself, I said, "Thanks, Anne. This was a fantastic idea."

"Visa, MasterCard, and American Express accepted," she said. "I paid for the rooms, you pay for dinner."

I laughed. "Sounds like I got the better deal."

"Tell me that after you've paid for breakfast," Anne said.

☽☽☽

"It brings back such incredible, if not happy, memories," Anne said as we entered the art gallery. "The fussing to look sensational, the expensive gowns, the shiny and tamed hair, fake nails, fake smiles, and then, the terrible disillusionment as the evening progresses. The only fire I see is in the eyes of the caterers and the artists. These functions are never what they appear to be."

I studied the crowd, trying to visualize it from Anne's point of view. Sure enough, many of the glamorously dressed guests appeared to be standing around, looking for something to do. They eyed the caterers as if the distraction of food and drink offered a way to occupy—and satisfy—their empty hands and minds.

A blonde woman, wearing a shimmering red gown that flowed like lava, had her eyes focused on the door. Was she waiting for someone, or planning her escape? Two men stood nearby, tuxedoed and manicured, joking with each other, while observing the shimmering blonde. An overweight woman, escorted by an equally overweight man, held a miniscule plate mounded with hors d'oeuvres.

"I haven't yet missed being rich," Anne said.

I reeled in my wayward thoughts and brought my attention back to my friend. "You never said anything about being rich."

She ignored me, which meant she wasn't sharing, so I said, "From where I come from, everyone wants to be rich. An evening like this is part of the fantasy." Again, I studied the crowd and, this time, locked onto a tall, broad-shouldered man, accompanied by a slim woman bearing the intangible charisma of a model. "Can you believe it? It's the Harley Guy. In a Tux."

Anne's attention, however, was focused elsewhere. "Oh, oh, it's the gallery curator. I should've warned you..."

A man in a slim-fitting suit and drainpipe pants danced toward us, arms wide. "Anne darling!"

Anne grinned and gave him a friendly hug. "Alfonso, it's so good to see you. Meet my friend, Marjorie Veil."

His busy gaze settled on me. I could almost hear a "bleep," as if he were scanning my bar code: age, nationality, income. "Welcome, welcome," he said. "I'm so glad you could come. Have you seen our fine new sculpture? It's brilliant, quite brilliant." He winked at Anne and motioned for a waiter. "How about a glass of bubbly to celebrate our new discovery?"

Next thing I knew I was holding a flute of champagne.

"You simply must take a look at our fine new sculpture," he said, prodding me forward with a light hand to my back. "It symbolizes the flow of life, with its ups and downs, its joys, and its heartaches."

We paused in front of a table on which rotated a multi-colored piece that looked eerily familiar.

"Notice the shades of red," the curator continued, "burnt red, symbolizing our mother earth; crimson and salmon, symbolizing fire, sunlight, and emotion; ruby, symbolizing the flow of blood in our veins..."

My mouth opened, and I turned to Anne.

"Sorry," she whispered.

"Where in God's name is he coming up with all this crap?" I whispered back.

Anne patted my shoulder. "That's the beauty of art, hon, especially this piece. Every time I see it, I see something new, as if it changes with my mood. All I know is that it makes me happy. It's as if you sent positive feelings or thoughts into the piece and they're flowing back to the observer. That's why it's so valuable. How can you put a price on happiness?"

Anne turned her attention back to the curator, who showed no offense at our rude whispers. "I do appreciate you displaying the sculpture in your lovely gallery. I understand that including a piece at such late notice isn't your usual policy."

Alfonso waved ringed fingers. "We were fortunate to discover this talented artist hidden within our midst. She was inspired by the gods, I'm sure."

I couldn't believe what I was hearing and that Anne was part of it.

"Will she be in attendance tonight?" Alfonso asked. "She's a real mystery. Everyone's waiting."

Anne looked at me, and I shook my head. "Afraid not," Anne said. "She's shy about displaying her work."

The pressure around my throat became painful and my body began to shake, so I looked for a place to sit.

Alfonso appeared to deflate in disappointment. "One of our patrons has made a generous offer on it already."

"It's not for sale," I said, annoyed at this smooth-talking man, with his streaked and spiked hair.

Anne tried to shush me, but it was too late. Alfonso had heard me and turned my way.

"Do you know her?" he asked, one perfected groomed eyebrow raised.

Anne piped in, "The artist expressed a deep reluctance in parting with her work at this time."

"Yes, yes, so you mentioned when you dropped it off," Alfonso said. "But money talks, you know. And I mean lots of money." His eyes brightened at the prospect, probably counting on a sizable commission. He winked at me. "We have ways to put on the pressure, you know. That's one of my jobs."

Anne pinched me before I could respond. "This is all new to my friend here."

Alfonso rubbed the tips of his fingers together. "I'm acquainted with many wealthy and influential people." Again, his eyes scanned over me as though adding up the cost of my gown: $400, ka-ching; pearl earrings: $500, ka-ching; good hair stylist, flawless makeup: ka-ching, ka-ching; no wedding ring. Good. Easier to manipulate.

I gave myself a mental shake. I was being unfair. He was just doing his job, talking up the sculpture. It wasn't his fault that he didn't know it was mine.

"It was so nice to see you again," Anne said, looking over his shoulder as if she'd spotted someone in the crowd.

"Oh yes, yes, I must go. Enjoy." Several air-kisses aimed our way and then the thin, wiry, sales-machine hurried off to make another contact. "Harriet, darling," he called before disappearing into the crowd.

"Alfonso is very successful at what he does," Anne said, "and is actually a nice guy."

Should I be angry or grateful? I couldn't decide. Anne had deftly taken the decision out of my hands.

"Be right back," she said, doing her own disappearing act, which gave me the opportunity to wander about the gallery on my own. I handed my half-empty flute of champagne to a passing waiter and meandered with no set destination, too upset to take notice of the fine exhibitions. That is, until I sighted the glass vase I'd admired on my previous visit.

"What do you think?" asked a woman from behind me. It sounded like Harley Guy's girlfriend, Claudia.

"I can't describe how I feel," I said without turning. "How about you?"

"I don't know."

"Who's the artist?"

She didn't answer.

All looks and no brains. "See how the forms are floating inside the vase walls?" I asked.

"They were sculptured by air while the piece was being blown," she said.

So, she knew something about art after all. "They appear to be moving."

"It's the light at play. The piece is transparent, but thick, so patterns of light develop inside, as well as on the surface."

I turned to face her, impressed by her knowledge. I had misjudged her.

Claudia's gaze remained fixed on the vase. "This piece was created for visual delight."

"That's a relief," I said. "I'd hate to think someone would actually put flowers into it."

Claudia's silence encouraged me to add.

"I wonder what the artist was thinking."

"I wasn't thinking, just feeling."

"You?"

She looked me straight in the eye. "Yes."

I liked that. She had a sense of humor. Claudia an artist? Yeah, right. I gave her an I-wasn't-born-yesterday smile, and she smiled back.

"Hey, Marjorie." It was Anne.

"Sorry, Claudia, I gotta go."

When I reached her side, Anne said, "So, you met the artist. Nice surprise, huh.?"

"What artist?"

"Claudia Moore. I just found out that she's the one who crafted that magnificent glass vase you so admired."

I looked over at Claudia and caught her smile. I shook my head and waved. My mistake. There was hope for her after all.

"Her boyfriend made the offer for your statue."

It took a moment for Anne's words to sink in. *Boyfriend? Offer?* "You're kidding, right?"

Anne grabbed a flute of champagne off the tray carried by a passing waiter and replaced it with an empty one. "Nope."

"How do you know?"

"He told me."

The sculpture represented an entry to my heart. And that entry wasn't for sale. "Did you tell the Mr. Living-Out-Loud Harley Guy that it wasn't available for purchase?"

She took a gulp of champagne and sighed in satisfaction. "Yep."

I looked around for Cecil, but he was hidden from view. "What did he say?"

"He wanted to know how I knew," Anne said, toasting me with her empty glass.

I grabbed Anne's arm as if warding off what I sensed was coming next. "You didn't tell him I was the artist, did you?"

"Hush. Here he comes."

"No, you hush." I released her arm and turned toward the exit, my heart beating in telltale fashion. Low, dull, quick. "You can either join me, or I'm calling a taxi."

Anne followed me out the door and pulled out her keys.

I grabbed them out of her hands. She'd had several glasses of champagne after all.

She tried to grab them back. No go.

I clenched my teeth until my jaw hurt. What else could go wrong? Was it too much to ask for a little peace and quiet?

I unlocked the doors, took the driver's seat, waited for Anne to get in, then steered the Volvo onto Highway 1.

"I knew you could only be pushed so far," she said.

Darn right. I got all dolled up like some metallic princess, shine and lace, pearls and sandals. For what? The curator's words still rubbed me raw. "Have you seen our fine sculpture? It symbolizes the flow of life..." Blah, blah, blah. Not that he was entirely wrong. I'd similar theories as to what the sculpture symbolized.

Maybe it wasn't a freak accident that this piece of clay affected people the way it did. But then Harley Guy, of all people, had to go and put in an offer to buy it. The only highlight of the evening had been meeting the creator of the glass vase.

Who would have known?

"What will it take for you to forgive me?" Anne asked, her voice wobbly from either emotion or drink.

I was driving too fast and took my foot off the gas. "For now, I'd appreciate it if you'd just stop looking at me."

"All righty," she said, and then turned on the radio and started singing along with Aretha Franklin, the queen of soul, "Chain, chain, chain; chain of fools."

I sighed. Anger solved nothing. Anne was a good friend, and although she got carried away at times, she had my best interests at heart. If I hadn't believed that from day one, I wouldn't have allowed her to lead me around like an organ-grinder's wharf monkey.

It wasn't until we were parked in front of the Big Sur Lodge that Anne announced, "I'd like to make this up to you."

Giving her the most gracious smile I could manage under the circumstances, I pulled the key out of the ignition and got out of the car. "It's okay, Anne, by morning I'll have forgotten about the whole thing."

Anne slammed her door and came around to my side for the keys. "I doubt that, but at least let me take you out for your birthday."

That got my attention. "How'd you know it was my birthday?"

She studied the keys I was holding as if they had turned into lucky charms. "Adam told me."

I pulled in my breath, followed by a choked groan. Adam knew things he shouldn't. And somehow it involved my mother.

"We could dress up again," Anne said. "And go out for a nice, quiet lunch."

My anger dissipated at her uncertain expression. She was a good friend. I dropped the keys into her hand. "I'll let you know over breakfast."

Chapter Sixteen

OKAY," I SAID the following morning at the Lodge restaurant while scarfing down a *Big Sur Scramble*, consisting of more food than I normally ate in a week.

"Okay what?" Anne mumbled, rather overindulging herself. Her plate was a colorful mosaic of scrambled eggs, grilled vegetables, pepper jack cheese, seasoned potatoes, and toast. Apparently, her low-cal, veggie diet was on break.

"You can take me out for my birthday."

"Well, thank God for that."

"Guess that means we'll be spending another night here," I said.

Nestled among redwoods and oaks, the dining room's floor-to-ceiling windows invited in the serenity of the outdoors. Fans whirred overhead, and the doors stood open, sending cool breezes our way.

Anne studied my face with a lift of a brow. "Do you mind?"

"Are you kidding? I could tolerate one more day of this."

"So, who's your tent sitter?" she asked, scooping up the last of her eggs.

The server came by to refill our coffee. We both took ours black. "Holly," I said.

Anne's fork cluttered to the table. "You trust that little tyke?"

"She's not guarding Fort Knox. I carry my valuables with me."

Anne gave me a knowing smile, alerting me that she was in my head again. "You figured she could use the responsibility, right?"

I took a long sip of coffee and stared out the window. Several people whisked by on bicycles, sending out a lazy, cricket-like trill. "And the money. She said her parents have summer jobs here at the park, but I believe they're in pretty dire straits."

"Why am I not surprised? Want to walk over there and check on how she's doing?"

Before I could answer, Anne stood and patted her stomach. "I could use the exercise."

It didn't take long to figure out that Holly hadn't spent any time in my tent. Everything appeared exactly as I had left it: rolled up sleeping bag; folded blanket; fluffed up pillow. And the strong euca-lyptus scent of my funky, tent-deodorant spray indicated that the en-trance had remained tightly zipped. I felt a tinge of alarm. Giving her permission to do what she'd been doing anyway, with the stipulation that she look after my stuff, had seemed like a good idea at the time. Had I gotten her in trouble with her parents? Or had an adventure turned into a paying job lost its appeal?

Anne brought her hands to her hips and shook her head, moon and star earrings swinging as though tolling a warning. "If Holly's family is in such dire straits, what's with all the camping gear?"

"I believe they may be living here for a while."

"That's not permitted."

My laugh sounded bitter, considering Adam, Anne, and I were doing the same. "I assume management made an exception, consid-ering the parents are temporary employees."

An expression ranging between exasperation and pity crossed Anne's face. "It never seems to end, does it...life's little tragedies?"

"And no one is spared," I said, reminding myself that valuable life lessons are often learned through adversity.

Even, it seemed, the life lessons of a six-year-old.

❯❯❯

Anne must've selected the most expensive restaurant in Big Sur for my birthday lunch. We sat at a table in Post Ranch Inn's Sierra Mar

Restaurant with dizzying views from the top of a cliff 1,250 feet above the Pacific. "This place is definitely worth all those stairs we had to climb getting here," I said.

Anne's eyes appeared to mist over, but I could've been wrong, considering the way natural light filtered through the plate-glass windows into a dining area otherwise lit only by strategically placed lamps. "This is one of the most romantic places on earth, a perfect getaway for you and Morgan someday."

My heart did a crazy leap in my chest. Why did she have to bring up Morgan, today of all days, when I was most vulnerable? "At nine hundred dollars a night? I don't think so."

"Don't exaggerate," Anne said. "The Butterfly House is a mere five hundred smackeroos."

"Plus, occupancy tax," I said.

"The building's shaped like a butterfly, I'll have you know, and has a private deck with a fantastic view. You also get a gourmet continental breakfast."

"In that case, I guess it's worth it," I said, holding back a smile. She made the place sound like a bargain.

"I heard they have beds you can lose yourself in," Anne said.

"I can lose myself just fine without the bed."

"You see yourself as a caterpillar," Morgan had said during our guided tour into the Los Padres Forest, "and I see you as a butterfly."

Caterpillar to butterfly. Yeah, maybe someday.

Anne sobered and placed her hand on mine. "Oh yeah, that's why you came to Big Sur. To find yourself."

My chin began to wobble. "It's very important to me right now."

She patted my hand and handed me a spare napkin from the table. "As it should be, hon. Are you ready to order?"

I looked at the menu and set it back down. "There are no prices."

She presented me with a stern brow and pursed lips. "It's prix-fixe, dear. Anyway, it's on me, remember?"

Did Anne know what she was getting into? This could cost her a fortune.

"The fruits, vegetables, and herbs are all organic," she said without consulting the menu. "And the meat is free-range. Sometimes they have to wait nine months to get a shipment. Almost like having a baby."

I shook my head. Organic Anne was back in full force.

"And everything is made in-house," she added.

Even if this was gourmet from heaven, I didn't want to annihilate Anne's bank account.

While Anne ordered for both of us—which was fine with me, considering the menu consisted of four courses, with at least four choices each—I stared through the expanse of windows at the panoramic view of the ocean below. From this distance, the surf seemed poised in a massive swell of foam, frozen for a breath of time, perfect as a picture.

For a moment, there was silence, so I figured Anne was also enjoying the view, but then she sucked in her breath and mumbled something that sounded like a curse.

The oceanic view lost focus. What was going to knock the earth off its axis this time? "Anne, we came here to celebrate my birthday. No more surprises, please."

She said nothing, just stared over my shoulder. I made to turn, but she nudged me under the table and gave me a warning look. "I wouldn't if I were you."

I turned anyway, a strange rebelliousness surfacing that I was beginning to recognize as part of a new me. "Of all the rotten luck," I said when I saw who it was.

Cecil and Claudia couldn't have been standing in the foyer for more than a minute before they were whisked past our table by the host. "Hey, they didn't even have to wait," I said.

"They must be regulars," Anne pointed out. "Big tippers, too."

I checked out Claudia from behind, with her how-to-walk-like-a-model strut.

"Jealous?" Anne asked.

Darn, I hated it when she read my thoughts this way. "It would be nice to be that rich for a day or two, just to try it out."

"Do they look happy to you?" Something in Anne's voice made me turn to study her face. She was staring at the churning ocean below as if she'd gone in search of the answer to her own question.

"Sure," I said. "They just try to hide it so people like us don't feel bad."

The host led Cecil and Claudia to prime-table seating. Cecil must have sensed our scrutiny because he turned and looked our way. His eyes widened, but to my relief, he raised a hand and took a seat, making no move to invade our space.

Claudia peeked in our direction and smiled.

"I want to hate that girl, but can't," I said.

Anne smirked. "A flower amongst the weeds."

Our first course arrived, and at my look of confusion, Anne informed me that it was living watercress salad. "The roots were cut just before it came to our table."

Although arranged imaginatively with appetizing texture, color, and aroma, the courses that followed were miniscule compared to our mega breakfast at the Big Sur Inn. A good thing, considering that a sedentary woman of five foot six, weighing one hundred and thirty pounds, should've called it quits for the day.

We finished our meal in less time than we'd waited for the table. I passed on dessert, having tea instead. Anne indulged in some sticky chocolaty conglomeration that made my teeth ache just looking at it. Health food to junk food with apparently no regrets.

"Why here, Anne? It's so—"

"Expensive?"

"Trail mix will never taste the same after this."

"I like to spoil myself now and then. Anyway, this place exudes positive energy, the kind you can plug into and draw inside to re-energize."

Ocean, cliffs, trees. Couldn't argue with that.

"Besides, Adam pays me well, and you've been helping him, too."

"I have? Doing what?"

"Making him happy." Anne signaled the waiter for our check.

"Oh, no, ma'am," he said when he arrived at our table. "The gentleman two tables down settled the bill for you."

My insides twisted. Not good.

"Saved me a bundle," Anne quipped after the waiter left.

"Yeah, but what will he want in return?"

I could tell by the frown on her face that she had considered this, too.

"I suppose we're expected to go over and thank him?" I said. Harley Guy rubbed me the wrong way, so sure of himself, so live-out-loud pushy.

Anne smiled and waved in their direction. "Nope. They're coming here. No sneaking out the door this time."

"Hello ladies," Cecil said, his cheerful confidence annoying.

I met Claudia's eyes. She shook her head as though trying to warn me about something.

"Care to join us?" Anne asked.

I kicked her under the table. Too late.

"Thank you." Cecil pulled out a chair for Claudia and signaled for her to take a seat. Instead, she walked over to a window shaped like a porthole, which spotlighted the view of the ocean below. Cecil gazed at her back, and, for a moment, I wondered if her action had made a small imprint on his psyche. He shrugged. Guess not. "You left the gallery last night before I had a chance to talk to you," he said.

I smiled, wishing I were anywhere but here. At least Claudia was keeping a safe distance. Lucky girl.

"About your sculpture," he said. "I was told it wasn't for sale. But surely you can make another." I started to shake my head, but he placed his hand over mine. "I'm making a very generous offer."

I retrieved my hand and placed it on my lap. "Sorry, it's not for sale."

Anne made a coughing sound. "Marjorie didn't want it displayed. I'm afraid, I entered it against her better judgment."

I heard the soft intake of breath. Claudia had turned from the window and was giving me a curious look. Our gazes held for several seconds before she shifted her attention back to the window.

"But why?" Cecil asked. "It could make you famous."

I touched my throat, felt my pulse throb. This was just the sort of thing that could plunge me back into the sort of life I'd been living before. By today's standards I'd been sitting on top of the world—a good job, money in the bank, a home of my own—but I hadn't felt successful in all that mattered. How could I explain this to a man like Cecil, who appeared to thrive on material success and fame?

Anne cleared her throat. "Thanks for picking up the tab. That was an unexpected treat."

"A small gesture of appreciation," he said, looking at me. "Your sculpture brought me a great deal of pleasure, more than I've felt in a long time."

"I'm sorry to hear that," I said.

He frowned before something approaching a smile crossed his face. "Yeah, me too." He glanced at Claudia, who continued to stare through the porthole and appeared not to be listening. "I wish I could explain it. How a glob of glazed and fired clay, containing no material of value and created by an unknown artist, could make me feel happy when little else can."

"Doesn't that concern you?" I asked, "that a worthless piece of clay can have this much power over you?"

He pinned me with his dark glaze. "At first, yes, but then I figured what the hell? Instead of asking questions I can't answer, why not enjoy what money can buy?"

I thought back to what I'd told myself when holding my completed sculpture for the first time. *Nothing outside of yourself can give you what you think you're missing.* "Do you have to own it to enjoy it?"

"Yes," he said.

He was missing the point—big time. He wanted to possess what the sculpture could only depict. And that just couldn't be.

The expression *You can't take it with you* came to mind. "Again, I'm sorry to hear that."

"You don't know me very well if you think I give up that easily," he said.

Claudia appeared at our table and placed her hand on his shoulder. "There are many forms of pleasure, Cecil, many of them free for the asking."

Smart girl.

Cecil gave me an odd look, which I couldn't decipher on such short acquaintance. Then he stood, put an arm around Claudia's small waist, and drew her close. "Guess you're right."

Claudia held the faraway look I expected to see on the faces of the *Dark Watchers* as they stared over a landscape, a look that contained wisdom far beyond what was normal for someone so young and so beautiful.

Chapter Seventeen

A NNE WAS AT THE WHEEL AGAIN—me riding shotgun—on our way back to the Lodge. But I hardly gave it a second thought. Not that her driving had improved, just that I had other things on my mind. "I should've mentioned it earlier," I said, "but with all the other stuff going on since my arrival, I nearly forgot all about it. Dr. Mendez signed me up for a four-day workshop at the Esalen Institute, starting tomorrow."

"Well, goody for you," she said, which surprised me. For some reason, I had expected her to make light of the plan. *Four days at ground zero for the New Age movement, meditating and soaking your way to nirvana? What are you thinking, hon?*

To be honest, I was a bit nervous about spending this much time with a bunch of people I didn't know. I'd heard rumors about nudity and drugs, but, according to Dr. Mendez, the workshop promised to touch on advanced behavioral and psychological concepts that I couldn't pass up. "Each experience you expose yourself to," he assured me, "and each relationship you forge, regardless of how trivial it may seem, provides an opportunity to unplug from the bonds of your old reality and change the manner in which you perceive the world."

"Esalen is great for exploring what makes you tick," Anne said, swaying her head to a heavy rock band on the radio. "I've been there for several forums myself, mostly to do with nursing and healing."

"I heard it's kind of New Age," I ventured between throbbing drumbeats and screeching guitars.

"Yeah, they often deal with stuff that lies beyond the imagination, with unrealized human capacities and that sort of thing."

I valued Anne's opinion and was glad to hear this. So far, at least, it concurred with what I'd learned about the place. "I heard some great writers and thinkers share ideas there."

Anne eased up on the accelerator, which brought the car's speed down to fifty around a curve marked for forty. "You heard right. It's sort of a blend of Eastern and Western philosophies. Did you know it was home to the Esselen tribe?"

"One of the reasons I agreed to go there. It's the tribe of my mother's people."

"Thus you."

I nodded, feeling a stab of pride.

Anne must have noticed we were losing speed because she floored the gas pedal, and the Volvo surged. "I read somewhere that there were no full-blooded Esselen left."

The thought saddened me. "According to my research, there are only a few hundred Esselen descendants of mixed blood. Some history books list the tribe as extinct."

"It's all experimental, you know," Anne said, doing it again, changing the subject and leaving me disoriented, yet curious, always curious.

"What is?"

"The stuff that goes on at the Institute. There are no guarantees."

I dug in my purse for some chewing gum and found a single piece, wrapper partially open. "Ha. Just like life."

"You're prepared, of course, that nudity is common in the hot springs, massage area, and swimming pool?"

I knew she'd get around to *that* sooner or later. "Are you trying to dissuade me?"

Anne turned and grinned. "You're blushing."

I put the gum into my mouth, needing a jolt of Juicy Fruit to quench my sudden thirst. "I don't plan on spending my time swimming or hot-tubbing."

Anne punched the accelerator. "Chicken."

"You've got that right." I said, wondering if she was just trying to get a rise out of me. "I'm staying out of trouble, with a capital T."

Hypocrite. Hadn't I concluded during my talk with Holly that "getting into trouble" was a necessary ingredient in life?

"Staying out of trouble isn't always the best way to go," Anne said. "You might miss out on something valuable."

I snapped my gum. "Naked bodies? I don't think so."

"You know, don't you, that you're chewing on aspartame and plastic," Anne said.

I bit my tongue. Ouch. "So now you're going to tell me that there's an organic version of gum, too."

Anne reached into a storage compartment in her dashboard and threw something onto my lap. "Certified one-hundred percent organic."

"Goody, and not even individually wrapped." I took the aspartame and plastic out of my mouth, put it back into its foil wrapper, and replaced it with Anne's *organic mixed berry* variety.

"So, what workshop did you sign up for?" Anne asked, peering at the winding road as if we were on a casual Sunday drive instead of racing the Indy 500.

"Something about healing the past and living in the present, using the Gestalt approach," I said. The fog was rolling in. Good thing we were almost back at camp.

Anne took her eyes off the road just long enough to give me a searching glance. "Unresolved inner conflict stuff?"

The texture of Anne's organic gum wasn't as bouncy as mine had been and the favor was fading fast. I wondered what it was made of. Tree sap? "Something like that."

"Let me guess. With parents and an ex-lover."

"You are too awesome," I said, trying to keep the sarcasm out of my voice. She was right, of course. My two mothers, my ex-fiancé, and my conscience all added up to deep inner conflict, hard, if not impossible, to resolve in a lifetime, let alone in four days.

Anne shook her head. "All that fear, anger, and guilt."

"As I said before, I need to deal with all that crap before I can move on."

To her merit, Anne refrained from chuckling. "So, you're going to find yourself through Gestalt therapy. I never did understand it."

"It's complicated," I admitted.

"Can you give me a definition in one sentence or less?"

"Probably not."

"Try anyway."

I looked out the window at the passing trees and greenery. I smelled pine, but suspected it came from the little tree-shaped deodorizer dangling from the car's rearview mirror. "Well...it helps you stand aside from your usual way of thinking."

"Which is?"

"Darn it, Anne. Don't interrupt. Now I have to start over."

"Sorry," Anne said, not sounding the least bit apologetic.

I gathered my thoughts to try again. How to explain Gestalt therapy? I was certain far greater minds had tried and failed. "You stand aside from your usual way of thinking—"

"Whatever that is," Anne slipped in.

"—so, you can tell the difference between what's actually being perceived and felt and what's only residue from the past."

Anne lowered the volume of the rock station charging the car's interior like a shot of adrenaline and cracked open a window, allowing the true scent of moist pine forest to flow in. "So, let me get this straight. What you feel and observe in the here and now—"

"—is real and important," I concluded.

"The goal being?"

"Insight," I said with great authority, though I had no idea what I was talking about.

"You've lost me," Anne said, lifting her hands and then dropping them back onto the steering wheel. The car swerved only slightly.

"A person somehow learns to become aware of being aware, or something like that."

"Okay, so if you've got to be present in the here and now, how does the past fit in?"

Darn it. She knew I didn't know, yet she kept egging me on. "Residues of the past affect the here and now."

"Oh, really?" she said with her own touch of sarcasm.

"Often our lives aren't based on the truth."

Anne pulled into the Pfeiffer Big Sur State Park entrance and slowed the car to a crawl. "So, what else is new?"

I wanted to cry. I wanted to throw up my hands as Anne had done earlier. Where was I coming up with all this crap? "Which leads to feelings of dread and guilt—"

"So, you're going to rediscover yourself," Anne said.

"That's the plan." We were back to the same old subject—self-discovery. It sounded so fruitless. Like the taste of this mixed berry organic gum.

"Want me to drop you off at the Institute?"

"No, I'll be fine," I said with more confidence than I felt. "But I'll need to give you Adam's journal for safe keeping while I'm gone. And... Could you keep an eye on Holly? Make sure she's okay?"

Anne pulled into the Inn's parking lot. "You're a glutton for punishment."

She noticed that I was looking for a place to dispose of my gum. "Throw it out the window. It's biodegradable."

Nope. Still litter to me. I put it into the foil wrapper with my discarded Juicy Fruit and stuck it into my purse to throw away later. "By entrusting Holly with the care of my tent, I hope she also gains the confidence to take care of herself in a world otherwise beyond her control."

"I don't have much faith in her parents," Anne said. "They may steal your tent and everything in it."

"You told me to shed the tent anyway."

Anne laughed. "You mean your security blanket?"

"Might as well start now," I said, though the thought of leaving was bothering me more by the minute.

"I'm going to miss you," Anne said.

My heart did a crazy flip flop, and I fought back tears. "It'll only be four days."

"And then you'll pack up and go home."

I wish. "No. I still have some unfinished business."

"With your birth mother?"

I took a deep, ragged breath, beginning to realize that this 'business' with Antonia probably couldn't be completed in the short time I was here. "Yep."

☽☽☽

After Anne left for her room, I felt alone and confused. It was my twenty-ninth birthday—a depressing thought. Three months ago, I discovered that I was adopted, was part Native American, and had an identical twin sister. Enough to blow anyone's mind. So, for the first time in over twenty-eight years, I was questioning who I was and what the hell I was doing on this earth.

Antonia, who had started all this with her freaky messages, was now remaining maddeningly silent. The woman who had awakened me from a comfortable, though aimless, life path and thrust me into a world of confusion seemed to have packed up and split.

Like I wanted to do.

"Thanks a lot," I muttered, knowing in my heart that Antonia had done me a tremendous favor. How else would I have met my twin and the two loves of my life, Morgan and Joshua? Yet, although Antonia had led me to the door of self-discovery, she wasn't about to walk me through it. I had to do that on my own.

Time for some reflection. Something I'd put off for too long.

After changing out of Anne's finery, I slipped out of my room and hiked to a nearby clearing just wide enough to set up my Medicine Wheel. I placed my marker stones in a circle, marking north, south, east, and west, then took my smudging tools from my backpack and lit the stick of herbs. Its fiery red tip glowed before I extinguished the flame, and as the sage, cedar, and lavender smoldered, I, too, smoldered, in a sad, lingering way. I fanned the smoke toward me and inhaled, visualizing the smoke blanketing me and penetrating deep inside. I waved the smudge stick above, below, and around me and finally placed it on the abalone shell where it could burn itself out.

Then I sat in the place of the South, eyes closed, thinking of how my Medicine Wheel symbolized the universe and my own personal reality. "I've come to seek the power of the Spirit of the South," I said. "To feel its energy flow through and around me."

According to what Ben, *Gentle Bear,* Mendoza had taught me, the Southern direction of the Medicine Wheel is the direction of the past, a place to set one's beliefs aside for a while, to get close to all living things, and to learn to trust and expect the best.

In order to follow the path of trust and innocence, I would have to awaken the child within me, not an easy task considering I was such a goal-oriented busybody. Maybe if I thought about Holly, the way she looked for the soft and tender in those around her, I could remember how it once was.

I reached into my backpack for my journal and pen, trying not to feel rushed. It was getting late. The moon was shining through the swooshing tree branches, its fullness waning, as if part of it had been scooped away. That meant its energy was waning, too, making it a good time to rid myself of the things that were holding me back.

I'm upset, Antonia, I wrote. *You upset me. Your emotions, your sorrow, are taking me down. Is your unhappiness linked to the past? Does it involve Bob, my birth father? I'm reaching out to you in the only way I know how. I can't move on until I know what you want and if there's something I must do.*

I zipped my jacket against the dropping temperature. I wanted to head back to my room, crawl into bed, feel warm and protected. What was I doing out here? "Damn it, I'm scared."

Someone started crying. I thought of Holly's shadow people and shivered. "Mother, I'm scared of what I can't see and what I don't know, and I'm scared of what you might tell me. But I'm not going to run from this. I'm not going to run from you."

As the crying continued, I felt a wave of emotion surge from my chest outward. What if I'd been getting the situation with Antonia all wrong? I'd been making it all about me, wanting to know what she wanted in order to shut her up and get her out of my life. What if she needed help to reach that place where dead people go, a place of purported peace and happiness? Was it possible that she'd been crying all this time for *my* intervention on *her* behalf?

It was almost completely dark now. Long fingers of fog were drifting in. I needed to get back to my room or risk getting lost. I gathered my marker stones, convinced I couldn't do this alone.

Call in your sister, a voice said.

Veronica?

I already had. But she hadn't shown.

Chapter Eighteen

I WOULD BE LYING IF I SAID I wasn't nervous. It was six in the morning and I was driving down Highway 1 toward a small hot springs resort on a cliff overlooking the ocean on the coast of Big Sur. I'd heard it called a pagan monastery, a school of the mysteries, and a kingdom of death and rebirth, where people fall flat on their faces in order to discover their souls. My only consolation was that the Esalen Institute sat on land that had once belonged to my ancestors, right smack in the middle of what had been an ancient Esselen burial ground.

There was no fog to obscure my view, yet I nearly missed the turn off. The sign marking the resort's entrance might as well have been nonexistent, miniscule as it was, with *Esalen Institute by Reservation Only* printed in equally miniscule letters.

This place was not user friendly.

As if to reinforce this observation, there was a guard posted at the gate. Was it his job to keep people out—or keep them in? Regardless, it felt as though I were entering a prison. He frowned and asked for my name. I frowned back and gave it to him. He consulted the guest list. I half expected him to ask for my ID. Instead, he said, "You're late."

"Yes," I said.

He pointed toward a building to our left. "Registration is at the Lodge."

Not exactly a warm reception.

The moment I stepped out of my Jeep, I heard the sound of crashing surf. The cool, salty air generated a moment of immersive, restorative, and invigorating peace. "I can do this," I said. "I need to be here."

I left my bags in the cargo hold of the Jeep—in case I had a change of mind—and headed for the Lodge. I glimpsed a pool nearby. Was this where guests swam nude? Currently, it was unoccupied, for which I said a prayer of thanks. I passed an old Hippie. His cheeks were flushed, his eyes glazed, and his hair...well, it looked like it hadn't been trimmed or washed in a while. "Can you feel the energy?" he asked. I nodded and walked on.

The woman at the registration desk looked normal enough. Her shoulder-length hair was styled in a shaggy bob with bangs—no dreadlocks, spikes, or pink dyes—and she wore snug jeans and a skinny white top. "Welcome to the Esalen Institute," she said, running the eraser of her pencil to the bottom of her list. "Veil? Marjorie Veil?"

"Thanks. Yes" —I looked at her nametag— "Pat."

"You're a bit late," Pat said as she handed me a folder stuffed with registration materials. "But I'm sure you'll still get a lot out of today's workshop."

I opened the folder and fingered the papers inside. Late? Heck, I nearly chickened out altogether. "I had a little trouble finding the place."

"No worries. You'll do fine." She pointed out a laminated map of the grounds taped to the counter. "There's a wooden bridge here that crosses the creek and leads to the Big House where you'll be lodging. That's also where they hold most of the lectures, including the Gestalt course for which you're registered."

"I didn't see much activity when I came in," I said, keeping my voice upbeat in spite of my discomfort.

"We currently have close to a hundred guests staying with us," Pat said, "in various teepees, yurts, and cabins. Most are attending workshops right now. Later on, as the temperature warms up, you'll find them dispersed all over the grounds."

The phone rang, a reminder that I was missing part of my first day.

"Come back when you've settled in," Pat said, picking up the receiver. "This is where the meals are served. The office also serves as a bookstore."

"You've just said the magic word," I said.

She grinned. "Meals?"

"No, bookstore."

Instead of retrieving my luggage from the back of my Jeep and locating my room, I hurried down the path toward the Big House and my first workshop. I slipped through the door labeled "The Gestalt Approach" and took a seat in back of the room. Most of the thirty or so attendees appeared focused on the instructor, who, to my relief, barely glanced my way. I allowed myself a quiet sigh.

According to the workshop description, the instructor's name was Hal Jones. He was talking about unresolved inner conflicts, which meant I was in the right place.

Before I had a chance to get out a paper and pen, he concluded his lecture. "Now, let's form a circle and begin applying some of the Gestalt exercises we've been talking about."

The participants burst into activity, shoving materials back into their folders and rising from their seats. The room vibrated with the buzz of conversation and the scraping and clanging of chairs as they formed into a wide circle. I glanced at the woman sitting next to me, wondering why she hadn't joined in. Her eyes had a distant, ominous look. "I'm thinking about packing my bags and getting out of here," she said.

"That bad, huh?"

"Afraid so."

"How about you stay long enough to clue me in, then maybe we can make a run for it together?"

She grinned. "Okay."

"I notice we have a new member in our group," Hal said above the ruckus. All heads turned my way. Some smiled, others grimaced, and the rest appeared blurry-eyed. Hal came to the back of the room and handed me a bundle of class handouts. "You must be Marjorie," he said, loud enough for the entire class to hear. "Glad you made it."

I nodded and accepted the stack of papers, hoping he would leave it at that.

He did.

"You're in for it now," my new friend whispered.

"You think?"

The corners of her mouth drew back in a mirthless smile, revealing neat bottom teeth. She shoved her class materials into her backpack and extended her hand. "My name's Jennifer."

"Nice to meet you," I said, giving her hand a squeeze.

"Likewise," she said. "Guess we better join the circle."

We slipped into an opening saved for us by one of the other class participants. "Howdy, Marjorie," the woman said. Her face laid claim to fifty, but she had the trim, firm body of a thirty-year-old. Her auburn hair stretched back into a ponytail that reached halfway down her back. Something told me she was a country girl, maybe into horses.

"Nice to meet you," I said, shaking her hand.

"The name's Kate. Glad you hooked up with Jennifer here. I think she was ready to bolt."

I gave her an affirmative nod. "I think you're right."

"I heard that," Jennifer said.

"You were meant to." Kate's lips quirked into a smile. "Hell, the best part is yet to come."

And in a way, she was right.

)))

When we broke for lunch, my brain felt dehydrated, not only physically, but mentally. After leading us through an awareness, meditative exercise, where we concentrated on our breathing, our movement, and the sensations in our bodies, Hal had asked for volunteers to the *Open Seat*.

I sensed this wouldn't be pretty, so was baffled when at least five hands shot up, including Kate's.

"She's crazy," Jennifer whispered.

Couldn't argue with that.

Kate wasn't selected, but three other volunteers were, and one by one, they related their stories. Instead of allowing them to concentrate on the past or speculate about the future, Hal prodded them into the present. "Imagine that you are there right this minute," he said. "What are you doing? What is your experience?" And they relived their anger, sadness, and irritation as if it were happening in the here and now. The entire episode was daunting and intimidating, and I shivered at the thought of what would be revealed when it came my turn.

"I know you came here wanting change or resolution," Hal said, "but the point is to make contact, not change. The more you try to keep things in the *why* rather than the *how*, the more you tie yourself up and remain the same."

All three of the volunteers ended up crying at some point, as did many of the group participants, including Kate. I envied their openness, wishing I could bawl my eyes out. How cleansing that would be.

Kate was now leading the way back to the Lodge for lunch. "It's easy to get turned off by all this."

Jennifer's eyes met mine, and we smiled.

"But don't let it," Kate said. "You've got to die before you can be reborn."

"The food's incredible," Jennifer said.

Kate gave her a hug. "Another reason for hanging in there."

I made no comment. My stomach did it for me. "Sorry," I said. "I didn't have breakfast."

"It's like a New Age summer camp," Kate said. "Wait till you soak in the tubs."

I tried not to grimace.

"Of course, I haven't been able to talk Jennifer into joining us," Kate added, giving her a poke in shoulder.

"I haven't come across anyone I care to see naked," Jennifer said.

"Then don't look," Kate said. "Hell, it's something you have to experience. Like Big Sur itself. What do you say, Marjorie?"

"I'm hungry."

Kate gave me a genuine, top-toothed grin. "Keeping me in suspense, huh? That's okay. One thing I've garnered over the years is patience. I break horses, you know."

"Come on," Jennifer said, taking off at a faster pace, "or we'll be last in line."

I scooped a colorful assortment of fruits and vegetables—strawberries, kiwi, melon, raw broccoli, celery, and carrots—onto my plate and topped it off with a bowl of barley soup. "This is incredible," I said after we'd taken our seats at a communal table and sampled the fare.

Kate rolled up the sleeves of her plaid shirt. "All the produce comes from the garden located near the kitchen, and it's picked fresh daily. The soil and climate are perfect here, plus the gardeners are first rate, so we're being fed physically as well as emotionally and spiritually."

Jennifer coughed and took a sip of water. "I asked Kate about the others in the group, and she told me most were psychologists."

"Oh great," I said.

Kate patted my back. "Just think. You can get all kinds of free advice."

I looked at Jennifer from across the table. "Are you a psychologist, too?"

"Oh, please," she said, as though tasting something bitter. "I teach Kindergarten."

"I'd say that makes you part psychologist, part nurse, and part mother," I said.

She set down her fork and gave me an over-the-shoulder, faraway look. "My problem is that I have a hard time releasing my emotions in public. Or anywhere, for that matter. I kind of keep things bottled up inside."

Kate shook her head. "You're just a damn chicken."

"I know exactly what Jennifer means," I said. "I'm nervous about exposing myself, too."

"Oh, shit," Kate said. "I'm stuck with two wusses."

"I'm sure you'll see it as a challenge," I added, "knowing how you break horses and all."

Kate shook her head. "People are different from horses."

"I certainly hope so," Jennifer said.

"Look at it this way," Kate said, waving her fork in the air. "All that garbage we're carrying around inside isn't good for us. It weighs us down, rots us from the inside out. I should know. I've had some crappy life experiences, both physical and emotional. Unlike horses, that kick ass or run like hell, we try to bottle things up. And you know what? Fear turns into trauma, which really screws with the brain."

I had to agree. I was carrying around my share of garbage, which was casting a shadow over my plans.

"I figure what I'm experiencing here will be good for me eventually," Jennifer admitted, "but the idea of sitting in the *Open Seat* and letting it all hang out drives me batty."

"The group is very supportive," Kate said.

"I know, but..."

All at once, I felt the determination to stick this out, if not for my own sake, then for Jennifer's. "We'll be there for one another."

Kate slapped her hand on my back. "Now you're talking."

Jennifer didn't look so sure.

☽☽☽

By next evening, over half of the group had been in the *Open Seat*. Boxes of tissue had made their way around the room, and many participants hadn't liked what they'd discovered about themselves. Some even freaked out, which lead to several tense moments, and I wondered how many would be absent the next day.

Kate's story had been gripping. Her only son had died of cancer at twenty-six and her husband of a heart attack a year later. They had a successful horse ranch, but without her husband and son's support,

149

she soon ran into financial difficulties. She sold the ranch at a pittance, to, of all people, her husband's best friend. "Ultimately, there was no one to turn to," she said. "I was all alone."

"Bring everything to the real and present," Hal reminded her, "as if it's happening now."

"I have no one to turn to. I'm all alone." As Kate said these words, she eyed her fellow workshop members, one at a time, and not one looked away. Their eyes mirrored her pain.

"I might be small," she said, "but I'm strong. I've learned to wipe my own ass."

"You've gone from dependence to independence," Hal said. "And now you're well on your way to interdependence, where you recognize your need for others, within certain boundaries, which is what we all seek."

Kate looked at Jennifer and me, her eyes bright. "Yeah, I guess so."

My heart seemed to reach out of itself, and I felt something warm expand within, something I recognized as far too great to contain.

))))

"Tomorrow may be your turn," Kate warned over dinner.

Jennifer gasped. "Heaven forbid."

"Hal said we didn't have to," I pointed out.

"Marjorie's right," Jennifer said. "No one's forced into the *Open Seat.*"

Kate cocked her head at the two of us. "What a shame. I found it freeing. Anyway, who's joining me in the hot tub?"

With a quick shake of the head, I voiced my excuse. "I'm spending some time in the book store, and then I'm heading to my room to read."

"Me, too," Jennifer added.

"That figures," Kate said, getting up from the table. "Guess it's time for me to hang out with the movers and shakers."

"Enjoy," I said. She deserved a good time.

"Wish I was more like her," Jennifer said after Kate had marched out the door.

"She didn't get there overnight," I said, knowing this to be true.

We watched Kate through the window as she headed down to the baths.

Jennifer sniffed. "I'm not getting it. I don't think I can find the meaning of life through academics."

"It's early yet," I said. "Although I don't see much progress toward spiritual health in this workshop."

"What do you mean?"

"Well, Gestalt deals with the physical part, you know, the breathing and getting in touch with your senses. And it deals with the emotional. At least while you're in the *Open Seat*, but—"

"I think I'm getting your drift," Jennifer said.

"The physical and psychological freedom people experience here may lead some to nudity, hot tubbing, and sexual encounters that feel very liberating—"

"Or are just an excuse for some dirty old men to get what they can't get at home," Jennifer interjected in a tone that suggested repressed emotion.

"But, I'd like to experience the liberation of spirit," I finished.

"Okay, so Gestalt may be a start," Jennifer said. "I agree with the part about taking responsibility for ourselves."

"You mean, wiping our own asses?"

"Yeah, and cutting out the blame and deciding instead to be happy."

"I guess you get what you truly believe in and want."

Jennifer peered through the window at the pool below. "Something like that."

I spied several tanned and bare bodies milling around the pool and allowed myself a cleansing chuckle. "Easier said than done."

Jennifer turned from the window and appealed to me with her wide brown eyes. "How the hell do I get to my unconscious mind, where all the crap is, the part that's screwing up my desires?"

"Which are?" I asked.

Jennifer's laugh expressed too many disappointments and missed opportunities for someone her age. "Not what you're probably thinking."

"Which is?"

"That I want to strip naked and jump into the hot tub."

"That's exactly what I was thinking."

"Sorry to disappoint you," Jennifer said.

"Hell, I'm not disappointed. If you went down there, I'd be all by my lonesome. Anyway, our subconscious is like a computer. It functions the way it's programmed."

"So how do I deprogram mine?"

"I think that's what Hal's trying to help us do with Gestalt, forcing us to change tracks."

"The imagination part?"

"Yes. And changing our thoughts and words."

"Are you going to take the *Open Seat* tomorrow?"

"You mean the *Hot Seat*?" I shivered. "I don't know. My situation is kind of weird."

Jennifer snorted. "That's what they all say."

"Some of the stuff in my head is pretty scary."

Another snort. "I find that hard to believe."

If only she knew.

Jennifer's gaze strayed to the window again. "Do you think the subconscious has a sense of humor?"

"Most definitely not. It can't reason, and it believes anything our conscious tells it."

"Then I'm in deep shit," Jennifer said.

"Aren't we all?"

Chapter Nineteen

A T FIRST, WE THOUGHT we had been spared. But near the end of the session, Hal announced there was time for one, maybe two, more in the *Open Seat*, and only Ted, Jennifer, and I were left. Hal looked us over, one at a time. "So, who will it be?"

Jennifer gripped my arm and started breathing in and out in short, shallow breaths. "Lordy, lordy, lordy."

I patted her hand and stood. "I'll go."

An ear-splitting whistle from Kate. "That a girl."

Hal addressed the class with a warning. "Remember, we're not looking for a break through, but a break-in. By invading Marjorie's privacy, we hope to help her re-establish contact with her lost and deadened feeling."

Good luck with that. I'd been trying to do so for weeks with no success.

"You'll do fine," Jennifer whispered, the color drained from her face.

"Of course, she will," Kate said.

Hal picked up a chair and placed it next to the *Open Seat*. "I'd like to try something new this morning." He gestured for me to come forward. "Marjorie, you'll be talking to an imaginary person, who'll be sitting in the empty chair in front of you. If it helps, you can move back and forth between the chairs as you act out the dialogue be-tween the two of you. Exaggerate it. Use ridiculous extremes if you like, but act as if you're talking to a real person."

"I don't think I can." My words came out low and a bit hoarse.

"You mean you choose not to?"

"Yes. I mean... No."

His smile was understanding and encouraging, the kind of smile a parent gives a child when she's first learning to walk. "You have to go out of your mind in order to use it."

I eyed the door, wishing I could make a run for it. "I don't know where to begin."

"Your unconscious can be programmed to do whatever you want it to."

I caught Jennifer's eye. She managed a shaky smile and gave me the thumbs up.

"You're going to talk to the personification of whatever or who-ever bothers you," Hal continued in a calm, hypnotic voice.

"The personification?" I looked him in the eye, hoping to make clear that I wasn't easy to put under, if that's what he was trying to do.

"Yes. Ascribe it with a personality. Give it a name."

I thought of Antonia, who bothered me plenty. Ascribing her with a personality wouldn't be that hard. Sad and outreaching. "Okay."

Hal smiled, nodded. "Now tell me, Marjorie, what would you like to accomplish?"

"I'd like to help my mother."

"Speak up Marjorie, so the class can hear you."

"Help my mother."

"In what way?"

"I want her to be happy."

"You can't do that for her," Hal said with a note of criticism. "She has to do that for herself."

"She can't"

"Why not?"

"She's dead."

Several of the workshop members laughed, some hooted and clapped, but Hal frowned and narrowed his eyes. "If she's dead, how do you know she's unhappy?"

"I hear her crying."

"A real psycho," sneered a male in the group.

"Shut up, Ted," Jennifer snapped.

Hal coughed—his way, I'd learned, of regaining the class's attention. "I'll ask everyone to refrain from such comments."

Ted's face reddened. "You told us to say what we feel."

"I also urged you not to judge. Judgment blocks expansion. We're here to support one another, remember?"

A shrug from Ted. "Yeah, whatever."

But Kate, dear Kate, wouldn't let it go. "You're here for all the wrong reasons, Ted."

The scowl on his face suggested he was anxious for a fight. "Oh yeah? And how do you know?"

"I saw you drooling over all those bare bodies last night."

"Not yours," he said, a cruel edge to his voice.

An impressive eye roll from Kate. "Oh, give me a break. I may be a bit long in the tooth, but my body's tanned and toned. Centerfold material."

Applause broke out, and someone said, "Way to go, Kate."

Jennifer leapt to her feet. "Wait till it's your turn in the *Open Seat*, Mr. Smarty Pants. I'll get you good."

Ted sneered. "I'm not getting into that damn chair."

"That figures," Kate said, her voice low and confident. "You piece of chicken shit."

"You've really got a mouth on you," Ted shot back, taking a step toward her.

"Come on," Kate said, putting up her fists. "I've fought bigger guys than you—and won."

"Kate, your behavior is not very lady-like," a female participant chided.

Kate gave her a piercing glare. "Lilly dear, ladies get fucked and fucked over."

Lilly puffed out her lips and turned pink.

I looked at Hal. He appeared to be following the altercation with interest, as if searching for clues, while the participants gave pieces of themselves away. As far as I could tell, he faced some critical choices as to his level of intervention. How much and when, for instance, should he limit what people were allowed to say or do? I tried to relax, curious as to how much divergence the group could tolerate and still function in a constructive and cohesive manner. For now, it seemed, there would be no holding back in this class.

"I had to grow a pair of balls," Kate said to no one in particular.

Jennifer clapped. "Tell it like it is."

I felt a slight thrill. Something important was happening here. No wonder Hal was allowing the scrimmage to play out.

"Next thing I know, they'll be calling me Katherine," Kate said under her breath.

No one commented on that, but Hal wrote it down.

"Back to Marjorie," he said, and all heads turned my way.

I faced the empty chair, not certain where to begin.

Then I heard someone crying.

My throat tightened. I strained to hear more. "Antonia?"

I'm here, Sunwalker.

Dear God, finally. "Mother?" I sat down facing the second chair and closed my eyes.

I'm so sorry.

I took a ragged breath. "Sorry for what, Antonia?"

Only your father knows.

"Knows what?"

Silence.

"Knows what, Mother."

More silence, then, *I still love him.*

"You still love the man who broke your heart? The man who tore our family apart." I felt angry for her, for me. "Do you still love me, too?"

More than you know.

I reached out my hands and groped in the air, but came up empty. "Touch me, Momma. Let me feel your touch."

But she was gone.

☽☽☽

"You should've been an actress, you know that?" Jennifer said on our way out of the Gestalt workshop. "Even though you didn't change seats the way Hal said you could and you never told us what your imaginary person was saying, you had everyone on the edge of their seats. It looked like you were really talking to someone."

"I was."

Jennifer's mouth clamped shut, and she stared at me as if I'd grown horns.

Kate slapped her thigh. "I knew you weren't acting. No one's that good."

We halted on the paved path leading to the narrow wooden bridge over the ravine, which divided the 120-acre Esalen property. "I wanted so much for her to touch me."

"Who?" Kate asked, her eyes radiant.

I pulled in a deep, reviving breath. "My mother."

Jennifer quit gawking at me as if I'd come from another planet, only to eye me as if I were a bit loco. "Why didn't we hear her, too?"

"The only other person who's been able to do so is my sister, Veronica." *And Adam.*

Kate whistled. "What a blessing to know there's an afterlife."

"You ever doubted it?" Jennifer asked, stepping onto the rickety bridge.

A group of guests carrying backpacks exited the bridge on the other side and appeared to be heading for the Buddha Garden. We were on our way to the Big Lodge, where we would grab a bite to eat and then go our separate ways until supper time. A good thing, because I felt exhausted and needed a nap.

"Why yes, dear," Kate said, following Jennifer onto the bridge. "If you've been through what I have, you'd have doubts, too."

Jennifer shook her head as if this were highly improbable.

"I hope my husband and son are happy," Kate said, just loud enough for me to hear over the rushing creek below and screeching hawk above. "Wherever they are."

I reached forward and gave Kate's shoulder a squeeze. "Me, too."

Kate turned to glance at me, but said nothing until we'd exited the bridge on the other side. "You really freaked Ted out, you know. I thought he was going to puke."

"And you should have seen Hal," Jennifer added. "He seemed upset about something."

We passed a circular meditation house where workshops titled *Modern Mystical Movement, Radical Aliveness, and Core Energetics* were in session. "Well, it shook me up, hearing my mother again. She's been hard to reach lately."

Jennifer paused to eye a stone Buddha surrounded by wilted flowers and beaded necklaces. "What did she say?"

The image of my mother formed in front of my eyes. My heart expanded as if to take her in. It had the room. Dear God, it had the room. "That she still loves my father and loves me."

"What are you going to do?" Kate asked.

I turned in a slow circle, taking in the churning ocean, the looming mountains, and the kinetic Esalen grounds, feeling a sudden restlessness, as if all were conspiring against me. "I don't know, but whatever it is, it can't be accomplished here."

"I think talk of the spiritual freaks out all the scientific types," Jennifer said.

Kate crossed her arms. "While you were staring at that other chair with tears running down your face, I got the shivers. It was obvious that something inexplicable was going on, but most of the group didn't get it. They didn't dare."

☽ ☽ ☽

Anxious as I was at this point to return to Pfeiffer Park and see what I could do for Antonia—and for myself—I also wanted to finish what I had started at the Esalen Institute. I'd come with the intention of exploring and healing some of my inner conflicts in a supportive environment and had only accomplished part of that. I'd watched others explore and had done a bit of exploring myself, but, as far as I knew, I hadn't done any healing.

So, that meant more Gestalt workshop.

Which wasn't easy, considering that most of the participants were distancing themselves from me. I would've done the same had I been in their shoes, but it made for some uncomfortable moments.

Jennifer and Kate, bless their hearts, stuck by me like bodyguards. They assured me that I'd helped bring out the spiritual aspect of their search for self and that the rest of the class consisted of fools if they couldn't see that for themselves.

"If the group is supposed to be a mirror in which we catch a reflection of our own personal style of interaction, as Hal teaches," Kate said the next morning as we headed for the Gestalt workshop, "we're in deep shit."

"The group mirrors my fear," I said. "I hate what's going on with my mother and would like to ignore it, too."

Jennifer raised her arms up and down like a bird having trouble on takeoff. "But these are hip and educated people. Teachers and psychologists. They're supposed to be open to glimpses of reality that most people never permit themselves to see."

"Yeah, like Ted," Kate said.

Jennifer snorted. "That turd."

Hal started class with another surprise. "In yesterday's session, this group failed miserably in coming together as a unit. Each of us was holding on to our own presuppositions, beliefs, and ideas. As a result, we sat back and watched Marjorie take the *Open Seat* as if she were putting on a show. We didn't give her our empathy, our support, or our strength. Today, with your cooperation and Marjorie's, I hope we can change that."

"Hold it," Ted said. "I'm an independent thinker, not a conformist. I refuse to become part of some Nazi groupthink."

"I understand your fear," Hal said.

"It's not fear—" Ted began, his face turning red.

Hal held up his hand. "Let me finish. You're afraid of losing your

individuality, or, worse yet, coming to some misguided group decision. But ask yourself. How independent are you really? Most of us
rarely have a truly independent thought. Our minds develop in relationship to other minds. They are not locked inside our brains. They
are fields that interact with one another." Hal waited a moment for
his words to sink in, "So if you think about it, you're already part of
a group mind."

"Of a collective consciousness," one of the psychologists in the
group said.

Hal stopped pacing the room, looking relieved that at least one
person comprehended his missive. "That's right, Nick, and it's radi-
cally different from groupthink. The individual isn't subordinated,
but enhanced and strengthened by participation in the group."

"Like the Blue Angels," Kate said.

Hal chuckled and resumed his pacing. "Yes, with everyone in
sync."

Nick spoke up again. "There has been increased interest of late
in mind/body healing, and I believe that collective intelligence has a
lot to do with its success. When a group finds cohesion, sometimes
magic occurs."

"Group magic." Hal scratched his head as if Nick's comment inspired deep thought. "I like that." He eyed each participant and
asked, "How about just for today, we practice a shared intention to
help Marjorie reach her mother. If we listen for something deeper,
we may learn something new."

"Communicate with the dead?" Ted asked, his voice an unpleas-
ant squall.

From the corner of my eye, I thought I saw Hal flinch. "Our intention is to help Marjorie reach her highest potential. We'll be creating a safe space in our center for her to do her work. We'll focus all
our attention on her goal and forget about our own personal agendas."

Hal turned to me. "Marjorie, are you ready to receive our support
and possibly receive another message from your mother?"

Yes, yes, yes. "Yes."

"Okay then." Hal picked up a chair and motioned the rest of the group to do the same. "Let's make this a healing place and let's attempt to explore a territory that is rarely, if ever, accessible to us individually."

As the group circled their chairs around me and I took the *Open Seat*, I eyed my fellow participants one-by-one. Several returned my look with blank expressions, others nodded, but most of their gazes drifted over my shoulder. Only Hal, Kate, and Jennifer seemed to be sending out any positive vibes. Ted sat with his arms crossed, his contribution a hard stare.

Facing the empty chair, I closed my eyes and waited, hoping to receive some sense of direction from the people gathered around me. Something warm blanketed me, but I had no way of knowing if it came from the group's unified intention or from my mother's presence.

"Antonia?" I said.

Nothing.

"Mother?"

I held you in my arms until the end.

"Oh, my God, Momma." I found it difficult to swallow. Someone handed me a tissue. I wadded it up and wiped my face. "What can I do to help you?"

Talk to your father.

"But I don't know him. And I don't know where he is."

First Dawn knows.

"Who?"

Your sister.

"Veronica?"

She knows.

"Momma?"

Yes, Sunwalker.

"Will we be together someday?"

We already are.

"Can you touch me?"

Something cool brushed my cheek, and I reached for it. But no one was there. No one I could touch or feel anyway. It was like loving and being loved by God, which, according to my present standards, fell short, a giving and receiving that was illusive, lacking, and incomplete.

When I stopped crying, I realized how quiet the room had become. I opened my eyes, afraid of what I might see. My gaze sought out Hal for guidance, but he was sitting in a chair with his face in his hands. Next, I eyed Kate and Jennifer, who both looked back at me, their expressions glazed. I scanned the other members of the group. Some were crying. Some were praying. Some just stared into space. Ted stood next to a window, looking out. I listened to my heart thud in my chest as I waited for Hal to break the silence. He coughed, stood, and said, "We heard her, Marjorie. We heard your mother."

"Thank God," I whispered, searching the faces around me for a glimmer of understanding and support. Nick nodded at Hal's words, the woman named Lilly smiled, and several others whispered amongst themselves, but only two met my eyes.

Jennifer and Kate.

Hal faced the class. "You just got a taste of something authentic, be it your deeper psyche, your soul, or whatever you want to call it. However, I must warn you, the experience will fade. At your current stage of development, you cannot adequately interpret what just happened here. You won't have that kind of self-understanding. But I do think most of you can appreciate the miraculous something that can occur when individuals quit fighting for airspace and come together in shared exploration."

"Here, here," Lilly cried out. She began to clap until others joined in.

My chest grew warm as I, too, brought my hands together. Quit fighting for airspace. Share the exploration. What wonderful concepts.

When the clapping ended, Hal said in a voice that shook, "I'll close this morning's session early so each of you can reflect on what has just been revealed to you."

Jennifer stood. "Hal, may I share a quote that applies to what we've experienced today?"

"Be my guest," he said, relinquishing the floor with a wave of his hand.

Jennifer turned toward Ted and considered him through narrowed eyes. "Abraham Lincoln once said, 'To believe in the things you can see and touch is not belief at all; but to believe in the unseen is a triumph and a blessing.'"

A scowl marred Ted's face as the class erupted with cheers and applause. He excused himself and strode from the room.

Hal smiled at Jennifer before directing his attention back to the group. "See you this afternoon," he said.

We all stood and went our separate ways.

)))

During the last session of our workshop, Jennifer and Ted surprised everyone by volunteering to take the *Open Seat*. Then Hal came up with another one of his evocative ideas. "We're going to have a face-off. I've noticed the antagonism between these two workshop participants. In fact, if I remember correctly, Jennifer told Ted that when it was his turn, she'd get him good. Now's her chance."

Everyone, except me, applauded. I hated confrontation. It made me nervous. And I knew it made Jennifer nervous, too. So, imagine my surprise when I saw the grin on her face. I'm ashamed to say I found myself leaning forward in anticipation.

"Let the match begin," Hal said, and as Jennifer and Ted took their seats, I swear I could hear the ring of a bell.

Jennifer took the first swing. "Okay, Mr. Independent Thinker, it's time you start participating in this group instead of stonewalling everything we're trying to do. What kind of psychologist are you anyway?"

"Psychologist?" Ted frowned. "What are you talking about? I'm an elementary school teacher."

He might as well have punched Jennifer, the way she went stumbling back to her corner. "Shit."

Ted's face turned the shade of anger. "You've got something against teachers?"

"Hell no. I teach, too. Kindergarten."

"Well, I hope you don't use such foul language around your students," Ted snapped, his face taking on a lighter hue as he gained some semblance of control.

"As a teacher, I figured you'd be more open-minded," Jennifer said, sidestepping his comment about foul language. "The way you expect your students to be."

"There's a big difference between being open-minded and just plain gullible." Ted thrust his jaw forward as if daring her to take a punch at it.

She did. "Gullible, my foot. You're scared."

Ted shot out of his chair, which flipped over and slid back, jolting the person behind him.

"Thanks a lot," said the injured man.

Ted ignored him, apparently intent on delivering a deciding blow. "Scared of what, some figment of Marjorie's imagination?"

I clasped my hands together. This guy's mercury level was reaching the boiling point, his face, his neck, his hands all the color of hot lava.

Jennifer, in contrast, appeared placid as a saint, as if outside the reach of all the pettiness of this world. "That's it big boy, show us your stuff."

Although Ted remained standing with his legs spread and hands squeezed into fists, I thought I glimpsed a look of respect in his eyes.

"What's got into her?" Kate whispered from the seat next to me.

I shook my head, baffled by Jennifer's transformation. One thing was certain; she was discovering a new part of herself, as I had hoped to do. I wondered if it was her subconscious speaking.

If so, it had no sense of humor.

))))

"Can you believe it?" Kate said later that evening. "Jennifer and Ted are in the hot tub together."

"No, actually I can't."

Kate smiled, probably wondering when I'd take the leap. "One minute they're in the *Open Seat*, kicking, screaming, and sobbing, just about ready to kill each another, and the next they're hugging like a couple of soul-mates."

"Yeah, that was kind of unexpected."

"In the process of yelling at each other," Kate continued with a trace of glee in her voice, "they discovered that they lived rather dull, unassuming lives, both elementary school teachers, single, and bored out of their skulls."

"Well, they aren't bored anymore."

Seagulls squawked overhead, drawing Kate's gaze away from the churning waves and upward. "I'd been wondering if any of these people would change in a significant way, if they would uncover some new strength, an unsuspected capacity for life. Now I know it's possible."

"So where do you go from here?" I asked.

"I'm signing up for the twenty-eight-day work-study program."

"You want more of this?"

"Yeah, why not? I've heard the program is emotionally and physically challenging, and rarely restful."

She had that right, more reason to stay away.

"Let me guess," Kate said "You're still set on helping your mother."

"You're psychic, right?"

She tapped her temple. "Bingo."

"Okay then, use your psychic powers to predict if we're going to keep in touch, because I'm going to miss you and Jennifer."

Kate's eyes grew teary. "I don't need psychic powers for that. We're going to keep in touch forever, even if we don't call, write, or e-mail."

My eyes misted, too. "I think I know what you mean."

"We meet, hopefully make a positive difference in someone's

life, and then move on," Kate said. "That's how life is. We ulti-mately travel it alone."

My smile was shaky as I stood and peered out the window at the pool and hot tubs below. "I'll never forget you, Kate." When she didn't reply, I turned and saw her wipe her eyes with the back of her hand. I gave her a hug and turned away. "See you in the morning."

"Not so fast," she said. "I'm headed back, too."

"Aren't you going to strip and soak in the tub?"

"It's Jennifer's night. I don't want to steal the show."

I laughed until my sides hurt. "Jeez, I love you."

"Love you back," she said.

Then we walked hand-in-hand over the bridge that crossed the creek leading to the Big House.

Chapter Twenty

I NOTICED IT THE MINUTE I pulled into camp. The Circus Campers were gone—tents, stoves, generator, and all. That meant Holly was gone, too. *Oh, dear God, Holly. Where'd you go? Are you okay?*

I parked the Jeep and headed straight for Anne's camp. She was supposed to keep an eye on Holly. She'd know if my little friend was okay.

When I knocked on and cracked open the door of Anne's yurt, she was sitting in lotus position in front of her altar, hands on knees, palms up, eyes closed. I sensed that I shouldn't disturb her, yet I didn't back away, drawn, but not mollified, by her calm, meditative state.

"Anne." My throat tightened. I tried again. "Anne?"

She turned and looked at me, her gaze unfocused as though I'd roused her from a deep sleep.

A force with the strength of restraining hands on both of my shoulders kept me from entering her yurt. "Holly's gone."

Enough candles flickered on her altar to cause the park rangers concern, but this didn't seem to bother Anne. She was wearing her white robe again. Incense and candle smoke swirled around her, and dim pools of candlelight illuminated the side of her face nearest the altar, causing her to appear mystical.

"Give me a few minutes, okay?" she said.

I stepped away from the yurt, made the sign of the cross, and pressed my hands together, palm to palm, fingertip to fingertip, the way I'd been taught as a child—prayer being the best way I knew at this moment to quell the pain in my chest and the questions running through my mind. "Please God, take care of Holly. Wrap your arms around her. Hold her tight. Keep her safe."

"Holly's gone," I repeated when Anne stepped out of the yurt.

Anne put her hand on my shoulder. "Sweetie, we need to talk."

I blew out my breath. "Yes."

"Pump up the fuel tank and light the stove," she said, "while I fetch some water for chamomile tea."

I moved like a sleepwalker, but managed to do what she'd asked. When Anne returned with the water, she asked, "You okay?"

I sank to my knees on her yoga mat, currently covered with dry needles and a dusting of dirt. "I feel as if I've just lost a member of my family."

Anne poured water into a pot and set it on the camp stove to heat. "I was trying to help her just now."

A log shifted in the fire pit, and I jerked. "With witchcraft?"

"Using the strongest *magick* I know."

The day was too bright for my dark mood, the bird chatter too cheerful. Holly's absence created a void in my life, yet left no mark on the world around us. "Did you talk to her before she left?"

"She was concerned about your tent and asked me to watch it for her. She also left you something." Anne stepped back into her yurt and came out with a mason jar decorated with acorns and dried flowers. "She said to write your problems on pieces of paper and put them into this jar so God can take care of them for you."

She'd made me a God jar, just as promised. Damn it. I took Holly's gift and pressed it to my chest in an attempt to relieve the gripping muscle tension beneath.

"Let it go, girl."

I lifted my shoulders and then allowed them to sag, a gesture too limp to pass for a shrug. "I only knew her for such a short while."

Anne stoked the fire and then settled on the yoga mat next to me. She asked no questions, nor did she attempt to make me smile, allowing me my darkness.

Finally, she said, "Holly was here to teach you."

My reply, another half-hearted shrug. My friend, Ben *Gentle Bear* Mendoza, had referred to the Southern direction of the Medicine Wheel as the way of the child. He'd explained that children grow in body and mind, yet keep the attitude of trust and innocence, and that spiritual maturity and the understanding of one's true identity come only by adopting these child-like attitudes.

Anne checked the temperature of the water with her pinkie. "Holly will do fine because, as you pointed out not long ago, she has spunk and stands up for what she believes in, but also because she won't interrupt the flow of happiness into her life with thoughts of unhappiness. She accepted the gift of love that you and Adam gave her and will use it to spread love to others."

Holly was a soul that had entered my life as a gift. Who was I to deny her the opportunity to move on and spread all the love she had stored in her spiritual piggy bank? If only I knew for sure she'd be okay. "But—"

Anne held a finger to her lips to silence me. "You made a big impact on her, too. I talked to her mother before they left. She quit drinking and was trying to spend more time with her kids."

Holly's mother quit drinking?

"She'd been thinking about what you said, about how her kids would never forget and how they'd stop coming to see her when they grew up if she didn't change."

I wiped my eyes and cleared my throat. "I told her things I should've told my mother, except I didn't have the guts."

"You were more worried about Truus's feelings than you were about your own, but in Holly's case, you saw the big picture. And it did Holly's mother good to see it, too."

"Do you think we'll ever see Holly again?"

"I doubt it. But at least she's safe for now. I had to call the police, Marjorie. Holly's dear Papa, while in a state of alcohol-induced psychosis, started complaining that his kids had placed poisonous ants in his tent. He decided to take off his belt and start whipping 'those little mother fuckers' to teach them a lesson. Holly's mother came to me for help. Since it was a case of domestic violence, the police called in Social Services. The kids and their mother are in good hands and will get the help they need."

Anne knew more about these things than I did, so I trusted her judgment. "I don't even know Holly's mother's name."

"Felicia."

"That's a beautiful name."

"Yes, and it turns out she's a beautiful person as well, doing the best she can under the circumstances. If it makes you feel any better, she and the kids will be able to stay together. The people at Social Services promised to help Felicia find a full-time job, maybe with a house-cleaning service while the kids are at school. The pay is good, and the demand is high, especially in Carmel and Monterey."

"Anne," I said in an attempt to forget about Holly, at least for a while. "Considering all your talents and abilities, why do you practice witchcraft?"

Anne stilled before answering. "There was a veil separating me from God, a veil consisting of guilt, rules, regulations, and misconceptions. With witchcraft, I split that veil down the middle, opening the way back to heaven."

"Why witchcraft?" I repeated, watching her pour steaming water into our mugs and drop in bags of tea.

"Why earth medicine?" she countered.

I raised and dropped my shoulders, trying to understand.

Anne leaned closer, and I sensed her penetrating blue gaze. "Are you afraid that *magick* is evil or that I might accidentally unleash something beyond my control?"

I thought about my adoptive mother's reaction when I tried to tell her about Earth Medicine and the Medicine Wheel. She'd been so spooked that she refused to listen. She had cut me off—and therefore out of her life—rather than try to understand. I returned Anne's gaze and smiled. "That's exactly what I've been programmed to think. But I'm willing to listen."

"Glad to hear that." She handed me a mug of tea. "Chamomile, to help you relax."

As the honey-apple flavored liquid slid down my throat, I prayed that I'd have the strength to open my mind and heart to what she was about to share.

Anne took a sip of tea, and the soft slurping sound calmed me. "Unlike some witches, I don't try to control nature or force nature to do my will. My prayers are less directed, more open-ended."

I released a cleansing sigh.

"*Magick* is being in harmony with nature, accepting its gifts, understanding its treasure, and being grateful."

That didn't sound so bad. In fact, it sounded a lot like the philosophy of the Native American, the way it concerned itself with our connection to the Earth and the forms of life with which we shared it.

"*Magick* is more like a communication, a bringing of one's own sacred power into expression. Your sculpture, for instance, is *magick*. Adam's art is *magick*. You've both aligned yourselves with the powers of the universe. You've given form to your spirituality."

"What about black magic," I asked, staring at my shoes.

"Everything can be turned into something ugly. Even love can be turned into hate. All spiritual paths share the tenet of not hurting others. So, too, *magick.* "

"If there's nothing wrong with *magick,* why couldn't I enter your yurt?" I'd read enough about witches to know she wasn't performing lewd and blasphemous acts or worshiping the devil. But what *had* she been doing?

"Do you like being disturbed when you're in the middle of prayer?"

"Of course, not."

"Does your church encourage visitors to walk in during the middle of its service?"

"Nooo."

"Through ritual, I drew a circle around me, like a protective bubble of energy, a world between worlds. It helps to hold and concentrate my energies."

I felt the flash of understanding and with it came inner warmth, like the warm aftermath of drinking Anne's chamomile tea. "You mean the way I put down stone markers to outline my Medicine Wheel, a sacred space that shouldn't be disturbed."

"Exactly," Anne said, her tone soft, careful. "A circle of knowledge and power, the doorway between the seen world of matter and the unseen world of spirit. If I understand correctly, you then cleanse and purify your Medicine Wheel through smudging."

"Yes, using the smoke from a burning smudge stick of sage."

"Witches use incense, which also comes in a stick."

"Is that why you're staying in a yurt instead of a tent, to define your sacred circle?"

Anne grinned. "You're such a smart girl."

Right then and there, I changed my mind about witchcraft, or whatever unconventional belief system Anne used to express what she was feeling within. The words and rituals may differ from what I was accustomed to, but the underlying threads were the same. Anne's mission was to help and heal. If witchcraft helped her accomplish that, more power to her. Maybe I wasn't like my adoptive mother after all.

"By the way," Anne said. "Holly left a note in your tent."

I put down my half-empty mug and got to my feet. "Can kids even write at her age?"

"I didn't say it was legible."

I felt the kind of dizziness that accompanies sudden good news. "Maybe she wrote where they were going and if they'd be coming back."

"Don't get your hopes up. They left in a hurry."

"Gotta go," I said, heading for my tent.

"Take your time," Anne called after me. "I need to check on Adam."

I turned and walked backwards without slowing my pace. "Will I see you later?"

"Are you kidding? I want to hear all about Esalen. Plus, I've got a surprise for you."

She'd already surprised me plenty for one day. I didn't think I could handle another. Anyway, I doubted she could come up with anything that would affect me as deeply as a gift from Holly.

An envelope addressed to me lay propped against my pillow. I opened it and withdrew the folded sheet of paper inside. A letter, plus, five ten-dollar-bills.

> *Deer Mrjure,*
> *I am sory I coodnt wotch the tent.*
> *Mommy sed we had to leve.*
> *Hear iz yor mune. I did not ern it.*
> *Luv, Holly*
>
> *PS I mis u.*

I stared at the letter, picturing Holly toiling over the words. By the looks of her spelling, it must have taken her a while to write as much as she did. I fingered the money I'd given her for watching my tent.

Sweetie, why didn't you keep it? Heavens knows, you could've used it.

I crossed myself and again prayed for her safety. Holly was a strong little girl with two older brothers and a mother at her side; but sometimes having the support of one's family wasn't enough.

While I unpacked my Jeep and tidied up my campsite, I continued to fret. What if Social Services separated Holly from her family, in spite of Anne's assurances? What if she was lonely and afraid?

It would take a hell of a surprise from Anne to rescue me from my conscience, a horrible oppressor, with no capacity for reason.

Twenty-One

"Y OU WANT TO TAKE ME DANCING?" I asked.

"You'll love it," Anne said. "Cross my heart and hope to die." She smiled as I imagined her smiling when about to administer a tetanus shot. *It'll only sting for a little while, and just think, it's for your own good.*

I backed up a step. "I don't think so." Next, she'd be circling my campfire, playing the tambourine and swirling her skirt in a torso-undulating gypsy dance, like Esmerelda in the *Hunchback of Notre Dame.*

"Anyway, that's not the surprise," she said.

"Surprise?" What else did she have up her sleeve?

She hesitated for what seemed like a full minute before continuing, kind of like dangling a worm in front of a starving fish.

I surveyed my campsite, looking for something to clean up, something to do, anything rather than take the bait.

Finally, she took mercy. "Your sister's here."

I thought my heart would stop, instead of performing wild gypsy moves in my throat. It was about time. While stuck in a cave in the Los Padres National Forest, thinking we may not live another day, Veronica had promised that, once we got out of there, she'd help me figure out what our mother wanted. "I think we'd make a great team," she'd assured me. Ha, some team, showing up at our point of rendezvous twenty-two days late. "Veronica?"

Anne chuckled. "Do you have any other sisters?"

"No, but—"

"She showed up the day after you left for your workshop at the Esalen Institute. Good thing you'd already told me about her or I would've freaked out when I ran into her at the Lodge. She booked one of the bungalow rooms, and, therefore, so did we."

Again? I sat down, so I wouldn't fall down.

"I figured you'd want to be close to her."

Anne functioned like a whirlwind, changing directions without notice, sweeping up all in her path. But this wasn't how I'd conditioned myself to operate, which required a sense of control, of balance, of stability. I took several deep breaths, waiting for my brain to thaw and kick into gear.

"You also need a decent place to shower and dress."

My neural-control center was still out of whack, quite a handicap in my current situation. Good thing I was sitting down. "And I suppose I'll be wearing another ensemble out of your anti-minimalist wardrobe."

Anne's bracelets glistened and jingled as she swung her arms wide. "All taken care of."

My mind whirled as I realized I wasn't getting out of this. Of all things—dancing. "Where's Veronica now?"

"Who knows? She's not as predictable as you are."

I grinned. "Isn't she something?"

"If you didn't look exactly alike, I'd never believe you were sisters. She dresses like a vamp, for God's sake."

"She likes red," I defended.

"And black leather and boots."

"She's got style. Just like you."

"So, who am I to judge, right?" Anne said, followed by a put-upon sigh.

"You're both too awesome for words," I said, and meant it.

））)

Veronica wasn't in her room at the Lodge, which didn't surprise me. She'd show up when she was ready, and not a minute sooner. Life

175

was never dull with her around. I was almost afraid to contemplate what it would be like with Anne added to the mix.

Spread out on my bed was an outfit I would never have chosen for myself and, as a result, would never have felt so thrilled about wearing. After a quick shower and some primping with my makeup and hair, I slipped into this dream-of-a-dress, and while twirling in front of the mirror, I began to suspect that it hadn't come out of Anne's wardrobe at all. Gold polyester and spandex fringed with loops of metallic thread just wasn't her style. The dress was also short and tight. Talk about vampy.

I searched for pantyhose to wear underneath, but found none. Guess the idea was for my legs to go bare. What was Anne trying to accomplish with this uncharacteristic transformation? She couldn't change me inside. Could she?

I slipped into the gold sandals, with their delicately braided straps, and clasped on the gold Cleopatra-style necklace and hoop earrings Anne had provided. A soft misting of her Coco Chanel perfume, and I was ready to go. Good thing Anne would be there to protect me, because this outfit screamed trouble, the kind I'd spent a lifetime trying to avoid.

)))

The minute we entered the lobby of the River Inn, I knew something wasn't right. For one thing, the admission was pricey. And then I noticed the crowd. The place was packed. The heavy rhythm of drums and something that sounded like wailing pervaded the air. It filled every nook and cranny in the room and vibrated through my body in a way that seemed primal. I wanted to ask Anne what the hell was going on, but the drumming, wailing, and chanting made conversation difficult. Some woman wearing a Las Vegas-style headdress was dancing with a sword! "Jeez," I said, ready to run for my life.

Anne grabbed my hand. "Oh no, you don't."

"No wonder Veronica didn't show," I shouted. "She probably knew where you were taking me and wanted no part of it."

Before Anne could respond, another dancer leapt from out of nowhere and grabbed my free hand. Anne whooped and gave me an enthusiastic shove. Next thing I knew, I was part of some crazy dance routine, fringed dress and all.

Other guests joined in, so I was hardly alone, but that didn't make me feel any better. In fact, I was seething. Anne had tricked me. Instead of spending a quiet evening with my sister, I was whirling around with a bunch of crazies, and that persistent drumming was doing funny things to my head. If I didn't know better, I'd swear I was on drugs.

"Now this is *magick*," Anne called out as she joined me on the dance floor. "Do you feel the kinship? Do you feel the high? These dancers are like shamans, taking us to an alternate world."

"I'm going to kill you when we get out of here," I yelled.

She shrieked with laughter, arms and hips swaying. "Let loose, girl. Forget yourself. Enter the flow state."

I saw visions of my mother, her stiff upper lip, her stern brow. Hadn't I told her to loosen up not all that long ago? I was being tested. Again. "Okay, smarty-pants. Just watch me now."

What followed on my part was undignified. If my mother had seen me, she would've disowned me for sure, and Cliff, my ex-fiancé, would've been convinced I'd lost my mind. But Morgan, sweet Morgan, would've been delighted. He once told me that he would love to watch me dance and sing. If only he could see me now.

I felt as if I were part of a mass consciousness, not unlike the group-mind experience I'd participated in at the Esalen Institute. Something that had been dormant inside of me was finding a release. A resurrection of sorts, another path to The Source. My hair was wet and plastered to my neck. The room smelled like sweat and cologne.

And I loved it.

"Art can save your life," Anne screamed above the ruckus.

"Yes," I screamed back. The music had entered me, accelerating my pulse by adding a pulse of its own. My hips undulated like a belly dancer, my arms swayed over my head, rhythmic as snakes. Life was good. Life was sweet. I was out of control.

So was Anne.

We were having one hell of a time. That is, until someone nudged me and muttered in a voice laced with sarcasm, "My eyes are deceiving me."

Great. Cecil, of all people. I smiled and graced him with my back.

"Nice ass," he said.

I ignored him. Talk about an ass.

Finally, Anne and I took a break.

"Water," she moaned as she headed for the bar.

I lagged behind her, my face and body moist with sweat, as if I'd just stepped out of a sauna. A tall cold glass of water, and I'd be ready to call it quits for the night.

I thrilled to the sound of tinkling ice cubes as Anne handed me a frosty glass of water, and I gulped it down as if I'd just spent a week crawling through the desert. "Did you see who was here?" I managed through iced lips.

"Yeah," Anne said after guzzling down her water. "We're caught between the devil and the deep blue sea."

Adrenalin coursed through me as if I were preparing for a race. "Let's see if we can make it out of here without running into him."

Anne grabbed my glass and set it on the bar next to hers. "Not so fast, hon. It took some doing on my part to get you here, so I'm not about to let Mr. Charming chase you off. Let's give the dance floor another try."

As luck would have it, Cecil blocked our path. "Well, if it isn't Cinderella and her fairy godmother."

"Eat doo-doo," Anne said, her tone saccharine sweet.

Cecil eyed us with the killer instinct of a prizefighter seeing his opponent on the ropes. "Quite the erotic dancers."

I thought Anne would punch him, but instead she gave her body a little shake. "I'm the floor sample, baby, want a demonstration?"

He turned on her as if eager for a verbal boxing match. "More like a floor show."

"Um," she said, looking him up and down. "That could be arranged, too."

My mouth didn't quite gape open, but did a close enough rendition to show my surprise. What had gotten into her?

Cecil's eyes brightened, and not in a good way. "You're not such a fuddy-duddy after all."

"Hardly," Anne said, taking a step closer.

They stood eyeball-to-eyeball, prepared to land beat-to-the-punch blows until one or the other threw in the towel, but then, thank goodness, Claudia appeared. "What's the holdup, honey?"

Saved by the bell.

I sighed in relief, but not Anne. She looked disappointed, as if someone had just swiped her favorite toy. Oddly enough, so did Cecil.

I looked at Claudia.

She shrugged.

Nothing was as it seemed.

Chapter Twenty-Two

ANNE AND I HAD FINISHED our breakfast at the Big Sur Lodge restaurant, yet the chair I had reserved for Veronica in case she showed up stood empty. I pushed away my plate and checked my watch. We'd been here for an hour.

Where was she?

Wanting to see my sister again had taken such a strong hold over me that I could think of little else. We'd met for the first time three and a half months ago in Carmel Valley and had parted soon after. Which meant we had a lifetime of catching up to do. I needed to ask her a zillion questions, darn it, discover how we were alike, how we were different.

Anne placed her hand over mine and gave it a squeeze. "Why don't you call her and see what she's up to?"

"No way. She'd consider it prying, and our relationship is still too fragile for that."

"Okay then, how about we go pick up your sculpture at the gallery?"

I grabbed my napkin and dabbed my eyes. "Sure, why not?"

Anything to get my mind off my sister, and the empty chair.

☽ ☽ ☽

Alfonso looked at us, wide-eyed. "We sold the sculpture. I thought you knew."

"You've got to be kidding," I said.

His gaze darted from Anne to me and back to Anne. "It brought an outstanding price."

An outstanding price? Was this man crazy? "I don't care what it brought. We want it back."

"That would be impossible, Ms. Veil."

"And why's that?" I asked. Art galleries didn't screw up like this, did they? They had their reputation to think of, let alone getting sued.

"It has already been picked up by the buyer."

"So? Call him and tell him to return it."

Alfonso took a step back, bumping into the counter behind him. "It wasn't a *he*."

Sometimes we need enemies in our lives to snap us out of our comfort zone. When we get tired of people pushing us around and rendering us voiceless, we rise up with decisive action to begin the process of maturation and growth. At least, that's what I hoped was going on. "Who cares? Get it back."

Anne cleared her throat and gave me a warning glance. "This is highly irregular, Alfonso."

"I agree," he said. "However, the buyer said she was a personal friend of yours."

"Friend? We don't know anyone from around here. Anyway, it wasn't for sale."

"What's her name?" Anne asked, her voice calm. I wanted to kick her.

"Claudia Moore, a fellow artist. I saw Ms. Veil speaking to her during the exhibit of her glasswork, therefore, the assumption that—"

"What did she pay for it?" Anne asked.

The curator beamed. "Ten thousand dollars."

"That little witch," I said.

"Hey, watch who you're calling witch," Anne said.

I paced back and forth, clenching and unclenching my hands. I hadn't realized until now how much the sculpture meant to me. This glob of glazed clay, which had cost me little in time and effort, embodied a passion that had been suffocating inside of me and had finally broken free. "What's her address?"

"That's private information—" Alfonso began before I cut him off.

"Anne, call the cops."

"No, wait," he said. "I'll look it up."

☽☽☽

It was a straight shot up Highway 1 to Monterey. We'd left Big Sur behind and were nearing Carmel. Hands gripped on the steering wheel, I felt back in control.

"She did it for Cecil," Anne said.

"That's what I was thinking. I doubt Claudia would've taken my sculpture on her own."

Out of the corner of my eye, I saw Anne turn toward me. "Why are you defending her? You don't even like her."

"Because she's an artist," I said. "Unlike Cecil, she knows it's not about possession."

Anne fiddled with her bracelets until they spun around her wrist like mini roulette wheels, but made no comment.

As we passed Carmel Valley Road, I looked into my rear-view mirror, wishing I could go back in time, if only for a while. I had so many precious memories of the three weeks I'd spent in Carmel Valley with Morgan, Joshua, Veronica, and Ben. I'd felt more alive during those dangerous and confusing weeks than I'd ever felt before. Or since. How is it that some memories stay forever etched in our minds, to recall at a moment's notice, triggered by a sight, a sound, a smell, while others fade away like dreams? Often, though not always, the etched memories hold special significance, highlighting as they do particular exhilarations or fears, turning points in our lives—Morgan plucking a dandelion and holding it to my nose. Joshua grinning at me from an upper branch of an oak tree. But that doesn't explain the mind's ability to keep these memories so vivid, so fresh, as if hard-wired into our cells, memories that we share with our children, take to our graves.

Anne lowered the window a crack. Cool air gushed in. "Cecil's missing the point. He wants to own what the sculpture depicts. You rendered something invisible, visible, Marjorie. You used your hands to transform something mysterious into something tangible. Maybe that's what Cecil wants to own."

"Now, it sounds like you're defending *him*," I said.

"Just trying to understand."

I took the Munras exit to Fisherman's Wharf, then swung into the parking lot entrance, retrieved a parking ticket, and pulled into a space facing the water. A gust of air, scented with seaweed and fish, greeted us like an over-zealous host as we stepped out of the Jeep. My hair whipped about my face as I locked the doors and jammed the keys into the pocket of my windbreaker. "Wonder how much one of those yachts costs."

"If you have to ask, you can't afford one," Anne said.

I released a slow breath and shook my head. "If a man with that kind of money still needs more..."

"It's called *Defiance*," Anne said.

"What is?"

"Cecil's yacht. The name should be displayed on its exterior."

I could understand calling a yacht *Defiance* to denote defying the dangers of the sea, but my guess was that Cecil's definition implied open disregard, contempt, and disobedience. "What kind of man are we dealing with?"

"A man darn proud of himself for making it big by resisting rules and authority," Anne said. "But there seems to be a spiritual vacuum in his perfect world."

We took the long ramp to the marina docks. It didn't take long to locate the mega-yacht with 'Defiance' written on its bow in swirling blue script. "There it is."

"Three decks," Anne said. "Quite impressive."

I heard the flap-flap of a flag, the *cah-wok* of a seagull, and the roar of a boat motor. "Is that a Jacuzzi on the upper deck?"

"Appears so, plus an area for sunbathing and a bar."

"Wonder what it looks like inside?"

Anne elbowed me and increased her pace. "Only one way to find out."

I followed Anne, my mouth dry and scratchy, my palms beginning to sweat. "What are you planning to do? Jump on board and knock on the door?"

"Yep."

"What if nobody's home?"

"Then we'll take a self-guided tour."

A man dressed for fishing, unlocked the gate to the marina dock and passed through. We caught the gate before it clicked shut and followed him in. Then we marched to Cecil's yacht, crossed the gangway to the port deck, and took the stairs to the covered-aft-deck lounge like a couple of rookie thieves. A set of glass doors leading to the main salon stood open—an invitation to enter. Cherry woods abounded in the yawning space, offset by ivory carpeting. An over-sized couch and matching armchairs in blues and whites faced a 50-inch plasma-screen TV. Next to the entry doors, stood a granite-topped bar.

"Holy cow," Anne said in a volume usually reserved for places of worship, though her words conveyed a less reverent tone.

"My sentiment exactly," I said.

"Check out the chandelier above the dining table," she said. "Looks like it weighs more than I do. Can you imagine all those leaf crystals clanging together in choppy weather? Last place you'd catch me during a storm."

"Can I help you?" asked an amused voice from behind us.

I jerked around, my stomach in sudden knots. Then I remembered to be angry. "I want my sculpture back."

Cecil had the nerve to smile. "Sorry, can't do."

"What," Anne said, swinging her arms wide to encompass the extravagant surroundings. "You have so little, you need to rob the poor."

"Poor?" Cecil raises an eyebrow. "Marjorie's not poor."

Anne hesitated for only a moment. "And how would *you* know?"

His smile widened.

Anne snorted before picking up what appeared to be a fishing-float paperweight from the bar and twirling it in her hand. "Seems you're possessed by what you wish to possess."

A cloud passed over Cecil's face, but he said nothing.

Anne must have sensed that she'd hit a sore spot, because she poked it some more. "Shiny new objects, self-absorption, and distraction. The spirituality of our time."

Again, no comment.

"Let's get out of here." Anne turned to me. "We're wasting our time."

It would be good to get off this mega-sized boat. It symbolized all I'd left behind in Menlo Park—stuff and more stuff—but not the stuff of life, which was free. I recalled a quote attributed to the Greek philosopher, Epicurus, who had lived three-hundred years before Christ. "If you want to make a man happy, add not to his riches but take away from his desires." How little had changed since then.

I glanced at Cecil. He stood with his back to me, staring out the window. Anne was wrong. Coming here had not been a waste of time. It took being here for me realize that creating my sculpture, when and how I did, had occurred for a reason. My mission wasn't to hold on to that burden basket of transformed clay, but to let it go. I had the power to shed the weight of ownership as well as that of anger and hate. I, not Cecil, was in charge of, and responsible for, the conditions of my life. He was a side issue, not the reason I was here. I would not allow him to steer my course, as I had allowed my mother and ex-fiancé to do for too long. I would donate the money he'd paid for the sculpture to Alzheimer's research, thereby turning something negative into something positive.

Anne threw the paperweight she'd been holding overboard. It splashed as it hit water, but didn't sink. Instead, it buoyed on the surface as though weighing nothing at all.

Cecil let us go without comment, which was a comment in itself.

))))

We found Veronica standing in the Big Sur Lodge Café/Expresso Bar eating a double scoop of Pistachio Nut ice cream. "You're lucky he didn't have you arrested," she said when we told her of our little escapade.

I gave her a hug and kissed both of her cheeks.

"Hey, watch my cone," she said, swinging it clear of my hair. "Want some?"

"All I want is to dominate your time for the next couple of days," I said, "so we can talk, talk, talk."

Veronica bit into her ice cream.

Watching her made my teeth hurt. "It figures you don't lick ice cream like everyone else."

"I don't do anything like anyone else." She turned the full force of her gaze on Anne. "Hi, want some?"

Anne had been standing by without comment, which surprised me. She had a strong opinion on just about everything and usually didn't hesitate to voice it. "Maple Nut, if they have it."

Veronica headed for the expresso bar. "Coming right up."

"How come her hair's black?" Anne asked.

"She said she hated being blonde. So, she dyed it."

I'd seen Veronica as a blonde in Carmel Valley when she pretended to be me in order to save my life. I could still feel the shock I'd experienced on seeing her for the first time. It was like looking in the mirror, except for her eyes. They'd been such a cold, cold blue.

"Good thing you're not having ice cream," Anne said. "You're shivering."

"Where have you been all day?" I asked on Veronica's return. I tried to keep the accusation out of my voice, but failed. Why wasn't she as anxious to see me, as I was to see her?

Veronica handed the double-scoop of Maple Nut to Anne. "Eat it quick. It's starting to melt."

"Mind if I take it with me?" Anne asked. "I have to check on a friend of mine."

Veronica shrugged. She'd purchased another double-decker of Pistachio Nut for herself and appeared intent on finishing that one, too.

"Toodle-oo then," Anne said as she headed for the door, licking the ice cream dripping down the side of her cone.

I didn't repeat my question, curious if Veronica would get around to answering it.

After downing half her ice cream, she smiled, her eyes thawing from cold cobalt to waves of summer warmth. "I completed a written assessment and a panel interview today at the San Francisco DEA Recruitment Office."

"How'd you do?"

"Don't know yet. Even if I pass both, I still need to go through a drug test, medical exam, physical task assessment, psychological assessment, background investigation, the works."

"That'll take forever," I said. Why was she was putting herself through all this? For the privilege of what? Getting inserted into hostile organizations? Getting herself killed?

"The whole process usually takes about twelve months. Hopefully, the undercover work I did for the DEA in Carmel Valley will fast track my acceptance into their training academy."

"Around here?"

"Quantico, Virginia."

Bad news. That meant we'd be separated again.

"Unlike you, I can't afford to sit on my duff all day," she said.

I laughed. Veronica had plenty of money. Her...our...father had seen to that. But being the type of person she was, she still wanted to work. And she loved working with the Drug Enforcement Administration.

People were staring at us. No wonder. Veronica looked like a Hollywood celebrity and I her pale reflection. She was the luxury model, with all the bells and whistles, I the stripped-down version, no power windows, no leather seats.

Veronica broke into a wide, soul-warming grin. "You're so needy, little sister. It's written all over your face. Makes me feel loved, though, the way only one other person can."

And that would be Ben *Gentle Bear* Mendoza, who had taught me about my Esselen ancestors, Earth Medicine, and the Medicine Wheel. "So, are you two still seeing each other?"

"What do you think?"

I smiled. It was hard getting a straight answer out of my sister. "I'm glad."

"How's Morgan?" she asked.

"Fine," I said, doing my own version of evading a question.

Veronica inclined her head. "Just fine?"

"I miss him."

"But you can't go back to him until you've solved the situation with Antonia, right?"

"She talked to me at the Esalen Institute, Veronica. She mentioned our father."

"What about him?"

"She said to ask you."

Veronica looked away.

"We have to help her."

"You don't have to plead your case with me," she said. "I'm here to help in any way I can, just as promised." Finished with her ice cream, she gave me a long overdue hug. Not the bear hug I would've preferred, but, with my sister, I'd learned to take what I could get. "I missed you, too," she said. "Come on, let's get something to eat."

"You just ate two double scoops of ice cream."

"Not so loud, Sis. People think I'm thin because I starve myself."

"As if you care what people think."

She nodded at the host who held up two fingers and motioned toward a table by the window. Heads turned our way as we took our seats. Veronica tossed her hair over her shoulder and opened her menu.

"How did it go with the interview part of the exam?" I asked unable to my control my curiosity. Her interest in becoming a DEA special agent fascinated me, petrified me. "You must have some idea..."

"You mean after they got over the shock of my appearance and actually looked at my resume?"

At my nod, she grinned. "I think I brought some excitement into that office."

"They'll be lucky to have you."

"Love you, too," she said. "Now let's talk about Antonia."

Chapter Twenty-Three

IT WAS AFTER FIVE in the evening by the time Veronica and I approached Anne's campsite. There were no swirls of dripping fog, no gusts of wind. The trees stood still like monumental totem poles to commemorate what we were about to do. The birds made no sound. All of nature seemed to be holding its breath, big and silent, except for the steady flow of the Big Sur River.

I drew my jacket more tightly around me, but couldn't shake off the chill I felt within. We were heading into strange and unmarked territory, about to ask Anne to guide us in a ritual that was foreign to us.

She'd explained to me that witchcraft wasn't anti-Christian or anti-religion. Wiccans, she assured me, believed in God and weren't linked in any way with the Christian summation of evil. Unlike what Hollywood would have us believe, Wiccan rituals weren't dangerous or evil. They, instead, sensed and used natural energies that weren't recognized by mainstream science as available to us all.

So, why was I now so terrified?

Anne sat on her geometric-patterned yoga mat in front of the fire pit, skirt tails caught up between her legs and tucked into her waistband and a jacket draped over her shoulders.

I ran unsteady fingers through my hair. "Anne, Veronica and I would like to..." I looked at my sister, but she waved away my silent appeal for assistance. "Veronica and I are joining forces in reaching out to Antonia and decided we needed your help."

Anne raised an eyebrow and patted the mat next to her. "Might as well sit down. Sounds like this may take a while."

Veronica did a quick visual search for alternate seating, apparently not keen on joining us on what had the look and feel of a magic carpet.

"You'll find a lounge chair and some pillows alongside my living quarters," Anne said, pointing toward the yurt, currently topped with a colorful afghan throw. No ho-hum nylon tent and canvas chairs for Anne. More like boho décor bliss.

Veronica picked up a turquoise starburst lounge chair, unfolded it, and tested it for strength.

"It's sturdier than it looks," Anne said dryly.

"Where'd you get this thing," Veronica asked, "at a Bohemian camp sale?"

"You can get just about anything online these days," Anne said.

I concentrated on the popping campfire and the smell of burning wood in an attempt to calm my fraying nerves. When that didn't work, I said a silent prayer. *God, please understand what we're about to do.* "Anne," I started again. "Could you help us contact our mother?"

Anne pulled in a relaxed diaphragmatic breath, followed by an extended exhalation. "I'm not a psychic, Marjorie, or a medium."

Even in the cold, I felt beads of sweat form on my forehead. "Given your knowledge about Wiccan ritual and its use for spiritual attainment and positive change, I figured you'd know what to do."

Anne glanced at Veronica before addressing me. "What have you told your sister about me?"

"That you've found the path on which your spirit is most content via the Wiccan religion," I said, "and that you blend different forms of spirituality to come up with your own rituals."

Anne blinked several times, and silence stretched like a rubber band chain. A breeze kicked in and the totem tree branches began to sway. A rustle in the bushes started me shaking, which I knew would soon become uncontrollable to the point of pain.

"Shocked the hell out of me," Veronica said, accompanied by a fine imitation of a befuddled hair scratch. "Marjorie hanging out with a witch? Never thought I'd see the day."

Anne bit her lip in what appeared to be a suppressed smile.

"Will we need bat's wings, eye of newt, and a cauldron?" Veronica asked.

My face burned. I wished she would stop.

But Anne was sharper than I had given her credit for and knew Veronica's teasing for what it was, a breaking of ice, an easing of fear. "What we'll need is courage and patience."

"Do we have to cast a spell?" Veronica asked, but this time, I sensed a note of genuine interest.

"We'll want to send our wishes into the universe, along with certain words and rituals—"

"Like in church," I interjected, trying to add a touch of normalcy to what we planned to do. "In an ask-and-you-will-receive sort of way."

"It's okay, Sis," Veronica said. "I think Anne's telling us that witchcraft is like prayer that you don't recite out of habit."

Anne and Veronica shared a look and appeared to come to a silent agreement—*I'm in, if you're in*—before Anne eyed me with the studied attention of a busy mind.

Another pause in conversation, but more comfortable, more elastic than before. The rickety lounge chair squeaked as Veronica shifted her weight.

She was watching Anne closely.

I recalled what Dr. Mendez had told me while trying to explain my psychic connection to Joshua. "We are not separated minds in isolated bodies, but part of a collective consciousness in which all minds are united." He compared us to beings without borders and said that, according to the holistic theory of the universe, it may be possible to tap into the collective consciousness, of which the minds of the deceased are a part.

Anne slapped her knee. "We'll form a circle."

I thought of our group experience at the Esalen Institute, the way we'd formed our chairs into a circle, with me in the center.

"There's a mental atmosphere that surrounds us, which is receptive to our thoughts," Anne said. "It has the power to do anything and is meant to be used."

I compared what I'd learned from Dr. Mendez's holistic universe and quantum physics theories to my experience at the Esalen Institute. "And we can multiply our effect on this power through our united consciousness, right?"

The lighthouse beam of Anne's eyes settled on me, and I swear I could feel its warmth. "Exactly. If we send thoughts into this spiritual intelligence, telling it what we want, we may be able to break through the veil."

"And help our mother," I said.

Anne frowned and stared into the leaping flames. "The Great Mind works in wondrous and mysterious ways."

"Okey-dokey," Veronica said under her breath.

Anne ignored her. "We'll perform a ceremony."

Veronica shifted in her chair. An owl hooted.

"A sharing," Anne said, "with ritual to help bypass the conscious mind. The mind of order—of the director."

Even from a distance, I could see Veronica freeze, which made me nervous, afraid of what she might say or do if provoked. Her face twitched, but she said nothing.

Anne continued. "In ceremony, one reaches out mentally to the unknown, the unseen, and feels the power of inspiration."

"I'm all for that," I said, though to be honest, I was growing increasingly uneasy about the whole thing. More than once, I'd experienced inspiration from the unknown, but I'd never intentionally invoked it. Except, of course, while trying to contact Antonia.

And see where that got me.

"What kind of ceremony do you have in mind?" Veronica asked, her voice soft.

Darn, I hated it when she got that distant look in her eyes.

"We'll make one up," Anne said.

"Oh, wonderful." Veronica's sarcasm caused my uneasiness to turn into downright dread. *Calm down*, I told myself. *You've done something similar with positive results using the Medicine Wheel. How is witchcraft any different?* Maybe Antonia's hopes, fears, and plans hadn't vanished after she died, but had turned into thought forms that had somehow been recording in the cosmic airways and could be accessed by other minds. What other explanation was there, except that maybe my mother's consciousness still existed in a parallel realm from which she was trying to reach us? Both theories sounded crazy. But the alternative was equally crazy, that the voices Veronica and I'd been hearing were an illusion.

"It's easy enough," Anne said, "as long as we take it seriously and follow our instincts."

I drew in a breath, always a comfort, but also a delaying tactic. I tend to judge and reject events before allowing them to unfold, often to regret my presuppositions later.

"If I understand correctly," Anne said. "You've been hearing your mother cry, Marjorie. Can you remember what you were doing at the time?"

"I heard her cry for the first time after constructing my Medicine Wheel. I was sitting in the position of the East, concentrating on the initial step of the Medicine Wheel journey. Awareness."

"And the second time?" Anne prodded.

"Sitting near a stream, looking into the water."

"Where?"

"In the Los Padres National Forest near Carmel Valley."

"Apparently both times you were in a tranquil, meditative mood," Anne said, "during which you surrendered your conscious mind, allowing your subconscious to send out feelers."

Anne turned to Veronica. "What about you? Have you heard your mother cry, too?"

"Yes, soon after coming to Carmel Valley and finding my mouse totem." She hesitated and looked at me.

I unzipped my pouch and dug out the small, smooth stone. "Veronica gave it to Joshua, and Joshua gave it to me."

"It's a long story," Veronica said.

Anne nodded, then asked, "Did you hear her cry again?"

"The crying stopped after I gave away the totem," Veronica said. "And to be quite honest, I was relieved. I didn't know at the time that the person crying was Antonia. I also didn't know that I had a twin." Veronica looked at me and smiled, which altered the appearance of her face from mean girl to loving sister. "It started up again when I followed Marjorie to Tassajara."

"What do you think your birth mother is trying to convey?" Anne asked.

"Haven't the foggiest," Veronica said. "Maybe she's lonely."

"She spoke to me at the Esalen Institute," I said, "in a way I could understand. Not that I could make sense of her message."

Anne stilled and looked at me, her eyes wide.

"Our instructor said our minds are fields that interact with one another. In one of our workshops, he had the participants form a circle around me. Then he asked them to focus their attention on my goal of communicating with my mother. It worked, Anne. It really did. Antonia talked to me."

"What did she say?" Anne asked.

"That she was sorry."

"For what?"

"I don't know, but she said our father knew."

Veronica slid from the lounge onto a bed of needles. "Shit."

"When I asked her where my father was, she told me to ask my sister."

Veronica stood and dusted off her jeans, avoiding my eyes.

"She said my sister's name wasn't Veronica."

The breeze rustled the lapels of Veronica's leather jacket and lifted strands of her hair.

"But First Dawn."

Veronica took a shaky breath and stared into the darkening sky.

"We've got to help her," I said.

"She's waited twenty-nine years to contact us," Veronica said, her voice toneless. "What's a few more days?"

"Days?" I said. "We can't wait days."

"We're headed for a dark moon," Anne said, "not a good time to practice *magick*. Instead we'll meditate and relax in preparation."

Meditate? Relax? "Till when?" I asked.

"To quote from the Wiccan Rede, 'When the moon rides at her peak, then your heart's desire seek.'"

"But that won't be until—"

"Actually, the full moon energy is available three days before the date of the full moon and three days after," Anne said, "which happens to be August first."

I shook my head. "So glad you cleared that up."

Anne's eyes twinkled like the stars now visible through breaks in the redwoods. "Anytime."

"I think I'll start calling you Sister Anne," I said.

She stiffened for a second, then quipped, "Oh dear, you've found me out."

We both laughed, but Veronica appeared thoughtful, as if she'd just been handed a piece to an unsolved puzzle.

Anne stood. "Sorry, girls, but I need to stretch my legs."

When neither of us spoke, Anne said, "I realize this is all new to you, but" —she dropped back her head and contemplated the misty heavens— "with practice, these new insights may become part of the way you think and act."

Veronica eyed her with that piercing blue stare that had on more than one occasion caused me to feel like I'd just exited a freezing pool of water. I held my breath, waiting for her verdict. I couldn't do this without her, but we needed Anne, too.

"It's hardly that simple," Veronica said. "I insist on the security of rules and regulations."

Wow, Veronica and I have more in common than I thought. "She's applying for a job with the DEA," I said, as if that explained everything.

But Anne wasn't buying it. "Rules and regulations are limiting."

"Can't argue with you there," Veronica said, "considering I break the ones that don't serve me all the time. Still, rules and regulations are made for our welfare and protection. They ensure our rights as citizens against abuses by other people, organizations, and the government."

"Okay then," Anne conceded, "maybe you'll agree to take just a wee little peek to what's on the other side."

Veronica folded up the starburst lounger and leaned it against Anne's yurt. Then she sat next to us on the yoga mat with its geometric angles and shapes, which, if you looked at them long enough, transcended language and the rational mind and produced visual and spiritual harmony.

Chapter Twenty-Four

WHAT AM I SUPPOSED TO DO in the meantime?" I asked over Annie's organic French roast coffee the next morning. Not only did I prefer her one-dollar-per-ounce brew to mine, but her campsite as well, so darn colorful, in an upcycled-from-Goodwill sort a way. A Steller's Jay voiced a loud *shaq-shaq-shaq* and the river rushed in the distance, now familiar and comforting forms of white noise. The air was crisp, scented with pine and wood-smoke. Paradise, yet... I dreaded the idea of spending the next nineteen days twiddling my thumbs, waiting for a full moon.

"You could stop thinking about contacting your mother for a while and concentrate on Adam," Anne said, her voice soft. "Sometimes we find answers in the most unlikely places."

I stared at her as if she'd just suggested going out dancing again. Adam didn't need my company, let alone my intrusive thoughts. What could I possibly do for him?

Anne patted my arm. "Be his friend."

Clasping my mug in both hands, I inhaled the chocolaty scent of Anne's artisan specialty, no comparison to the coffee I served up at my campsite, which Anne compared to sipping pesticide. "He's got you, Brock, and his coyote friend, Buster."

With anyone else, I would've considered the sudden contortion of Anne's eyebrows an expression of anger, but by now I knew she accepted me as I was and she didn't anger easily. "You blow hot and then cold when it comes to Adam," she said. "One minute you're arguing his case as if your life depended on it and the next you back off. If I didn't know better, I'd say you were more concerned about his art than his soul."

Her comments hurt, but that's usually how it is with the truth. If nothing else, she was making me stop and think.

"Allow yourself to be The Great Spirit's instrument," she said.

Adam would likely reject any gesture of friendship on my part, considering that he lived in a world of his own, in which I was not included. But the part about being God's instrument worked for me. "Okay."

Anne stood and released the hem of her skirt from the belt around her waist. "I need to check up on him. Want to come along?"

I set my mug next to hers and stared at it for a while before shrugging and rising to my feet. Next thing I knew, I was jogging to keep pace with Anne's energetic stride. "I've always wanted to bring the spiritual back into nursing," she said without slowing down. "I want to prove that nursing programs need to integrate religious studies and spirituality into their coursework."

I managed to adjust my step to hers, unwilling to admit that I had difficulty keeping up with a woman at least ten years older. "What do you mean, you want to bring the spiritual *back* into nursing?"

Anne pulled in a deep breath, more likely due to my continued questions than physical exertion. "In the days of old, spirituality was a big part of healing. People relied on priests, shamans, medicine men, and—"

"Witches," I said, catching on.

Anne grinned. "Some very wise witches."

I brushed strands of hair off my face and tried to control my rapid breathing. This woman had super powers, and it took more stamina than I possessed to keep up with her. "Adam's lucky to have you."

Anne halted, then turned to face me. "For Adam, the past and future are dissolving into a sensorial present that embraces him and makes him feel whole and secure. His present moments are very large, and I don't want to take that away from him."

I took in the redwoods that soared to dizzying heights, the musty odors that managed to smell good out here, and the birds that chirped and screeched in chaotic chorus. In an institution, he would be cut off from all this.

"We can't fix him," Anne said, "but that doesn't mean we can't help him heal."

At that moment, a wall of doubt evaporated from inside of me. *Not fix, but heal.*

"As far as I'm concerned, this is holy ground," Anne said. "A place of compassion, honesty, and love, of emotional and spiritual health, of passion and purpose."

The flow of the Big Sur River greeted us as we entered Adam's camp. As did Buster. He yipped, sprang to his feet, and ran toward us.

I froze.

"Sweet, isn't he?" Anne said when he halted in front of her and pinned her with his yellow-brown gaze.

I waited for my heartbeat to decelerate.

Anne rubbed the coyote's head and behind his ears. "Hey, Adam," she said. "Whatcha doin'?"

He sat in a grassy clearing, playing with a deck of cards, and didn't look up.

"I gave him Tarot cards to aid his memory," Anne said as we headed his way. "Each has an image of a different saint. He plays with them for hours."

A pagan divination tool based on Christianity? My mother would consider putting saints on Tarot cards as irreverence to the sacred. Yet, in this case, what she would call sacrilege filled me with hope. Maybe my dream about all religions uniting wasn't naïve after all.

Adam spread the cards in front of him, doing a pretty good rendition of a Las Vegas dealer, though more slowly and with a tremor in his hands.

"I thought Tarot cards had pictures of fools, magicians, and priestesses," I said.

Anne's eyes danced to the tune of another one of my brilliant comments. "St. Francis was a fool for Christ. St Nicolas was a miracle worker. St. Mary Magdalene was the First Papesse. The way I taught Adam to use the cards doesn't involve memorizing their meanings. All the information he seeks is already in his subconscious, which the cards help bring to the surface. They serve as reminders, friends, and meditative tools. Anyway, they're beautiful and he loves them."

Adam selected a card from the spread and held it up.

Anne laughed. "St. Anne. Yep, that's me."

He passed his right hand over the cards, once, twice, then selected another.

Anne leaned in for a closer look.

"She wiped the face of Jesus with her veil," Adam said.

I stared at Adam, feeling a strange sensation come over me like a chilly mist. Only one saint I knew of had wiped the face of Jesus with her veil.

Adam picked up the card and ran his finger over its surface. "He felt so alone..."

"Anne," I said. "Did you tell Adam about my sister?"

She looked at me, her expression sedate, restrained. "No, sweetie, I didn't."

Of all fourteen Stations-of-the-Cross commemorating Jesus' long and painful journey to His crucifixion, I'd always been most fascinated by the sixth, depicting Veronica's veil with the face of Christ imprinted on it. I'd made a point of sitting in the pew below the sixth station each time I went to Mass as a child. I hadn't known back then that I had a sister named Veronica, and now I faced yet another mystery. Who told Adam?

If Antonia had communicated with Adam about me, she may also have communicated with him about Veronica. But why refer to either of us? What would compel her to reach from the other side to a complete stranger with AD?

I met Adam's eyes, but found no answer there. I did, however, sense a thirst for intimacy. Anne was right. I could be Adam's friend. Not by nagging him or telling him what to do, but by providing him with company and the gift of a listening ear.

While Anne fixed Adam's breakfast and gave him his vitamins and medication, I hunched next to him and watched as he sorted through his cards.

Anne glanced at her watch—an astronomical contraption that she wore on a chain around her neck. "Would you stay with Adam for a while? I won't be gone long."

"I don't think that would be a good idea," I said. "I'm not very good at—"

Buster nudged me with his nose, and I lost my train of thought long enough for Anne to wave and take off in the direction from which we'd come.

I sighed and turned my attention back to Adam. "Tell me about your sculptures."

It took a while for me to realize that he wasn't going to answer. Either he hadn't heard my question or it got lost in his mind like a missed target. I detected a slight angling of his head and a momentary scrunch of his brow before he asked, "How are you?"

"Fine," I said. "How are you?"

No answer.

Then it hit me. "How are you?" was a question that came easily for him, a question he'd asked thousands of times during his lifetime and therefore slid from his mouth as automatically as a recorded message on an answering machine. But when he was asked the same question, no prerecorded message, so no response.

"I'm going to die," Adam said.

The suddenness of his words jarred like the blast of a bullet. I wanted to tell him that we were all going to die, but didn't. It makes a big difference when you're not sure of the when, where, and how. I looked at the ring of keys attached to his belt, keys to his car, his home, his safe deposit box, his totems, reminders of the possessions that no longer mattered to him. While the rest of the world continued to grasp for more.

"Let's go visit Kathleen and Anthony," I said.

Adam looked at me and smiled. "Okay." He put the Tarot cards back in their box and placed the box in his coat pocket. Then he stood and, with Buster at his side, headed for the grove that held the possessions still dear to his heart: the sculptures of his wife and child.

As I followed, I was struck anew at Adam's talent. By freak chance—or miracle—I'd created a single sculpture that struck a chord within those who saw it, but I could never replicate it. Adam, on the other hand, produced masterpiece after masterpiece.

Had he started the statue for the gallery showing? Maybe he would be more inclined to create a piece if the profits from a sale were used for Alzheimer's research?

☽☽☽

"Sell one of Adam's sculptures for AD research," Anne repeated when I presented my brilliant idea on her return. "I don't know. If it generates a lot of money, the pressure would be on for him to produce more. He can't be forcefully inspired."

I got what Anne was saying with my mind, but not with my heart. Something told me that it was important to preserve some of his work. "No one would be forcing him to do anything. He said he'd do one, remember?"

"Don't you see?" Anne said. "The demands and pressures of recognition and celebrity are exactly what he's been trying to avoid."

I thought of my one venture into the world of an artist. What was the truth behind what appeared to be an undesirable outcome? "How about if he donates a sculpture anonymously?"

Anne sighed and shook her head. "Okay, I'll discuss it with Adam and his attorney, considering Adam has already expressed an interest in donating funds to AD research. As I said, he only creates when he feels inspired. Speaking of which..."

"What?"

"While you were at the Esalen Institute, Adam created a magnificent replica of Kathleen and their five-year-old son, Anthony."

I stared at her, speechless.

"Anthony is sitting on Kathleen's lap and she's reading to him. His eyes are wide and his mouth open, his little hands clasped in delight."

Adam had shown me his work only an hour previously, but I hadn't seen anything like this.

Anne laughed, apparently amused at my baffled expression. "It's in my studio."

"How'd you get it to there in one piece?"

"I didn't."

My hopes crashed.

"Before the clay fully dried, I separated the sculpture at key junctures, then encased the pieces in plastic and reassembled them at the studio with the help of some water and potter's glue. The clay we gave him was reinforced with fiberglass, which made it especially strong."

"Did you fire it?" I asked, finding it hard to breathe.

"Not yet. It still needs to dry. If I get it into the kiln by Wednesday, though, Thursday at the latest, and, if all goes well, I could deliver it to the gallery in time for Saturday night's showing. I'm sure Alfonso will be happy to exhibit it. Especially if, this time, the piece will be for sale."

☽☽☽

"Keep your fingers crossed, hon," Anne said as we entered her studio Friday morning. "Anything can happen during the firing stage. Pieces of this magnitude and complexity have been known to explode in the kiln."

We approached the giant oven, paused, and took several deep breaths.

Anne disengaged the latch and opened the door.

Our eyes meet.

"Looks like we have a winner," Anne said.

Chapter Twenty-Five

MORE EXCITED ABOUT the exhibition of Adam's work than I'd been about my own, I anticipated Saturday night's showing with unconcealed relish. More than once during the week Anne had mentioned that I appeared to be walking on air, and she was right. I hadn't felt this giddy about an upcoming event since I was a kid.

My sister was rarely around, probably due to her knocking them dead at the DEA. At least she'd given us the spare key to her room—now that Anne and I'd checked out of ours—which we were making shameless use of to prepare for the night's showing. This time, however, I insisted on wearing something comfortable, not about to let Anne doll me up again in one of her slinky—albeit elegant—outfits.

"Wear it yourself," I told her when she held up the form-fitted open-back vest with matching pants. It had eight crisscross straps in back and a low V-neck front and was made of a polyester crepe material that looked sexy as hell.

"Black's not my color," Anne said.

"Then why'd you buy it?" For the life of me, I couldn't figure out why someone who favored roomy skirts and tops—embroidered or appliquéd with flowers, vines, moons, and suns—owned such elegant, eye popping finery.

Anne shrugged and held up another creation for me to drool over, an ankle-length, fitted dress with cap sleeves, made of sheer floral silk with a pale pink lining. Florals weren't my style, but this dress did *floral* so delicately that I could practically smell its sweet, Dutch-garden scent.

Anne grinned when she saw the look on my face. "Try it on."

I did.

And as I twirled in front of the mirror like a make-believe Cinderella with her fairy godmother looking on, I wondered out loud, "Why don't *you* ever wear this stuff?"

"They're from another life," Anne said. "I can't bear to wear them anymore."

"So, doesn't it bother you to see them on me?"

"No dear, it makes me exceedingly happy. As to what I'm going to wear..." She pulled out another of her bohemian-style ensembles.

〉〉〉

As we stood in the doorway of the gallery surveying the crowd, Alfonso hurried toward us, arms outstretched. "Anne. Marjorie." He and Anne hugged, air kissed, and touched cheek-to-cheek. The third time around, Alfonso caught Anne on the nose.

Then he turned to me, gaze probing.

I looked away, not quite ready to forgive and forget his mishandling of my sculpture. Yes, even though I'd decided to let that that particular burden basket go.

He touched my arm. "I'm still trying to get your artwork back."

"Lots of luck," I said. "That Cecil is an odd one."

"If he wants any future dealings with this gallery, he'll cooperate."

Alfonso gestured toward Adam's sculpture. "The exhibit is quite a success and the evening is still young."

A number of people had gathered around the clay mother and child, so I excused myself and shouldered my way through the crowd. A discretely posted sign beneath the exhibit urged spectators not to touch, but the wide-eyed look on many faces conveyed that more than one itched to do just that—including me—which bode well for a profitable sale.

I turned from the sculpture and caught Cecil and Claudia standing near the entrance where I'd left Anne and Alfonso only moments before. Claudia, as usual, clung to Cecil. And this, as usual, rubbed me the wrong way. She was allowing him to dilute and absorb her through his bullying, as I'd allowed with Cliff.

Cecil caught my eye and blew me a kiss.

What nerve.

I didn't know the hows and whys, but I knew there was going to be trouble. I also knew that I couldn't stand being around him for long. Sure, I'd convinced myself not to hold on to an object that had cost me little or nothing. But still... He'd taken my one and only, never-to-be-repeated, creation, and there was nothing I could do about it without spending a lot of time and money. And time had become too precious for that.

Anne's grounding lavender, white sage, and frankincense scent preceded her as she came up from behind me. "Guess who just walked through the door."

"Yeah," I said. "You'd think we were Cecil magnets the way he keeps showing up wherever we are."

"There aren't many must-visit places in Big Sur," Anne said. "You can hit just about all of them in one day. But I know what you mean. It does seem like you, in particular, are attracting him in some inexplicable way, as if there's some kind of psychic connection. Random and meaningless events sometimes become un-random, in a synchronistic way. It's how the spiritual world tries to speak to us."

"I'll go with the 'there aren't many must-visit places in Big Sur' theory. Beats thinking his showing up all the time is some kind of meaningful coincidence. You'd think he'd at least be embarrassed to make an appearance *here*."

"Apparently, he doesn't embarrass easily."

"Well, if he covets Adam's sculpture, the way he did mine, he's welcome to it. Especially if he's willing to part with some of that easy money of his to pay the hefty price attached to it. Trouble is, I don't think this one will be to his liking."

Anne's frown implied that she didn't agree. "I'm glad we labeled the artist as anonymous. Adam needs protection from the likes of Cecil."

The crowd parted, as if rolling out the red carpet for this flashy couple, guiding them directly to Adam's statue.

"Uh-oh," Anne said.

I held my breath, certain Cecil would make some scathing remark—*How touching, a mother and child*—so I wasn't prepared for the way his eyes widened and his face paled as he neared. For a moment, it looked like he might pass out. His hands opened and closed in what appeared to be helplessness before he reached for the statue.

I blocked his path. "The sign says, 'Don't touch.'"

Cecil stepped around me.

I grabbed his arm. "What the hell's wrong with you?"

Instead of turning on me in a fit of rage, Cecil stared at the statue, lips parted.

Anne touched my shoulder and whispered, "Watch it, Marjorie. Something's not right."

The crowd grew still and silent, transformed into cardboard cutouts in my befuddled brain. Even the background music seemed to recede.

"What's wrong?" I repeated in a gentler tone.

No answer. Not even a sign that he'd heard me. Instead, Cecil spun around and headed for the gallery exit.

I turned to Anne. She shrugged and shook her head.

Sure, I didn't like the guy, but I was invested. He'd paid a huge chunk of change for a sculpture created by someone without an ounce of talent and then freaked out at the mere sight of a sculpture created by a true artist. Either he was a basket case, which I doubted, or something else was going on. Something that involved Adam.

Curiosity, and a touch of sympathy—though he didn't deserve it—had me following Cecil out the door.

He stood outside the gallery entrance fumbling with a cigarette and lighter. He lit up and then ran trembling fingers through his hair.

"I don't know what's going on here," he said, "but...that sculpture is of my mother and me."

I opened my mouth to speak, but nothing came out. *No way.*

He took a deep drag of his cigarette and released the smoke through flared nostrils. "She passed away thirteen years ago at the age of fifty-one. Too young to die."

Still, I said nothing. Kathleen's son? Anthony? This was too strange.

"Call me a mama's boy, but I loved her. For loving me. When I was most unlovable."

"How about your father?" I asked, fearing that I already knew the answer.

Cecil's smile didn't reach his eyes. "You'll get a kick out of this, being that you like me so much and all."

"I doubt it," I said.

"Good ole Dad disappeared four months ago. He left a note saying he was taking a trip and not to worry."

I aimed for calm and neutral, but my ragged intake of breath caused me to miss target—big time.

Cecil's eyes narrowed. "Do you know something about what's going on here? Does it have anything to do with my father?"

I didn't blink or look away, my silence, my answer.

"Son-of-a-bitch." He leaned closer. I smelled tobacco on his breath. "Where is he?"

A slight shake of my head, a dead giveaway, of course, that I was withholding a secret.

"Of all the...you and that fairy godmother of yours... How are you involved in this?"

What could I say? That his father had AD and didn't want to see him, and that I thought he was a lousy son and wouldn't tell him where his father was for all the frickin' tea in China.

Cecil took one last pull on his cigarette, then tossed it onto the pavement and crushed it beneath the sole of his shoe, probably what he wanted to do to me. "At least I know the old fart is alive and well. Guess I can be thankful for that."

Alive, but not well.

I stood with the blank-eyed pose of a display dummy, unsure what to do. It saddened me to see Cecil this way. In fact, it scared me. All that money and power, and he could still be brought to his knees by love. Or the lack thereof.

Was there no security in this world?

I returned to the gallery, leaving Cecil behind in the dark.

"How's he doing?" Anne asked when I reached her side.

"Not good."

"Did he say anything?"

My stomach cramped. I thought I was going to be sick.

"Are you okay? Did he hurt you?"

"He's Adam's son."

"But...the kid's name was Anthony."

"Want to bet that Anthony's middle name was Cecil?"

"It's hard to believe that cute little kid grew up to be Cecil."

"And even harder to believe that Adam is his father."

It took Anne a moment to reply. "Actually, not. Adam was a lot like Cecil in his younger days. I know, because he made a few confessions during the time we've spent together. Did you tell Cecil that Adam created the sculpture?"

"No, but it's pretty obvious he knows there's a connection."

"And that we know where his father is."

"Yes. At least he suspects it."

Anne whistled softly. "We've got to hide him."

Chapter Twenty-Six

NEXT MORNING, Veronica was still nowhere in sight. So again, I joined Anne when she set out to check on Adam. The path to his camp was familiar now and one to which I would never grow tired. After leaving behind the cool, dense canopy of redwoods that surrounded the campground, we hiked through sunny patches of earth supporting what Anne pointed out to be sycamores, alders, maples, and cottonwoods. As we climbed the gentle slope into more rugged landscape, Anne drew my attention to the underbrush of redwood sorrel, hedge needles, and sword ferns that soon gave way to the more fragrant and sun tolerant rattlesnake grass, sticky monkey flower, and vetch.

We crossed several ravines and creeks, caught glimpses of the bright blue Scrub Jay, and heard the mockingbird-like song of the California thrashers, followed by a startling flutter of California quail as they took off in flight. I breathed in the complex nature scents—resinous, woody, lemony, floral—and listened to the air moving through the trees, feeling their calming effect take hold. "No wonder Adam loves it here."

"It's as close to paradise as we'll get here on earth," Anne said.

We found Adam in a shady grove bent over a mound of mud, his wet hands sliding over the clay's surface. But today he was building something different. It wasn't a rendition of a woman or a child, and the feel of it ran counter to the usual blitheness of his work. This clay figure sat crouched with his head cradled in his hands. I couldn't bear to look at it.

Anne shook her head and closed her eyes as if she, too, found the sculpture disturbing. Her lips began to move in what I assumed to be prayer. As I waited for her to finish, I added a prayer of my own. *Dear God, please bless and comfort Adam in his final journey. And forgive me for any part I may have played in negatively impacting that journey.*

"Adam," Anne said in a tone so gentle it brought tears to my eyes. "What's your son's name?"

"Anthony," he said without pausing from his work.

"And his middle name?"

Adam didn't answer, just continued pressing, pulling, shaping. I focused on Anne, and my heart drummed my unease in skipped and racing beats. Was she going to tell him about Cecil?

Anne plunged on. "Is it Cecil?"

Adam's head jerked up, and he broke into a genuine, crow's-feet-around-the-eyes Duchenne smile. "Ce Ce."

"Cecil was quite upset when he saw your sculpture."

Adam's hands froze, and then, slowly, he straightened and looked at Anne. "Cecil?" His voiced sounded strained, as if he were testing the name after long disuse.

Anne's face showed no expression, but I could imagine the wheels in her head turning. "He recognized the sculpture of himself and his mother," she said, "and wants to know where you are."

Adam rinsed his hands in a pail of water and drew them through his grizzled hair, but said nothing.

"We'll have to hide you."

"I won't," Adam said. "I can't."

"He'll find you."

Adam's gaze darted to the crouching figure he'd been working on. "I love him."

"I understand," Anne said.

Adam stretched his leg. It appeared to be shaking. "I didn't want to...to..."

"Burden him, I know," Anne said.

If only I hadn't insisted on showing Adam's sculpture in public. If only Cecil hadn't been there. What were the chances? My heart had told me I was doing the right thing. How could good intentions have gone so wrong?

"Actually, this may work out for the best," Anne said.

Her words surprised me. I had difficulty imaging anything involving Cecil turning out for the best.

$$)))$$

It was time to tidy up my campsite. The tent and its contents smelled musty. Small wonder. I eyed the pile of clothes that needed laundering. This wasn't like me. I was turning into a slob.

Anne appeared out of nowhere, as usual, rescuing me from what would have been an afternoon of productive cleaning. "She's back."

I didn't have to ask who she was referring to. Veronica had a way of disappearing for hours, days, months, with no explanation. I, for one, always welcomed her back, knowing better than to ask where she'd been. "It's about time."

"Let's corner her before she disappears again. We need her tonight for our circle."

"It's only the twenty-second," I said. "There's no full moon."

Anne took off and called over her shoulder, "We're going to do a practice run, and for that we'll need your sister."

"But I'm not ready," I said, following her at a slower pace.

"You'll never be ready," she said without turning. "Might as well take the plunge."

We found Veronica in the Big Sur Inn dining room—eating.

"How can she stay so slim when she's always stuffing her face?" Anne asked in a tone that implied admiration rather than condemnation.

"Heredity," I said. Yet, if my attempt at humor was true, I'd been starving myself all those years for nothing.

My sister's hair fell past her shoulders in thick, silky waves. No extensions. The real thing. I knew, because my hair was equally thick and silky. Only difference, mine was still the natural honey blonde we were born with.

"She looks like a dang fashion model," Anne whispered, checking her watch. "And it's only noon. I think I hate her."

Veronica motioned us over. "The *Angus Burger* is to die for."

Anne shrugged and took a seat. "We need to talk."

Veronica lifted a neatly shaped brow and reached for the menus racked at the side of our table. "Make a selection. Lunch is on me."

The server approached carrying two glasses of water and did a double take on seeing me. "Wow. Twins. Cool. You look exactly alike, except for the hair and—"

"Yeah," I said, to prevent her from going on. *Except for the hair, the makeup, the clothes, the carriage.* "People say that all the time."

Veronica laughed and bit into a seasoned red potato.

The server swiveled her head back and forth between us. "This is so amazing."

Anne cleared her throat and glanced at the server's nametag. "Helen, dear, I'll have the Vegetarian and some iced tea."

Helen fumbled for the pad and pencil still tucked in her apron pocket. "Oh, yeah. Sure." She took Anne's order and turned to me.

"I'll have the *Chicken Reuben* and a club soda."

"Coming right up," Helen said before heading for the kitchen.

Anne got straight to business. "We're going to practice some of your earth medicine tonight, Marjorie."

"We are?"

"We're in the time of the waxing moon. Energies are building up quickly, making this a good time to launch new ideas. We'll start out by demonstrating the similarities between Native American and Wiccan rituals, to set your mind at ease that witchcraft isn't a perversion of Christianity."

"Hold it, I never said anything about—"

"I suspect Anne's little demonstration is for my benefit as well as yours," Veronica said. "Just so you know, I'm open to clearing up some common misconceptions about what most people consider a dark and dangerous subject." A dramatic shiver. "Human sacrifice, orgies, devil worship, the whole nine yards."

On catching Veronica's last words, the busser nearly dropped the drinks he was carrying. The conversation died while he set down our glasses and hurried to the next table.

"Well, that was effective," Anne said.

Veronica raised and lowered her shoulders in a display of indifference, which I now recognized as part of her mask. Her shrugs were easy to miss, unless you became a close observer, as I had in the short time I'd known her. You can say that my antennae were fine-tuned as far as my big sister was concerned. "Bet he doesn't come back with refills," she said.

I took a sip of club soda.

"Marjorie will be in charge tonight," Anne said.

My throat seized. Bubbles of carbon dioxide burned my nose. In charge? No way. This was supposed to be a practice run to launch new ideas, Anne's department, not mine.

"Marjorie's going to set up her Medicine Wheel, and we're going join her in some meditation and prayer. Are you okay with that, Veronica?"

"Can't wait. When and where?"

Chapter Twenty-Seven

W E CHOSE A CLEARING off the Pfeiffer Falls Trail surrounded by an understory of sorrel, hedge nettle, and sword ferns and topped by a dense redwood canopy. As I listened to the ground hum and the Pfeiffer-Redwood Creek breathe, I started to assemble my Medicine Wheel as Ben *Gentle Bear* Mendoza had taught me during my stay in Carmel Valley. "We'll be using five directional aids," I said, locating a spot facing north with my compass. "To help us envision an encircled cross symbolizing the four-directional Medicine Wheel, which, of course, exists only in our minds. What I'll be showing you is not a literal version of American Indian ritual. Consider it an adaptation for modern times, one that encompasses the spirit and intent of the ancients."

I set the first stone on the earth's surface. "The white marker represents the North, the direction of receiving." Then I placed the yellow stone facing east. "East is the direction of determining."

A quick glance at Veronica's intent gaze confirmed that she was listening to, if not completely following, my condensed introduction to the Medicine Wheel.

"The red stone marks the South, the direction of giving," I said, situating my red stone at the base of the circle. I moved to the fourth direction of the wheel and put down my black stone. "West is the direction of holding." Lastly, I set the green stone in the middle of the circle. "The Center is the place of stillness, where energy is generated from within. The Medicine Wheel also represents the four primary elements, air, fire, water, and earth, which are linked symbolically with every energy pattern."

"May I interject here?" Anne asked.

"Sure," I said, glad for the breather.

"In witchcraft, we cast a *magick* circle, a protective area to work in, similar to the Medicine Wheel. Both spheres are meant to hold and concentrate our energies."

The similarities between the two spirit traditions comforted me. I was no expert on the Medicine Wheel and its teachings. Using this device to expand my awareness and find my own perception of the truth in learn-as-you-go fashion seemed harmless enough, but sharing the system with others felt like the blind leading the blind.

"But in witchcraft," Anne said, "instead of using stones to define our circle, we make a mark on the ground in chalk or with a length of rope."

We didn't share enough history for me to recognize the subtext behind Veronica's closed-off expression, though by studying her over the past few months, I'd come to a somber conclusion: My sister had suffered and her mask of indifference covered up a bruised heart.

"We also make use of the four elements, earth, air, fire, and water," Anne said, "and each has a color and direction. Earth is green and its direction is north, which is associated with growth, nurturing, and abundance. Air's color is yellow and its direction is east, which is associated with communication, education, and the realm of the intellect. Fire's color is red, the direction of the south. It represents the passion and desire that burns inside us all. And finally, water is blue, its direction west, which is associated with emotion, intuition, and cleansing."

Anne motioned for me to continue.

So, I did. And as she inserted bits and pieces about witchcraft, I discovered that, like the smudging of the Medicine Wheel, the *Magick* Circle also needed to be cleansed of negative energy using smoldering incense, and that both circles served as places to receive and make magical calls without interruption.

With my introduction to the Medicine Wheel out of the way, we sat within the sacred circle to begin our work. I lit a white candle and prayed that we end darkness and become open to love and light. I hesitated, unsure how to proceed.

To my relief, Veronica chose that moment to speak. "Since Antonia told you to ask me about our father, I think this might be a good time to share what I know."

Was my sister finally going to divulge the information she'd withheld since we first met? I closed my eyes, preparing to memorize every word.

"Nearly thirty years ago, our father came to Monterey on a business trip and decided to extend his stay by a few days to take in the sights. He drove the 17-mile road along Pebble Beach and stopped at the site of The Lone Cypress. That's where he first caught sight of our mother."

The fleece-lining of my jacket didn't insulate me from the chill I felt at my sister's words. I'd heard my mother's voice for the first time while visiting The Lone Cypress on what was meant to be a romantic day-trip with my now ex-fiancé, Cliff. From that point on, my life had taken a drastic turn.

"She stood there, facing the ocean," Veronica said, "with the wind blowing through her long, black hair, and he couldn't look away."

"But he was married," I said.

"Yes." Veronica swallowed before continuing. "He told me that he didn't know how long he'd been watching her before she turned to leave—it could have been minutes, it could have been hours— but when she smiled at him, he was lost."

It took no stretch of the imagination to guess what happened next. Same tired old story: man on business trip gets lonely; cheats on wife; figures no one will ever know; business trip over; man leaves *other woman*; goes back to wife; fun while it lasted; guilt sets in; wishes he hadn't done it; girlfriend gets pregnant...

"He extended his stay for an additional week and told his wife, Elizabeth, that it was for business. He and our mother ended up spending the entire week together. Her name was Antonia Maria Flores. She was nineteen and trusted him completely."

"Did he tell her he was married?" I asked. So many lives affected by this single, misguided affair.

"Not until he was about to leave. He claims it broke his heart to do so."

Oh, Mama. You gave up everything for the man you loved. As I almost did. Until you showed up in my life. Were you trying to warn me?

"Nine months later, Bob got a telegram. *I gave birth to twin daughters. Love, Antonia.* He took the next flight to California."

What Veronica said next sent another wave of chills through me. "Elizabeth hadn't been able to conceive, so when Bob saw the two of us in the hospital nursery, he couldn't leave us behind. He told Antonia he would take us both."

I found it hard to speak. "How could he be so selfish?"

"Because he also loved Elizabeth."

"He loved two women?"

Veronica's scowl softened. "Yes, he also loved his wife, who later became my adoptive mother."

"And what was Antonia's reaction?"

Veronica ran a hand through her hair, then rubbed her face as though washing it. "She loved our father and wanted him to be happy, but couldn't give us up." Veronica hesitated, as though weighing the effect of what she was about to reveal. "He said he'd force her to let us go. He knew Antonia had little money and that she lived with an elderly aunt and her parents were both dead."

"Oh God," I said.

"Our mother didn't scream or fuss, just cried. And, in the end, our father couldn't bear to follow through with his threat."

Everything was quiet, except for the trickle of creek water and rustle of air flowing through redwood branches, sounds which, to me, proved more therapeutic than those produced by Himalayan singing bowls. I felt my mother's pain as if it were my own. And in a way, it was. Veronica's and mine.

Veronica's face tightened. "He agreed to take one twin and leave the other."

"So, he took you and left me behind with our mother," I said, feeling numbness set in.

"Much later, Bob discovered that Antonia had died soon after leaving the hospital. Her passing had been unexpected. She didn't have time to contact him. He believes that Antonia would have wanted us to be together."

"So, that's how I ended up in the hands of a midwife with babies for sale," I said in a voice that sounded distant to my ears.

"And you were adopted within weeks."

"Why wasn't I taken in by our mother's people?"

"You mean by the elderly aunt? What do you think?"

"But Antonia belonged to a huge, extended family."

"Yet she was alone."

"It's also possible that her extended family was never notified," Anne said, her voice soft. "Maybe the people responsible for putting you up for adoption thought they were doing you a favor, believing you'd have a better life if adopted by a family with means."

Or maybe my adoption had been illegal.

Veronica lifted the green stone that marked the Center of the Medicine Wheel and cupped it in her hand. "Whatever the circumstances, by the time our father found out about your adoption, the so-called experts warned that you and your new parents had become accustomed to one another and to take you away would traumatize you all. So, he let it be and tried to forget you."

"Did he?" I asked, bracing for her answer.

"He claims that he thought about you every day."

Every day? I doubted it. After hearing of our mother's death, he could've kept in contact through my adoptive parents. Not just for my sake, but for Veronica's as well. "Did he think of our mother, too?"

"I'd like to believe he did. And here's the strange part. Dad said that on the day they met, our mother told him she was hearing a voice."

The air left my lungs. *Oh, God. Just like me.*

"He advised her not to listen, but she said that the voice was trying to warn her about something."

Anne made the sign of the cross.

"Veronica," I whispered, eyeing the darkening landscape around us. "I think someone has joined us."

"Yeah, I feel it, too."

We turned to Anne for guidance, but her eyes were closed, her body swaying.

Someone started to cry.

"Here we go," Veronica said under her breath.

Anne's eyes shot open. "It's time, girls."

We scooted together, joined hands.

"Look at the candle," Anne said. "Squint until you see light stabbing in all directions. Then relax and breathe in...

"Hold... Breathe out... Pause... Breathe in... Feel the power rising within you."

I peered at the candle. The light, indeed, appeared to be shooting in all directions. I squeezed Veronica's hand, then Anne's, waiting for the feel of rising power.

There was none.

"Think of Antonia," Anne said. "What is it you want to say to her? Breathe in. See her in your mind's eye. Hold on to that picture. Breathe out. Feel yourself receiving Antonia's message. Put all your senses to work."

It was easy to picture my mother. She looked just like Veronica. What proved hard, was opening to her message.

Anne adjusted her position next to me. "Let's activate our thoughts with the power of will. Say out loud with me, 'As we wish, so it shall be.'"

Our voices joined to repeat the words, "As we wish, so it shall be."

"Before Antonia can manifest herself to us, she must exist in our thoughts," Anne said. "Breathe in and sense the world for her, so she can feel it, too."

I strained to become aware of the world as I was currently experiencing it. The air rustling through the trees with its fresh, piney smell. Warmth radiating from Veronica and Anne's hands and from their bodies huddled against mine. I felt a deep sense of love for my friend and for my sister, a reciprocal love, the kind of love that makes life worth living. My mother no longer had a body with which to experience these things. She could only experience them by remembering. Maybe I could help her remember true love by encountering and manifesting it through my body. But did I have enough love within me to share?

"The wind contains the spirit and breath of your mother," Anne said. "Do you feel it? Open up to it; give your mother a voice."

Again, I heard someone crying. It sounded lonely, riding on the wind.

"Mother, please let Veronica and me help you. Tell us what you want. Tell us what you're trying to say."

Veronica jerked her hand from mine to point at a spot outside our circle. "What's that?"

Following the direction of her finger, I thought I detected movement. A cloudy shape materialized in the late-morning air. It appeared to be reaching out to us.

"Mother," I cried.

Veronica said nothing, but I felt her body quiver against mine.

"Mother," I said again.

But she was gone.

We sat frozen, waiting for her to return.

Anne was the first to recover. "Time to shut down."

We can't give up now. She's here. Separated by the thinnest of veils. A veil we almost penetrated. How many more chances will we get? This is driving me crazy. I don't know how much more I can take. I want to go home to Morgan. I want to go home to Joshua. Damn it, I want to go home.

"It's okay, Marjorie, we'll try again," Anne said, taking hold of my hand and pulling me up.

Antonia. Come back. I've been trying so hard. What more can I do?

"Marjorie," Anne said. "It's okay."

Veronica stood and dropped the green stone she'd been holding back into the center of our circle. "So, that's it?" Her voice mirrored my disappointment, though *her* eyes remained dry.

Anne offered a tired smile. "We actually did good."

Veronica brushed off the back of her jeans. "Well, isn't that just great?"

"Next time we'll do even better," Anne said, letting me go and snuffing out the candle, "because we'll have two more powers on our side."

Veronica spun around to face her. "Which are?"

"The full moon. And Adam."

"Who's Adam?"

"Our gateway," she said.

Chapter Twenty-Eight

TALK ABOUT HEAVEN," Anne said, eyeing the simple fare on her plate. "Roasted hotdogs and toasted buns, garnished with ketchup, mustard, and relish."

Although equating the contents of a meal soaked in sodium and fat to heaven was said in jest, Anne was right. Sitting under the canopy of oaks and redwoods at her camp munching on beef wieners was indeed paradise.

Sheets of sunlight filtered through the leafy tree branches like the fingers of God, highlighting the understory of ferns and vines below. The sound of water rushing in the nearby Big Sur River and the occasional *shaq-shaq-shaq* of the Steller's Jay did wonders for my spirit, which was currently riding low.

It had been two days since my sister had shared with me what she knew about the circumstances of our birth and separation, and two days since we'd heard our mother cry. Why wasn't Antonia sharing her message? What was holding her back? When I participated in the group circle at the Esalen Institute, Antonia had instructed me to talk to my father, the man who had broken her heart—and abandoned me. What was I supposed to talk to him about? Even Veronica seemed perplexed. What could he possibly know that Veronica didn't, having lived with him most of her life?

Anne and I had been taking it easy, doing little more than eating, hiking, sleeping, and taking care of Adam. A good thing, because I was still trying to absorb the new prologue to my life story. A prologue that had brought more pain than enlightenment.

Veronica had more or less disappeared. Again.

"My sister doesn't know what she's missing," I said.

Anne dabbed at a glob of ketchup that had dripped onto another one of her bohemian maxi skirts. "Veronica has her own take on wonderful." She poured bottled water onto her napkin and rubbed at the stain.

"You can hardly see it," I pointed out. "It's camouflaged by all the yellow, purple, and pink in your skirt's patchwork design."

Anne rubbed harder. "But like a thorn in my side, I know it's there."

Footsteps crunched on packed vegetation, causing me to wonder which of our fellow campers was out and about? In exception to the departed Circus Campers, the Pfeiffer State Park residents had been amazingly quiet and had pretty much left us alone. Surprising, considering there were about two hundred RV and tent sites available—all occupied.

For Adam's sake, Anne had avoided getting chummy with the neighbors other than to say hello. No use encouraging the predictable questions: "Where you from? Whatcha you do for a living? How long you staying?" Anyway, most campers came and went like vehicles sharing the freeway, entering and exiting via conveniently placed on-and-off ramps.

However, this wasn't a fellow camper.

Talk about a thorn in the side.

"What took you so long?" Anne asked. She crumpled the napkin into her fist, indicating that she was more disturbed by Cecil's unsolicited visit than her words implied.

"I had some background checking to do," he said, grimacing at the remnants of hotdog and condiments on our plates. "I'm an attorney, you see, and that gives me access to a wide variety of research options. In other words, I'm privy to the personal information of even the lowliest, most nondescript, most insignificant citizen. But you, Sister Anne, caught me off-guard. Yes, even a hard-nosed attorney like me can still get hit between the eyes."

Anne paled, but said nothing. Another surprise. She loved butting heads with this man.

"What I discovered was" —a pause while Cecil stared at Anne, apparently to add a little Hitchcock suspense before releasing his bombshell— "unexpected."

What could he have dug up that was giving him such satisfaction?

"Hey, Marjorie," he said. "Did you know that your friend here was a nun?"

Anne set down her plate and stared at the stain on her skirt. *Like a thorn in my side, I know it's there.*

"Her superiors compared her to Hildegard of Bingen," Cecil said. "Guess ole Hilda had special powers, too."

Anne placed one hand over the stain as though protecting a wound.

"Hildegard heard voices, had visions, and could tell the future," Cecil said, taking a step closer to Anne. "She even wore a pentagram. Do you?"

"What do you want?" Anne asked.

"Did they kick you out of the convent, or did you desert?" Cecil persisted.

The serenity of Anne's features had the transcendent feel of Hildegard of Bingen—herself no stranger to controversy. Her face appeared lit from within, her expression untroubled. "Did your research into my apparently not-so-private information make you feel better, Cecil?"

His smile was one of amusement. "Actually... Yes."

Smart-ass. I pulled in my breath slowly so as not to attract Cecil's attention. How could this turn into anything positive? What was there here to learn?

"So, what is it *you* want, Sister Anne?"

"Trust, respect, love."

He gasped and brought his hand to his chest. "Gosh, is that all?"

"No," she said. "I also want honesty."

Cecil's eyes dulled, and his smile turned into a sneer. "You ask too much."

She smiled. "I know."

"Where is he?" Cecil demanded, as if losing patience with his cruel, one-sided game. "I need to talk to him."

Anne's eyebrows shot up. "Need?"

He reddened under his tan. "I *want* to talk to him."

"That's too bad," Anne said, giving each word a staccato punch. "He doesn't want to talk to you."

For an instant, Cecil froze. But like the robotic villains on TV, he recovered quickly and shot back. "I bought the statue."

"Goody for you," Anne said, and I applauded the way she was holding on, despite the frustration she must be feeling.

Cecil aimed his gaze at me. "I don't know what my father told you, but, knowing him, it was a line of bull. He's quite the con artist, you know. He'll play on your emotions and do just about anything, if it's for his own good."

Following Anne's lead, I tried to remain calm, but my heart was bouncing off the walls of my chest as if preparing for a sneak attack.

Cecil surveyed Anne's camp with the condescending expression of a tourist on a slum tour. "So, where is he? Living it up in one of those Big Sur Lodge cabins? I wouldn't put it past him. The only one he ever loved, besides himself, was my mother. That son of a bitch left without a word."

I pictured Adam and saw only kindness and love. How could Cecil misjudge his father in this way? "He left a note. You said so yourself."

Cecil pulled back his lips and exposed even white teeth. "Except he failed to mention where he was going or how long he'd be gone."

"He didn't want to burden you," I said.

"Oh, please. He burdened me plenty. I've been searching all over for him. Even took time off work—" Cecil slapped his forehead with his palm. "Hold it. Are you his whore?"

It took two eye blinks on my behalf before comprehension set in. Of all the nerve. I itched to slug him.

Maybe if I caught him by surprise...

"Your anger is making you small," Anne said.

I flushed. Did that include me?

"He's got you eating out of the palm of his hand," Cecil said.

Frustration seemed to be building inside of him, reminding me of a pressure cooker without a release valve. Something had to give.

"I don't think we're discussing the same person," I said. If anything, we were talking about Cecil, not Adam. Buying my sculpture when it wasn't for sale labeled him a con artist in my book. Someone who would do just about anything if it was for his own good. On top of that, he owned a mega yacht. Come on, who was the one living it up?

Cecil grabbed onto my comment as though hungry for a lead. "Then let me see him."

"You have no idea what you're asking," Anne said, her eyes bright with wisdom tempered by wrinkles of concern.

"I'll take my chances."

Anne's face cleared, as if she'd decided to give up her fight for trust, respect, love, and honesty. "Okay."

Cecil's eyes narrowed. Anne's easy submission likely struck him as suspicious. "You'll take me to him?"

Anne stood. "Sure."

"When?"

"Right now."

What was she doing? This spoiled man could destroy Adam if he chose. Then again, it was Adam's son we were dealing with. Anthony, the cute little kid depicted in Adam's sculptures, trying to catch a butterfly with his doting mother looking on. Did that sweet child still exist somewhere beneath Cecil's caustic exterior?

Cecil looked at me, and I shrugged. What did I know? I was the one who got Adam into this mess. *Good work, Marjorie. See where your interference has led?*

"Follow me," Anne said.

ꛃꛃꛃ

Adam sat on a floor of leaf litter, eyes unfocused, stroking Buster.

"Hi Adam," Anne said.

He didn't look up or smile at Anne's greeting.

"Is this some kind of joke?" Cecil blurted.

"No joke," Anne said.

"Where's my father?"

"Right in front of you," I said. Was he blind?

Cecil snickered. "That bum and his mangy dog? What kind of idiot do you take me for? Anyway, my father's name isn't Adam."

Adam got to his feet, a rather slow and painful-looking process, and walked off with Buster at his side. We watched in silence as they disappeared into a break between the brambles and vines.

"So, you don't believe me," Anne said.

Cecil puffed out his chest. "Quit wasting my time. That's not my father."

Anne stared at him for several seconds before saying, "Follow me."

I trailed behind them, dreading the scene that was about to unfold.

The shaded grove and pond looked like a playground, its occupants frozen in time: Mother with child, child at play, mother staring off into space, child asleep. Sculptures everywhere. True signs of Adam's love.

Cecil jerked to a halt. His head swiveled back and forth as if trying to take in all at once. He dropped to his knees and released a moan that sounded more animal than human. I thought of Antonia. Did her pain come from the same place?

"Damn it," he said. "Damn it. Damn it."

Finding Cecil's pained reaction too disturbing to watch, I turned away and met Anne's troubled eyes. "I'll wait at my camp."

She nodded. "That might be best."

"Do you want to talk to your father?" I heard her say.

"No," Cecil said. "Dear God, no."

I prayed that Adam wasn't around to hear.

)))

Waiting for Anne was misery. I paced, cleaned, fetched, and brooded, to no avail. Guilt had taken hold of me and wouldn't let go. I'd come to Big Sur to step into my own life story, not interfere with someone else's. What had I set in motion with my stubborn insistence that Adam share his work? How could good intentions have gone so bad?

If only I could go back and start all over, knowing what I knew now. Of course, if life came with a rewind button, how many rewinds would it take for me to finally get things right? And how would I ever move forward if I was constantly revisiting the past? Time to fess up. My actions had contributed to the mess Adam was in. Now, I had to step forward to help get him out of it.

"How's Adam?" I asked on Anne's return.

She sat on one of my tripod camp stools and reached for the pot of coffee. "Not good."

Hopefully, in her current mood, she wouldn't notice that the coffee was cold and had lost its flavor. "And Cecil?"

She poured the coffee into a mug, took a sip, and winced. I handed her packets of creamer and sugar. She passed. "He's a coward like the rest of us during unexpected moments of crisis. It takes superhuman strength to face some of life's cruel realities, even more so when it involves the people we love."

Sometimes Anne's wisdom seemed aimed directly at me. I hated to admit it, but when it came to cowardice during unexpected moments of crisis, Cecil and I had a lot in common. "Did you tell him that Adam has Alzheimer's?"

"Yes. And he asked why his father wasn't in a medical facility getting treatment. I tried to explain about his participation in an experimental program to relieve the symptoms of AD, but he wouldn't listen. I think he'll be back with the cops."

"Poor Adam."

Anne nodded.

We sat in silence until I changed the subject. Anything to get my mind off Adam.

"Anne, about being a nun..."

"It's true," she said. "I made the mistake of sharing some disturbing visions with our mother superior. I was scared and thought she could help."

"Why didn't she?" I asked, then remembered my mother's reaction when I told her about the voices I'd been hearing. Shock. Disbelief. And later on, verbal abuse.

"She believed that I was seeing and hearing things all right," Anne said, "but that the visions and locutions were coming from the devil. So, she limited the time I spent alone, giving me extra work to prevent such dangerous nonsense. I had no objection to that. Anything to stop the voices and visions.

"For weeks, then months, I hoed weeds, scrubbed floors, and did double kitchen duty, until every bone and muscle in my body ached. But the voices and visions continued. The other sisters started avoiding me, crossing themselves whenever I was near, fearing for their own spiritual contamination. Thus, forcing me into a form of solitary confinement. All the while, I was terrified that my soul was damned and my mind infected by the devil. In time, the things I'd heard the voices predict started coming true and, despite Mother Superior's assertions that it was the devil communicating with me, I started wondering if the voices were coming from a beneficent source."

Anne paused to catch her breath, which sounded ragged. "I don't blame Mother Superior completely. She was doing her best to save my soul. In the end, what it amounted to was that she didn't believe in the afterlife, except as outlined in the Bible. She believed in unexplainable events that happened thousands of years ago, but not that they could happen today."

"Instead, you're considered crazy or evil," I said with the confidence of at least partial understanding.

Anne traced the quote on her coffee mug, a gift from Truus, my adoptive mother: *Courage, dear heart*. Words I'd longed to hear from her the day before I left for Big Sur. "Since then I've learned to be careful," Anne said, "with whom I share my experiences."

My nails pinched my palm as I balled my hand into a fist. "Did they kick you out of the convent?"

"No. I left."

"Why?"

"There are subtle forms of punishment, Marjorie, that are quite effective. One is withholding love." Anne dumped the remainder of her coffee into the fire ring. "There was only so much loneliness I could take."

"But all those clothes you shared with me and your talk about getting burned."

Anne looked up, her eyes blue fire. "After I left the convent, I rebelled against my vows of poverty and of chastity, big time."

I pressed my chin onto my clasped hands. How lonely, how desperate Anne must have felt. Talk about journeys of self-discovery. "But why turn to witchcraft?"

"I figured if what I was hearing wasn't coming from God and if that made me some diabolical threat to society, it was my responsibility to discover where the communication *was* coming from. So, I took to studying the lives of other women who didn't fit into society, who were banished, so to speak, for their visions and their intuitive, holistic ways of seeing things."

"Witches," I said.

"Exactly. And what I discovered astounded me. Did you know that during the late Middle Ages as many as sixty thousand women were burned at the stake as witches?"

"That many?"

"And most of them were midwives who helped ease the pain of childbirth and women who used herbs for healing and had knowledge of nature's way. They included women who were smart, unmarried, childless, or owned property. The list goes on. And you know what?"

I shook my head.

"With witchcraft, I've found a place where womanhood is elevated to the place where it rightly belongs, where the intuitive, imaginative part of one's self is respected not condemned, and where one is able to connect with the invisible world through symbols and creativity. In other words, I found my home."

"You've been through hell," I whispered.

Anne straightened her shoulders. "I am the master of my fate, the captain of my soul."

The words hung like a dark cloud between us. My throat swelled with tears. Regardless of all my recent affirmations about lessons to be learned in this journey we call life, at that moment, I felt no hope.

Chapter Twenty-Nine

I T WAS AUGUST FIRST, four nights short of a full moon, but we could wait no longer. Anne, Veronica, and I had gathered on a secluded north-west bank of Pfeiffer-Redwood Creek to form a circle, as sisters, for the well-being of Antonia's restless spirit.

"First, we need to take a ritual bath," Anne said, aiming the beam of her flashlight over the surging black water, "in order to cleanse ourselves of negative energies. A nice warm soak with herbs, scented oils, and Epsom Salts would be preferable, but we'll just have to make do." She propped the flashlight on a boulder facing the creek. Then, calm as you please, she stripped off her white velvet cape and tossed it a safe distance from the slippery rocks on which she stood. The chill night air closed in on her naked body, but she waded into the waist-deep water without so much as a whimper.

Veronica whistled between her teeth. "No burning candles? No incense to set the mood?"

Anne didn't answer. It was too dark to be certain, but I suspected goose bumps had gathered over her bare skin by now. No human—except maybe those living in the world's 'frigid zones'—could saunter into ice-cold water at nine in the evening without major discomfort.

"Getting into that creek buck naked is crazy," I said, feeling my back grow rigid. "It's too cold and, besides, it's indecent."

Veronica set her flashlight next to Anne's, then turned to me and smiled as she unfastened her black-hooded cape and let it slither to the ground.

All she had on was a black thong, no better than naked as far as I was concerned.

Anne splashed water at Veronica. She yelped as liquid ice smacked her unprotected behind. Then she swung around to face her tormentor, her stance that of Artemis, Goddess of the Hunt and the Moon: independent, yet feminine; swift; decisive; quick to rescue—and to punish. Lickety-split, she dove into the creek and yanked Anne's feet from under her. Anne, rather like Hecate, the goddess of intuition and psychic wisdom, of *magick* and divination, landed with a splash. I stepped back, distancing myself from this out-of-control twosome.

Veronica paused from her war game with Anne. "Whatcha wearing, Marjorie? Thermal underwear?"

My teeth chattered in spite of the sumptuous cape—compliments of Anne—still wrapped around me. "I wish."

"Your turn," she said, edging toward the bank of the creek.

I took another step back, waving my flashlight. "You two are nuts. Tomorrow you'll both have pneumonia."

"Drop the cape," Veronica said, "or I'm coming after you."

She was serious. She would pull me in and enjoy doing it. I was shivering. Heck, I was shaking so hard I found it hard to stand. This wasn't a ritual. It was torture.

Veronica rose from the water, her wet hair plastered against her face and shoulders, her nakedness shimmering in the moonlight, the visage of a proud, dark goddess. "Drop it. NOW."

I aimed the beam of my flashlight toward the trees, vines, and bushes that edged both sides of the creek. The vegetation looked dark and shadowy, even more threatening than the icy water and its two lunatic occupants. I fumbled with the ribbon at the collar of my cape, stalling. It was too far to hightail it back to camp, especially wearing a long cape and with bare feet. Plus, it wouldn't be smart. I'd be labeled, "chicken" for life.

Veronica stepped out of the water and onto the bank.

I set the flashlight on a flat rock, making sure it faced at right angles to the beams shooting from Anne's and Veronica's flashlights, so we could see what was coming from alongside the creek. Just in case.

Then I dropped my cape and edged toward the bank of the creek. Veronica jerked to a halt and bent over laughing.

"What?" I said.

"I can't see," Anne cried. "It's too dark. What's going on?"

"She's wearing a cream bra with matching panties," Veronica shrieked, "probably with the day of the week embroidered on them."

I looked down at my lacy briefs and serviceable bra and, for a moment, forgot the cold. Okay, so they weren't Victoria's Secret, but...

Someone pushed me from behind. *Veronica!* I flew into the ice-cold river, head first. Couldn't scream. In order to scream, I would have to breathe in. I came up choking and spitting. No sympathy from my companions. Oh no. Their cackling even disturbed the birds. A hawk screeched. An owl hooted. Or maybe it was Anne. I didn't know, or care, too busy gagging, shivering, and planning my revenge. I unhooked my bra and barely had time to appreciate the carrying capacity of two Double-D cups before filling them with water and flinging the icy liquid at the two crazy women with whom I was sharing the creek.

"Thatta-girl," Anne said, clapping her hands.

Veronica let out a between-the-teeth wolf whistle. "You look pretty good, Sis. Did you get a boob job?"

In spite of the cold, my face grew hot. As I turned to refill my make-do weapon with liquid ammunition, I saw movement near the bank of the creek. I crossed my arms over my exposed 'boobs' and squinted into the darkness. Even with my flashlight's beam aimed at the creek's outer banks, all appeared a grainy black and gray.

"Adam?" Anne said, her tone hopeful.

So, she had seen something, too. Double damn. Of all the rotten luck. Three naked, defenseless—stupid—women with someone, *Dear God let it be Adam*, lurking in the shadows. I eyed my flashlight.

It would serve as a better weapon than the cotton and spandex one dangling from my hand.

Someone started to cry.

"Shit," Veronica said.

I turned toward the sound and gasped. A second figure wavered in the darkness. It was of average height, nebulous, and appeared to have a blanket over its head. Anne's and Veronica's flashlights were of no use. They illuminated us, the defenseless, in all our glory, while the unwelcome gawkers remained no more than shadows.

The weeping pulled at me. It sounded like my mother. But how could that be? We hadn't yet formed our circle. Or consecrated our space. Or channeled our collective wisdom and power. Already chilled, the cold now went deeper. My aura felt like the inside of a Popsicle. I longed for a towel, a cape. I longed for my mother. The hazy figure withdrew its blanket, and I gagged on my quick intake of air. Even in near darkness, I knew...

"Ver-on-ica," I sputtered. "Look."

Veronica thrashed through the water to my side, then grabbed my arm for support.

"Oh my," Anne said. "I was concentrating on Adam."

Without taking my eyes off the cloud of energy I knew to be our mother, I said, "Are you sure it's Adam?"

"Yeah. They're both here, Adam *and* your mother."

I edged closer to the bank. Dr. Mendez had told me about an author named Michael Talbot, who speculated that the conscious is not contained in the brain, but is a plasmic holographic energy field that permeates and surrounds our physical bodies. The past, then, is not lost, but still exists, recorded in the cosmic airways, and can be converted into holograms by our minds. Was Antonia a three-dimensional recording from the past? Were her emotions—her hopes, her fears, her plans—recorded in the cosmic hologram? Was the spiritual part of her reaching out to us from a different realm that we could somehow connect to at the quantum level and where the past, present, and future existed all at once? Darn, if only I could reach my flashlight and aim it where it would do more good.

"Looks like Adam's in some kind of trance," Veronica said, still clutching my arm.

"Likely a self-induced one," Anne said. "To close himself down."

"You think he's giving up?" I asked, my teeth chattering.

"More a matter of connecting with a different kind of power, a higher power."

I jumped at the hoot of an owl. My throat hurt. Tears stung my eyes. *Adam, please help Antonia accept the light, so it can pull her out of the darkness.*

Antonia appeared to embrace Adam. They faced each other for what seemed a long time. Adam pointed in our direction. Antonia shook her head. Adam motioned again. Our mother turned to face us. Veronica squeezed my arm. It hurt. But I didn't mind. It reminded me that I wasn't dreaming, that this was real. Adam guided our mother to the bank of the creek. Her face caught the full beam of my flashlight. I gasped. "God help us."

Where her eyes should have been, there were two black holes.

Veronica's icy hand went limp, and she leaned against me. "She can't see us."

"Oh, she can see you all right," Anne said, "just not through her eyes."

Veronica made a guttural sound as if clearing her throat.

The creek's flow gained force. My knees felt weak. "Mother. We love you."

Antonia brought up her hands. Then dropped them.

"We heard you crying," I said. "Is there anything we can do?"

A nod. Or was it? Maybe my imagination was playing tricks on me.

"Is it about our father?"

Another nod? Hard to tell.

"We know you were a good mother," I said. "You did everything you could to protect us."

She reached out her hands and wailed as I had heard her wail in the cave near Tassajara during my guided tour through the Los Padres Forest. The sound had been high, weird, and powerful, like that of a hurricane-force wind, and it had saved my life.

I took a step forward. Anne pulled me back. "Don't go near her."

"Our father loves you, Mother," Veronica said.

For a moment, Antonia seemed to solidify.

"He hopes to see you on the other side. Will you wait for him there?" She nodded as before.

"Will you wait for us, too?" I asked.

She said, *Yes.* I was sure of it.

Veronica swayed against me, as if sapped of all strength. I supported her with my arm, afraid she might fall.

"Then go there now, Mother," I said, "and be happy."

As Antonia's image began to fade, her words—*Your father. Your father*—coursed through the air like ripples on water.

"What about our father?" Veronica asked. "What does he know?"

I tried to step forward, wanting one last look into her hollow eyes. This time, Veronica held me back. My eyes felt hot and scratchy, my nose wet. I sank into the creek making heavy, noisy sounds. The freezing water felt oddly warm.

"What about our father?" Veronica repeated. "What's he got to do with this? With us?"

No answer. Our mother was gone.

Veronica sank to my side and pressed her cold body against mine.

"You two stay here," Anne said. "I'll get the towels."

The water flowed on as if attempting to carry Veronica and me from the security of the creek bank to the Big Sur River, and from there to the vast Pacific Ocean, connected only by the golden thread of love. I rested my head on my sister's bare shoulder and clung to her wet, icy hands. "It's okay, Sis."

Anne returned, speaking in a low murmur. She urged us to stand and draped us with towels. Still clinging to each other, Veronica and I sloshed to the creek bank.

"She can't break through," Veronica said.

To which I added, "Or we're blocking her."

"How," Veronica asked.

"For one thing, I think we're trying too hard. Antonia isn't our own private genie, who we can summon at will, simply by rubbing a magic lamp or performing a ritual, no matter how focused and powerful. For another, we can't understand a language we haven't yet learned."

Anne gave my sister's back a vigorous rub, then began massaging her arms. "Are you saying you're not ready for what she wants you to know?"

"I can't speak for Veronica, but there's more for me to learn. I have to become more like our mother, I mean, really empathize with her and make space for her in my heart, before I can understand her message. I've been making this all about me, missing out on a message that's carried by vibrations that can't be caught through the eyes and ears."

I felt a moment of sudden joy as though a shaft of light had shot past my mind straight to my soul. My muscles stopped shaking. "Her message will become clear," I said with conviction that could only have come from an outside source. "Not as we expect, but as the need arises, in a form that at first will confuse us. Antonia wants us to look into our hearts where real life happens, where the secrets of life are hidden in plain sight. She wants us to open our spiritual eyes and ears."

"Hey," Veronica said. "Where'd that come from?"

"I don't know."

I closed my eyes as Anne's strong, capable fingers began working the circulation back into my arms. "Will Adam be okay?"

"I think his little talk with Antonia has done him a world of good," Anne said.

The vision of Adam and the spirit of our mother embracing would forever stay projected on my mind like a three-dimensional holographic memory that could be relived in vivid detail over and over. "I wonder what they said to each other."

Anne made the sign of the cross. "I doubt we'll ever know."

Chapter Thirty

I WOKE TO A DEEP CHILL in the air. The steady drip, drip on the roof of my tent indicated that fog had condensed on the flat needles of the redwoods overnight and was now oozing onto the ground below. I lingered in my sleeping bag. I wanted to go home—to Morgan and Joshua. I wanted to be coddled, spoiled, pampered, and loved. Why was I making it so hard on myself? Morgan would take care of me. My only mission would be to make him and Joshua happy. Which would be easy—because I loved them.

Maybe I would never be able to unblock the energy field that existed between Antonia and me. Maybe now that she'd done her best to relay her message, she would find contentment in the after-life, where consciousness resides. And Veronica? She hadn't been able to get away fast enough after last night's ordeal. Neither she nor Antonia needed me. Not anymore. If they ever had.

I checked my watch. It was nine o'clock. By now, Morgan would be in for breakfast. His mother would be frying bacon and eggs for her husband, son, and grandson, while they discussed the chores still to be tackled that day. Equipment would need to be serviced, calves to be fed, corn to be irrigated one last time before harvest.

I grabbed my for-emergency-use-only cell phone and punched in the ranch number. Joshua answered on the second ring.

"Joshua?"

"Marjorie! Hey Morgan, it's Marjorie! Are you coming home?"

I wanted to say yes, but something nagged at the back of my mind. *Not so fast. You still have things to do.* "Soon, honey."

"We miss you."

My throat. It hurt. "Miss you, too. And sweetie... I love you."

"I know."

Silence.

"How's our stray?" I asked.

Joshua laughed. "He's getting fat."

"Oh dear."

"Morgan says he hasn't seen a mouse or rat lurking around the place since Gabriel came to live with us."

"Well that's good anyway." Joshua, my precious Joshua, with his straight black hair, his deep brown eyes, and Gabriel, the scrawny tabby, my backyard stray. What a picture they made. Once orphaned and voiceless, now best friends.

"Morgan gave me a baseball cap to keep the hair out of my eyes," Joshua said. "And a pair of rubber boots for when we feed the calves and irrigate the corn, and...and...cowboy boots for when we go to the feed store...and to the part store for repairs."

I laughed, absorbing the joyful music of his voice.

"Uh... Morgan says it's his turn to talk." A pause. "I love you."

"Love you, too, sweetie."

"Marjorie?" It was Morgan.

The timbre of his voice sparked a toe-curling jolt of pleasure. Good thing I was still bundled in my sleeping bag. "Marjorie?"

I started to cry

"Honey, are you okay?"

"I don't think I can take this anymore."

Silence.

"Tell me to come home, and I'll head out today."

Morgan's long inhale and exhale sounded close, rather than two hundred miles away. "If it was just about me, I would," he said. "Nothing would make me happier."

"Tell me you can't go on without me, that no one's holding me back but myself."

"You can't give up now," he said.

Tell me to come home. That we need to get married right away.

"I want you here," he said. "Joshua wants you here. We all do. But you have to finish what you've started."

I closed my eyes, tightened my grip the phone. "I don't know if I can."

A sigh, so close, so far away. "I'd love to pull you into my arms and make it all better, but..."

"We'd regret it in the morning."

"Afraid so."

I sat and pulled up my knees, the sleeping bag still wrapped around me to keep out the chill. "I've been in contact with Antonia twice since coming to Big Sur. Yesterday, she spoke to us, and I think... I hope...she'll be okay."

"Us?"

"Adam, Anne, Veronica, and me—"

"Adam and Anne?"

"New friends. Oh, Morgan, a lot has happened since we last talked."

His chuckle spanned the distance, its energy reaching inside of me, where it most mattered. "No surprise, with Veronica around."

A flashback to our ritual bath in the creek caused me to shudder. "We saw her. We saw Antonia."

Over the phone, across the miles, Morgan's quick intake of breath and its slow release relayed that he cared. "I can't honestly say I understand," he said. "I've never experienced the kind of things you're experiencing. But I'm glad, Marjorie. I'm glad."

"And that got me thinking that...that...I could..." Damn, I was stuttering.

Morgan chuckled, but otherwise remained silent, giving me a chance to get a grip, and blurt, "That I *could* call it quits and marry you right away."

"When you come home and we marry, I won't be able to let you go again." Morgan's voice caught. "That's why you have to be sure."

"I know," I said.

"Think about it for a few days. Make sure you're not leaving something undone."

"Do you miss me?" I asked. *Stupid question.*

"More than you know. I'd give just about anything to hold you in my arms right now and make all your troubles go away."

"Thank you, Morgan. It helps to hear that."

"When you come back, it will be forever. Okay?"

"Forever," I said before ending the call.

The weather hadn't changed during my talk with Morgan. A quick peek through the vestibule of my tent revealed air still heavy with moisture and clouds still hanging low, endless gray clouds that obscured the sun. But the lack of sun and blue skies no longer darkened my mood. I dressed, recharged with a cup of coffee and an energy bar, and headed for a destination unknown, confident that the answer to the nagging question of why I must stay would make itself clear.

My insulated jacket, plus the vigorous walk, turned my shivering body into a sweaty one. The walk turned into a jog, my shoes hitting the earth in a *plat, plat, plat*. The wind chilled my cheeks. My breath became puffs of steam. A stitch in my side caused me to slow to a walk, then halt and inhale rushes of air. I dropped onto a grassy clearing, rolled onto my back, and closed my eyes. *Tell me what to do.*

You already know, a voice answered, though this time the voice didn't belong to an ancestor or to my birth mother.

This time, it belonged to me.

Until I cleared a channel for my intuition to grow sharper and for me to become braver; until I gained enough confidence in my own life story to make room for love; I would be of use to no one. I needed to take some risks and do things I'd never dared do before, things that risked being wrong, but needed doing anyway. I needed to access the holographic field where Antonia's consciousness resided. No more trying to direct her life story or, for that matter, emulate Veronica's. Antonia's message had something to do with my father, and, for some inexplicable reason, my relationship with Adam held the key.

I stood, invigorated by the new direction my thoughts had taken me.

Antonia would contact me when *I* was ready.

Chapter Thirty-One

I FOUND ANNE, no problem. Her brown and yellow skirt billowed and fluttered against the background of green forest like a butterfly. She looked up at the sound of my approach. "Thought you'd be packed up and hotfooting it home by now."

I took a deep breath and exhaled into the shaded stillness. "Morgan stopped me."

She handed me a mug of hot water with a tea bag steeping inside. "He must be a far-sighted man."

"I'm very lucky."

Anne nodded, but made no comment.

As I eased into a camp chair next to her, I caught the scent of turmeric, ginger, cinnamon, and honey rising with the steam from my mug. Anti-aging, anti-inflammatory, antioxidant, anti-everything that ails you. Just what I needed.

Silence, except for the ambient nature sounds that never grew silent.

"Marriage isn't for the weak-hearted," Anne said. "You've got to be strong. Hell, you've got to have guts. I mean you really stand naked when you marry someone. There's not much you can hide." She stared off into the distance, yet appeared to be looking inside. "You have to stand up for yourself, and at the same time be willing to compromise."

Her words filtered through my mind, but I didn't try to capture them. She leaned forward in her chair and set her mug on the fire pit ring. "With the right person, marriage can be heaven. It's like a rebirth. You help each other develop in areas where you're weak. But

God help you if you marry the wrong person." She shuddered. "It's how I envision hell."

A glimmer of pain in her eyes had me offering, "Love means letting go of fear."

Anne blinked, but said nothing.

"Anyway, I can't leave now," I said. "I care about you and Adam. You've helped me mend some gaps in my worldview, making me feel better about myself and making me realize that my passage on this Earth isn't an individual one, but a team effort. Observing Adam's treatment of his son, and vice versa, has helped me understand Truus better, that her strict, even restrictive, parenting is done out of love and that I've been judging her too harshly. Plus, you've helped me open up to Antonia. How can I ever thank you enough for that?"

Anne smiled, her radiance warming my heart as the tea and campfire warmed my body. "Your love is enough."

Her mood was hard to gauge. She appeared a bit down, which was unlike her. No matter what the problem, she always seemed to land on her feet. Had Cecil's cruel words brought back memories difficult for her to shrug off? The past has a way of slipping back in when we least expect it, wreaking havoc with our lives.

"Cecil scares me," I said. "He's like an out-of-control bulldozer, about to destroy everything you and Adam have accomplished during your stay here. Adam appeared to be doing so well, as though part of him had accepted and made room for the next phase of his journey. Look how his mind extended to Antonia's. That's got to mean something."

Anne rested her elbows on her knees and stared at me. "Cecil stirs things up. That's for sure."

"How could Adam have fathered such a son?"

Anne turned her intent focus from me to the fire. "Actually, Adam and Cecil are like two peas in a pod."

Impossible. Unacceptable. No way.

"You didn't know Adam before," Anne said, her eyes shifting

back to me with a hint of the fire she'd been observing. "In his own words, he was an arrogant, bossy, pain in the ass. In a way, Alzheimer's has made him a better man."

Anne wouldn't make up something like this, but still... Adam arrogant and bossy? I shook my head. I was a planner, a doer. I wanted to press forward, get results. But that wasn't Anne's style, and she, more than anyone, had Adam's best interests at heart. "What can I do for him, where do I begin?"

"Visit him."

"That's it?"

"Unless you have a better plan."

I handed her my empty mug. Some would call Anne's patience a lack of drive, but I suspected that she had found peace and, more than that, contentment.

After rinsing and storing the mugs, Anne pulled a plastic container out of an ice chest and put it into an insulated backpack cooler. "My Popeye blend," she said at my questioning gaze. "I mix it up special for Adam."

"What's in it?"

"Juiced apples, spinach, parsley, carrots, celery, and beets." She pulled out another plastic container, which she added to the backpack cooler. "I also fixed him a memory mender. Since AD is believed to be caused by an accumulation of toxins in the brain, I try to eliminate all packaged and processed foods. Maybe if he'd been eating like this all along..." She shrugged. "Anyway, there's no going back. The best I can do is try to prevent more of his autonomic nerve cells from being destroyed."

"Where'd you get hold of a juicer out here?"

"They're letting me make use of the kitchen at the Inn," she said, handing me the backpack.

I tested the pack's weight—heavy—before sliding it onto my back.

"You got the light one," Anne said, grabbing another backpack cooler with contents unknown. She flexed her muscles in a bodybuilder pose before yanking the burden onto her back. "Beats going to the gym."

Weighed down by my backpack, the hike to Adam's camp took more stamina than usual. I was out of shape and it showed. Anne, though, wasn't even breathing hard when we reached our destination.

We found Adam sitting as still as one of his sculptures. Buster sat next to him and whined as we neared.

Anne dropped her backpack and placed a hand on Adam's arm. "What's wrong?"

"I lost my keys," he said.

"Aren't his keys rigged up with some kind of computer device," I asked, "that beeps like a pager or intercom locater?"

"Yep." Anne pulled out her own key ring. From it swung a small black gadget that looked like a remote car door opener. She pressed a red button and a loud *beep* came from the direction of the grotto.

I dropped my backpack and ran, following the beeping sound until I reached Adam's grove of sculptures and located his ring of keys.

On my return, I felt pleased with my small contribution to his peace of mind.

"They're heavy," he said after I handed them to him.

No wonder. At least five keys, a sapphire-and-diamond-encrusted BMW emblem, and a mini- computer hung from a thick, gold ring.

Adam sat up straighter and peered at me. "I don't need them anymore."

"That's true," Anne said. "Unless they make you happy."

Adam fingered the keys one at a time before holding the BMW emblem up to the sun. Sparks of light shot in all directions. "Kathleen bought this for me," he said, before the light of illumination disappeared from his eyes. He handed me the keys. "They're heavy."

I handed them back. "Yes, they are."

Adam stared at them and shook his head. "I don't want them anymore."

"Marjorie will keep them for you until you need them, okay?" Anne said.

"Okay," he said, eyeing Anne's backpack. "I'm hungry."

I was already keeper of Adam's journal. Now I was also respon-sible for his keys, adorned with gold, diamonds, and sapphires, and no one seemed to want them.

Chapter Thirty-Two

I HARDLY HAD TIME to appreciate the purity of the next morning's air or the sheer brilliance of the sun penetrating the canopy of redwoods, before Anne bore down on me with bad news.

"Adam's gone."

Why was I was not surprised? "Have some coffee," I said through gritted teeth. "Nothing organic about it, but it's fresh, and I can vouch for its rejuvenating qualities."

"Sometimes coffee is as sacred as holy water," Anne said before accepting my offer and sitting on a log next to me.

She lifted her face to the sun, her gray curls wafting in the breeze like a halo.

"Bet Cecil took him," I said.

"Lord, yes. He even left a note saying his father was now in safe hands." Anne lowered her head and peered into her coffee. "Adam went along without a fuss. There were no signs of a struggle."

"Struggle?" I dug into my coat pocket and pulled out his key chain and mini-computer. "Darn it, Anne."

Anne made no move to take the burden from my hand. "The computer wouldn't have helped."

"But he might have been able to set off the alarm."

"I doubt he would have."

"What about the sensors in his clothing?"

"Useless," she said. "I found them in his tent."

My insides grew hard and unyielding. "I think I hate him."

"Who?" Anne asked. As if she didn't know.

"Cecil." His name conjured up foul and poisonous feelings within me, the part of me that judged and pronounced guilt without a trial.

Anne grunted, as if in agreement, but not as fighting mad about it. "I assume he feels the same about us."

"Us? What have we done?"

"Let's look at it from Cecil's point of view," she said. "He finds his arrogant, meticulous, and very rich father living like a bum and chumming it up with a couple of total strangers who are hiding him and selling off his sculptures. What would you do if Adam was your father?"

"I'd freak out and place him in a care facility lickety-split."

So much for speaking my mind. I had just sided with the devil.

Some kind of bird, maybe a blackbird, definitely not a Steller's Jay, sang out as if to remind me, "Do not judge!"

"Poor Cecil," Anne said. "He's grieving the loss of his relationship with his father."

It was hard for me to think of Cecil as poor in any shape or form, except maybe in manners and consideration, but yes, chances were that he was as devastated as Adam initially was about the ravages of AD. I looked at Anne's kind face, struck anew by her wisdom.

"Although Adam has deteriorated physically and mentally," she said, "his condition hasn't accelerated enough to put him in a nursing home. We could've put that off for months, maybe even years." She shook her head, signs of regret etched all over her face. "Now he won't get the holistic diet I was providing for him, nor the individual attention."

Despair weighed down on me, not knowing what to do, even questioning my right to do anything at all. "I wonder where Cecil took him."

"I know exactly where."

"How?"

"Brock caught Cecil leaving the park with Adam and followed them."

"Knowing Cecil, he probably selected a place that's expensive, thus exclusive," I said.

Anne poured herself another mug of coffee. "That probably

would've been the case if the best care homes in town didn't have waiting lists of up to six months. Decisions made in a hurry usually end up in poor choices."

"Are you saying what I think you're saying?"

"Afraid so. The facility Cecil selected wouldn't have been my first choice. That said, even the top-rated nursing homes have doctors who are responsible for hundreds of patients at numerous facilities. It'll take vigilance and involvement on Cecil's part for Adam to comfortably live where he's been placed."

"Confined to a hospital bed or a wheel chair? Please say no."

The deepened frown on Anne's face was my answer. "My guess is that he'll be placed in the mental health unit of the nursing home. It'll be traumatic for him after the independence he's used to. He considered this his home, his paradise. He had his clay, us, and—"

"Where's Buster?" I asked.

"At Adam's camp, looking lost. Coyotes, in my opinion, should be kept wild. Adam didn't do Buster any favors by feeding him. He's become too dependent on handouts, and, I hesitate to say, on human love. I'm beginning to suspect that Buster is a coydog, the result of breeding between an abandoned dog and a coyote, but that doesn't make domesticating him right. Anyway, I gave him something to eat and left him there for now."

"What are we going to do?"

"Visit Adam and try to encourage the staff to see past his ailments to the man he is."

"Can we get him out?"

"With the help of his lawyer, maybe," Anne said, her expression tight. "Guess it depends on the shape he's in."

I got to my feet and poured the dregs of my coffee onto the campfire. "Then what are we waiting for?"

"I'm not sure Adam's strong enough to withstand the ensuing battle," Anne said. "We'll need to talk to Cecil first."

"A lot of good that'll do." I took Anne's mug and plopped it next to mine to wash later. How could she remain so calm?

Anne stood and did a slow stretch. "It's worth a try."

"What if I give Cecil his father's journal, so he can read for himself what Adam has been going through and why he made the decisions he did?"

Anne smiled, but her eyes didn't join in. "Good idea. There are a few things I also need to share with Cecil."

))))

We arrived at the care facility at 1:05 p.m. A staff member led us through several long corridors that opened into room after room of aged, sick, and shrunken people. Some sat slumped in wheelchairs, some shuffled along with walkers hooked up to IVs, and others lay in bed with vacant stares. The crying, the moaning, and the occasional screams and mirthless laughter sent shivers over my skin.

"Is this what it all comes down to?" I asked. Many of these people were spending their last days guided by bio-engineers rather than by caregivers trained to know the difference between curing and healing.

Anne halted. "They ache for home."

I wrapped my arms around my chest to quell the shivers racking through me. "It smells so...so strange in here, like stale urine, greasy disinfectant...and death."

"Death awaits us all."

Not a comforting thought. "Jeez, it's so degrading."

Our guide shot us an impatient look. We trailed behind her by at least six feet, probably a good thing, since our conversation would not be to her liking. "Ladies?"

Anne smiled an apology, and we resumed our walk. "Are you beginning to understand, that during our short stay here on earth, we need to prepare?"

"How can anyone prepare for this?" I asked.

"We can't, not fully," Anne said. "Most of us won't leave life in the exact way we choose. But we *can* eliminate one of its heaviest burdens...regret. During our lifetimes, we can resolve our conflicts, heal our relationships, and reach our potential. In other words, live each day as if it were our last. So, when it comes our turn, we're ready."

"You mean die in peace?"

"Our greater reality is untouched by change, decay, and death. The patients you see here are releasing their minds and their lives in preparation for a grand adventure. Death is like a reset button, a fresh beginning, a reacquainting with God."

"All I see is suffering," I said, though I was beginning to understand where Anne was going with this.

"The transformation can be painful. That's why it's so important for patients to participate in their own illness."

"How?"

"By not attaching to a particular outcome, but allowing for what is most right."

We found Adam sitting in a wheelchair next to a sliding glass door that led to a courtyard exposed only to the overhead sky. His hair had been cut short, his beard shaven. He looked sleek and intimidating, not at all like the Adam I knew.

"What the hell do you want?" Cecil demanded from his sentry position next to the door.

"When it comes to Adam, probably the same thing you do," Anne said, her voice calm, as if he hadn't just startled her as much as he'd startled me.

What was he guarding against? Entry? Or escape?

Cecil's bloodshot eyes flared. "You had him wired up to a computer like a damn dog."

Anne shrugged. "If you had bothered to ask, I would've told you that your father was participating in a remarkable study about which he was quite excited."

Cecil shot out of his chair. It hit the wall with a thud. "You had him living like a goddamn bum."

"That was his idea," Anne said.

"You expect me to believe that?"

"You'll find what you need to know in here," Anne said, handing him a thick manila envelope. "It's his advanced directive, otherwise known as—"

"I know what an advanced directive is," Cecil said.

"The papers were written up between Adam and his attorney."

"Without telling me?"

"It appears so."

"That son-of-a-bitch."

I stepped forward with Adam's journal raised like a weapon. "That son-of-a-bitch didn't want to burden you." I jabbed the journal against his chest. "This will explain what the legal documents don't."

Cecil blinked several times before taking the journal from my shaking hand. He let it fall open and drew in his breath. "It's in his handwriting."

"Well duh, since it's *his* journal. Although, in time, Anne had to step in and take dictation."

"Ce Ce?" Adam said.

Cecil jerked and the journal nearly slid out of his hand. He managed to retrieve it and clutched it to his chest as though safeguarding a treasure. "He didn't recognize me before."

"And he may not recognize you five minutes from now," Anne said.

"That bad?" Cecil asked, staring at his father.

"We've been able to slow the progress of the disease down, but he's had his bad moments."

Cecil looked like someone had punched him in the gut.

I glanced at Adam. Our eyes met.

"Antonia?" he said.

"No—"

"Let him talk." Anne said.

Adam stared at me as though I held a lifeline and he were drowning. "I can't get out. The doors won't open."

"I'll help you," I said. "Like you helped me."

He smiled for the first time since we arrived. "Will you help me find my boy?"

Cecil gasped.

"I'll try," I said.

Adam cocked his head and frowned. "He's all alone and afraid. We have to find him."

I looked at Cecil. His expression was wide-eyed, as Adam's had been only moments before. "We will," I said.

By the time I refocused on Adam, his face had the appearance of a blank plastic mask.

I was the one to look away.

"Go someplace quiet and read Adam's advanced directive and journal," Anne said to Cecil. "Then pick up Claudia and meet us back at Adam's camp."

"Claudia?"

Anne's gaze didn't falter. "You're going to need her to help decide what to do."

Cecil took a ragged breath and drew his hand through his hair. "I suppose you want to take my father back to Pfeiffer State Park."

"Moving here was a shock for him," Anne said, "a major setback. Hopefully by tomorrow, we'll know what steps to take."

"Did *you* read his journal?" Cecil asked, addressing me.

"Yes," I said. "And it nearly broke my heart."

"I assume I'm not going to like what I'm about to learn."

"You're right," I said, "but it'll explain a lot."

Chapter Thirty-Three

A NNE AND I were in for another nasty surprise. During the short time Adam had been gone, someone had vandalized his camp. His tent and sleeping bag lay in shreds. Toilet paper waved from bushes and trees. Shaving cream and toothpaste formed graffiti-like markings on the flattened earth, and his belongings were scattered like party trash. Even his treasured deck of Tarot cards.

"Adam's sculptures!" I raced toward the grotto without checking to see if Anne followed; just charged ahead, leaping over gopher holes, exposed roots, vines, and duff, praying the vandals hadn't found his precious sculptures.

They had.

It looked like a war zone with decapitated and mutilated bodies of clay strewn in grotesque imitations of death. Adam's family, and memories, were gone. I sank onto the dark and wet detritus on the forest floor—dead plants and animals, bacteria and fungi, necessary for the birth and survival of new forms of life. I noticed for the first time how the canopy of trees soaked up all the sunlight, leaving little behind for the vegetation below. Life and death, struggle and survival.

With a sob, I let go of the detritus that had taken up all the space inside of me: guilt, anger, judgment, blame, the sense of limitation and unfairness of things. It had served its purpose. Time to allow for the birth of something new.

Anne knelt beside me and dropped her face into her hands. Her shoulders shook as she, too, succumbed to her grief.

I don't know how long we sat there crying before we noticed

Buster's presence. He lay with his grizzled head on his paws, eyes dull. "Here, boy," I said. He scuttled over. Both Anne and I scratched the coyote's head and ran our fingers over and through his hair, drawing comfort from this gentle earth creature.

"He's not much of a guard dog," I said, my voice hoarse.

Anne looked at him with a trace of a smile. "He prefers to guide and comfort, not defend. Right, Buster?"

I stared at the pointless destruction around us. "I never got around to taking any pictures."

"His art has served its purpose," Anne said. "And thanks to you, one of his works survives."

"And Cecil has it, thank God." I wiped my eyes. "We have to prepare him."

It took effort for Anne to stand. In fact, it took two tries, as if she'd aged ten years in a matter of minutes. I didn't fare much better. Anne grabbed hold of my hand and pulled me up. "Prepare Cecil or Adam?" she asked.

"At the moment, Cecil. It would be too cruel to let him walk into this."

"Too late," Cecil said from behind us. He leaned on Claudia's arm for support as he stared at the desecrated grotto that had once been sacred to his father.

"Would the two of you like to be alone for a while?" I asked.

Cecil nodded, and as Anne and I headed back to Adam's camp, we heard him weep.

"It's hard to dislike a guy when he's in pain," I said, realizing how easy it was to judge—and to misunderstand.

)))

"We can't bring my father back here," Cecil said when he and Claudia returned from Adam's grotto. "It wouldn't be the same."

"It doesn't have to be the same," I said, surprised at the conviction behind my words. Something was urging me on, and I wasn't questioning the source. "It's still his home."

I met a wall of skepticism, in the form of Cecil and Anne, but went on in the camp's defense. "We can fix it up even better than before."

Anne and Cecil continued to frown at me.

"Don't you see?" I said. "It may all seem new to Adam anyway, considering his limited memory of past events. We can restore the grotto to the way it was when he first discovered it. Maybe he'll sculpt again, maybe not, but it'll still be a comfort to him, the trees, the ferns, Buster..."

"I, of all people, don't want to detract from the benefits of nature in slowing down the progress of AD," Anne said. "But Adam will need closer supervision now. He has lost ground. And soon, he won't be able to sculpt anymore, due to the numbing effect of neuropathy on his fingers and hands. As it is, what he's been able to accomplish is quite miraculous."

Well, that pretty much clinched it. Without Anne's optimism and support, there was no way I could talk Cecil into extending Adam's stay.

"I would love to have the opportunity to get to know Adam better," Claudia said, "before—" She halted, bit her lip. "Once we return home, I'm afraid the opportunity to do so will be lost. Adam's regression may accelerate, and Cecil and I will feel pressured to go back to work."

I gawked at Claudia in surprise. I'd only heard her express an opinion once. When we were alone.

A smile crossed Cecil's face. "Well then, guess, it's worth a try."

☽☽☽

We worked the rest of the day and most of the next before the reconstruction of Adam's camp met Cecil's approval. Much had to be replaced or upgraded, and Cecil made numerous trips into town for the needed supplies. For once, I didn't resent what money could accomplish, especially when it was being used to help Adam.

We left Adam's sacred grotto untouched, except for burying all traces of the broken sculptures.

"Adam took matter from the physical world," Anne said, "and now it has returned. Ashes to ashes..."

It was time to bring Adam home.

☽☽☽

As so often happens, the best-laid plans are prone to failure, or at least what we perceive as failure. On our return to the convalescent hospital, it appeared as though Adam had given up. His body was there, but his mind seemed to have left the room.

"It's only been three days," Cecil said, his sense of helplessness unspoken, but evident in the way he repeatedly opened and closed his hands. "How could he have slipped this far?"

Anne used her middle and index fingers to check Adam's pulse. "In dementia, so much depends on the patient's attitude. Staying here with convalescing and declining people must have brought home, quite traumatically, that he was sick and dying."

"Wasn't he aware of that before?" Cecil asked.

Anne's eyes flashed, but her voice remained calm. "Aligned with the power and intelligence of nature, he seemed to have risen above it. He forgot about what happened in the past, let go of what might happen in the future, and made room for the quiet space in between."

Cecil let out a breath. "Thanks, Saint Hildegard."

"Sorry," Anne said. "I tend to get carried away. Anyway, Adam is still Adam regardless of what happens in his life. He's here now, unchanged, regardless of AD."

I crouched in front of Adam's wheelchair. "Do you hear that, my friend? You're still Adam inside and always will be. We love you, and we're here for you. So, don't give up."

He didn't respond.

"You said that Adam has forgotten about what happened in the past," I said, "so maybe he'll also forget what he experienced here."

Adam looked at me and then looked away. I felt encouraged by this small gesture.

"His name isn't Adam," Cecil said. "It's Russell."

"Not anymore," Anne said. "He renamed himself as a sign that he accepted the new person he was becoming. AD forced him to forget the man he thought he was and make room for the man he actually was."

Cecil closed his eyes, releasing a stream of tears.

I searched for a flicker of life in the man slumped in the wheelchair in front of me. "Adam, it's up to you."

If he heard me, it didn't show.

"Let's get him out of here," Cecil said.

☽☽☽

We'd been on the road for nearly an hour, and Adam hadn't spoken a word. Cecil, who was at the wheel—a rented Mercedes E-class Sedan this time, instead of a Harley—kept peering at his father through the rear-view mirror. I sat next to Adam in the back seat, occasionally glancing out the window at the abundance of pines, ferns, and wildflowers speeding by.

"It'll be okay, Ce Ce," Claudia said from the front passenger seat.

I felt Adam stiffen at my side. "Ce Ce?" he said.

Cecil swung his head around, nearly losing control of the car. Gravel shot up from the shoulder of the road and splayed the sedan on all sides. Cecil corrected the wheel, and with a series of short thumps, got the vehicle on the pavement again.

"Pull over, Cecil," I said, grabbing hold of Adam's hand and giving it a squeeze. "Don't let his lucid moment pass."

Cecil did so and turned in his seat. "Hey Pops, remember how you used to call me banana head?"

"Banana head," Adam said.

"And how Mom said she'd kick my butt if I didn't behave."

"Kathleen," Adam said.

"And she called *you* potato head."

"Potato head."

"Especially when you wore those silly navigator glasses."

262

"Dork," he said.

"Yeah, you looked like a dork."

"Ce Ce?"

"Yeah, Pops, that's me."

"Take me home."

Cecil's hand shook on the steering wheel. "Okay, Dad. Will do."

Adam leaned back against the seat and closed his eyes.

☽☽☽

Adam stared at his campsite as if seeing it for the first time. That is, until Buster ran up and nearly him knocked down. "That a boy," Adam said, patting the coyote on the head.

"We got you a bigger tent," Cecil said, his voice unsteady.

Adam walked up to the tent and ducked inside. Cecil had been careful to purchase duplicates of everything destroyed by the vandals, including Adam's cot and sleeping bag.

We held our collective breath as though the slightest inhale or exhale would shatter the protective bubble we had tried so hard to produce.

Adam came out of the tent carrying his ring of keys. He held it up to the light and smiled. I'd placed the keys on his pillow, next to his God jar—which had miraculously survived the destruction to his campsite—hoping they would bring back good memories. Although the only key that would be of use to him now was love. "They're heavy," he said and put them into his pocket. He then pointed toward the tent next to his.

Cecil placed a hand on his shoulder. "That's for Claudia and me. We're staying with you for a while."

Adam scratched his head and headed for the grotto.

"Shit," Cecil said, hurrying after him.

Anne, Claudia, and I stayed behind, caught in a state of suspension.

At first, there was silence. Then, "Kathleen! Anthony! Where are you?"

He had remembered after all.

"Cecil's with him. He'll be okay," Claudia said with a frown that contradicted her words.

"Come on," Anne said. "Let's lend them our support."

Cecil and Adam sat shoulder-to-shoulder near the bank of the pool of water.

"Talk to me," Cecil said. And miraculously, Adam did. His words didn't all make sense, but Cecil seemed to follow along just fine. Adam talked about Kathleen and Anthony, how they had played together and how much he loved them. He talked about leaving home so he wouldn't burden his beloved son Ce Ce. He talked about losing his mind.

"I never thought I'd see the day when Cecil would let down his guard in this way," Claudia said. "He's really a good person, once you get past his tough exterior. Aggression is his way of defending against rejection."

Anne and I shared a look. You bet it was a surprise to see this new side of Cecil.

"He tends to use up all the energy around him, making people feel like he's sucking them dry."

"Including you?" I asked in a tone meant to express understanding rather than judgment.

Claudia looked at me as though she sensed that I knew exactly how this felt. "It shows, huh?"

"Let's go fix lunch," I said.

We left father and son alone—together.

Chapter Thirty-Four

S NUG IN MY FLANNEL-LINED sleeping bag, I welcomed the ease with which sleep overtook me.

I am standing alone in the center of a large Medicine Wheel, the flicker of candles the only source of light. Trees, thick and wet, surround me like motionless sentinels. As I squint into the black night, my heartbeat aligns with the energetic beat of the Earth. A new sense of awareness warns that change is on the way. I anticipate that change with excitement instead of fear. I even know the direction from which it would come: West.

"Marjorie." The voice sounded familiar. "Wake up."

I didn't want to wake up. I wanted to go deeper.

"Marjorie," the voice said again. "It's cold out here. I'm coming in."

I grabbed my flashlight and switched it on.

"Stop that!" Veronica said. "You're blinding me."

I brought the flashlight to my thumping chest. "What are you trying to do, give me a heart attack?"

"Make room," she said, wrapped in what appeared to be the comforter from her bungalow bed. Someone was in for a big dry-cleaning bill.

I scooted my sleeping bag over as far as the tent would allow.

Veronica touched my shoulder with a trembling hand. "We need to talk."

About time she instigated the conversation for a change.

"Antonia. She" —Veronica took a deep breath— "she told me to get my head on straight. At least that was the gist of it."

Good for you, Mother. "She did?"

Veronica positioned her comforter next to my sleeping bag. "I knew, just knew, she wasn't through with us."

News flash. Why do you think I've been hanging out in a wet, foggy, and not all that comfortable campground, rather than hightailing it home to Morgan and Joshua? Like it or not, Antonia and her two daughters had unfinished business to attend to. "She's waiting for us to pay attention. I mean, really pay attention."

"I thought we were already doing that," Veronica said. "What more does she want?"

"Well, for one thing, we've been scurrying around and missing out on much of what's important."

Veronica's intake of breath hastened me to add, "Before you get all pushed out of shape, notice that I'm including myself here. It feels safe keeping too busy for emotional commitment."

Veronica tucked the edges of the comforter underneath her. "I have my career to think of, thank you."

I turned off the flashlight. "Oh gee, and I thought it was something important."

"My future happens to be important to me," she said.

"You need the money?"

"What's money got to do with it?"

"Then why?"

She squirmed in her sleeping bag. "Why what?"

"Why do you disappear all the time?"

"I don't like attachments or commitments. They feel like chains."

The conversation was making me ache. I, too, craved freedom from attachments and commitments. But during my stay in Carmel Valley, I realized that to be completely free, I would have to stay single—and alone—all of my life. Which wasn't an option. Not after falling in love with Joshua, Morgan, and Veronica. Life would be empty—intolerable—without them.

"I suppose that includes me," I said.

Veronica didn't answer.

"Ben, too?"

"Especially Ben. Love scares the crap out of me."

The tent lit up as if someone had switched on a spotlight.

Seconds later, a clap of thunder.

"Sounds like we've really pissed Mom off," Veronica said.

My laugh sounded hoarse. "Guess she doesn't want us to continue on this way."

"You mean unloved...the way she was?"

Ben loves you. I love you. "Why, Veronica? Why are you so skittish about emotional commitment? You're free, independent, and strong. I feel the power of your energy whenever I'm around you. You inspire me."

"Seems there are some things you don't know," she said.

Another flash of light. Darkness. More thunder.

"About our father?" I asked.

"Yes."

"Did he hurt you?" *Please say no.*

"Not physically." Veronica's words were nearly drowned out by another clap of thunder. "It was the way he looked at me. I understand, now. I'm a duplicate of our mother, and he loved her in his own selfish way."

"The guilt must have been unbearable," I said, trying to understand what my father and Veronica had gone through.

"And the pain," Veronica spat out.

Lightening, brighter than before.

"Darn it, Veronica, you said he didn't hurt you."

Veronica made a cackling sound. "I sensed something wasn't right from the time I was small. As did my step-mother. And she resented me for it. Though, bless her heart, she never took it out on me in a noticeable way."

My insides rumbled along with the thunder. "Anne told me that withholding love is a form of punishment."

Veronica sighed into the momentary silence. "Anne must have suffered to know that."

"I think she has."

Veronica touched my hand.

"I was dreaming when you woke me up," I said. "About a big change. Coming from the West."

The tent lit up. Seconds later, a blast of thunder seemed to explode on top of us.

"Shit," Veronica said. "That's what Antonia told me."

I squeezed Veronica's hand and held tight. "Then we're in this one together, Sis."

☽☽☽

Next morning, I woke with a start. Veronica was no longer lying next to me. Gone again.

The smell of coffee, bacon, and eggs.

Veronica singing, "Row, row, row your boat..."

Not gone after all.

I rolled out of my sleeping bag, fumbled into my clothes, and crawled out of the tent, which suddenly felt too small to contain me. What had previously served as a sanctuary, now whispered of confinement. I was ready to break free, test my wet wings.

"Thank you, God," I said, "she cooks, too."

Veronica checked out my disheveled state and grimaced. "I don't live on a starvation diet if that's what you mean."

"Considering our eating habits, you'd think one of us would be fat," I said, giving her a head-to-toe once over.

"Maybe you've been torturing yourself for nothing," Veronica said. "I've got the perfect metabolism, and since we're twins—"

"Okay, then, give me the works." Just thinking of all the delectable treats I'd given up over the years made me want to cry.

Veronica mounded my plate with scrambled eggs and bacon. Then added a bagel, spread with at least half an inch of cream cheese. "Why have all this crap in your ice chest if you don't plan on eating it?" I didn't answer, too busy drooling over the breakfast in front of me. "Anyway, how's Adam?" she asked.

"Ah, so you do care about him," I said.

"Give me a break. I hardly even know the guy."

"Then why'd you ask?"

"Here," she said, shoving the plate at me.

"Someone vandalized Adam's camp and grotto," I said. "All of his statues were destroyed."

"Not *all* of them," Veronica said.

My egg-laden fork froze in midair.

"I've got connections with the DEA, remember?"

You said you were still in the pre-acceptance stage. Screenings, examinations, assessments, and background checks. That's not exactly what I'd call having connections."

"A special agent in the San Jose resident office recognized the name on my DEA application due to my undercover work in Carmel Valley. Seems not many people volunteer to put their lives in danger for free. Anyway, when he read that I was temporarily staying at Pfeiffer State Park, he introduced me to the little bastards who were responsible for the vandalism of Adam's camp. Apparently, they were booked on an unrelated charge."

"Drugs?"

"Meth bust."

I shivered. We'd bathed naked, not far from where the vandalism took place. "How'd the DEA know that the delinquents they arrested for meth were involved with Adam?"

"Because the twerps had the amputated head of one of his sculptures in their possession."

"But how did any of you know it was Adam's work, when you never saw it before?"

"The face on that head looked exactly like me. Minus the eyes, of course."

"Antonia."

"Yep. According to the special agent, the pranksters thought the head looked spooky, sort of fit into their odd take on life. You should've seen the look on their faces when I walked in. Oh, Lordy, what a sight."

I grinned, appreciating the humor of the situation.

"The employees at the resident office kept staring at me, and, for the life of me, I didn't know how to explain. So, I didn't. Which adds to my mystique."

I laughed. She probably drove them crazy with curiosity. "I'm surprised the head didn't crumble when it was removed."

"Yeah, pretty amazing."

"Adam must've used sturdier clay from some other location," I mused. "According to Anne, the quality and texture of the mud varies depending on where it comes from. Maybe it can even be... Oh my gosh, you should show it to Anne and—"

"Not so fast. The DEA can only release it to Adam or Cecil."

I took a bite of the scrambled eggs. Cold, but delicious anyway, adding to the warm satisfaction I felt inside.

Veronica set down her still empty plate and jabbed it with her fork. Plastic hit Styrofoam with a popping sound. "Life sure has taken a turn for the strange and unexplainable. Either we're crazy or very different, Sis, and I don't like either explanation."

"It would be nice to feel normal again," I said.

"You bet it would."

"Except then we'd be stuck in our own separate ruts," I said. "Unaware of what life was really all about."

Veronica stood and dumped her plate into a large plastic bag. "I'm still unaware. How about you?"

"I thought I'd find myself here, but—"

Veronica appeared to be hanging onto my words as if they held untold significance.

"I've taken such baby steps. I tried to rush it, but couldn't."

"So, what have you learned?" Veronica asked, holding out the plastic bag.

I tossed in my trash. "That it's not just about me."

Chapter Thirty-Five

THE LOOK ON CECIL'S FACE when Veronica and I walked into Adam's camp made me smile. I swear, his eyes practically bulged out of their sockets.

"Holy crap," he said, "there's two of you."

"Double the trouble," Veronica said as she surveyed the group sitting around the crackling fire. She nodded at Anne and Claudia before her gaze settled on Adam.

From Claudia's rapt expression as she scrutinized my sister, it was obvious that she sensed Veronica's power and strength. Sometimes I forget how truly commanding my twin is. "Veronica has some good news," I said.

The attention already focused on my sister grew expectant. She shrugged. "All in the line of duty."

I gave her an impatient nudge. "Tell them."

"The DEA apprehended the delinquents who destroyed your campsite," Veronica said, addressing Adam, "and were able to re-claim the head of one of your sculptures."

Adam smiled at Veronica. Not, I assumed, because he under-stood what she was saying, but because she was directing her an-nouncement to him.

"The sculpture appears to be of—"

"Antonia!" Adam said.

Veronica blinked, momentarily speechless.

"He thinks you're Antonia," I said.

"Who's Antonia?" Cecil asked.

"Sorry," Veronica said when she noticed the tears running down Cecil's face. "I didn't mean to make you cry."

He held up his hand, shook his head. "Who's Antonia?"

"Our mother," I said.

"Your—"

"We'll clue you in later," I said, hesitant to clarify. There was a limit to the amount of information he and Claudia could be expected to absorb all at once. Especially when it came to the unexplainable.

"Would you care to accompany me to claim the property?" Veronica asked Cecil.

He wiped his eyes. "And bring it back here?"

"Marjorie thinks Adam might have used some kind of special clay for this piece and that maybe it can be fired," Veronica said.

Anne pushed to a stand. "I'll go along and check it out. If it's salvageable, we can stop at the studio on the way back and keep it there for safekeeping."

With that, Veronica, Cecil, and Anne were off, leaving Claudia, Adam, and me behind.

The camp was meticulously organized, the surroundings cool and serene. Insects buzzed, birds called, water flowed, and the scent of pine and fermenting soil carried in the breeze. Claudia took the opportunity to probe me with questions about my sister. Apparently, Veronica's power and independence fascinated her. Like me, Claudia had spent far too many years under someone else's thumb. The door to her cage stood open. She was perched at the threshold. Would she remember how to fly?

While Claudia and I talked, Adam moved to the grotto. We paused our conversation to check on him, only to find him sitting beneath a sheet of sunlight, facing the trickling pond, head bowed, as though worshipping at a shrine commemorating his encounter with God.

"I agree that being surrounded by nature is good for Adam," Claudia said, "but Cecil can't stay much longer. He has already stretched his away time to the limit. Turning off his phone was a novelty, but..."

"Does he need the money?" I asked, repeating my earlier question to Veronica.

"When it comes to money, and power, there's never enough," Claudia said.

"And there never will be."

Claudia smiled. "I'm beginning to suspect that's true. Cecil needs to keep adding to himself in order to be himself. He's deathly afraid of losing. In his eyes, losing makes him less of a man." She drew in a deep breath. "He's wealthy, but when it comes to true wealth, he might as well be a pauper. It breaks my heart to see him look outside of himself for fulfillment and validation." A quick glance at Adam. "What does all that money and power amount to in the end?"

"It may keep Adam out of a nursing home," I said.

She gripped her hands together. "Yes, but for how long?"

I had no answer for that.

Adam turned to face us, a soundless acknowledgment of our presence. Claudia's eyes filled with tears. "Cecil wants to take his father home."

"That may be best," I said.

"Cecil loves his father and is hurt, really hurt, by what he sees as Adam's desertion. That he turned to Anne, a complete stranger, rather than to his own son during his time of need is, to Cecil, incomprehensible and unforgivable. Adam left behind a lot of unresolved emotional baggage, and, now it seems, it's too late to do anything about it. Two, hard-headed men haven't been able to break the wall of misunderstanding that separates them or express their love for each another."

Talk about hard-headed, she could've been talking about my adoptive mother and me.

"Adam's got a lovely place, you know. It's too big for him now, but a lot can be done to rearrange things." Claudia looked around for a moment, then continued, her voice lifting a notch. "We could build him a grotto like this one. He could keep Buster, even the tent."

They would probably need a special permit to keep a coyote on the premises, but I didn't say so. They would figure that out for themselves soon enough. "Sounds ideal."

"Yes, doesn't it," Claudia said.

☽☽☽

Cecil returned with an announcement. "Anne says the sculpture of Antonia's head can be fired, which means we'll have one more reminder of Dad's tremendous talent."

"And love," I said, wishing there was a way for Adam to express his deep affection for his son as he had only been able to do in his journal and through his art. I had a sense that the kindest thing we could do for him now was to help him say goodbye to his beloved son, and the kindest thing we could do for Cecil was to help him hear it.

Anne glanced from Claudia to me. "Why so down?"

Claudia shrugged. "We were just talking."

"About Adam?" Cecil asked, a touch of irritation in his voice.

Claudia's shoulders tensed.

Was it habit for her to stiffen this way when Cecil frowned at her, or did she feel hesitant about expressing her opinion?

Silently, yet with all the energy I could muster, I urged her to speak up and share what was on her mind.

She looked at Cecil with a lift of her chin. "We're worried about your father."

"I've already discussed it with Anne," Cecil said. "We're taking him home."

"I figured you would," Claudia said, "and I think that's a good idea, but... I think something has been left undone."

Anne stood next to Adam, watching him play with Buster. "I agree."

"Cecil," I said. "There's no doubt your father wants to be with you and that he's not thinking clearly enough to see himself as a burden anymore. But something has changed in him, and I'm not sure he'll get it back."

"Maybe I could take him on a cruise to Alaska," Cecil said. "He always wanted to see—"

"No," Anne said.

"How about therapy? We can afford the best."

Anne smiled, but shook her head.

"Then what?" he asked.

"How about we perform one of Anne's rituals?" I said.

Everyone stared at me in silence. No problem. I was following my gut, letting it speak. "The problem with Adam is spiritual, right?"

"Yes," Anne conceded.

"Then we need a spiritual solution."

Silence.

"During my time at the Esalen Institute, our Gestalt workshop instructor said that when a group finds cohesion, magic occurs. By performing a ritual together, we could focus our collective attention on helping Adam resolve any internal conflicts he may have and allow for what's most right, when it comes to his disease."

After what felt like a long silence, Veronica said, "I'm the first to admit that the rituals Anne introduced me to during my stay here stretch my concept of reality. But if it helps Adam in some way, I'm in."

"What kind of ritual?" Claudia asked.

Veronica laughed. "Girl, sometimes it's best not to ask too many questions and just go with the flow."

"Anne combines a variety of time-tested spiritual practices with roots in numerous religions," I said, "that fit her unique sense of connection and which she's now willing to share, if we're willing to bypass our—"

"Anne's a witch," Veronica said, "who uses Wiccan rituals to open a crack in the door to our minds."

Claudia brought her hand to her throat.

"The rituals Anne performs can help us send our wishes into the mental atmosphere that surrounds us," I added, "which is receptive to our thoughts and meant to be used. In short, her rituals are a form of prayer."

I couldn't tell if Anne was amused or offended by Veronica and my quick summaries of the spiritual pathway that fed her soul.

"You don't have to participate if you don't want to," she said. "And neither do you, Cecil."

"Me?" Cecil said. "I wouldn't miss it for the world."

☽☽☽

"Why witchcraft, when there are so many spiritual practices to choose from?" Claudia asked as we gathered around the campfire for our evening meal. Cecil had prepared a feast of baked potatoes, corn on the cob, and barbecued ribs.

"Why not witchcraft?" Anne countered as she filled up her plate.

Claudia straightened her shoulders and proceeded to present all the reasons why not, including how it was one of the least understood practices of our time.

Between mouthfuls of food and the waving of hands and plastic utensils, Anne and Claudia argued, debated, and eventually came back to, "Why not?"

"Okay," Claudia said. "Do what you have to. I'll participate through prayer."

"Fair enough," Anne said. "We're all praying to the same Source, anyway. 'When two or more are gathered in my name...'"

Claudia closed her eyes. "I can't believe this is happening."

Veronica laughed. "Believe."

Chapter Thirty-Six

IT WAS IMPOSSIBLE not to appreciate the sheet of sunlight piercing through the redwoods, cottonwoods, and big-leaf maples lining the pond near where we sat. I raised my hands as though seeking the sun's blessing on what we were about to do.

Only a few months before, I would have been horrified at the very thought of participating in a Wiccan ceremony. All I knew about witches came from television and movies, children's stories and fairytales. I had no idea until Anne clued me in that Wicca was one of the fastest growing religions in the United States, that it honored a deity divided into male and female spirituality known as God and Goddess, and that it gave reverence to the Earth. Now, I was about to join Anne, Veronica, and Cecil in a *magick* circle, in hopes of sharing with Adam our combined love, energy, and intent and help him allow for what was most right when it came to his spirituality and his disease.

"Big Sur is an unusually powerful place," Anne said, drawing me out of my reverie. No argument there. The area's geophysics, if nothing else, made it a healing place. Anne stood and turned to Claudia. "If you'd like to learn more about the *magick* circle, you can help me set one up now."

"Knowledge is power," Claudia said.

I started to rise from my crouch next to Cecil, but Anne waved me back down. "Since you've already taken your ritual bath and are wearing—" she rolled her eyes "—your bath robe, better stay put."

Anne wore the usual white velvet cloak, impractical for outdoors, but impressive as far as rituals go. She handed Claudia a broom and put her to work cleansing the sacred space for the circle.

"I can understand why Claudia won't participate," Cecil said with what sounded like admiration in his voice. "She's Catholic, you know."

"That might actually be a good thing," I said.

Cecil threw me a sideways glance and raised brow that appeared to question my sanity. Couldn't blame him. I'd been doing my own share of sanity questioning lately. "The Catholic religion accustoms its congregants to ritual," I said. "See the way Anne is walking around the circle with a bowl of water, cleansing and consecrating the ground?"

He glanced her way, but I could tell by the restless movement of his hands that he was only partially listening.

"On occasion, Catholic priests walk into the congregation and mist holy water over the parishioners to bless them and cleanse them of their sins. Now, check out the way Anne's carrying the censer with smoldering incense in it. Catholic priests do that, too, as a form of spiritual cleansing. I've come to love the sweet, cloying scent of the burning resins. They're a mild sedative, you know."

Cecil shifted his weight and stretched his leg. "Do the priests walk in circles?"

I nodded. "I've seen them walk around the altar and around a coffin. And see that altar in the middle of Anne's circle?"

"Okay, I get it," Cecil said.

"Did you enjoy your ritual bath?" I asked, feeling the urge to rib him a bit. How tame today's dip in Adam's pond had been compared to my immersion in the creek with Veronica and Anne twelve days before. This time we'd worn bathing suits. This time, we'd only sprinkled ourselves with water. And this time, we'd run for cover as soon as the cold set in.

"Nearly froze my ass off," Cecil said. "Damn, I wish that blasted wind would let up."

"It's only a breeze, you wimp."

"When that witch-saint-pal of yours tried to make us wear those spooky velvet capes, like damn Halloween costumes, and put on *magickal* jewelry, I nearly called the whole thing off."

"*Magickal* clothing and jewelry help focus the mind," I said. "They create a mood and enhance energy."

"Bathrobes work just fine, thank you." Cecil twisted around and frowned at Anne. "No wonder Claudia's nervous. She thinks we've all lost our marbles."

"She's stronger than you give her credit for," I said.

"She's full of surprises, that's for sure."

I studied the handsome man I hadn't been able to stomach only days before. He needed a haircut and shave. He was letting himself go. "Aren't we all?"

Veronica, Adam, and Buster lay on an area of wild grass a short distance from where Cecil and I sat, absorbing the last rays of sunshine. Crows, jays, and blackbirds flitted around them looking for food and voicing their complaints at not finding any. It struck me that the crow's wings only show their iridescence when hit just right by rays of the sun That's when you see that they're not really black. They only appear black to the blind.

"It's time," Anne called.

Cecil practically leapt to a stand. "Summoned at last."

Veronica and Adam trailed behind as we headed for the ceremonial site.

"Claudia has opted to stay outside the circle," Anne said as the four of us reached her side. "She knows she can't enter it later. Doing that would break the circle and allow whatever energy is in it to get out. The same goes for those inside. Once in, we can't leave until the ritual is over. We must hold in our personal power until we're ready to release it."

We all nodded, except Adam, who stared over Anne's shoulder.

"What about Buster?" I asked.

"He stays outside of the circle with Claudia," Anne said. "Got that, Claudia? Don't let him into the circle."

"Got it," Claudia said.

"How do *we* get into the circle?" Veronica asked.

Anne raised the double-edged knife she held in her hand. It had a black handle and was at least six inches long. "With this *athame*, I'll cut a door in the energy that makes up the circle and then seal it once we're inside."

The frown on Veronica's face suggested that her "openness to the new" was being stretched to the limit. Her sense of humor, the little there was of it, seemed to have evaporated.

"Claudia and Buster can guard the door," Anne said.

"From what?" Claudia asked.

"From anything that approaches our circle."

"Like what?" she asked.

"Squirrels, chipmunks—"

"Skunks and bears," Cecil added.

Claudia bit her lip.

"Don't let Cecil's teasing get to you Claudia," Anne said. "Soon it'll be too dark for you to see much beyond the circle. Consider it a symbolic job."

Claudia gave Buster a pat on the head. "We could always use the broom for protection, right boy?"

Once Veronica, Cecil, Adam, and I were seated within the circle, Anne said, "The moon is waning, a good time to get rid of the negative things in your life. I wish we had the power to get rid of Adam's illness, but we don't." She paused and winked at Adam. He responded with a slight narrowing of his eyes. "But we may have enough power between us to help him in some other way yet to be discovered.

"We summon the energies of earth, water, fire, and air to join in our ritual. We summon the archangels—Michael, Gabriel, Uriel and Raphael—to watch over us and protect us. We summon the spirit of the trees to help us bend, forgive, and adapt. We summon our Lord, God, and our mother, Mary. And finally, we summon our ancestors, Antonia and Katherine."

Adam jerked at the sound of his wife's name.

"Everything is energy," Anne continued, "a rock, water, wood...our bodies... And we're all part of the huge energy field of the universe. The repercussions of our thoughts and actions ripple out, connecting us to all things, including the higher realm. We must send our intentions to our subconscious minds and to the spirit."

I closed my eyes and tilted my head to the darkening sky.

"We need to build our energy into a cone of power," Anne said, her voice hypnotic. "Let's concentrate on our outcome. See it as happening in your mind." She started to beat a drum. "Let our energy build."

With Anne's rhythmic beating, I thought about Adam. What did I want for him? A cure? No, that was impossible. Peace? Tranquility? Reconciliation? Yes. I wanted father and son to bond and heal while there was still time. And I wanted for Adam and Cecil to find peace.

Anne put down the drum. I opened my eyes. She struck a match and leaned over the altar. "With the lighting of this candle, I will direct all our stored energy out to do our work."

It was nearly dark. I could barely make out the faces of those in our circle, let alone that of Claudia, sitting in the beyond. I rubbed the mouse totem in my robe pocket, Joshua's gift, a reminder to touch—and be touched by—my surroundings. Night wind whispered through the vast energetic field that surrounded us. I took a deep breath and exhaled, imagining a cord of light energy descended from the base of my spine into the core of the Earth, and the Earth's energy traveling back up that cord into my body.

"My father told me I was a loser," Cecil said, "and that I wouldn't amount to shit!"

Now, that was unexpected. I waited for Anne to reprimand him, but she remained silent.

Okay, so I knew how much it hurt to have a parent attack me verbally, but, somehow, I thought Cecil was above such hurt. I peered through the dimness at Adam's downcast face and couldn't reconcile him with the image Cecil portrayed.

Veronica blew out her breath. "Dr. Jekyll and Mr. Hyde."

"I proved him wrong, though," Cecil said in a strangled voice. "An empty victory, since he no longer knows or cares."

Adam looked at Cecil, but said nothing.

"What Dad? Not even a tear of regret?"

Adam stared at his son, but remained silent.

An owl hooted. What a lonely sound.

Cecil threw up his hands. "What's the use?"

"Exactly," Anne said. "There's no going back. The only way is forward. The Adam behind the false mask that he once presented to the world is still here with us now, the Adam behind the ego. We have with us his spirit and soul, alert and conscious, not bogged down by guilt, regret, or disease."

Could it be true? Was Adam's spirit aware of what was going on? Was it above and beyond guilt and regret? Was that fair?

"Oh God," Claudia screeched from beyond the circle.

I jerked and turned in the direction of her voice.

Buster growled.

Cecil leapt to his feet.

"Stay put," Anne said, blocking Cecil with her outstretched hand. "Don't leave the circle."

"What is it, Claudia?" Cecil asked.

The swoosh of a broom. "Stay back!"

Anne stood. "Calm down, hon. You've got Buster. Anyway, she won't hurt you."

"She?" Claudia shrieked.

"Come closer to the circle, Claudia, so we can see you."

A dark shape scampered toward us.

"Thatta girl. Now sit and close your eyes. Try to ignore what's happening."

Claudia huddled near the edge of the circle and appeared to make the sign of the cross. It was too dark to see if she'd closed her eyes.

"Are you okay?" Anne asked.

"Yes," she said, her voice trembling.

"Have you closed your eyes?"

"No. I want to watch."

Anne sighed. "Is Buster there with you?"

Right on cue, Buster gave a high-pitched whine.

"Then let's be still and wait."

Had Antonia come to participate in our ritual? Did she and Adam share space in the depths of the Sacred that couldn't be grasped with the eye or the mind, only the heart? Trouble was, we hadn't yet explained to Cecil and Claudia who Antonia was and her deep connection to Adam in another realm.

It takes a huge stretch of faith to put yourself in the hands of the invisible, but I was willing to try. In order to reach through the portal in the fabric of time to the level of awareness where Antonia's consciousness dwelled, I would have to quit trying to figure everything out. I would have to open my heart, open my mind, and relax into a trusting, effortless state of being. In other words, in order to touch the energy of the Universe, I would have to stop being who I thought I was.

Like Adam.

As I refocused on the flickering candle and watched the small stream of smoke waver, I allowed myself to fall into the space of alignment, deeper, deeper into the depths of consciousness, deeper, deeper into the unifying field underlying physical existence. I bypassed my shadow self, the naysayer, the judge, the blamer. Deeper, deeper. No more quivering, no more stammering, no more stuttering. I had a story, but I was not my story. I was the detritus on the forest floor, necessary for the birth and survival of Antonia's message. Whatever that message might be.

I felt the force of my mother's presence extend from outside the circle as if an invisible chord stretched beyond and through the boundaries between us. I heard what sounded like a thousand cricket wings rubbing together. Power surged inside me, filling a space that was once empty. No more weeping, no more doubting, no more questions. No more forcing the situation. I would accept whatever I could decode from Antonia's message. No more. No less. And then move forward from there.

"Antonia?" Adam's voice reached my ears, but didn't pull me from the place of pure consciousness, where emotions, body, and the external world recede.

"Why did you come?" Adam asked.

Silence.

"No, you don't owe me anything," Adam said.

I couldn't hear what Antonia was saying, which was okay. This wasn't about me.

"Ce Ce?" Adam said. "No. He's not here."

A groan from Cecil's direction; the only indication that he'd heard his father's words.

"Ce-Ce?" Adam asked. "Here?"

"Yes, Dad, it's me," Cecil said.

"Son?"

"Yes, Dad."

"It's him," Adam cried. "Antonia, it's my boy! He's back!"

"I see something," Claudia screamed. "It's...it's—"

Buster's bark covered up what she was about to say.

"Hush, Buster," Anne said. The coyote obeyed. "Claudia, Antonia won't hurt you."

"Antonia? Who's Antonia?"

"We'll explain later," Anne said.

"My dear son," Adam said as though he were as lucid as the rest of us, instead of experiencing the later stages of AD. "If I failed you, I ask for your forgiveness."

What must Cecil be thinking and feeling on hearing his father's words?

It broke my heart to consider that I had misinterpreted my adoptive mother's love for me as manipulative and overbearing, when she, like Adam, had only been parenting the best way she knew how. She must have felt abandoned when Antonia began speaking to me and taking up all the room in my heart. No wonder the name calling, the anger.

"I love you more than life itself," Adam said, "and always will."

"I love you, too, Dad," Cecil said, his voice a broken whisper.

When my stay at Big Sur was over, I would cut Truus some slack and show her my appreciation for the good mother she was. *I love you mother. I love both mothers.*

"Call me by name and speak to me about your daily life," Adam said. "I will hear you."

Cecil started to sob and embraced his father.

Another surge of energy. Time stilled. Boundaries dissolved. It felt as though Antonia were embracing me, too, yet passing through me, leaving love in her wake.

Don't try to grasp or understand, I told myself, *just feel.*

Veronica and I will do our best to live the life you missed out on, Mother. We'll feel the sun on our skin for you. We'll sing and dance for you. We'll marry and have children and feel love for you.

Antonia began to cry, but this time it had a joyful sound, rather than that of unabated grief. Veronica slid next to me and took hold of my hand.

"Sunwalker," Adam said. "You need to talk to your father."

He paused as if waiting for further instructions. "Ask him—"

Veronica tightened her grip on my hand. "Our father? What the hell does he have to do with all this?"

Silence.

Chills and goose bumps coated my skin. I listened with my body as if it were my ears.

Fallen Light, Antonia said. *Ask your father about Fallen Light.*

"She wants us to ask our father about Fallen Light," I said.

Veronica gripped my hand so tightly I thought it would break. "Fallen Light? Who or what—?"

You must complete the circle.

"She wants us to complete the circle."

"What circle?" Veronica asked.

The sound of cricket wings rubbing together began to fade. As did the connection I felt to my mother. But power continued to surge through me—electrifying power—in the form of love.

Rest in peace, Antonia

The pain shooting up my arm reminded me that Veronica was still clutching my hand.

"What was that all about," she asked, releasing her grip.

I shook my hand to regain its circulation. "Seems you need to introduce me to our father."

Her reply, "Dear God, give me strength."

Chapter Thirty-Seven

I HAD BEEN IN BIG SUR for over seven weeks now and had experienced only three days where the temperature reached past the seventies. And this wasn't one of them. Veronica and I sat at a table in the Big Sur Lodge restaurant staring at the remnants of our breakfast. Neither of us had been hungry. My sister wore her hair in a slack ponytail. Her eyes appeared large and vulnerable without the distraction of shadow, liner, and mascara. Emotions played across her face that I'd never witnessed before, as if our mother's strange request to ask our father about Fallen Light had stripped her of a mask behind which she'd been hiding.

"Why'd Antonia have to meddle in our lives this way?" she asked. "This'll change things. Forever."

Antonia's so-called meddling had brought about change all right. Like a flash flood that sweeps you up in its current and carries you to destinations not of your choosing. I hated change. It made me feel vulnerable, off balance. But our mother had made one request—just one. How could we ignore it?

I eyed my sister's unusual attire. The fact that she even owned pink sweats meant she had a soft side, which gave me hope that we could be friends—as well as sisters. I put my hands over hers, amazed at how cold they felt. Mid-morning or not, the best place for her right now was in bed. "We'll talk some other time."

"You mean it?"

"Darn right, I mean it. Let's get you back to your room so you can lie down."

She looked like she might float away, and I'd wake up to discover this had all been a dream and that I didn't have a sister after all.

"Come on," I said. "I'll tuck you in."

☽☽☽

Anne was waiting for me at her campsite dressed in wide-leg chino pants that looked at least a size too big, a heavy black overcoat, and a matching knit beanie. You would think she'd just raided a distribution center for the homeless.

What was going on here? First, Veronica switching from black leather to pink sweats and now Anne trading in her boho skirts and sandals for safari-type clothing and army boots.

She sat in front of her camp stove, humming a tune I didn't recognize and steeping a cup of what appeared to be tea. She waved me over. "Hey girl. How about taking the edge off with a synergistic shot of theanine?"

Theanine? I blew out a puff of air, which fogged the front of my face like a cloud of grievance. "Only if it's tea you're offering and only if you have something non-organic to go with it."

She pulled out a bag of assorted chocolate miniatures. "For special occasions, I keep certain foods on hand that don't quite make the health food grade."

Special occasions? What did she have up her sleeve this time?

She tossed me a Milky Way *Midnight Dark* chocolate. It plopped at my feet. "Cecil's taking Adam home," she said, "and I'm going along as his nurse."

I stared at her, unable to muster a sense of joy at the news. What had I expected? That she and Adam would stay here forever, while I came and went as I pleased?

"Cecil did some checking, but couldn't find anyone trained in the holistic and spiritual aspects of Alzheimer's. He could've saved himself the trouble if he had asked me first, but... Oh well, it looks like I'm in. Being an oddball, a renegade, a traitor to the medical community makes me a perfect fit for the job."

"You're a renegade, all right."

"Coming from you, that's a compliment." Her words held the humor mine lacked. She looked me up and down. "You okay?"

I tore open the Milky Way's silver and black wrapper and popped the bite-sized chocolate into my mouth, resulting in a euphoric rush, taste buds tingling. Leave it to Anne to have comfort food on hand when most needed. "When do you leave?"

Anne tossed more candy my way, as though they possessed some kind of pain-blocking super powers. "In a couple of days. Cecil's arranging things as we speak."

I stared at the cheerful heap of chocolates.

"They live in Los Angeles," she said.

I shuddered at the thought. Traffic congestion, smog, Santa Ana winds, earthquakes, flooding, wildfires, crime. "In the city?"

"Bel Air, actually."

"Oh." My mind automatically shifted from visions of crowds, gridlock, and shootings to ones of palatial homes in the Santa Monica Mountains, spectacular views of city and ocean—fires and Santa Ana winds.

"Cecil told me that Adam owns a Rolls Royce and his own private jet," Anne said, "and that he belongs to the Bel-Air Country Club."

Try as I might, I couldn't picture the Adam I knew surrounding himself with such things. "Not much use to him now."

"No, thank God."

"Does Cecil live like that, too?"

"Afraid so."

I thought about Cecil's yacht, his Harley, and his toffee-nosed, I'm-so-superior, attitude. "What kind of attorney is he?"

"He practices entertainment law. According to what he told me, he's one of America's top 100 power attorneys. Quite an exclusive group."

"He must be brilliant," I said grudgingly, amending my previous judgment of him as a spoiled drifter.

Anne pursed her lips. "He must understand how Hollywood works, that's for sure."

I picked up a mini Snicker and tore open its wrapper. My mother used to make a dessert called *Snickers Candy Bars*, with milk chocolate chips, butterscotch chips, peanut butter, marshmallow cream, caramels, whipping cream, and salted peanuts. It was amazing I had any teeth left. "What did Adam do for a living?"

"He was CEO and managing director of one of the fifteen talent agencies that run Hollywood. In other words, he was one of the most powerful people in the entertainment industry. From what Cecil told me, being an agent is a dirty, cutthroat business. The pressure is incredible, Hollywood being such an uncertain place."

"A spiritual desert," I said, biting into the Snicker.

"And we're taking Adam back to it a changed man," Anne said.

"Are you okay with all this?"

"Marjorie, in most cases AD leads to death in seven to ten years. Adam has already surpassed five. Soon he'll become unaware of his condition. No desires, no aversions, no hatred, no tenderness. From that point on, the one who'll suffer most is Cecil. Watching his father deteriorate will be horrifying. My job will be to provide Adam with as much security and predictability in his otherwise uncontrollable and meaningless physical surroundings. But just as importantly, if not more so, I'll try to provide Cecil with an understanding ear and heart. Pray for them both."

It took a moment for me to get words past the tightened muscles in my throat. "I really, really hate Alzheimer' disease."

"It most definitely tests the spirit," Annie said. "Be grateful that you'll be spared witnessing Adam's final days."

She was right. I'd had the good fortune of getting to know, learn from, and love Adam when I did. "Annie, I'll miss you both."

"Bet you'll never forget us."

"You've definitely opened my eyes to a thing or two."

"And you, mine."

An assortment of tea bags lay strewn on a tray. I was about to select an orange-cranberry, when Anne shooed my hand. "It's got to be green tea for that shot of theanine I promised. Relaxation without sedation." She sprang into action. "Hot water coming up."

After pouring steaming water into a mug and dropping in a bag of "the best green tea on the market, besides the loose variety, of course," Anne asked, "Have you talked to Veronica about your mother's request?"

"No chance. She looked dispirited, so I put her to bed."

"Don't discount Veronica's current disheartened mood to simple lethargy or fatigue. It may be more than that. In fact, I'm sure of it. She's going through some kind of spiritual surrender, allowing her imagination and emotions to take reign for a while. Which I'm sure is not her natural state."

Darn right it's not. Not my strong, powerful sister.

"Odd," Anne said, "for your mother to make the request she did."

"From the dead, of all things," I said. "I can't believe this. After everything our father has done to her, she still loves him and wants us to contact him."

"Apparently, he holds a secret," Anne said, motioning for me to sit in one of her shabby boho camp chairs.

I sat. Accepted her curative mug of tea. Took a sip. Not bad. "I wonder if it has anything to do with completing the circle that Antonia talked about." I paused, groping for the missing piece of the puzzle. "Something's wrong, Anne. Veronica doesn't want to take me to our father. He must be a monster."

"Is that the impression you get from her?"

The mug in my hand was shaking, so I set it next to the metal campfire ring. "She's sending out some pretty negative vibes."

"Which means another delay," Anne said.

"Or lesson. Maybe there's more for me to learn before taking that step. Speaking of which... Anne, according to what Cecil said, you can see and hear things. Can you—"

"What I see and hear is my personal cross to bear. Trust your own inner voice. It'll lead you where you need to go."

The sound of running water and wind swooshing through the lower branches of the trees added credence to her words. "I hope you're right."

"You've learned a lot during your stay here," Anne said. "I can tell even in the short time we've spent together. For one thing, you've learned to stop asking why. And you sense the deeper good in seemingly senseless situations You've also learned compassion and trust and to love more deeply. Take these lessons with you and apply them when you go to Pacific Grove to meet your father."

Cold numbed the tip of my nose and my leg was falling asleep. I uncrossed my legs and twisted in my chair to improve my circulation, then picked up my mug and took a reinforcing sip of what was left of Anne's synergistic shot of theanine. "I've learned a lot from you, Adam, and Cecil, and my brief acquaintance with Holly, Claudia, and the participants in the workshop at the Esalen Institute, but I'm not sure I'm through asking why. Do you think seekers ever become finders?"

Anne's gaze seemed to penetrate to where I hurt. "Life is not about pursuing certainty, but greater understanding."

"As far as the deeper good..."

She chuckled. "You think too much. Unhappiness and disappointments are just surface ripples. Let them pass over you. Inside, you'll be undisturbed."

"Anne, is that what Adam has done? Has he entered the place of peace within himself where his environment no longer determines his happiness? I'd like to believe that. I mean, I'd like to believe he can go on without wants and fears, without his sculptures, his grotto, and without us."

"You go, girl," Anne said. "Adam has been introduced to the presence of something that transcends our current understanding of things. He's remembering where he's from and where he's going again. Now, how about applying what he has taught you to your own situation. Enter that place of peace within yourself."

"Where my environment no longer determines my happiness?"

She nodded.

"I'll give it my best shot," I said. "If for no other reason than to help Veronica. Our mother's request to contact our father has really shaken her up. I get the feeling she needs me."

Chapter Thirty-Eight

ON ENTERING VERONICA'S room the next morning using the spare keycard she'd given me, I found her sitting on the floor next to her bed, legs pulled up to her chest, forehead resting on her knees, still wearing her pink sweats. It looked like a tornado had touched down on her bed and ripped through the rest of the room, hurling clothes, shoes, and decorative pillows in all directions. Her sheets and blankets formed a twisted heap on the center of the mattress. Her suitcase lay open in the middle of the floor. Messy, sloppy. This girl needed a personal maid. Or an intervention.

I picked up two pillows and put them on one of the armchairs facing the unlit fireplace. Her knee-to-chest pose was one of low spirits rather than one taught in a basic yoga class. "Hey, Sis." Our roles had apparently reversed. The mention of contacting our father had drained Veronica of her strength and activated mine.

"He's in Pacific Grove," she said.

"Pacific Grove," I echoed, caught off guard by her comment. "Who is?"

She lifted her head with the slightly disoriented look of someone who just woke up. Her gaze tracked my face as though she expected me to read her mind.

"Who's in Pacific Grove?" I asked.

"Our father."

My knees began to buckle. I sat on the bed. Was he tall? Was he short? Was he handsome? "So, does that mean I finally get to meet him?"

"If you want to," she said, her voice throaty, raw.

"Want to? Of course, I want to." *He's part of who I am.*

"I knew you'd react that way."

"Jeez, Veronica, I've been looking forward to this day... No, dreaming of this day, since...since—"

Veronica held up her hand. "Hold it."

Why was she acting this way? There was obviously bad news ahead. And since it concerned Veronica, and my father, it concerned me.

"He's an alcoholic," she said.

She might as well have doused me with ice water, the way my body went into chill mode. "How bad?"

"It's affecting his health."

"Cirrhosis?"

"Not that I know of, although I wouldn't be surprised. He looks a lot older than he is. He's thin and his skin..."

I stood, walked over to the door leading to the exterior deck, and opened it. A refreshing, pine-scented breeze rushed in, along with the singing of songbirds, the hammering of woodpeckers, and the harsh cackling of crows in a spirited forest symphony. However, the light was dim, due to the cloud of vapor that drifted and swirled through the neighboring redwood forest as though pumped in by a portable fog machine. I turned my attention back to Veronica and the cheerless room. "We need to help him."

Veronica picked up a pillow and punched it with her fist. "Don't you think my step-mother and I have tried? You have no idea what we've been through. And are still going through. He's a disaster."

"I'm so sorry."

After a brooding silence, Veronica said, "I think it all goes back to feelings of guilt. Of what he did to Antonia, to you, and to my stepmother."

"And to you," I said.

Veronica hesitated, then seemed to decide on something. "I've tried to detach myself from him, you know, keep an emotional distance. But he keeps pushing my buttons and hanging on. I can't make him go away. He follows me, Marjorie. At least when he's sober enough. It's amazing how much he can accomplish while under the influence."

"Why?"

"Beats me. Maybe he still thinks I'm his little girl, kind of like with you and your adoptive mother, Truus." She dropped her face into her hands. "It's as if he perceives me as his personal property and that his every wish is my command. I don't know how much more of this I can take."

Her words echoed my words to Morgan and Anne less than two weeks ago—a lifetime ago. I'd felt then as Veronica did now, as if I were in a spiritual black hole in which everything solid was vaporizing. She was in darkness, and seeing her this way broke my heart. It also pointed me toward a new purpose as I neared the end of my journey along the second path of the Native American Medicine Wheel. No more wasting my life energy on judgment and blame. No more idling in neutral, distant and emotionally uninvolved. No more wallowing in the anesthetizing fog of disconnection and a closed heart. In Big Sur, the land of my mother's people, I'd retrieved a part of myself that I'd forgotten, and now I would use that part of myself not only to fulfill her strange request to meet with my father, but to support Veronica in her search for the light.

"Does he know where you are?" I asked.

"He knows that I'm applying with the DEA."

I drew up the blinds covering the windows facing the deck. No brilliant burst of sun light, but light just the same. Softened by fog. "How?"

Veronica's laugh sounded hollow. "He's quite the detective when he puts his fuzzy mind to it. Anyway, he doesn't have anything better to do."

My chest ached at the sight of my sister, my hero, sitting there, back bowed, sinking into the feelings she'd been trying to outrun, searching for a way out of what our mother had asked us to do. But our mother must have had a reason. And we'd promised.

"Do you still want to meet him?" Veronica asked.

"Yes," I said. I couldn't keep waiting for more knowledge and more skills. I couldn't wait for more support from the world. "It's what our mother wants."

When Veronica didn't reply, I added, "We'll share the burden."

☽☽☽

The morning fog had lifted, but the sky over Anne's campsite looked unsettled. Long, flat-topped clouds with the appearance of black-smith's anvils were forming overhead.

Anne followed my gaze and stated the obvious, "Thunderclouds."

"Bring them on," Veronica said before plopping down next to Anne on her yoga mat. Then in a voice without the slightest inflection, my sister began telling her about our father.

Anne listened, sighed, and nodded, but said little, as though the best thing to do at this point was to sit with the information, hurt, and anger Veronica was sharing and allow for the mud to settle.

How strange. At times, while Veronica was describing herself—her rigid self-sufficiency and perfectionism, her avoidance of close relationships, her intolerance of uncertainty and change, and her inability to express emotion—she could have been describing me. Yet, the father who had raised me had been kind, supportive, and addicted only to love. What was it that shaped us as individuals? Events? People? Circumstances? Heredity? Or did our "shaping" have more to do with how we reacted to our yesterdays and used them as a foundation for our tomorrows? Could the clay of our past still respond to the molding of our hands and minds, as long as we kept it wet and fluid and didn't expose it to the fiery temperatures of judgment and guilt? Could we use our history to our advantage, instead of allowing it to get in the way?

When Veronica finished, Anne said, "You've just taken the most difficult step in the healing process of what you've been through. Openly identifying the problem and talking about your sadness and anger. Well done."

"You can thank my shoulder angel for that," Veronica said with a quick tilt of her head in my direction. "She drove me to it."

"Yes, Marjorie has that effect on people," Anne said with a grimace. "So, how about we take a look at the flip side of what you've just shared? From what your sister told me and the little I've observed since meeting you, you're not afraid of other people and authority. You don't depend on others to tell you who you are. You stand up for yourself. And you've just done a darn good job of unburying your feelings and expressing your emotions. In other words, you've been through a lot and prevailed. That's what I call progress."

"Thanks, counselor," Veronica said. "Are you implying that my father made me who I am."

"Strong and powerful," I said.

Veronica chuckled. "Love you, too, Sis. I'm addicted to danger and excitement, which gives me the feeling of control. Maybe that's what you see when you think of me as strong and powerful. I'm the daughter of an alcoholic, who has let me down so many times, I've lost count. Forgive me if I don't look forward to seeing him again, let alone introduce him to someone precious to me, who I don't want to share. Discovering that I had a sister was one of the best things that ever happened to me. I won't stand by and watch my father destroy her, too."

Precious? Best thing that ever happened to her?

I was so shocked by what Veronica was saying that I couldn't speak.

Anne smiled, her eyes reassuring. "Marjorie's stronger than you give her credit for."

"Yeah," Veronica said. "She demonstrated that when we were stuck in that cave in the Los Padres National Forest. Incredible. You should see her in action."

I felt like a fly on the wall listening to a conversation that was making my head spin. *Don't stop now, Veronica.*

"The situation you're labeling as bad might hold a deeper good," Anne said. "Challenges often become opportunities."

Veronica shot her a look that matched the stormy clouds above.

"Anne may be right," I said, finally finding my voice. I felt antsy, as I had in Veronica's room, wanting to wash windows, scrub floors, run a mile. Instead, I took a seat on one of Anne's wobbly camp stools, which had about as much stability as one of those animal spring riders you find on park playgrounds and did little to offset my fidgety mood. "She's given me some sage advice a time or two."

My sister looked unconvinced. "Elizabeth and I have lived with Bob's illness for years. We've tried everything and, as far as I'm concerned, exhausted all possibilities. He's a walking time bomb. If he doesn't kill himself, he'll kill someone else. In the meantime, he goes along his merry way, oblivious to the path of destruction he leaves behind."

"Do you hate him?" I asked.

Veronica looked at me as if part of her were dying. "Yes. Sometimes I do."

$$\text{)))}$$

This would be my last hike before leaving Big Sur and heading for Pacific Grove to meet my father. I planned to make it a memorable one. I would stop often to look and listen. I would allow the silence to blanket me. I would pay attention to the space between the drip of the fog, the squawk of the crow, and the peck of the woodpecker. I would lean against trees, smell the perfume of their leaves, needles, and bark. I would put my toes in creeks and ponds. I would be there as fully as I could.

While I climbed the Mount Manuel Trail toward Vista Point, beyond, underneath, and above the shady oak woodlands and exposed chaparral came the sight and smell of decaying leaves and decomposing matter. Death and life, hand-in-hand, one feeding the other.

I thought about how life kept rearranging itself, how it went on, and how we were dissolving at every moment. Leaving Adam and Anne behind would be a small death for me. There would be an empty space left inside. Maybe, with the right attitude, I could find peace in that space. Maybe I could make room there for my father and his secret.

Apparently, he had wasted twenty-nine years punishing himself for the mistake of falling in love with two women. Such pain and suffering over something that couldn't be fixed. It had settled in his mind and caused him to decay from the inside out.

And with him, he had dragged his wife and his daughter.

In many ways, I had been spared.

As I crested Vista Point, I noticed the strips of bare soil between the coastal shrub and grassland, otherwise known as *bare zones*. California sagebrush and black sage produce toxic chemicals that inhibit the germination and growth of the seedlings of competing plant species, sometimes even inhibiting the germination and growth of their own. Add to that the lack of sunlight, due to the dense canopy of their branches, and the area appeared uninhabitable indeed. I took in the sweeping 360-degree panoramic view extending across the entire Big Sur area. What had nature taught me about survival in the bare zones of life, the seemingly barren patches of the in-between?

As I took another slow turn, scanning the Santa Lucia Mountains, the rugged coastline, and the sheer coastal cliffs, I decided it was time to find out.

)))

Cecil, Claudia, Anne, Adam, Veronica, and I settled on logs in a circle around the campfire in what was left of Adam's camp. It was dusk and almost everything, except for the tents and sleeping bags, had been packed away for the group exodus to Los Angeles.

I glanced at Cecil, who sat at my side. From the start, I had disliked his strut, his wisecracks, his unapologetic display of wealth, and the way he lived and acted from a place of inner authority. I had misjudged him. He and I were more alike than different, and were ultimately seeking the same thing—he with the massive chrome headlight of his Harley lighting the way, and me weighed down by the stuffed cargo hold of my Jeep. Cecil's inner strength, his money, his connections, his ability to live life out loud would serve his father well during the last chapters of his life. I hated to admit it, but since Cecil and I had let down our surface barriers, with the purpose of helping Adam, we had connected in some inexplicable way. I thought of Holly, Kate, Jennifer, Claudia, Adam, Anne, Veronica, and, yes, even Buster, each a traveler on the road of life, each a teacher, each a messenger.

Cecil poked me in the side and presented me with a wide grin. "I'm returning your sculpture."

Sculpture? With the turbulence generated by Adam's disappearance, Antonia's strange request, and news of my father, I'd forgotten all about it. Like Adam's ring of keys, the sculpture now served as a symbol of what had once mattered: a useless possession, something that would only weigh me down.

Cecil laughed. "Cat got your tongue?"

I opened my mouth to speak. Then thought better of it. What could I say? He had paid $10,000 for my creation and was offering it back to me. Too late. I no longer cared.

"I'd like to see it," Veronica said, perking up at the news. "It must be something special, for Cecil to steal it. Right?"

"Actually, it's rather coarse and amateurish," Cecil said.

I felt myself bristle, but said nothing. He was right. I had been dabbling with clay, untrained in the medium, unaware of what I was doing.

"But the darn thing hit me in the gut," Cecil said. "Either Marjorie got lucky, or I have exceptionally bad taste in art."

Everyone laughed. Except me. "I really hated you, Cecil."

"He hated himself," Claudia said, her voice soft, but sharply focused. A simple acknowledgment and acceptance of fact. It occurred to me that she accepted Cecil for who he was without the need to change him. How amazing was that? What I had perceived as needy clinging and insecurity on her part was in fact a sign of her unwavering support. Her love, like the light of the sun, was not selective. She, the silent watcher, was possibly the most enlightened among us.

Cecil gave her a swift look and lifted his brow. "I know it sounds crazy, but I was trying to turn a mystery into something material, something I could own and control. Your sculpture was like a port-hole into the unknown, Marjorie, into which I wanted to take a peek. It had nothing to do with workmanship."

A flash of lightning, lit up the sky with a sheet of light.

"Maybe it was God speaking to you," Claudia ventured.

Go Claudia.

Cecil gave a mirthless laugh. "I don't believe in God."

Buster whined, followed by the clap and rumble of thunder, bringing to mind the sharp inhale and extended sigh of nature.

"Guess this is as good a time as any to start on a new path," Anne said into the sudden silence.

"The old path brought me here," Cecil said, "but I know what you mean. It's hard to understand, or accept, what I've experienced in the past weeks without believing in something."

The warmth in Cecil's eyes as he looked at Adam made me won-der if I'd ever look at my father in this way. Or would he be beyond reach, as Adam nearly was?

The blackened sky lit up with a flash of lightning, followed sec-onds later by another clap of thunder.

Odd, how often we gathered in darkness, only to experience light.

"Anyway," Cecil said. "I'm pretty good at getting people to do what I want." He shrugged and presented another of his smartass smiles. "That's why I'm successful at my job."

Yeah, using manipulation, control, and intimidation. "Do you think you could use that special talent of yours to get someone to buy my sculp-ture?" I asked with an equally smartass smile.

Cecil, Claudia, Veronica, and Anne stared at me as though I were speaking a foreign language.

"Sell? What for?" Cecil asked.

"For Alzheimer's research. Add to that the $10,000, minus commis-sion you already paid me for it, and it'll amount to a tidy sum."

The collective sigh of approval that followed felt like a supportive wind behind my back. I looked at each member of our circle, sensing so much love I felt I could fly.

"I could organize an auction," Cecil said, rubbing his forehead with both hands, "which brings out peoples' competitive spirit and their sense of fun and generosity." He glanced at his father. "Maybe even Dad and Buster could help."

Adam's gaze settled on Cecil from the opposite side of the campfire like the touch of a butterfly, gossamer on steel, and I swear, even with only the illumination of the fire and moon, I glimpsed comprehension in his eyes.

Cecil frowned and shook his head. "It'll take some doing. Actually, it'll require a whole new frame of mind on my part. I'll have to call in some markers in favor of a good cause, instead of my own pocketbook for a change. It'll also take cooperation and trust. Not my forte, I'm afraid." Cecil looked at Claudia, who squeezed his hand. "Guess you can say, the life I've been leading thus far has been rather stagnant when it comes to personal relationships."

"You can bet your Harley boots on that one," Veronica said. "You were in a foul state when I first met you, and, from what I understand, you nearly dragged your father down with you."

The angry tone in Veronica's voice, suggested that she was comparing Cecil to our father.

"And I have the opportunity to set things right again," Cecil said.

He cocked his head and looked at Veronica with the sharp eye of the entertainment lawyer that Anne claimed him to be. "You and that sister of yours are like two sides of a coin, one side dark, the other light, each setting off the other, each necessary to form the whole."

"Antonia implied that the circle isn't yet complete," I said, unable to shake off my mother's words. *Fallen Light. Ask your father about Fallen Light. You must complete the circle.*

"Then Fallen Light may be the center," Anne said.

Chapter Thirty-Nine

IT WAS TIME to say goodbye to Adam.

As Veronica and I entered his camp for the last time, I wondered if he would recognize me. The tents were gone, everything packed, leaving not a single trace of Adam's stay. Cecil and Claudia sat in a head-to-head huddle, deep in muffled conversation, so occupied with each other that they failed to acknowledge our presence.

Anne, in contrast, looked relieved to see us. She waved us over. "They've been like that all morning. You'd think they just united after years of separation. Anyway, if you're looking for Adam, Marjorie, he's in the grotto."

Was she trying to get rid of me?

She turned to Veronica. "Okay, out with it. Is it true that the DEA instills fear in physicians, concerning how they treat their patients and what they prescribe?"

I'd been dismissed.

"Don't worry," Veronica said when she caught me frowning. "We'll be fine."

I wasn't worried, just miffed. But I could take a hint.

Adam sat in the center of his evacuated grotto, arms resting on raised knees. His hair was trimmed, his face clean-shaven, thanks to Cecil this time instead of Brock. Brock's employment as Adam's personal care aide had come to an end. And not a moment too soon, according to Anne. After Adam's return from the care facility, he'd become even more averse to water. Washing and showering had turned into a battle. Though Brock and Adam had forged a companionable relationship, the assignment had stretched Brock's resources to the limit, and he was eager to move on to a less challenging position.

Adam's clothing appeared to have materialized straight out of a Banana Republic catalog. He looked like a normal, well-outfitted camper. Except for the vacant stare.

I sat next to him. He glanced my way, then looked back at the barren circle his grotto had become. Hawks called to one another as they perched in the sycamores, alders, and redwoods that encircled the pond—from which Adam was now keeping a guarded distance. Apparently, the water spilling from the outcropping of rock and trickling into the pool no longer evoked in him the peace and tranquility it once had.

I closed my eyes and took a deep breath, my mind settling into a waking-dream state. Spirit surrounded us; I sensed It everywhere. So, I appealed to It for Adam. *Please God, help Adam in his final journey.*

Adam touched his fingers to mine. I turned my hand over, palm up, and he clasped it.

The words Adam had written in the final pages of his journal returned to me as though carried on the whiff of perfumed air coming from the wild flowers interspersed between the shrubs and ferns.

The last thing I'll lose is love. I may forget people's names, where I am, and what I'm doing, but I will remember love.

Buster rested his furry head on our joined hands.

)))

Anne swept raised arms over the vacant camp. "All is ready. Accept what is."

For me, it wasn't that easy. I'd never had many friends, never made the effort, never felt the need. But now I felt as if part of me were leaving. Anne would say it was the part of me I'd given her as a gift, making room for what I was still to become.

She pressed a ring of keys into my hand. "I own a home in Pacific Grove where you're headed. The house is kind of..." She shook her head as if lost for words. "It'll be a good home base for meeting with your father."

The assortment of keys jingled as I inspected them. Not tokens of power or possession. Not something to hoard or tie one down. But a gift meant to be shared and enjoyed.

"Stay as long as you like," she said. "As a matter of fact, keep the keys for whenever you're in the area, which I hope will be often." She looked at Veronica, and her face softened. "We're sisters now. What's mine is yours."

A home in Pacific Grove. I squelched the questions that threatened to ruin the moment. *Accept with gratitude and generosity. It's part of the plan.* Her generosity was beyond comprehension. I didn't know what to say.

"Actually, you'll be doing me a favor," Anne said, "sort of like house-sitting. The key to the art studio in Monterey is on the ring as well, in case you feel the urge to play some more with clay. And my closets... They're packed to the hilt with clothes that'll fit you both, many with the tags still attached. I'd love to know you were wearing them."

All those clothes. Questions again sprang to mind: Where'd she get the money, the clothes, the house? Again, I squelched them. They would be answered in time.

We hugged. I sniffed in Anne's ear.

"Stop it," she said. "That tickles."

I sprang back. "Sorry."

A smile from Anne. "You're expressing emotion. See how far you've come?"

True, my emotions were flowing more freely now, if not at full force. All these years of storing them up—as if releasing them would amount to bleeding—had taken their toll. I glanced at Veronica. Her eyes were bright with unshed tears. Tears? Talk about coming far.

She reached for Anne's hand.

"Oh, no you don't," Anne said, pulling her into a bear hug.

Cecil had likened my sister and me to two sides of a coin, one side dark, the other light. I, instead, envisioned a coin imprinted with Janus the Roman god of two faces, one face looking backward, the other face looking forward, both on the same side of the coin. What appeared on the other side would, for now, remain a mystery.

I thought of my father, the man I was about to meet in Pacific Grove, and felt my heart contract. Could Veronica and I uncover and live with his secret? Could we release our dark *yesterdays* and uncertain *tomorrows* and open to the avenues and surprises that lay in the light of the present? Or would we remain stuck in our private worlds, ruled by our own narrow perceptions, sealed from the hidden meanings of life?

I put my arms around my *two* sisters, confident that it was the former rather than the later.

With love, anything was possible.

Acknowledgments

MY DEEPEST THANKS TO:

My husband and family for their continued patience and support while I wrote and revised yet another novel in my "Enter the Between" series. Two more to go, and I'm done. Promise.

My line and content editors Judith Reveal, Moira Warmerdam, Marianne Chick, Linda van Steyn, and Jodine Turner. Thank you, thank you, for finding those pesky typos and setting me straight when I veered off course.

My critique partners, past and present, for their valuable suggestions: Jo Chandler, Lee Lopez, Dorothy Skarles, Natalia Orfanos, and members of the *Amherst Writers and Artists Group*, directed by Gini Grossenbacher, especially Judy Vaughan.

My sister, Theresa Adrian, brothers, John and Ron van Steyn, and friends, Kathy Simoes and Louis Silveira, for your faith in my writing. I wish I could express in ways other than words how much this means to me.

For fellow authors and members of the Visionary Fiction Alliance, Jodine Turner, Victor E. Smith, Eleni Papanou, Sandy Nathan, Saleena Karim, and Jim Murdoch for your help in bringing the genre of Visionary Fiction into the public eye.

My cover artist, Clarissa Yeo of *Yocla Designs* and Jonnee Bardo of *Gluskin's Photo Lab and Studio* for my author photo.

So many books were helpful in researching for this novel that I can only mention a few: *Earth Medicine* and *The Medicine Way*, by Kenneth Meadows, *Dancing the Dream,* by Jamie Sams, *The Field,* by Lynne McTaggart, *Spiritual Emergency*, by Stanislav and Christina Grof, The Natural History of Big Sur, by Paul Henson and Donald J. Usner, *The Person with Alzheimers's Disease*, edited by Phyllis Braudy Harris, PH.D., *The Truth about Witchcraft Today*, by Scott Cunningham, *The Map of Heaven*, by Eben Alexander, M.D.

About the Author

Margaret Duarte's parents immigrated to the United States from Holland (the Netherlands) with her two older brothers the year before she was born. She grew up on a series of dairy farms in California into what became a very large family—seven brothers and two sisters.

When she entered high school, her fascination with creative writing began. She was fortunate to receive excellent instruction, plus a great deal of encouragement from her English teachers.

Scholarship in hand, Margaret entered California State University, Sacramento, where she earned a degree in English and a secondary teaching credential. Then she did something she swore she would never do—married a dairy farmer.

Over the following thirty years, she helped on the family farm, raised two sons, taught at a local middle school, and dabbled in an assortment of hobbies, but did little writing other than in her journal. It wasn't until her sons were grown that she finally returned to what her teachers had encouraged her to pursue while in school—writing.

Though it delayed her career as a writer, she never regretted her decision to marry and raise a family. Her years as wife and mother taught her about love and selflessness and fueled her for the years of writing that lay ahead. They also uncovered what would become the driving force behind her work: the call for spiritual and emotional freedom. Through her novels, which synthesize heart and mind, science and spirituality, Margaret hopes to inspire people to activate their gifts, retire their excuses, and stand in their own authority.

For more information on Margaret and her books, visit her website at: http://www.margaretduarte.com

Book one of the "Enter the Between"

Visionary Fiction series

Silicon Valley resident Marjorie Veil has been conditioned to ignore her own truth, to give away her power, to subjugate in relationships with others, and to settle for the path of least resistance. But she has many surprises in store, for there are synchronistic forces at work in her life that, if she listens, will lead her to her authentic heart and happiness. The seemingly impossible happens in the wild of the Los Padres National Forest where Marjorie goes on retreat to make sense of her life when she thinks she has gone insane. The innocence of the Native American orphan Marjorie befriends, as well as more mystery and adventure than she bargained for, show her how love can heal in what turns out to be a transformative spiritual quest.

Book three of the "Enter the Between"

Visionary Fiction series

When Marjorie Veil takes refuge at a friend's Victorian mansion in Pacific Grove, otherwise known as *Butterfly Town USA,* she seeks answers to two burning questions. Why had her biological father abandoned her at birth? And why is her mother sending messages from beyond the grave, shedding light on agonizing secrets she took with her when she died?

Despite plans to enjoy Pacific Grove's quaint bookstores, ocean views, and butterfly sanctuary, Marjorie's stay is anything but replenishing. She senses something disturbing beneath the mansion's outward calm. Soon she begins seeing and hearing things that cause her to question her sanity, and she unearths a backyard labyrinth that reveals its own powerful secrets.

A psychological-supernatural tale of an ordinary woman in extraordinary situations which she resolves in remarkable ways.

Book four of the "Enter the Between"

Visionary Fiction series

Medicate or nurture; reform or set free? These are quandaries rookie teacher Marjorie Veil faces when she takes on an after-school class for thirteen-year-olds labeled as troublemakers, unteachable, and hopeless. Faculty skeptics warn that all these kids need is prescribed medication for focus and impulse control. But as Marjorie soon discovers, behind their anti-conformist exteriors are gifted teens, who are sensitive, empathetic, and wise beyond their youth. They also happen to have psychic abilities, which they have kept hidden until now. Can Marjorie help them do what she has been unable to do for herself: fight for their spiritual and emotional freedom?